IGNIS

TRACY KORN

IGNIS | Book Four

Cover Design Copyright © 2018 by James Korn

Photography by J.Korn Photographics

www.jkornphoto.com

ISBN: 978-1-946202-75-8
www.TheElementsSeries.com

Library of Congress Control Number: 2018909463

Edited by Amy McNulty

Summary: The rebels at The Seam have been defeated thanks to the alleged treachery of one of their own. It won't be long before a manhunt ensues for Jazz's entire crew, and given what they know about Gaia's secret project, they won't be prosecuted...they'll just disappear. With Liddick still missing and the port-cloud stronger than ever, they haven't come this far to give in now. When Jazz announces she's going after Liddick herself, she draws a line in the sand she may not be able to erase. Arco has no choice but to let her go, but how does he lead everyone forward with the past holding him back? Outcast. Hunted. Lost. Success will demand a sacrifice.

On the edge, a leap of faith could save them all.

First Paperback Edition
Printed in the United States of America

Snowy Wings
PUBLISHING

For Ryan.
Fellow pilgrim, partner, and friend.

"I'm a pilgrim on the edge, on the edge of my perception. We are travelers at the edge, we are always at the edge of our perception."
~ Scott Mutter

"We, the people of The American Preserve, hereby organize under the articles of the Global Civic Council as agents for public health and commercial responsibility. Herein, we shall investigate and hold accountable by legal due process any organization, regardless of affiliation, which interferes with ecological sustainability."

Mission Statement for The Society for Environmental Accountability and Management (The S.E.A.M.)

CHAPTER 1
Phase Three
Jazz

The Boneyard is never empty. No matter what time of day or night, someone is always here.

If Vox and Lyden are eavesdropping on my thoughts like they usually do, they don't say anything in reply. I guess everyone is too focused on trying to find out what to do now that the pro-Gaia propaganda they say Liddick wrote is bleeding through the virtuo-cines, seeping into the subconscious of anyone with even the slightest Empathic inclination. It will be harder than ever to convince the public that the port-cloud is literally killing the world now, and no one will believe The Seam's claims about Gaia genetically experimenting on the people they've abducted or blackmailed.

It took us days to patch those glyphs, and someone has been at the consoles surrounding the column of light on the main floor of the Boneyard ever since. It was a gradient of rotating colors, each one representing a new script for the virtuo-cine that was pulled up...*before* Liddick reset the server and locked us out of the network anyway.

I watch the flat, gray cylinder jutting out of the platform in the distance. It's hollow, dead, which is exactly how I feel when I consider the possibility that maybe the others are right. Maybe Liddick really did betray us.

I turn away from all of it, but especially from that thought, and look out the window panel in this corridor. It's been closed until now. The milky port-cloud haze sits like a rising fog under the field of stars that extends into oblivion. Earth is under that cloud somewhere. That's what they've been telling us, but they've been telling us a lot of things.

"When did three in the morning happen?" Arco asks, walking up behind me. He lifts his chin to the hovering blue hologram display over my head when I squint at him. It reads, *3:04 a.m. State Standard, American Preserve.*

"I don't know how anyone lives up here. It's always dark." I stare out at the haze and fold my arms over my chest, biting my lip to keep a yawn at bay.

"Calyx said there are bunks at the other end of this corridor. You should—"

"Arco, *crite...*" I let go of all the breath in my lungs as if it's what's weighing me down. "*You* should really stop telling me what to do."

His eyes are wide when I look up at him, but then they fill with pity. All this does is light a fire under my skin.

"Sorry..." he says, then presses his lips into a line. In the light of the window haze, I can see shadow smudges under his eyes. *He hasn't slept at all either,* I think, and the fire under my skin cools. "I'll be down that way then." He gestures past the main floor to the other end of the corridor where the bunks are supposed to be. "There's nothing else we can do until they figure out how to get back onto the Grid."

I nod at him but don't follow when he turns to go. I just watch him, knowing he's right about there being nothing else we can do right now. My dad, Calyx, Eco, and Tark, plus at least twenty more people behind consoles, are trying everything they can to regain access to the virtuo-cine network, but the feeling of hope slipping away is starting to thin the air. I know in the pit of my stomach they're not going to be able to reverse the pro-Gaia propaganda Liddick wrote. Right this minute, it's leaking into the subconscious of any Empath participating in a virtuo-cine, and it will eventually propagate to reach everyone, Empath or not.

Crite, sand dollar...lighten up, Vox thinks. My heart jumps into my throat at her loud voice suddenly in my head, especially since I can't see her. I hear her snort in the direction of the main floor at my left, and when I jerk my attention that way, she snorts again.

"Go away, Vox. Go to sleep," I say out loud.

"Been trying. Your pity party is *too* wild."

I roll my eyes at her, regretting that I didn't insist on Liddick showing me how to close off our thoughts back in the Vishan tunnels.

"Do you think he did it?" I ask after another minute. Vox slides around the corner with the back of her head leaning on the wall.

"No," she says, and I notice her eyes are closed when she comes into the light. "But he definitely stepped in his net somewhere."

"And now he's tangled in it..." I say to myself.

Vox gives one giant nod, then overly exaggerates her response, letting her mouth open like gravity is pulling at her chin. *"Yup."*

"We have to convince them that he's innocent."

She shakes her head from side to side, still without opening her eyes or moving her head from the wall.

"Quit bothering yourself with that." The immediacy and certainty of her answer sends a spike of heat through my chest, but she interrupts my thoughts before I can say anything. *And before you bark at me for hovering like I'm Arco, stow it,* she thinks. *Nobody said you're a delicate flower. We do, however, think you're being a skag.*

"Really. Who's *we?*" I hiss at her, and now she opens her eyes just long enough to drop her chin and stare at me like I've suddenly burst into song at three in the morning.

"Telling you to get some rest was *boyfriend* for 'you're being a skag.' Everything isn't about you, sand dollar," she says, then heaves a resigned breath before I can respond. *"Aaaand* if you're all done lamenting now, I'm going back to sleep in the chairs Sparkles told me to get out of."

I fight the laugh in my chest at her nickname for Eco, wondering if she's been trying to get the *neural-whatever-they-are* lights in his face to go from a pulse to a steady stream of red. She pushes off the wall with the back of her head, then heads back down the corridor to the main floor with her arms stretched out in front of her.

Open your eyes! I shout after her in my mind. She throws a thumb up in the air but doesn't turn around... or lower her arms.

I look back out the port window at the haze below and remember the Vishan Lookout Pier...the zephyrs that came together to hover over the Bale field looking like simple fog instead of the razor-toothed tornado monsters they actually were. Arco brought me up there to talk about how distant I was being then...and he was right. He was right about all my doubts just being my own fears that I was projecting on everyone else. I thought he was the one who doubted me then with his constant hovering, but it was me...those were my own doubts the whole time. *Did that just happen again?* I wonder. *Maybe I am being a skag...being angry feels better—not right, but better,* I remember. *It's better than feeling helpless.* I close my eyes and shake my head. *I'm an idiot. I have choices. I don't just have to watch all this happen.* I remember the invisible panel door that leads out of here is close, and I stretch out my hand, immediately feeling the difference in air pressure. *It's right there. I could leave right now and find Liddick myself.*

All at once I feel a weight lift off my chest. I turn and walk directly into the main room with the circle of uplink chairs. Tark and Calyx are talking with my dad. Eco, Liam, and Lyden are typing like mad men at their consoles, and Arwyn is saying something to Arco, who looks like he doesn't want to hear it. I clear my throat.

"I'm going to find him," I announce, then set my shoulders, waiting for the deluge of rebuttals to crash into me.

"*What?*" Jax finally says the word frozen on everyone else's lips. Arco blinks at me, trying again to say something, but nothing comes out.

"I'm not leaving him out there. He didn't do this," I say, turning to look at my brother. His eyebrows shoot up as he gapes at me.

"Uh, did you miss the part where they have a *record* of him resetting the server and erasing all your work?" Jax chuffs a laugh. "You saw him with your own eyes, Jazz. You saw him pull that lever."

"That doesn't mean he planned to sabotage us. You didn't see his face when he realized it was me in that virtuo-cine. He thought someone was playing games with him in there... We just need to let him explain what happened."

"Mr. Wright had a storyboarder credential," Mr. Tark says, blowing out an exasperated breath. "He wrote that pro-Gaia propaganda thread *and* the subliminal glyph code that now incriminates you and Mr. Hart." Tark's golden eyes are stony when he pulls a big hand over his mouth and down his chin, dropping the sentences on the floor like they're made of lead. I clench my teeth to keep from yelling my response.

"I don't care how it looks. He wouldn't betray us. I know there's more to this story, and I'm going to find out what really happened," I say, turning toward the door at the end of the corridor. I only get a few steps before it hits me that I have no idea how to get out of here once I'm through the first panel door, let alone where to even begin looking for Liddick.

"You're just going to go?" Arco says so quietly I wonder if it's actually a thought in my head. I look back and see him slide his hands into his white jumpsuit pockets, his broad shoulders seeming to dip under the weight of something heavy. Everything that's been rigid about him for so many weeks—or has it been months now?—slips away. He raises his chin just a little and asks me again. "You're just going to leave? That's it?"

"I have to," I finally hear myself say, the edges of the words crumbling like dry leaves, which is exactly how everything inside me suddenly feels: brittle...breaking.

"And where will you go?" he asks, pressing his lips into a line and narrowing his eyes at me, genuinely interested in my answer.

"I don't know; what were Liddick's last coordinates?" I manage, shooting my focus at Eco. The lights in his cheeks flash green as he laughs out loud.

"You can't just walk into the Mainframe Office, Jazwyn. *We* can't even get into that place."

"How do you know that? Have you ever tried?"

Eco opens and closes his mouth, then looks at Calyx.

"Well, no, but that's because we already *know*—"

"You don't know. You don't know because you've never tried."

"Jazz, are you listening to yourself?" Jax asks. "If The Seam can't get into that place, neither can Liddick, even with all his connections. Someone had to let him in there —someone he's obviously working for."

"And are *all* the people who work at the Mainframe office pro-Gaia? Pro-Biotech Global and Carboderm Corporation? Are they all against The Seam?" I turn to my dad. He crosses his arms over his chest and sighs.

"No, minnow, but at best, the ones who aren't have to appear neutral. It's dangerous to bite the hand that feeds you at that level." He struggles to say the last few words, like he's suddenly in pain now too. *What is this? More pity? I don't need pity from anyone. I need answers!*

"What if Liddick didn't realize what he was doing? What if he's in trouble?"

"Jazz," Arco says with the last of a breath. "What if he's *not?* What if he just he saw his opportunity and took it?"

"Opportunity for what? To be a storyboarder? He doesn't care about that! He wouldn't betray us!" I force out the last words as my throat constricts.

"I know you want to believe that, but look at his track record over the years."

"He was trying to help his brothers, Arco. You *know* he wanted to keep the rest of us safe."

"All he managed to do was either use people or alienate them. What is it going to take for you to see that he just doesn't care what *happens to you?* Why can't you see that I'm—" Arco breaks off his words like a branch over his knee...hard and sudden. The silence that follows snaps me in the chest, and all I can do is shake my head at him, waiting for the rest of what he was going to say. He pushes his hands through his hair and turns away from me.

"Look, I know you don't like him. I know you don't trust him," I say. "But I'm not asking you to do either of those things. I'm asking you to trust me."

Arco doesn't turn around. He clasps his hands behind his neck and sighs. The muscles in his back flinch behind the thin, white jumpsuit fabric, and I can feel him trying not to scream at the top of his lungs. He blows out another breath and slowly turns around.

"It's not that I don't trust you," he finally says very quietly. "Hell, Jazz. If I had to bet on anyone, it would be you."

"Then what is it?" I look around the room at all the wide eyes...all of them looking at me like I'm some kind of shivering puppy. *Pity...again. Why can't anyone see the very simple problem here!?*

"Just let her go," Vox says, shattering the silence like a hammer through a window. She slides off her virtuo-cine uplink chair and shoves her hands into her jumpsuit pockets, then shrugs at Arco. "Let her go."

"Vox, she can't just—" Jax starts, but Arco holds up a hand.

"No," he says with a small nod, then looks directly at me. "You know what? She's right." His eyes narrow like he's trying to see something far away, something far behind me. "I need to let her go." He nods again in answer to a question I haven't asked, and then I realize it's not my question he's answering at all—it's his own. A sharp pain runs through the center of my chest, and then a searing heat. It's so real I look down to see if something has actually just stabbed me.

"And what the hey, I'll go with her," Vox says, jackknifing the heaviness in the room and startling everyone, including me. "Better than waiting around here for The State to come vaporize us, right?"

"Wait, what?" Avis says.

"Go look at your blippy stuff." Vox pushes her chin at him, which sends Avis scurrying back to his console screen.

"I'll go with them," Liam says. "This whole thing is my fault."

"It's no one's fault," Calyx says, exhausted, then looks

from Liam to me. "You don't know what you're undertaking, Jazwyn. People's lives are wrapped up in this—they will lose everything if the port-cloud comes down. If Liddick is involved with anyone who—"

"If he is, it's that much more important to get him out," I say, turning to Liam, and eventually, everyone else in the room. "Look, I'm not asking anyone to go with me. I'm not asking for anyone's help, but I know that I'm not the only one here who thinks Liddick is innocent, despite however it seems." I glance at Lyden, who's been uncharacteristically quiet. He nods to me and opens his mouth to say something, but Calyx cuts him off.

"Before you get any ideas," she says to him, "remember our plan."

He closes his eyes in a long blink, then nods slowly at her.

"I know."

"Your plan for what?" Avis asks, stepping out from behind his console panel. "They're already tracking us. I didn't think it would be so fast."

"Then we need to get out of here now. We have to go to Phase Three," Lyden says.

"What? Why? You just narrowly avoided going there last I checked." Arco's eyes flash and blood flushes his cheeks as he takes a step in front of his sister. Arwyn threads her arm through his.

Mr. Tark shrugs at Lyden when he hesitates in answering.

"You might as well tell them. They'll know soon enough anyway—we don't have a choice."

My dad interjects. "I think they've all been through

enough, don't you?"

"I agree," Azeris says. "We need to wipe their prints from the Grid and erase their location flags, then get them out of here. Who's working on that?"

"No, first, what do you mean? What will we know soon enough?" I scan them all for the answers they're taking turns trying to hide.

"Jazwyn, it's better that you don't—"

"Azeris, *stop* trying to protect me!" I shout, and this time I don't care who hears me or who's offended. "I'm not blindly following some scripted path ever again. Does everyone understand that?" Blood pounds in my ears and my throat closes again with the threat of ears I refuse to choke on. "We aren't safe anymore. We never were safe, but the difference is now we know who are enemies are. We are *not* helpless. Just *tell* us your plan."

CHAPTER 2
Letting Go
Arco

Jack pushes his hands over his face and sighs. "All right, Jazwyn," he finally says, taking a seat on the console behind him. "We can't risk the port-cloud getting even more protection and support than it does already, but not for the reasons you may think. It has to be taken out manually because it isn't just a pollutant—it's the outer layer of Phase Three."

Everyone seems surprised by this answer. Jazz tries to talk a few times before any words finally come out.

"Outer *layer?*"

"It's not the same size as the port-cloud," Jack explains. "Phase Three is only about the size of this building, but it's tethered to the inner layer of the cloud. They're connected...symbiotic. If we can take down the facility, the cloud will also die." He pushes off the console and slips his hands into his white jumpsuit pockets.

"Why hasn't The Seam already destroyed it then? How have they let it stand if they've known about what's happening to people at Phase Three?" Jazz presses, wide-eyed and shaking her head in amazement.

"It's not just a matter of flipping a switch." Jack straightens, holding up a hand like she's going to argue with him. "We've come at it from all angles over the years—gradual political and social pressure was the option that yielded the least number of casualties, but those seem unavoidable now." He shakes his head at the floor like it's somehow all his fault. I'm actually starting to wonder if it is.

"So, how do we bring down the facility?" I ask, trying to cut through all the guilt and move this forward. Jack's eyes jerk to mine.

"We're not doing anything. You have all been through enough," he fires, then turns to Jazz when she starts to protest. "Listen, the only people who can get into Phase Three either work there or are being brought there to be worked on." He looks at Calyx directly. "We are *not* risking your lives out there."

"We made our way out of Gaia Sur, and all the way through the Rush... We can—" Jazz starts to protest again, but Tark cuts her off this time, suddenly impatient with everything.

"Before anything else, you need to understand something. Phase Three is different from Gaia Sur, and even from the Phase Two facility at the end of those biomes," he says. "It's connected to the port-cloud by four umbilical columns that pull in the organic matter needed to create the physical structure of the building. We need to get to *those* and upload the Ignis Archive—" He stops and blinks a few times when he sees our reactions, then exhales. "It's the DNA strand you know as *Vishan*. We need to get that into those columns. Once the atoms are infused, the sun will trigger their disintegration throughout the entire facility, which will cause a chain reaction in the port-cloud itself. But there are a lot of guards and a lot of weapons between here and there."

Everyone gapes at Tark, and Jazz shoots her father an incredulous look.

"Is *that* really what you've all been planning the last few hours? To blow up the whole thing with volatile DNA while the rest of us just stared through the window of The Seam building? How many times are we supposed to go through you being *incinerated*, Dad!?" Jazz's voice pitches, then cracks, and I can't just stand here watching her like this anymore. Her fists clench at her sides. I step between her and Jack and put my arms around her, which only makes her immediately push against my chest, trying to get past...trying to get in front of her father again to make him face her, but I can't let her go.

"Take a breath," I whisper through her hair. "Let him explain."

"Jazwyn..." he starts, but can't get the rest of his words out.

Calyx finally speaks up for him. "It doesn't have to be a suicide mission."

"No? Then do tell how you get that *Ignis* whatever you said—the Vishan DNA—into the port-cloud and get out before everything fires? That stuff has an *instant* reaction to sunlight...trust me." Zoe narrows her eyes at Calyx. Azeris wraps an arm around Zoe's shoulders, and I wait for an answer that makes sense. But how could there be one? They want to drop a match in the middle of an oil pit and expect to get out before it all goes up? I start getting pulled into the idiocy of it all until Jazz's erratic breaths and her heart pounding against my arm chase the thoughts out of my head.

"Look, they think I'm a mole here at The Seam," Calyx says after a minute. "There's a ship that brings port-carnate transfers from Phase Two. They're picked up at a hub in Admin City and flown in for the next phase of their experimentation. We have a contact who can get us aboard one of those ships. From there, I can pretend I'm delivering Lyden and Arwyn, and Eco can act as a guard escort."

I hear this like a balloon popping next to my ear. "You want to use them as *bait?* Do you know what they'll do to them there?"

"I'll make sure they don't get trapped in the labs— Arwyn will need to get the test subjects stabilized for transport while Lyden and I hack into the system to trigger the columns. Right now, they're embedded, and it will take at least two hours to raise them. Then Jack and the rest of his team can get inside and load the Ignis archive into the columns."

"And then how does everyone get out? Let me guess —that ship is just going to wait outside for you to blow everything up?"

"Our contact will leave the ship with Tark...with *you.*" Calyx looks at me squarely.

"*Me?*" I repeat, nodding my head and trying not to laugh at her. "You really are split."

"It's no joke. We won't be able to get another team in place with all the security alerts on the Grid now. Monitoring will only get tighter until they catch you all, so we need to move. Your crew is our only chance at finishing this."

"*Crew?*" Eco laughs out loud, raising his eyebrows as high as they'll go. "What could they possibly do but get in the way?"

I get two steps toward him before Jack starts again.

"No way. These kids need asylum. They've done their part."

Calyx tilts her head. "Your son is an Omnicoder, Jack. More than that, he's *your* strand of Omnicoder."

"No! I won't put—"

"*Plus*, we'll need another biodesigner to lace the organics with the archive if Liam is going after his brother," Calyx adds, nodding to Fraya and Myra. The blood drains from their faces.

"Are you hearing me? This was never part of the plan!" Jack shouts.

"That plan was from when we had time. All their warrant flags are up, Jack, even the ones who never went into the Grid—see?" Calyx points to Avis's console, which has little red blips at the end of each line of code. "They're not safe here, and our asylum contacts are probably already compromised. The safest place for them now is in the mouth of the wolf."

No one moves at this. The words hang in the air and choke us all. I want to move, to run straight up the walls, but I'm suddenly in one of those dreams where your feet are stuck in the mud. From the bloodless looks on everyone's faces, they feel the same thing. *They really are going to burn it all down, and they want us to light the fire.*

"What about the rest of us?" I finally break my paralysis and look at Jazz one more time, scanning her face for any indication that some logic is getting through to her. Her mouth is still set in that line as she shakes her head and crosses her arms. *Crite, why are you so stubborn!?* I want to scream at her, but I swallow it and try to be rational. "You just heard her, Jazz. They'll be looking for you, and they won't stop until they find you."

"That's a risk I'll have to take," she says, and I feel sick at the same time I want to punch something.

I take a deep breath, trying to beat back the urge to give in...to tell her, *Fine, all right, if it means that much to you, I'll go with you—I'll keep you safe.* I swallow that whole thing like a pile of nails because Jazz doesn't care about being safe. She only cares about finding Liddick. She just stands there with her eyes on fire. Nothing will change her mind about leaving. *Who am I to keep standing in her way?*

Eco breaks the silence, holding up his hands to the group like he's trying to slow down the whole show. "So let me get this straight. You're going to storm Phase Three, even though we have nothing ready and no one in place to reprogram it?" The lights in his cheekbones flicker blue and red as he turns to Jazz. "And *your* plan is to walk right into the Mainframe Building and what, find Liddick just sitting at a console or something? Is that it?"

Jazz squints at him like he's the biggest mollusk she's ever met, and while I wholeheartedly agree with that sentiment, I bite the inside of my lip to keep the smile off my face.

"We won't know until we get in there," she says, clearly trying to sound calm.

"*We?* So you *are* planning on our help," Eco adds with

a smug smile, then laughs in her face. Jazz sets her mouth in a line just like in the tunnels when she went off, thinking I was doubting her.

"You know what I'm tired of, Eco?" She squares her stance and tilts her head to the side as he raises his eyebrows, mocking her.

"Oh, I'm sure you'll tell me," he says, and I stop fighting with my composure. *Here it comes.*

"I'm tired of your sneering, Eco, and your *better than everyone* attitude just because you think you've seen more than the rest of us. Newsflash: You haven't. You've just been playing dress-up in a world that can be shut off when it gets to be too much for you," she says. He gapes at her. "I'm also tired of your overcompensating self-importance all because you didn't get invited to the information party about this whole stupid mess we're in. And you know the biggest thing I'm tired of, Eco? Your *whining.* Your incessant, entitled, no-way-it's-going-to-work whining. Pay close attention because this is the last time I'm going to say that if I have to find Liddick by myself, *I will. That's* my point. I *will* figure it out, so if you're not going to help me, then at least have the decency to shut your vent because I don't need your negativity, all right?"

Her chest is heaving by the time she's done with him, and her teeth are locked in place just like when she was kicking and throwing punches at Dell for not telling us about that shuttle-sized alligator back in the swamp. I watch it all unfolding like a flat-cine, resisting the pull to jump in and stop it. I stop myself instead. I'm not getting involved this time. Let her burn him down. Let her burn it all down.

Eco chuffs like a horse, then tries to laugh.

"I don't have to take this," he says, slashing his holographic keyboard out of the air. It disappears, and he makes a beeline for the corridor. No one stops him, not even Calyx.

"She's not *wrong*," Avis says to no one in particular once Eco is out of earshot, and Calyx falls into a nearby chair with a heavy sigh.

"I'll talk to him. His problem is with me, not any of you," she says.

"Don't bother. We don't have time for drama." Tark's voice is tight and thin when he answers. "You have a team to lead, and the clock is running." He steps away from Jack with a nod. Jack pulls in a long, slow breath, but then seems resigned. "Ms. Ripley..." Tark continues, clapping his hands together like he's about to make some kind of announcement. "I applaud your bravery in wanting to find Mr. Wright, but I'm afraid I don't have any resources I can spare. If you leave this facility now, you're on your own."

Jack starts to say something now, but Vox cuts him off.

"As long as you spare some of those coats? I'm not going out there in these underpants." She looks down at her jumpsuit and raises her tattooed arms to her sides. There are a few chuckles here and there, and the break in tension loosens the knot in my chest. At least for a second.

"We can help you with that, Ms. Dyer," Tark says with a wide smile as he glances at Jack. "We can definitely help you with that."

"Right, so this is just happening?" I ask, shaking my head and staring straight at Jazz. Bile inches up my throat at the thought of how much Liddick Wright has obviously never cared about *her* safety, and here she is again trying to run interference for him. *Crite, wake up, Hart,* I think. *Just let her go.*

"We need to find out what really happened, Arco," Jazz says in a soft voice.

And that's it. There really isn't anything else to do. I look from face to face for an answer, but everyone is just looking at the floor or somewhere off to the side.

"And what if he's not even in that Mainframe Building anymore?" I blurt out before I realize what I'm saying—a last-ditch effort to show Jazz how split this whole idea is.

"I was thinking the same thing," Azeris announces from the corner like some kind of giant taxidermy bear come to life. "All things done, he'd try to find me next. I have all his virtuo-cine equipment. He'd try to hack his way back in to the Grid to make things right—to find everyone again."

"So you think he'd be at your hab in the Badlands?" Jazz asks, hope spreading over her face, which makes my gut twist. *Let her go…*

"I think that would be his endgame," Azeris says with a decisive nod. "There's the little matter of getting off this ice cube first, though."

Zoe wrinkles her forehead, seeming to decide something. "But *we're* not on the Grid, so whoever is coming after you all won't know about us. We can go back to the Badlands, maybe even figure how to sync up with Cal. He's got that NET artifact you said you could maybe rig to?" She looks at her dad. Azeris nods. "There are still people in that Phase Two lab, and if this is all going down, we need to get them out before things get locked up tight."

"Wait...are we splitting up? Is that what's happening?" Myra asks as Fraya hooks her arm with hers. Jazz takes a deep breath and lets it out slowly. She pushes her hands over her face, then moves them to her hips, looking at us all.

I catch her eyes and nod. "Yeah. We're splitting up."

CHAPTER 3
Open Doors
Jazz

Arco looks through me more than at me, and I feel hollow. There's a whole conversation hanging in the air between us, and neither of us are going to touch it. Maybe that's how it should be. I need to stop living my life *around* everyone else...making decisions based on the least number of people I'll make uncomfortable, or on what their expectations are of me. It's exhausting. Arco looks exhausted too, and I know it's my fault. He's really not coming with me this time.

"You'll go in with Skull," Calyx says, turning to Arco. "Avis and Ellis will run your systems once our contact releases the ship."

"You can't be serious, Calyx. You want to throw a handful of cadets into Phase Three and expect them to execute a military grade operation? Have you lost your mind?" My dad grips the sides of the console he's standing behind and leans over the hovering hologram screen. *How is my own father doubting us now?*

I scowl at him and start to protest, but then I remember I'm not even going with them to Phase Three. I'm going to find Liddick.

"You know as well as anyone that if we're going to strike, it has to be now," Calyx adds. "Are their location signatures erased?"

"Ma'am, the coordinates were locked when we were kicked off the Grid. I can't edit them," a woman at a console says.

"Can you delete them?"

"No, I can't access them at all."

Tark growls low in his chest, then turns abruptly to Calyx. "Get them out of here while they can still leave... they need food and rest. Get some rest, but stay off the shifts. I'll be in touch with a rally point," he adds, but he doesn't look like he's totally confident in what he's saying. A wild panic suddenly pushes through me as it hits me...we're going out there. I'm going out there, but the people I love are not going with me.

"Wait—" I protest as all these pieces start taking shape. "When are we meeting back up and how?"

Everyone in the room just looks at me like I'm supposed to have that answer. I meet my dad's eyes, but the feeling that hits me isn't one of security like it always is when I look at him. This time, it's...*fear?*

"We're about to get that sorted out," he says, trading glances with Tark, who nods.

"If all goes well, we'll come back here to The Seam building. If you're really taking a team to find Mr. Wright, we'll need to fit you with offline locators," Tark says, turning to Arwyn.

"I'll put them together," she says, then looks at Arco and nods just a little. He presses his lips together in a ghost of a smile and lets out a breath.

"I don't like this," Myra says, her gaze frantically jumping around from person to person like everywhere is too hot for it to land.

"I don't either...but, I don't see another way," Fraya says. "If anyone can find Liddick, it's probably Jazz."

Jax looks at her in surprise, but then his expression softens. Our dad is clasping his hands behind his neck, and I know he realizes this is out of his control. A hollow spreads in my stomach like I'm slowly being washed away from the inside...helplessness. *His* helplessness. I hate that feeling more than anything.

"We'll be OK. We made it through the Rush. We made it this far," I remind my dad, my brother, and Arco, but the hollow feeling in the pit of my stomach only seems to get deeper.

"We were *together*," Arco says in a low voice. I meet his eyes for a second. His are bloodshot, which turns the normal hazel into a deep green.

"We'll find a way." Vox raises her chin. "And if we don't find one, we'll make one."

This sends a jolt of electricity through my teeth as I glance at the maps on her arms and realize all the ways she has *in fact* made in her life so far. I don't know anything about that world... *Can I really do this? Can I really go out there without knowing anyone? Without knowing where I am or where I'm going?*

All you need to know is where you've been, sand dollar, Vox thinks. *You figure out the rest when you get there.*

I turn to her, actually a little grateful that she was eavesdropping on my thoughts this time because I actually feel a little better. Arco's face is pale when I look up at him, and the hollow in my stomach collapses into a forever-falling abyss. The muscles in his jaw jump when he realizes I'm watching him, and almost in the same second, the hollow feeling stops. He swallows hard and sighs, resigned. He scrubs a hand over his face, then hooks it on the back of his neck.

"When are we leaving?" he asks Calyx.

"I need to make some arrangements. Give me ten minutes, and we'll go out the back of the building."

Arco nods, but then turns away from everyone and walks back to the windows in the corridor. Jax is in front of me in two strides, his huge hands planting themselves on my shoulders. He just looks at me for a second trying to find something to say, but nothing comes out. He lowers his forehead to mine, and the hollow I felt minutes ago fills with warmth...with strength.

"Come back," he finally says, but it's so quiet, I almost don't hear him. My throat closes up immediately, and all I can do is nod. I swallow hard, wrestling with myself for control of my composure.

"I will," I say. "Stay close to Dad. Don't get separated again, promise? He has to come home to Mom...and Nann." I choke, and then pull in a deep, sharp breath.

"We all do. We all will," he says, and a warm, strong feeling swells in my chest. "Say it..."

"We all will," I repeat, my voice cracking in betrayal on the last word. Jax nods, then gives Liam a knowing, warning look. I roll my eyes and almost guffaw, but swallow the laugh bubbling up in my chest, It's not because the look is so funny, but because his big brother overture is such a manic feeling in comparison to the heaviness surrounding us. I close my eyes in a long blink, then let my forehead fall onto Jax's chest. He squeezes me, and I laugh. I laugh until I feel the sob chasing close behind, just waiting to rush out and flood the room…to drown everyone, and I quickly swallow it back down. Jax gives me a final nod, then crosses to Liam and Vox.

My dad is talking with Calyx when I look over at him, so I turn to find Arco. He's halfway down the corridor with his hands in his jumpsuit pockets, just staring off into the black oblivion beyond the window. I take a deep breath and walk over to him. I feel my feet land in each step, then randomly think about all the steps I've taken since the interviews…since the long walk home watching Arco throw stones into the ocean trying to understand his interview—his reactions to Rheen forcing him to make decisions about people's lives. About *my* life. He's never been able to let that go, not really. And I don't know that anyone could.

"Hey," I say, slowing to a stop next to him.

"Hey…"

"Arco, I—"

"Jazz, don't," he says, but he's not angry or even frustrated. He just seems very tired. "Sorry. I just—I can't do this. Not right now." He swallows as the muscles in his jaw jump again like the strings of a piano.

I want to go to him, to hug him or hold his hand, but I know—like I knew during the same moment sitting in the courtyard with him after our interviews—that it would only make things worse. Right now, he's caught in the middle of wanting help and fighting to convince himself that he doesn't need it, and all I can do is watch him. The pull from both ends just tightens the knot forming in my chest, and then I realize, maybe for the first time, that this isn't just his feeling. I'm caught in the middle too.

CHAPTER 4
The Line
Arco

I turn away without looking at her. I force myself not to look at her because I know if I see her face, I won't be able to turn away at all. I'll just insist on going with her to find Wright, which is the same as volunteering to keep living in his shadow. I've been up and down that road, and it's not going anywhere. At least not for me. I used to think love was about what you could give—about who *you* loved rather than about who loved *you*. Maybe part of me still believes that. I don't know. Right now, I just want to fight for something that might actually make a difference.

"Arco!" she calls after me, and her voice feels like an arrow hitting between my shoulder blades. I press my teeth together and keep moving down the corridor, bracing for the next shot. It doesn't come.

I scan the main floor for Tark and head toward him, but he just tries to pin me in place with his unblinking lion-stare. I keep walking toward him because I don't care what he thinks or does anymore as long as he gives me something to do. Now.

"Mr. Hart?" Tark says, quirking an eyebrow at me when I don't stop. Our eyes connect.

"When are we leaving?" I ask, once I do finally stop

about two feet from him. He looks at me for a second like he's trying to remember a question to ask me, but then he abandons it and nods.

"Calyx is taking you all to a—"

"No. I mean when are we leaving for Phase Three?"

"I'll have more details in the morning. Get some rest between now and then. Get organized. You're all leaving with Calyx in ten minutes," he says.

"Mr. Tark, I—"

"I said, *get some rest*, Mr. Hart. You're going to need it."

Tark just nods at me before he walks away, and I want to rip one of these consoles out of the floor and throw it across the room. At least something would happen then. At least there would be input and reaction...we wouldn't all just be standing around like droids waiting for programming.

"You all right?" Jax asks me, gripping my shoulder. He cocks his eyebrows in surprise when I jump a little. "Whoa, too much coffee?"

"No." I let myself smile, then feel the adrenaline hit my bloodstream. "I'm just tired of standing around here waiting for something to happen."

"Looks like we're heading out...somewhere?" he says, nodding to Calyx as she starts signaling at everyone to come with her.

"Finish getting the trackers installed—we only have a small window for travel," Calyx says, and I feel panic hit me. There's no more time. I always think there will be time—*one more day, and she'll get it*—but that's all done now. This is really the line.

Jax slaps my back a few times, then gives me a knowing look.

"She'll be all right, man," he says, and I catch myself staring at Jazz right where I left her near the window in the corridor. I force my attention back to Jax.

"Yeah, I know," I lie.

"She's stubborn and smart, and she knows how to fight now," he says, nodding. "That's what I'm telling myself anyway. That, and she won't be alone. Vox will gut anything that comes near them, and Liam seems to know his way around up here."

I nod back at him like that's what I've been thinking the whole time too, but the truth is I don't believe it's all really happening. I can't believe she doesn't even seem to care we might never see each other again. She went on for hours about never seeing another stupid sunset that last day topside, but this, now...maybe never seeing her brother and father again, or me? All so she can go find *Liddick?* He's only ever caused trouble for her.

My stomach churns the more I go over it, so I close my eyes and tell myself when I open them again, that will be it. I can't carry this around and do what needs to be done.

"So we just push this or what?" Vox growls, stupidly reaching for the back of her neck. She can't seem to find it and winds up looking like she's doing some kind of interpretive dance. I choke a little on the laugh in my throat.

"Be still; it's not implanted yet," my sister says, pinching her face like she's trying to focus. She wipes the back of Vox's neck with a small white square of cloth, and half a second later, Vox swears a blue streak. Some of the words don't even sound like English.

"Whoa! What's wrong?" Avis's mouth hangs open. His eyes dart everywhere like he's trying to gather information. Vox is still swearing as she marches toward the corridor.

"Wait for us!" Liam yells after her, then follows in her wake when she doesn't even remotely slow down.

"What's that?" Jazz asks, approaching the group.

"A tracker. It's so we can find each other...after," my sister says again. "Neck or wrist?"

"Huh? I mean...wrist, I guess," Jazz says, holding out her arm as her eyes follow Vox down the corridor. Arwyn slides Jazz's bracelet cuff all the way down to the base of her hand, then swabs the inside of her forearm with another little white square. She positions a needle-like piece of brushed metal about half the length of her thumb on Jazz's forearm. "On three, OK? One...two..."

Jazz sucks in a sharp breath and holds it when she jerks her attention back to Arwyn. She blows it out and glares for a second before her face relaxes. "So much for three?"

"Sorry...it hurts less sometimes if you don't see it coming."

Jazz turns to me when Arwyn says this, and my guts churn all over again.

"Check it out!" Avis shouts, putting his hands straight into a 3D hologram materializing in his hand. It shows Vox flailing her arms at nothing in particular in a tunnel of some kind and Liam trying to keep up with her. He stops and doubles over every few seconds, and I take a closer look. *Did she hit him with something?*

"I think he's laughing," Jazz says, starting to chuckle herself.

"He is!" Fraya confirms. "Every time her hands fly up…she must be ranting."

Everyone starts to laugh a little at this, and for a second the rock sitting on my chest dislodges.

"They're in E corridor. You have to go through three walls to get there." Lyden grins, and even Jazz's dad cracks a smile. He's been either stoic or adamant up until now. Nothing in between.

"Your turn. Wrist or neck?" Arwyn says, now at my side.

"Can we all do that afterward? Pull up the hologram?"

"If you put the tracker in your wrist, yes. If you put it in the back of your neck, you'll see it in your head if you close your eyes. Everyone's locator will load in your peripheral vision."

"That seems more tactical than pulling it up out in the open," I say, but if Jazz is really going, I know I won't need that thing in my neck to help me see her when I close my eyes.

"It just hurts a little more…" Arwyn adds. And that pretty much seals the deal. I turn around and look at the floor over my shoulder.

"Do it."

***

After everyone has a tracker injected and Liam manages to bring Vox back from her field trip, Calyx calls a quick meeting. We all move toward the center of the room as she stands in front of the dead, gray column that used to be active with virtuo-cine plots. Now, it just looks like a sea tossing in a storm. Calyx clears her throat.

"Skull is working on mobilizing our sleeper cells on Earth, at Gaia Sur, and even at The State so they are in place when we go into Phase Three," she says, which makes everyone else in the room cheer. I'm surprised to hear it since I'd completely forgotten anyone else was here except for us, but there they are in all different-colored jumpsuits standing behind their consoles.

"Burn it down!" someone yells, which inspires another roar of cheering.

"But we're getting everyone out first? You said there were others in there…like you?" Myra turns to Arwyn, raising her voice over the noise.

"When we go in, we'll let them out. Arco and Skull will come for them."

Adrenaline hits my blood for the second time in what can only be an hour. But this is what I wanted, right? I wanted to do something that matters. I nod at my sister.

"And we're the wings? Whatever that means?" Ellis asks, turning to Calyx.

"Yes. You'll act as relays, bringing the people Arco and Skull extract back here where they can be stabilized, then transported to our contacts at The State for protection," she answers, then meets my eyes. "Your missions are critical."

"It's just the three of them with Tark going in to extract those people? They won't have help? What if they're caught?" Jazz asks in a rush, which puts me back a step.

"Once we're all inside, we'll clear a path and seal off most of the facility. They'll have a clear trajectory," Arwyn says, but Jazz's eyes are still sharp, cutting from my sister to Lyden. She relaxes almost immediately, so I look over to Lyden and notice his brows working. He nods at her, and I feel a weight hit me in the stomach again. I hate their stupid telepathy.

This puts Liddick back in my head, his smug face... the fact that he's nothing but a selfish, entitled coward.

"When are we leaving, and what are we flying?" I ask, pressing my teeth together to grind this thought to dust before I swallow it.

"We have one *Class A Wraith* and two *Class B Sojourners*," Calyx answers. "You and Skull will take the Wraith through the barrier, and the Sojourners will attach below. When each Class B ship is full, they'll head back here, and we'll board the Wraith. With any luck, we'll be back here in time to watch the light show," Calyx says.

"What light show?" Myra asks.

"The port-cloud and Phase Three burning up in the sun."

CHAPTER 5
Waking Up
Jazz

My forearm throbs where Arwyn injected the tracker, but it's nothing compared to the pounding behind my eyes. I stop fighting it and just sit up in the dark, disoriented until I realize we're at Calyx's hab. I have no idea what time it is, or how long we've all been asleep, but it feels like it's been at least most of the night—or, what's supposed to be night around here. I carefully make my way to the wall-sized window, which is only about ten feet away. Everyone else chose to sleep on the far end of the hab since it feels like you could fall out of the sky right here, but it reminds me of the Vishan Lookout Pier. I watch the brighter stars twinkling as if in protest of the port-cloud haze and remember that night on the dune before we all left for Gaia. The stars were fighting to be seen that night too.

"Hard to believe these have always been there, just blocked out..." Arco says, moving into place behind me. Heat radiates from him, and I can feel his warm breath on my shoulder.

"Did I wake you up?" I ask, and he shakes his head.

"I couldn't sleep."

We stand there in silence for a few more seconds just watching the stretch of infinity before us. I look down at the white haze underneath us knowing Earth is down there somewhere. It's all so surreal, I almost think I'm not actually awake yet after all. "How could so much have changed in such a short time?" I finally manage.

"Nothing has changed, Jazz. We just finally see it all for what it is." He says this from somewhere far away as he studies the stretch of black and white that folds into forever just beyond this glass. I suddenly feel like I've just walked through it…that anything stable under my feet has just fallen away.

"We're going to fix it. We're going to make it right."

Arco doesn't answer until I turn to look up at him, and then it's clear to me we're not just talking about The Seam and The State, or Gaia and Phase Three. His eyes dart to the ground for a second before his mouth twitches with a smile like a spark that just won't catch. He nods.

"I thought so…" He takes a deep breath, and my chest starts to ache. "There's a lot out of our control, a lot of unknowns…"

"That's how it's always been, though," I say, looking for something, anything, to break this tension between us now—something to close this gap that just keeps getting wider, but instead, the stupidest thing I could possibly say comes out: "I never would have imagined any of this when I sat for my interview."

"Crite, that seems like forever ago…" He finally laughs a little to my surprise. "I felt like such a mollusk when Jax and I accidentally busted your lip on the shuttle. I actually think it was my elbow that hit you."

"You were so concerned about my stupid lip when everything else around us was turning upside down." I smile back at him. He looks at me and brings his hand to my face, then strokes my bottom lip with the edge of his thumb.

"Seeing you hurt is the only thing I can't handle."

My chest aches even more now, but this time it also floods with heat. I turn into him and lay my head on his chest. His heart pounds against my cheek as he folds his arms around me and rests his chin on my head.

"So you don't hate me for this...for going to find Liddick?" I say, letting my eyes close like that will somehow create a buffer in case he protests. He chuckles a little instead, then lets out a long sigh.

"I could never hate you, Jazz. I love you." He says it like he's never coming back again, and the warm ache in my chest turns cold and hard and heavy. "I've always loved you."

Hot tears track my face, and no matter how hard I squeeze my eyes shut, I can't stop them. My throat swells shut, choking off anything I could think to say.

He pulls me more tightly against him, solid and steady, and I swallow as hard as I can in an effort to talk, but it doesn't help. I curl my fingers into his shirt and press into him, wondering how it's possible he can still smell like the sea...like home.

He clears his throat and loosens his hold around me, then moves his hands to my face.

"What?" I look up at him, scanning his face for the source of his sudden urgency. He shakes his head like he's fighting himself over whether to answer me or not, but then seems to settle it. He takes another breath and brushes his thumbs across my cheeks.

"Just tell me you love me," he almost whispers, and it's the last thing I would have expected him to say right now.

"Arco, you know I..." I start to say everything in my head at once, scrambling for all the explanations I know he deserves about why I'm going, how it has nothing to do with my feelings for him, but nothing else comes out. There are too many words and not enough all at the same time.

"He drops his hands from my face and looks back out the window, then crosses his arms over his chest like he's suddenly freezing. "I wish we never got on that sub..." he says to himself, shaking his head again before he chuckles humorlessly and takes a deep breath.

"If we hadn't, we wouldn't be in a position to fix the world right now."

Arco looks at me for a long time as the corner of his mouth tacks to one side.

"You know something..." he starts, then smiles to the floor. "I'd tear the world apart myself if it meant I could just fix us."

The same spike of heat I felt through my chest at The Seam building stabs me again, and I can't get a breath.

"What are you saying?" I ask, but the hollow in my chest is all the answer I need.

"I don't know how to be this close to you while you're so far away," he starts, searching my face for something he lost. He swallows a few times and straightens, pushing a hand through his hair. It falls in a series of small waves as he shakes his head again like he's fighting against whatever is trying to come out next.

"I thought it was Liddick who was always here with you, even when he wasn't, but you're the one who's with him."

His words are quiet, strangled, and they burn in my chest.

"It's not like that, Arco. If it were you out there—if it were you everyone thought betrayed us, I'd come for you too. I wouldn't let them write you off like they're doing now with Liddick."

He nods knowingly, and my words just fall around him like so much rain.

"Jazz, do you really think for one second I'd ever let anything take me away from you like that in the first place? That I'd ever let myself be in a position that would put everything at risk? I'd burn down whole worlds to stay in yours, Jazz. But I can't make you stay in mine."

"Arco, don't you see I just can't let everyone believe something that's not true? What if he's in trouble? What if he's hurt?"

Arco's expression doesn't change from absolute conviction. His sharp features cut the shadows made by the muted glow of the port-cloud outside the window, making him look like a statue come to life.

"Nothing would keep me apart from you," he says without missing a beat. "Nothing except you always running the other way."

"I'm not running the other way! *Why* is this so black-and-white for you? He might need help. Can't you see there are some things that are just out of our control?"

His smile sparks again, just enough to light his sea-green eyes for a fraction of a second before it fades just as fast.

"I'm still trying to make peace with that," he says, then gives me a small nod.

A ring of light begins to glow around the perimeter of the ceiling, illuminating everyone still asleep around the living room of Calyx's hab. She walks into the room already dressed in her white jumpsuit and long, white coat.

"Good. You're up. Rally the others. It's time to move."

CHAPTER 6
Sojourner
Arco

I was awake most of the night with my eyes closed, just watching her breathe through this tracker implant. It puts everyone in a little box in the corner of my vision somehow, just to the left and right. I can minimize each box to the bottom or drag one to the center like it's all on a screen. Whether this is a good thing or a bad thing, I haven't decided yet. Arwyn was right when she said it would hurt more. She just didn't mention when it would stop.

We're in coats and moving out the door in minutes. I overhear Liam saying something to Calyx about using *the slide*, which doesn't sit well with her at all. They exchange a few more words before he pulls Lyden into the conversation, and I strain to make out what they're saying. Lyden's expression tightens, so apparently, he doesn't like whatever Liam is talking about either. I take a few quick strides so I can hear them better, but Jax walks into my path and then falls in line with me.

"My dad said Tark has the ships ready. They're not far from here."

"How are they not conspicuous? Aren't there patrols or something here?"

"I think so. He said they're sending one of the B class

ships to take us there, and we only have a window of a few minutes before it will have to leave again. Must be weaving through a rotation."

I nod to him before he makes his way up the illuminated path to Avis and Ellis, then notice Liam walking a wide line with Vox and Jazz a few steps ahead past the cylindrical buildings in the distance. I watch the gap between them and us grow. I watch her get farther and farther away. Every step I take creates the vacillating feeling of either wanting to run as fast as I can after her, or ripping my eyes away and pushing forward.

I press my teeth together against the frigid air. The edges of her long, white coat whip behind her as she walks down the glowing white street, the light bouncing off the cylinder buildings like it's all some kind of perfect virtual reality wasteland. She turns around, and the wind blows her hood back. Her dark hair flies all around her as she clutches the coat around her neck. A breath stops in my chest when she holds up a hand and waves. I almost break away. I almost chase her down just so I can put my arms around her one more time. But I know if I do that, I'll never let her go again.

I nod, then force my feet to move in the opposite direction. When I look back over my shoulder after a handful of steps, she's gone.

She's gone, and I let her go.

"Arco! *Helloooo!*" Avis chirps at me from somewhere up ahead. "You coming?"

Everyone is about fifty feet in front of me, and I have no idea when that happened. I jog to catch up and notice Azeris and Zoe aren't with our group.

"Where are Zoe and her dad?" I ask.

"They went back to The Seam building to transfer to Azeris's hab in the Badlands. Where have you been?" Ellis chuckles, and I feel like a mollusk. *Get it together, Hart...*

"The Sojourner will be here in about three minutes. Is this everyone?" Tark says, coming from around the corner of the smooth, cold building to meet us.

"Azeris took his daughter back," Calyx informs him. "Everyone else is here, except...Liam took his group to the Slide."

"*What?*" Tark's expression sharpens.

"I tried to stop him. But in all honesty, it's the only chance they have."

"He went *where?* Did you say he took them to the Slide?" Jack crosses the room in a few long strides to Calyx and Tark.

"He'll handle it," Calyx tells him, holding up a hand to Jax, Myra, and Fraya so they stop advancing to catch up to Jack again.

"No, we need to go pick them up right now."

"There's no time. They'll be all right. Liam has... *friends* there," Lyden says.

"What the hell happened to your checks and balances? We were up all night configuring the workaround *specifically* to get them into the Mainframe Building and back out. They won't make the next rally point if they're not using that!"

"Liam doesn't think Liddick is there anymore," Calyx says. "And Jack, he's probably right."

"That's not the point! They were supposed to go there

just to be sure, then meet us at rally two tonight. *That* is what he told us they would do if we built that workaround." Jack's eyes are wild as blood crashes into his cheeks.

"He knew you'd stop him from searching if he didn't agree," Lyden says.

Jack rounds on him and grabs his shirt. "*You* knew about this? You knew he was just letting me think we were designing a simple little out and back, all so he could take my daughter to *the Slide?*"

"What the hell is the Slide!?" I shout. My heart hammers in my chest, and suddenly no one looks honest. No one except Tark. I take a few steps toward him and ask again. "*What* is the Slide?"

He sighs, then glares at Calyx and Lyden before turning back to me. "It's the underbelly of the Grid—a port-carnate hub to the deep net. The last access port was configured between the shift tracks here in Admin City, but it always changes."

His words just keep slamming into each other in my head, jockeying for position. For meaning.

"What do you mean, *configured?* It's an extension of the deep net or something?"

"Or something," Jack answers, then scrubs his hands over his face in obvious frustration.

"It's made from syphoned port-cloud atoms, and it's constantly shifting so the patrols can't find it," Tark adds calmly, but Jack is about to pull his hair out.

"So they're in danger? Is that what you're saying?" I ask, trying to get him to spit it out.

"It's a slip link from Lima, but—" Lyden finally says,

and that's all he has to say because that, I understand. Everything in me ignites. Lyden meets my eyes and holds up a hand like he's trying to walk me back from the edge of a building. I glare at him.

"You let your mollusk brother take Vox and Jazz to a deep net portal with *prisoners* from Lima?"

"Listen, I know it sounds bad, but he has allies at the Slide."

"Do I look like I give one fresh pile about your *skod* brother's allies!?" I yell, pushing toward him until Jax moves between us. I clench my hands into fists and focus all my energy on swallowing the rest of the bombs exploding in my lungs.

"We just have to go back and get them," Jax says, turning to face Tark.

The tops of two Sojourner ships surface just beyond the illuminated track we're all standing on. They settle onto it after Tark taps something into the console on his forearm.

"No time," he says. "We have sixty seconds to board and sixty to get clear of the reconfiguring perimeter seal before the sweep comes. We'll figure this out, but not here. Come on!"

"We can't just leave!" I shout.

"They're already *gone*, Mr. Hart! We'll find them, but we have to get out of this sweep path right now!"

He grabs my shoulder and something in me cracks. "Get off me!" I yell, pushing him as hard as I can.

He stumbles backward, then narrows his yellow lion eyes at me as he straightens. He puts his hands in the air at his sides, then lowers his voice and angles his head toward the bullet-style mini-ship in front of us.

"Mr. Hart, you have about forty seconds to get on that bus if you don't want to end up in Lima yourself."

"Good! Then there would be at least one person there who wouldn't be aiming to sell Vox and Jazz to deep net bottom feeders!" I spit the words at him, moving away again until Jax crosses to block my view.

"Come on—we can't do anything here," he says. "We'll circle back…"

I take one step, then another, feeling acid push through my veins. Before I know it, we're moving quickly down meshed metal steps. Calyx takes everyone down a few more steps, and I follow Tark, Ellis, and Avis to seats near the long, narrow cockpit window. I blink hard a few time to be sure, and then I am sure—Eco is behind the pilot's console.

"*You?*" I say, trying to stare a hole through the center of his light-up head.

"Yeah, me. You gonna help me fly this thing or what?"

CHAPTER 7
Friends in Low Places
Jazz

I forgot how cold it was here.

The wind keeps pushing my hood back and whipping my hair into a frenzy, but if this place is sealed, I'm not sure where the wind is even coming from.

"What's this blow about?" Vox asks Liam, likely eavesdropping in my head like she tends to do.

"Air circulation. This place exists for the servers underneath, not for people," he answers.

"Where are we going?" I ask, noticing how he seems to be walking with a purpose. I almost have to jog to keep up with him.

"A place I know that can help us. We're not going to find anything going through The Seam's channels. Just keep up."

Vox and I exchange glances. *I don't have a good feeling about this,* I think toward her. She raises a burgundy eyebrow.

What could happen?

I don't know. That's why I don't have a good feeling about this.

The streets—or, the wide, illuminated paths that pass for streets up here—are nearly empty. The occasional person with peacock blue or lavender eyes walks by wearing the same kind of long, white coats we are, but there aren't nearly as many of them as there were when we all first arrived.

"Where is everyone now?" I ask. Liam looks back over his shoulder at me, then scans the building behind me. He signals at us to catch up to him, so we do.

"Just keep your eyes ahead of you. Don't look at me while we talk, OK?"

"Why not? Where are we going?" Vox asks, not even giving him a second to explain.

Liam sighs, annoyed. "Because I don't want to draw any attention." He looks over his shoulder again at the tall, smooth cylindrical building that's getting smaller in the distance, then faces forward again. "We're going to a place called the *Slide*. It's connected via slip link to Lima prison."

"Wait, what?!" I ask, turning to him abruptly before I remember his instructions to keep looking forward. I jerk my eyes back to the edge of the illuminated path ahead. "And what's a *slip link*?"

"It's a port-carnate hub with jumping coordinates," Liam explains. "Untraceable. The whole place is no bigger than an oxygen bar. I know some people there who can help us find who hijacked Liddick's transfer from Azeris's hab, then pulled him offline after he reset the Grid server."

"Didn't the people at The Seam already say they traced him back to the Mainframe Office?" I ask.

"That won't help us find him—we need to see where he went after he left there."

"And we're supposed to do that how?" Vox asks,

trying, like me, to keep up with his long strides. "Does this place close in ten minutes or something? Slow *down.*"

"It's going to move soon. We need to hurry."

"Move where? Will you just explain this all at once already?" I ask, hearing the impatience in my voice.

"Crite, look—the Slide is a big room, OK?" Liam says, now walking even faster. "It's made from syphoned atoms from the port-cloud. The whole place dissipates, then reconfigures somewhere else about every six hours, which is about how long it takes for all the levels of the port-cloud to cycle, so the regulators never know the atoms being syphoned by the Slide are missing—it's essentially a place that never exists," he adds, exasperated.

"If it assembles and disassembles just like that, how do they have a port-carnate hub there? Those are... complicated," I ask.

"You understand Lima is populated by criminal geniuses, right?" Liam clips his words, and I get the distinct impression something else is going on here.

He's not telling us something, I think toward Vox. She nods quickly at me.

"And these are your *friends*?" she asks.

"If we hurry. I don't know who will be there after the coordinates shift, so we need to be in and out before that happens. It's here—come on." Liam heaves a relieved sigh, then leads us to the edge of the illuminated street. He turns to face the open black sky, which fades into the gray haze of the port-cloud below. He holds a small, black disk straight out in front of him, then turns it and takes several steps to the right before putting the little disc back in his coat pocket. "OK, we need to jump."

I gape at him. "Jump...*where?* There's nothing out there!"

"Yes, there is. There's an opening in the ion dome here—this section is just a placeholder to keep the atmosphere in check. We can move through it."

"I'm not jumping into space, Liam. Are you split?"

"Jazwyn, we don't have time for this. Trust me. The Slide is directly below us, and the only way in there is if you *jump with me.*"

A stream of heat shoots up from my chest and floods my cheeks. His voice is Liddick's. So is his face and the set of his mouth when he insists. I shake my head to clear the image and refocus.

"But then how do we get backup here!?"

"We—" he starts to answer, but then stops abruptly when Vox runs past us and leaps off the edge of the illuminated path, hugging her knees to her chest like she's cannonballing off the rock ledge into the ocean back home.

"Vox!" I shout after her, but Liam immediately covers my mouth with his hand and pulls me into him, then throws us both over the edge. His hand muffles my scream, and all I can do is grip his wrist as we free fall.

The black stretching out before us quickly turns to a translucent white haze, then a solid white sheet. I start to struggle, to reach out for something, but there's nothing there. After another second of this, it feels like the air around us thickens to the consistency of water, and we slow down. I grip Liam's shirt and look up into his eyes, which are deep blue, also just like Liddick's. His dark brows flinch, making the scar through the left one jump. He nods twice to me, apparently trying to make sure I'm done screaming. I nod back at him, and he removes his hand. He wraps his arms around me to contain my flailing, and I eventually stop when we slow down a little more. He pulls a finger to his lips and looks around frantically when we...*land?*

Vox's wild hair is the first thing I see when she takes a few steps toward us. She starts to laugh, then say something, and Liam immediately covers her mouth too.

"Ow!" he hisses and yanks his hand back, then swears. "Did you just *bite* me?"

Vox shrugs and whispers back at him. "Where are all your criminal friends?"

Liam rolls his eyes and pulls in a long, slow breath. "Follow me, and keep your mouth shut."

I can't see anything in any direction except solid white with patches of more translucent haze where it looks like the clouds have just descended on us—the thickest fog that has ever been. It reminds me of the fog that enveloped us in the last biome underneath the ocean floor, and the thought of this makes my heart hammer in my chest.

I grip the back of Vox's coat so we don't get separated.

Do you want me to hold your hand? she thinks, then snorts in my mind.

Stow it. Why did you just jump? You could have died!

Awww. I didn't know you cared, sand dollar.

I close my eyes for half a second and just shake my head.

You're going to get us all killed one of these days.

The haze starts to dissipate the second we start hearing conversation and music. After a few more seconds, people start taking shape. Some are sitting at a long counter, and some are talking with green-haired women along the side walls. Some are doing more than talking...

"Whoa," I say under my breath, and Liam gives me a warning look. Vox smirks at me and shakes her head.

You're so precious, she thinks.

Just stop talking to me.

"Well, look what the droids dragged in," a woman's sharp voice says from somewhere. "You must be Liam Wright."

"And you must be Dot," Liam says.

We keep walking through the last of the haze until we see a green-haired woman sitting at a small round table with a few hazardous-looking men. She's wearing a stark white jumpsuit like all the others, except for the extremely tall women along the sides of the room, who are barely wearing anything under their draping, white coats.

The people at the table—at all the tables, as I look around—are tapping away and swiping at holographic keypads hovering over the tables. Others at the long counter are exchanging what look to be metal pieces of machinery. To our left, a buzzing sound fires to life as a bright light flashes. After a few seconds, someone who wasn't there a second ago walks off the round, silver platform on the ground, then heads straight to a table.

"Last I heard you were a lap dog for Eros Styx," Dot says, looking Liam up and down. She looks at me, then does a double take when she sees Vox. "Who are the puppies?"

"These are my brother's friends," Liam says as we get closer. Dot raises an inky eyebrow and pushes her thin, red lips to one side. She clicks her teeth disapprovingly at Liam.

"Lyden didn't say you'd have company."

One of the oily, tattooed men sitting with Dot pushes out of his chair and crosses to Vox, grinning.

"This one looks like my type," he says, reaching to grab her face. She catches the base of his thumb and jerks it to the outside just like Cal did to Tieg back in the Vishan tunnels. He drops to his knees.

"You're not *my* type, skod..." she says, then *knees him in the nose.* He falls backward, bringing his hands up to his face. They fill with blood as he tries to get to his feet, but he apparently doesn't care since he drops his hands and advances on her again. Liam steps in front of her, but Dot shouts them both down.

"Get me a drink, Web!" She blows out a breath and rolls her eyes. "And clean yourself up before I tell everyone this little dragonfly broke your face." Dot gets to her feet and dusts the shoulders of Liam's coat, then grips the lapels gently before looking directly at him. She runs her thumb over the scar through his eyebrow and smiles. "Now...what can I do for you, Liam Wright?"

CHAPTER 8
Pit Stop
Arco

The controls on this ship are almost the same as on the Leviathan, especially the yoke that sits in the middle of the wrap-around control panel. I stare into the never-ending black through the window and pretend it's the sea, which at least helps me have an excuse for this heavy feeling—like it's just the miles of water pushing in and down, holding me in place like a bug under somebody's thumb.

"You got the hang of this pretty quick," Eco says, trying to make nice as we coast. I can't even look at him.

"A ship is a ship."

"I've been to the slip link—the *Slide*," he says, but I just keep looking out into the black. "It's not as bad as Skull and Jack think. People keep to themselves unless they have business with each other. You can be a ghost there."

I give him a side eye and decide that he's going to be chatty. "People from *Lima*," I manage to say, then wonder why I'm talking to him. I liked him better when he was a condescending know-it-all. "Why are you even here?"

He just shrugs as the lights in his cheekbones blink red. I don't have the energy to get into a conversation to find out the real reason, and I don't actually care.

"Skull said you were a pilot at Gaia."

"He seems to think so. It was all just simulations."

"Perception is reality." Eco doesn't turn from looking out the wraparound window in front of us. Maybe that's why he's here. Maybe he wants to see if the reality matches his perceptions from all his test runs in the virtuo-cines.

"How do you know how to fly this thing? Alpha-channel testing?" I ask, then remind myself I don't care. He nods.

"I've been many, many pilots and have flown many, many ships. Though this is a little more complicated without the widgets in my peripherals." He laughs to himself.

"You have widgets in your *vision?*"

"Right here," he says, holding out a hand to the left of his face. *"Pause, Review, Log, Enter.* I always catch myself trying to tap a button in real life... But you can't pause real life."

I never thought about how much easier my life would be if we could do just that...what I would do if I could just freeze time to think before having to make a decision. If for once in these last idiotic months I could just stop the world and plan.

"Fortunately for everyone," Tark says, walking onto the small deck behind us. "We already know what we know—doubting that is what gets people killed."

Eco forces a huffed laugh. "Analysis paralysis..."

"Indeed," Tark replies, walking in behind us and slapping Eco on the back. "We need to make a pit stop before we get to the Wraith. Make sure everyone below is secured," he adds. Eco raises an eyebrow at him, waiting for more explanation, but it doesn't come.

"Skull, I wanted to...apologize for—"

"No need. Calyx told me you spoke. I'm glad we're back on the same page." Tark claps Eco on the shoulder again, and the seatbelt dissipates from his shoulders in a scatter of black particles as he gets up, just like the seatbelts on the Leviathan. Once he goes below deck, Tark drops into his vacated chair and starts pushing buttons.

"What's the pit stop?" I ask, checking the grids on the gauges in front of me to see what Tark did. All the stars have disappeared from the map.

"I need to see a man about a fog."

I feel my face pinch, then glance over as he changes more settings on the floating control panel in front of him.

"You mean about a *dog?*"

Tark drops his chin at me like I'm a champion mollusk. "Mr. Hart, what would we do with a dog on this airship?"

I roll my eyes. "So we're going to get a *fog?* That's what you said? Because that makes more sense?"

Tark's white smile peels across his face. "Yes. It's a fundamental ingredient in the mutation you know as a *zephyr,*" he says, like it's some kind of lingo thing—like maybe I just call it a bubbler or a pooler...or a split, *flesh-eating wind!* I gape at him.

"Zephyrs? From the tunnels? Those things *killed* Joss, and you want to go pick one up?" I fight to keep my voice level.

Tark nods solemnly, then adjusts another setting on the digitized, floating control panel to his left.

"This one will be more amenable," he says, finishing his button pushing. He meets my eyes. "Mr. Ripley and his father will be programming it for us. We need to buy a little time."

I close my eyes in a long blink. Why can't anyone here just spit out what they're talking about all at once!? I take a deep breath through my nose, slowly, then hold it for a second until I'm sure I'm not going to blast him.

"And why do we need to program killer wind, exactly? Where are we even going to get it? Those things are miles under the seafloor in the Rush."

"The port-cloud has been draped in a security layer sometime in the last twenty-four hours. Phase Three must be on alert. We need a diversion that can be investigated, but not detected. At least not right away," Tark answers.

"And a *zephyr* is supposed to—never mind," I say, shaking my head. "Fine...so, where are we supposed to get it?"

"We're not going to get it, Mr. Hart." Tark smiles. "We're going to make it."

I shake my head at him, then push my hands through my hair in exasperation. I lean my head back against my chair and close my eyes. This whole thing is impossible.

Suddenly, the Sojourner picks up speed, but then seems to drop all at once. My ears pop, and my stomach jumps into my chest like I've just fallen over the edge of a solar coaster.

"Hey! Where are we going?" I grip the yoke in front

of me and feel it vibrate in my hand.

"Down..." Tark laughs, pushing his yoke all the way forward, and the Sojourner dives.

"Tark!"

"Keep her straight, Mr. Hart. This won't take long."

"Where are you trying to go? There's nothing there!" I shout, scanning for something, some destination on the grids, but there's nothing on the scopes.

"Then we must need a little more speed." Tark laughs again like some rabid brush dog, then pushes another button just beyond his yoke. The Sojourner surges, and my ears pop again. After a few seconds, a huge mass appears on the floating, green grid in front of me, and I nearly swallow my tongue when I see we're heading right for it.

"Obstruction! Correct course—" I start, then see the numbers juxtaposing in the corner of my vision. Sevens kicking out ones, decimals jumping between numbers, then disappearing all together. "Forty-seven degrees starboard; span twelve seconds!" I say, but I don't know how I know what to input...I just say the numbers.

"Override system command!" Tark shouts over me, his teeth barred in a psychotic smile, his wide, yellow eyes blazing like he's about to rip the throat out of something that he's finally chased down. "What do you see, Mr. Hart?"

"*What!?* That's mass, man! Can't you see it!? We're going to crash right into it!"

Tark rips out another laugh. "Not if we don't speed up!" He pushes the far button again, and the Sojourner begins to whine as another surge pushes up from somewhere below us, and my stomach dives.

"Stop! Abort!" I shout through my teeth. "System authorization override: six, seven, nine! Hart, Arco! Protocol: seven blue, remove instructor Skellig Tark for operations!"

For a split second, everything in my head is quiet— just for that one second when the thrusters disengage, but the inertia breaks have not yet kicked in...before the hull almost groans with the relief of slowing momentum. Everything stops except my breath hitting the bottom of my lungs and the periodic, distant cannon fire in my chest. I look up, and the sky is littered with stars.

The mass on the grid still isn't visible until we coast a few more seconds, but then I see it in the reflection of the ship lights. It looks like the walls of the Vishan Lookout Pier—long, smooth, black shards of glass all pressed together into a massive platform of some kind. A chill runs down my spine when I register what that thing would have done to us. "We'd have been ripped in half..." I whisper, still only partially back to reality.

"Glad to see you've been sharpening your skill set, Mr. Hart," Tark says with a chuckle in his voice like this has just been some split training simulation. Everything about him right now is almost painfully stupid to me. I squeeze my eyes shut, like that's going to distill it somehow, then just shake even the image of him out of my head.

"Are you *trying* to kill us?"

"Not at all," he says, letting a grin hook the corner of his mouth. "But if I were, isn't it nice to know you wouldn't think twice about stopping me?" He lets the other side of his mouth tack up, then gives me a knowing look.

"Are you telling me you just bluffed all that? You just put my *whole team* at risk to play a *game?*" I say through my teeth again, trying to keep my voice in check so no one below can hear what's happening. I push to my feet, catching the scatter of black seatbelt particles falling away in the corner of my vision.

"A game you needed to win if we're going to have any chance of keeping everyone alive for the next level of the mission, Mr. Hart." He stares straight into me, and I can almost feel the hole drilling into my chest. "Don't think. Act. Trust your vision. Trust your gut," he adds with a nod. "Because now you know you can."

The drill biting into my chest stops stinging, only to be replaced with prickles running up the back of my neck and down my arms. I did stop him...and I didn't think about it. I look out onto the floating slab of black that's glinting in the distance, then notice a series of lattice lines catching the light from our ship as we slowly drift toward it. I look back at Tark.

"There's a dock in there?" I ask, then nod, answering my own question before sliding back into my seat and grabbing the yoke. All right. I can do this. I already *did* this... "System command, six, seven, nine...Hart, Arco. Resume trajectory at two percent original speed. Sojourner class auto align. Take us in..."

CHAPTER 9
CEO
Jazz

Liam gently folds his fingers around Dot's wrists and smiles, then leans in just a little.

"Well, since you asked," he says, winking, and I am mesmerized once again.

He's just like Liddick. Like, exactly, I think toward Vox, but don't hear so much as a snort in reply. I tear my eyes away from Liam and Dot, but I don't see Vox anywhere in the room.

"What seems to be the malfunction with your little pet?" I hear Dot say behind me as I push through the crowd scanning for Vox.

"Jazz!" He grips my arm, but I pull loose.

"Vox is gone. We need to find her."

Liam swears under his breath, then abruptly nods. "There..." He starts walking with purpose to our left, where the crowd of people is the thickest. A very dark woman takes out one of her eyes, shakes it, then puts it back in and blinks furiously. A young man next to her takes out a tooth, then unscrews the bottom of it. He taps it until a small metal square falls out, which he then hands to yet another man who deposits the square into a small incision that he pulls open just under his eye. When he removes his hand, the incision completely disappears again. *What the? We need to get out of here.*

When we finally clear through most of the people, I see Vox standing over a wiry man leaning backward in his stool so far that his head touches the counter. Vox is standing over him with some kind of knife that she's using to...*mark his face?*

"What are you doing?" I ask once we finally get close enough, but from the looks of it, she's giving the man the first of an arrow tattoo just like hers over the bridge of his nose.

"He asked how I got mine. I told him. He wanted some. Here." She tosses me a little bag. "Hey, what's your name?" Vox stops inking and asks the man.

"Frenchie," the pale, skinny man says, looking up at her like she's some kind of divine being. I feel the bubble of pre-roarf nausea rise in my stomach, then distract myself by looking in the little bag.

"French-Fry gave me those," Vox informs me.

"Biochips?" Liam says, and the man laughs.

"You got your sub six automators, some Skyboard biochips, a few tracker bots, some—"

"Hey, stow it and be still, or you're getting a unibrow," Vox scolds, but the man's whole face just melts right back into an adoring smile.

I look up at Liam and hand him the bag. He shrugs, then shoves it in the pocket of his long, white coat.

"Vox, we need to go," he says just as Vox wipes her pick knife on the man's shirt, then slides the little bowl of ink away from her. She spits on a napkin, then wipes it over the fresh tattoo. The man winces until Vox moves her hands to her hips and admires her work.

"There you go, Stretchy. I only had time for the two arrows."

"*Frenchie...*" the man corrects, holding an imager disk under his chin until an exact holographic copy of his face appears in front of him.

"Whatever," Vox mumbles as she walks back toward us, leaving Frenchie to admire himself. He pokes at the two chevron style lines on the bridge of his nose in his holographic reflection. Both he and the hologram flinch. "Are we done yet?" Vox asks, falling into stride with us.

"We would have been if we didn't have to come and find *you*," Liam says.

Dot is back at the table, but this time, she doesn't have company. Liam slips into the chair across from her and kisses her hand. She raises a dark eyebrow, then rolls her eyes.

"So get on with it then," she says, pulling her hand away.

"Somebody cloaked my little brother without his knowledge. He's a ghost on the Grid now, and I need to find him. Can you run a scan for the last forty-eight hours for anyone coming from the Mainframe Office?"

"That's all you want?"

"And run a sweep that will also bypass any implanted organics?"

Dot nods a few times to herself, then jerks her chin for Liam to follow her.

"Come on, and bring your puppies."

***

We move to the other side of the room and go behind the bar, then down a small staircase that sinks right into the floor. At the bottom is another small room with the entire back wall comprised of nothing but endless stars. There must be a window there, though everything is so seamless, it just looks like the room opens up to outer space.

"Julius," Dot says to the air, and seconds later, a sophisticated man's voice replies at the same time green, crisscrossing lines stretch the length of the window.

"Good evening, Ms. Cavanaugh. Shall I access your queue?"

"Not yet, Julius. Bring the Grid online—Mainframe Office, all ports for the last forty-eight hours."

"Channeling," the Julius voice says.

Dot turns back to Liam and starts stroking the back of his hair. "Now then..." she says, moving closer to him.

"Um, we're still here," I say, clearing my throat. Liam flinches when she yanks a few hairs out of his head just as she smiles obnoxiously at me.

"Don't I know it, puppy," she adds, then turns back to the console station in this small, dark room and holds up the hairs she pulled from Liam's head. A blue beam of light falls over them like the med bay scanning laser back at Gaia Sur. Code starts scrolling on the console screen, and Dot leans her head sideways like she's trying to read from a new angle. Just before I can ask her what she's doing, she turns around to face Liam again.

"So?" he asks impatiently. "Do you see him?"

"When did Lyden get back? A few others here would be interested in having a word."

"I'm not here to talk about Lyden. Do you see Liddick in the DNA correlation or not?"

"This side of the atmosphere?" She cocks her head at the scrolling code again. "Yeah. He's here. Or at least he was."

"What do you mean, *he was?*" I ask, taking a few steps toward the console. "Where is he now? Who was with him in the Mainframe Office?"

Dot sticks out her bottom lip and nods at me but talks to Liam. "Don't know why you need me if your poochie here can sniff out your boy."

I glare at her, but before I can say anything, Vox slips behind her and jabs her pick knife behind Dot's ear. She sucks in a sharp breath and straightens.

"We don't have all day, prison lady..." she says, exasperated.

Dot winks one gray eye, then disappears in what looks like several puffs of smoke, which reassemble closer to the console. Vox gapes at her.

"Leash your dogs, Wright," Dot says, glaring at us just before she turns back to the console. Liam shakes his head at Vox and holds up a hand.

"Just be patient, OK? I'll handle this>" He takes a few steps toward the console. Dot flicks the air with her fingers, and Lyden's 3D image—his head, shoulders, and torso with three obvious gills cutting around each of his sides—appears, along with a series of words under his name:

Lyden Wright
State Cryptonics, Classified
Phase Three Candidacy approved: Amphimorphics
Status: Organics not received

"So, big brother torqued off the wrong Frankenstein?" Dot snorts to herself. "I was wondering how long he'd be able to play in that sandbox without getting dirty. Your handiwork?" She gestures to Lyden's gills.

"He's *not* dirty," Liam says through his teeth. "It's complicated, and I'm trying to straighten it out, but I need to find my little brother before I can do that, OK? Do you see Liddick in that babble or not?"

Dot waves Liam off and nods.

"All right, all right...zone before you trigger the adrenaline alarms and *poof* us all back into the cloud," Dot answers, then nods in my direction. "A girl can never be too careful with tech dogs—pro tip. Do you like my place here, puppies?"

"You made this place?" I ask, still not sure if it's actually a place at all.

"I wrote and programed the original code...after I had a little help," Dot answers, raising a quick eyebrow at Liam. She turns back to her display and swipes panel after panel of code with her fingertips. "This place is iteration, oh...four million something, something, and something. My baby's evolved into such a big, handsome AI system." She sneaks a wry grin over her shoulder at me. "Don't you think?"

"Strapping, can you hurry up?" Vox asks, earning a nasty glare from Dot. She's about to say something when Liddick's 3D image pulls up. He's wearing his blue Gaia jumpsuit...it's his cadet file.

Liddick Wright
Diplomacy path, Cadet Class
Phase Two Candidacy Suspended: Amphimorphics
Status: Private Contract Assignment. LTC: GS.
Authorization 379846 Key 4.

"Phase Two candidacy?" I say under my breath, then turn to Liam. "They were going to take him? They were going to send him to that volcano Gaia no matter what... just like you and Lyden?"

Liam nods, then swallows. "Probably the rest of you too. Where is he now?" he asks Dot. "Who's the private contract?"

"Must be a high roller for him to have a Long Term Clone standing in for him at Gaia Sur," Dot says. "See it? *LTC: GS?* Just like his big brother...how is the good doctor up on the Skyboard hill?" She smiles at him. "Say the word, and I'll push the button...scatter your doppelgänger to the four winds?"

"Can you *please* just get the private contract listing?"

Dot rolls her eyes, then looks back to the data display. "I give you some of my best hacking, and you won't let me blow up their toys." She flicks away several panels of code. "Oh, not you. Get back here." Dot reaches far to her left and grabs at the air. A code panel appears in place of the previous one, and she starts nodding. "Huh...*Van Spaulding,* you dirty old dog."

"*Spaulding!?*" I nearly swallow my tongue. "Tieg and Dez...are they?"

"His perfectly engineered prodigies? Yes, along with Zed, Bev, Lief, Leo, and Pitt," she adds to herself, then spins around. "Want to explain to me how he can order splicing for all those brats, but they send me to Lima for processing the exact same tech? Excuse me very much, Mr. Biotech CEO, if you can't appreciate a little *competition*," she almost shouts.

"Dez's father is the *CEO* of Biotech Global?" I hear the words in my own voice, surprised since I was sure I'd only thought them.

"And he seems to have taken an interest in cine tech these days...we've got a storyboarder credential here, a port-carnate override key, and even a little hab overlooking the Milky Way under the name *Ludwig Sprague*...how lovely," Dot adds, tapping away again at the code panel. "I'll download it all for you—then you need to take his stink out of my hub."

"Dez and Tieg's father did this? He took Liddick?" I can't make it stick in my head. "Why?"

"That's my question too. Why did he want that server reset, and why is he still keeping Liddick?" Liam asks the ground, then sobers abruptly and trains his eyes on Dot. "Where's the hab?"

CHAPTER 10
Piranha Wind
Arco

"What is this place?" I ask, watching the black glass slabs below expand around us.

"It's The Seam's outpost hub...we like to call it The Hole in the Sky," Tark says. "The magnetic field from the volcanic slabs disrupts the field scans, so it's invisible to The State or anyone else looking for trouble." A second later, another little Sojourner vessel glides into our path at the other end of what is quickly becoming a tunnel. A slab of volcanic rock slides into place behind the other craft, then another behind us until we're completely enclosed by it.

"So, The Seam built this place?"

"No, we just found it...by spectacular accident." Tark chuckles.

"You almost crashed into it too?" Tark makes a clicking sound with his mouth and sends me a wink.

"Spectacularly."

I start to laugh but swallow it just as another pilot kills his starboard lights and switches on the hull floods. I squint and do the same. After the initial blast of light, a soft glow bounces off the slick, black walls. Tark stands up and motions for me to follow him.

We move toward the airlock, and I scan the area for a

helmet. Tark keeps walking.

"Hey! You're just going to walk out there?" I ask

"The field is contained, Mr. Hart." Tark cocks an eyebrow as if to tell me this isn't his first time on a spaceship because, hey, we do this every day. *Crite...*

The airlock doors open, and the air is noticeably thinner—like altitude simulation training back at Gaia Sur. My lungs squeeze, and I remind myself to take shallow breaths so I don't start hyperventilating. The door to the other vessel opens in the distance, and a very tall, very slim, very pale man walks toward us. Instantly, the virtuo-cine back at The Seam building flashes through my head...the Transcendents with their long limbs and pale skin.

"What the—?" I start, but then suck it back in before I say something stupid.

"Look familiar, Mr. Hart?" Tark asks like he's reading my mind, and both he and the tall, pale man laugh.

"Like it?" The man holds out his unnaturally long arms to his sides, then pats his face with one of his hands. "Dr. Cave—best in Admin City if you're ever in the market for concepting. Tell him Fargo sent you."

"Uh, that's—you're...*engineered?*" I stutter, then bite the inside of my lip before I ask more questions with obvious answers.

"Naturally!" the man says through a guffaw. "Heh! Filter what I said there? *Naturally*? Only it's anything but? Get it?" He laughs again, and I look around, waiting for someone to jump out and say this is all some kind of joke. I close my eyes in a long blink, then turn to Tark.

"Does he have what we need?"

Tark cinches his composure back into place, then crosses to the lanky man and slaps him on the back. Dust puffs from the man's white jumpsuit and dissipates in a scatter of glinting particles.

"Careful, it's a loaner!" The man snorts, cracking himself up all over again.

Is this happening? I think. *Maybe I never really got out of that virtuo-cine chair.*

"Tell Cave he does good work. Briggs would be proud."

"Briggs *Denison?*" I ask, cutting an eye at Tark.

"You're a Gaia grad?" The tall man's eyes flash to me, and I mean they literally flash a white-blue light that makes me stumble back. The man laughs. "Sorry, sorry! Just had that installed. Triggered by adrenaline levels. The ladies love interactive tech, you know?" He elbows Tark.

I blow out a breath, exhausted by all this.

"You have something we need, apparently?" I ask, hoping my tone pushes this whole idiotic thing back into some semblance of sanity. Tark grins at me, then turns back to the man.

"This is Morris Fargo," he says, extending an arm to the cine character.

I raise two fingers to my forehead, then let them drop without fanfare. "Nice to meet you."

"So, building some piranha wind, eh?" Fargo asks us conspiratorially, taking a flat, white box from his pocket and sliding it through the air to Tark. I do a double take, watching it just sail over to him in slow motion like it's on an invisible conveyor belt. He takes it, flipping the lid back with one thumb. I can't see the contents from here, but whatever is inside seems to be impressive. Tark nods, then flashes Fargo a big, white smile.

"Just a little one. What's the density report?" he asks.

"The absolute thinnest blanket coordinates are embedded in those chips," Fargo says, lifting his chin to the little box he just gave Tark. "Just let them do their thing, and try to keep up. Should only be just a few clicks from here, if you want to get into position as best you can."

"Are they masked?" Tark asks, studying whatever is in the box again.

"Only from my *personal* obsidian reservoir—would I give you live wires? I'm hurt, Skull."

I cross to Tark, fresh out of patience for trying to put the pieces of their conversation together. I stare into the box in his palm and see three black squares, shiny and textured like the walls, floor, and ceiling in whatever this enclosed hub is.

"Nice doing business with you, Fargo," Tark says. "As always."

Fargo makes a clicking sound with his mouth a few times, then turns to get back into his Sojourner.

"Nice *not* seeing you today, Skull…" he says over his shoulder, then waits, raising a white eyebrow.

"Copy that. Never a pleasure…" Tark nods, then laughs a low, graveled laugh from somewhere in his chest. He closes the box as he slips it into his jumpsuit pocket, then slaps me on the shoulder. "Let's get this back to Ripley and his son."

"You going to tell me what *this* is first? And what that

was all about? Why do you need a density report on those chips?"

Tark nods to the air in front of us as we make our way back to our craft. "Because the thinner they are, the harder they will be to trace when we use them to make a hole in that port-cloud barrier. It won't take as long for them to fuse with the atoms and reprogram them."

"That's an organic barrier…these chips are embedded with assassin code?"

"Well, good to see you were paying attention in class, Mr. Hart. Yes, that's what's on them."

"And…that's illegal."

"Well, not outside of *A-sym* patches for cannibalizing damaged cells, but hey, that's why they're masked." Tark looks at me again like he's waiting for me to catch up.

"I assume you have a plan for deflecting the gaping hole you plan to make in the port-cloud with these then?"

"We won't actually be leaving a hole," he says, opening the hatch to our Sojourner. "The zephyr will occupy the space it leaves after consuming the organic matter in the barrier, just like an *A-sym* patch. It will simply shift to mirror the rest of the cloud."

"Do you actually think it's going to stop at eating just a little hole?"

"It will if Ripley and his son do their job right," Tark answers as the door seals behind us.

"Where did you go?" Avis asks, nearly running into us when we get back on deck. "You went through the airlock, and the front window just went black."

"Fargo must have launched a security barrier." Tark

half-laughs. "Can't be too careful up here."

"Did you get it?" Calyx asks, ascending the mesh stairs that go below deck.

"We got it—take these to Ripley and tell him what we need...he can build on the Wraith. Get everyone else locked down so we can launch."

Calyx nods, taking the little box from Tark before she heads back down the steps. Eco moves out of his seat so Tark can sit in it, and I get back into mine.

"All right, what are the coordinates for that Slide place?" I ask, but Tark doesn't answer me. He just starts pushing buttons. "We need to get Vox and Jazz out of there. That's no place for them to be—for *anyone* to be."

"Liam won't let anything happen to them," is all Tark says after several impossible seconds. I start to protest, but the Sojourner fires forward and forces the words back down my throat. I press my teeth together and start punching in an all-stop code, but nothing registers on my console.

"Did you disable my controls? Six, seven, nine...Hart, Arco; initiate operations sequence," I say.

"Authorization denied," a female voice says from... everywhere.

"Are you split!? We can't leave them there!" I yell once I realize what Tark is trying to pull. I punch more sequences into my console, which only activates the stupid computer voice again.

"Authorization denied...authorization den—"

"All right!" I shout, then push back from the console and try to take a deep breath. *What are the odds this will be OK? What are the odds anything will be OK in a prison hub with Liam Wright...* I think, and immediately numbers and signs I don't recognize storm into the corner of my vision. "What is this?" I say out loud, pushing the heels of my hands into my eyes, which only makes the numbers and symbols flood everywhere. "What *is this?"*

"Running probabilities on your chances of knocking me out of this chair? Don't waste brain cells, Mr. Hart— this rig won't respond to you without my authorization." Tark laughs to himself, and I just feel heat...*violence* in every cell in my body.

"Something is wrong. I'm getting Arwyn and Fraya," Avis says from behind me somewhere. I hear Ellis right in front of me a second later.

"Hart—take your hands down and look straight ahead," he says, his cold fingers wrapping around my wrists. "Breathe in through your nose and out through your mouth, or you're going to seize. Do it now," he says, and I try to listen to him. I snap my teeth together again and force the exhale through them, but it doesn't offset the acid in my lungs or the throbbing that has just started behind my eyes. *Is this what it feels like to want to kill someone?*

But then I see a flash of Jazz in a white room with the back end cut off, like half of it is just hanging in space. She's with Vox and Liam, and some green-haired woman in a white jumpsuit. "Is that the Slide? Where are the prisoners?" I hear myself ask.

"Ah, you see them now! I told you, they're all right. Liam has it under control," Tark says, which makes the image of Jazz and the others fade into another tornado of numbers and symbols. I feel the acid explode in my chest again, shooting through my arms and into the veins in my hands. *I will kill him,* I think, then push to my feet, even though I can't see anything but these *stupid* numbers!

"Arco, hold still; you have to listen to me," my sister says, now inches away from me. "You have to keep your adrenaline levels down. It disrupts the tracking interface."

"All I see are numbers and symbols! Where did Jazz go? I just saw her!"

"I know, *I know*...you can see her again, but you have to relax or your brain will shut everything down and you'll seize. Are you listening to me? Take a deep breath."

"We need to get them out of that place. Did you know too? Was it just his brothers, or did you know about the Slide too? *Tell me!*" I shout into the number storm.

"Arco, get level, and I'll explain everything to you, OK? You have to level first. Just breathe."

I take in a few deep breaths and push them through my teeth until the numbers start to slow down in the corners of my eyes. They're almost gone except for a series of coordinates that just keeps flickering.

"Atmospheric 90 12.17 16.7...what are those numbers?" I ask, lowering my hands from my eyes. I blink, and my sister comes into view. "What are they?" I ask again, turning to Tark. He just watches me for a second with an open mouth. "What *are* they!?"

"Those are the coordinates to the Slide right now," he says quietly.

I punch them into my console, but the asinine ship

voice is all I get in reply.

"Authorization denied."

I feel the heat in my chest light again, but Arwyn immediately starts talking.

"Arco, listen...by the time we'd get there, they'd already be gone, OK? The coordinates are going to shift in eight minutes, and that slip link will close. The Slide will show up somewhere else. They're going to leave right now, all right? Calm down. You have to breathe."

Everyone is above deck now, standing along the back wall and watching me like some kind of split sideshow. My hands start shaking, so I ball them into fists at my sides to make them stop.

"You're a Nav/Coder hybrid, aren't you?" Lyden asks, taking a few steps toward me.

"Get away from me."

I see Tark nod at him out of the corner of my eye, and before I can shoot him down too, my sister is in front of me again with her hands up like I'm some kind of rabid dog. I look past her at Avis, who's looking at me the same way—in fact, everyone is looking at me like I've just bitten the head off something.

"Arco, hold still, OK?" my sister says, then raises a cloth to my nose. When she pulls it back, it's smeared with blood.

CHAPTER 11
Leaving the Slide
Jazz

Dot punches something into her console, and a miniature white, 3D cylindrical building with a few lines of text underneath it appears on the illuminated grid. She reaches for the building, then *presses it all into a tiny square* and hands it to Liam. I look at Vox, who is just as shocked as I am.

"Here are the hab coordinates. I suppose you'll be needing new bioprints?" Dot sighs as Liam slips the square into his pocket.

"Ah...well these biochips—" Liam pulls the bag Vox got from Frenchie out of his other pocket.

"*Those* will get you and your puppies locked up like the rest of us in here. Hasn't Lyden taught you *anything*, Dr. Wright?"

"Yeah, well Rheen and the rest of her psychopaths have kept him busy the last few years. What's the problem with the chips?"

"Aren't you adorable? That's a bag of spare parts you have there, sweetheart. Meant to be taken apart and put back together again. Swallow any one of those as is, and the first shift track you board will bring a patrol down on you so fast, we could continue this meeting in person tomorrow back at Lima." Dot holds out her hand for the bag, and Liam hands it to her. "Julius!"

"At your service," the system voice says.

"Tell Neri I need three biochips for Admin City, one male, two female...Skyboard class, designer clearance."

"Of course," the low voice says again.

Liam tacks a smile to one side of his face. "I didn't know you cared, Dot."

"I don't," she says quickly before taking in a long, bored breath. "Your big brother gave me the cycling schedule that let me tap into the port-cloud in the first place—did you know that?" She rifles through the contents of the little bag with two fingers. "If it weren't for him, Lima really *would* be a prison, so I owe him, is all."

Liam nods and puts his hands in his pockets. "He said you'd been allies for a long time...and that you'd help us. Thank you."

Dot takes her fingers from the bag and raises them in a sloppy salute, just like Dell and the rest of the Badlanders.

She's from Seaboard North... I think, and Vox rolls her eyes.

"Do you have any channel filters she can swallow or something? Some that will let her keep her random epiphanies to herself?"

"Vox!" I hiss, but it's too late. Dot raises a dark eyebrow at me just as a tall woman with wide stripes tattooed over half her face comes in the room. She holds out a little box for Dot but is ignored.

"Readers, eh?" Dot asks me, then smiles when I hear her voice in my head. *Welcome to the club...*

You're from…Gaia? You're a Reader? I think.

She nods. *Used to be. Same class as Lyden. We ran in… different circles.* She shrugs, then smiles at the tall woman, who blows out an exasperated huff and abruptly sets the little box she's holding on top of Dot's console.

"Like I have all day?" the tall woman says. "The green one is male—you're *welcome.*" She turns on a heel and heads back through the door with a pinched look at Vox and me.

Dot sends an air kiss to her back. "You're a dream, Neri!" she adds, then picks up the box and tosses it to Liam. "Swallow the green one. The other two are for your puppies here. Any of you get pinched, I can't help you."

"We understand. Thanks, Dot," Liam says. "We better go."

"Yeah…" Dot looks at the band on the inside of her wrist. "Got about a hundred twenty seconds." She laughs, and all the blood runs out of Liam's face.

"Come on, *come on!*" he says, pulling back the coat sleeve to check his own wrist cuff. We run through the door behind us into the main room, which is filling with fog. Liam swears as we push through the dissipating crowd. "We just have to get across the threshold. The dome pocket will lift us back to the platform. Hurry up!"

"Or what?" Vox shouts up to Liam.

"Or we run straight out into space, freeze, and die! *Move!*"

Vox and I pick up the pace until we're on Liam's heels, the haze around us getting thicker and more disorienting. I almost slow down to get my bearings but know if I do, the next step I take could turn me into a block of ice. I forget about this, though, when everything starts to vibrate.

"What's happening?" I shout, now completely blinded by the opaque white haze in every direction.

"It's the dome pocket. It's starting to move!"

"Are we in it!?" Vox yells from somewhere to my right.

"Almost! Keep running!" Liam answers in the distance.

Of all the times I've been afraid in my life…when that giant bullet ant was crawling on my face in the Rush, when I sat for my initial Gaia interview, and even when that jellyfish stung me the night we sneaked away from Liam's port festival…this fear, now, is the worst.

"Aghhh!' Vox shouts, which snaps my attention back just in time for my ears to pop…hard.

"Ow!" I say out loud, and both of us start rubbing our ears.

"A little warning next time?" Vox says, punching Liam in the arm.

"Hey!" I point at the ground, then look around frantically. *The streets are glowing, and there's the tall, salt pillar buildings… We're back,* I think.

Salt pillar buildings? is all Vox has time to say in my head before Liam is barking at us.

"Crite…" he hisses, then grabs both our arms and pulls us in close. We need to get to the shift transports.

***

We walk about ten minutes along the illuminated street when Liam holds out a little yellow triangle to me.

"*That's* a biochip?" I ask. "I thought they were square."

"Foreign ingestibles—easier to hack. Just swallow it; we're almost to the shift platform."

I take the yellow triangle and bite it once, then put it under my tongue. I cut a glance at Vox. *Don't chomp this one,* I think, remembering her coughing fit after she tried to chew the one they gave her back at The Seam building so we could go into the virtuo-cines.

Yeah, thanks, she thinks in reply, narrowing her green snake eyes at me. "So what happens to the other bio-whatever they gave us already?" she asks Liam.

"This will override it."

"How do we know what these say about us?" I ask. "Dot never said anything except that the green one was male,"

Liam shrugs. "We can find out in the vanity district if we have time, but it's in the opposite direction as this hab," he says, holding out the miniature building in his palm. A small, holographic map radiates from it with a moving, blinking blue light."

"That's us?" Vox asks, trying to touch the dot. He waves her hand away.

"Yes, what do you think? We're almost there. Just don't talk or do anything, OK?"

Liam puts the little building map back in his pocket and pulls the wide collar of his coat closed around his neck. He blows out a breath and pulls in another long, deep one. Everything about him is on edge.

"We're going to find him. We're going to bring him back," I say. He looks down at me for a second and nods, and even though his expression doesn't change, the knot he's become seems to loosen a little.

The shift station on this...level—*plank*...? What did they call it before?—looks exactly like the other ones we were on with Eco and Calyx when we first arrived in Admin City. The pillars of light all have glowing names like *River Plank* and *Solar Plank* hovering at the top of them, and the illuminated street just widens like an old-time parking garage.

"Which one of these light poles are we supposed to walk into?" Vox asks, walking a few yards ahead.

"Just stay back here. I don't have time to chase after you if you get sucked into the wrong column—here, come on."

Liam steers us to *Nova Plank*, and I try to remember what Lyden said about getting into a shift. *Put your head against the back wall, hold your breath, close your eyes...*

Are the both of you going to Mom-and-Dad me this entire time or what? Vox says in my head as we walk into the column of light.

"What?" I say out loud just as the shift starts to push us, and my face is immediately frozen. Vox's neck extends stupidly halfway up the shift column like some kind of funhouse reflection. Her mouth is frozen in a wide, open laugh and all I can think is how I'm going to strangle her as soon as we get off this thing. My stomach lurches as we turn a corner, and I feel like we've just dropped off the edge on a solar coaster.

Finally, the shift starts to slow down, and Vox's head returns to a respectable distance from the rest of her body.

"I love those. Your head was way up there!" she says, pointing to the sky. I narrow my eyes at her.

"I hate you," I mumble and try not to roarf. "Where are we?"

"Nova Plank—come on, the hab is right here." Liam pushes his chin at a tall, white building and starts walking.

"We just walk in? What if there are guards or something?" I ask, assuming Liddick is being held against his will.

"Just trust me, and stay quiet," Liam says as we approach the building. Like all the buildings here, there doesn't seem to be a door in sight until he flattens the palm of his hand on the building. "Ludwig Sprague," he says out loud, and the door materializes in front of us. Liam raises an eyebrow at me and nods.

The inside of the building is colorful with an open seating area surrounding a white marble fireplace. The flames are blue, green, purple, and orange, and they remind me of the Vishan's fire.

"May I help you?" a tall, thin man with *actual waves of water* for hair says to us. I can't stop staring at him. The water looks just like it's lapping against the shore of a beach, only the beach is his forehead. I blink, trying to remember I'm supposed to belong here.

"Ludwig Sprague, please. We have a...*confidential* matter," Liam says covertly.

The man raises his eyebrows, which causes a shift in the current of his hair. A small wave rises and crashes on the side of his head. He snaps, then begins typing on a holographic keyboard, which appears in front of him.

After a second, a 3D image of Liddick with his hair slicked back appears alongside someone about his age, with dark hair that falls loose around his shoulders.

"I'm afraid he's already departed for his research sabbatical," the water man says.

CHAPTER 12
Push On
Arco

"It's OK," Lyden says, taking a few more steps toward me again, and for a second everything slows down. I sit down hard. "That cortisol must have flooded the tracker in your spine and synced your spheres—the part of you that's Navigator class, and the part that's Coder class," he adds, checking my eyes. I pull back from him. "It's why you saw those coordinates without knowing where we were as a reference."

"Well, that's good, right? He's psychic now!" Avis claps a few times and nods at me.

"*No*, that's not good, you mollusk!" Ellis snaps. "Didn't you read *any* of the literature they gave us at Gaia?"

"It's called a *surge*," Lyden explains, then drags a hand over his face and off the end of his chin. "It's the highest evolution the nanites you received at Gaia can bring about in a person."

"Sooo…that's *good*," Avis says again, this time widening his eyes like everyone has missed the obvious.

"The process is supposed to be gradual over the course of a career, but sometimes a surge can be triggered by a perfect storm of brain chemicals and a biological conduit—in this case, the tracker. "

I stare at Lyden, like everyone else, waiting for him to drop the other shoe.

"And…that *means?*" I finally ask when he doesn't do anything but look at me.

"It just means you may experience things you're not quite…able to handle yet. Your abilities will outweigh your experience right now."

"That's it?" Avis asks. "OK, how is he not a superhero again?"

Tark finally speaks up. "It's dangerous not to know your limitations, Mr. Ling."

"Not to mention the mental and physiological stress…" Arwyn adds, dabbing at my nose again. I take the cloth from her because I'm not seven years old, and decide that I'm done with this conversation.

"Could you just punch in the coordinates for the Wraith? We need to keep moving forward." I fire a look at Tark, and after a second, he nods.

"It's all yours." He finishes entering the numbers, and my controls are released. I turn around and face the long, wide path in front of us with the jagged black slabs of rock glinting in the hull flood lights. I inch the Sojourner forward.

No one says anything else, though everything they're *not* saying thickens the air until they finally go below deck. Tark doesn't say anything else as the Sojourner pushes toward the rock in front of us, which has apparently opened to let Fargo out and then close behind him.

I press my teeth together and try to remember what Dr. Denison said when I was pulling the Leviathan toward the retainer wall back at Gaia for the wet run... *push on...it will clear...*

Only this wall doesn't clear.

Everything in me wants to pull back on the yoke to slow us down, but instead, I push it forward. I feel the protest taking up space in my throat, growing until I almost choke on it, but I don't stop. Maybe it's because part of me actually wants to crash into the wall, but I know better. I would never risk everyone else's life like that. *Though...I'd just throw away my own?*

I push on.

"Mr. Hart?" Tark says in a thinning voice.

"It will clear."

We pick up speed when I engage the first level thrusters. I swallow hard to dislodge the questions and doubts and all the rest of the whining that wants to be heard in the back of my mind, but I'm done with it. I'm done being unsure of *everything*.

"*Mr. Hart!*"

"It will *clear!*"

And finally, it does. I engage the last two levels of thrusters, then align the ship with the flight plan in the projected green display on the window in front of me. I watch the stars do absolutely nothing as Tark exhales hard through his nose.

***

The Wraith is waiting for us as promised, but I wouldn't have seen it without the scopes. The hull is black, and from what I've read about this ship, it's also refractive, so it just looks like more stars in the distance instead of a two-ton ship. I take a deep breath and tell myself it's just like the Leviathan.

"The docking bay is an easy miss—just get starboard and wait for a hail. They're waiting for us," Tark says, and I want to know who *they* are supposed to be.

"Where's the other Sojourner?" I ask, scanning the perimeter for it, but it's nowhere on the scope.

"Likely already docked. There. Hold steady," Tark says as we both watch a patch of white open in the sky in front of us.

"What the—?"

"Hell on the brain to watch a window in space open up like that." Tark laughs. "Mark your scope—see the outline of the Wraith?"

"I see it," I say, pushing our little ship into alignment with the docking trajectory. After a second, I don't have to push anything. A hydraulic sound whirrs to life, the vibration of it resonating in my teeth and ears.

"Locked on. Good to see you, Skull. We were getting nervous," a woman's voice says…and it's familiar.

"Well, we couldn't let you have all the fun, Luz."

"*Luz?* Is that Ms. Reynolt?" I ask, narrowing a glance at Tark.

"The one and only, Mr. Hart," she says over the comms. "Bring her in, and we'll get you up to speed."

"How many other teachers are with The Seam?" I ask Tark.

"Not enough, unfortunately."

He barely finishes his sentence when the console projections thump, then glitch in and out before they return to normal.

"What was that? Error report?" I ask, entering my

clearance into the console.

"We're synced with the loading trajectory," Tark adds. He pulls up a perimeter scan, but all we see is the outline of the Wraith and the white loading zone guide beams that form the cradle for our Sojourner.

"Organic interference at the starboard hull," a female computer voice says.

"*Organics?* Out here?" Tark shakes his head and swipes away screen after screen like he's looking for a specific one. "Luz, what's happening up there?"

"You wouldn't believe me if I told you. We have some company. Standby—securing the docking field, but it might get bumpy down there."

"Are you going to tell me what—" I start, but the man jumping directly onto the front of our ship, pressing his hands to the glass like some kind of frog climbing a jar, stops the words sideways in my throat. "What the hell is *that!?*"

He's not wearing a suit so much as a skin, which is silver. His face is nearly as light with a blue tinge and seems to be covered in a thin layer of ice.

Tark's eyes narrow. "That's an Organic...hold on, Mr. Hart."

"What's an *Organic?*"

"Phase Three rejects—failed test subjects. He's not even human anymore."

None of what Tark is saying will process in my brain. Not while this man is crawling around the outside of our ship like some kind of bug on a windshield. He starts hammering his fists against the hull, his milky eyes unblinking. The console grid shakes and glitches again, this time going out entirely for several seconds. Another man and three women land on the hull behind him like they've just jumped from a platform above. I look up, but nothing is there and nothing shows on the scan.

"Where are they coming from?" I try to keep my voice level, but it's loud all the same.

"Nowhere. And everywhere..."

"What is *that* supposed to mean!? People can't just be out there like that. There's no life support whatsoever. They don't even have helmets!"

The Sojourner shakes violently before he can answer.

"Are you all right?" Ms. Reynolt says over the comms.

"We're all right. What's the containment percentage?" Tark asks. "They're in here with us, Luz."

"I know. We're trying to extract them without damaging your ship. We're at forty percent secured. Just hold tight; we're working on it."

"We can take about two more knocks like that before they push us off-trajectory. We won't be able to outrun them if they pull us loose."

"Copy that. Get everyone locked down. We may need to rattle your cage a little," another man says over the comms... *Is that Denison?* I shoot a glance at Tark and ask him as much. He gives me a quick nod, and everything starts coming together. *We had more help than we thought getting out of Gaia.* "Everybody, get secure," Tark says over the internal comms. "Calyx, we've got Organics. Make sure everyone is strapped down. Briggs has some fireworks for us."

"Oh, great," Calyx says. I shake my head, feeling

useless.

"What can I do?" I ask, trying not to stare at the actual *people* crawling on the starboard hull.

"Get locked in and hang on tight. It's going to get bright in here in about twenty seconds.

"Electric anomaly detected," the ship's computer voice says much too calmly for what's going on all around us. One of the Organic women bangs her head on the windshield several times, causing a split down the center of her forehead. The blood freezes immediately, but she just keeps banging.

"What are they supposed to be?" I ask, feeling repulsion and fear wrestling for control of my voice.

"The Phase Three rejects…the ones they could not get to sustain long-term oxygen deprivation and cold."

"Uh, it looks like they're sustaining both just fine to me," I say as one of the other women moves closer to the first, this one pounding on the hull with her fists.

"Sometimes, they're disposed of when testing indicates they won't be able to meet future test requirements. It's a damn waste of life." Tark enters a final combination. "Their minds are gone."

"Stabilizers engaged," the ship voice says, and a little hum shoots through my ears again. A few seconds later, blinding light floods the window in front of me and the Sojourner begins to shake.

"Hold on!" Tark says. "We've got two more of those, and then we should be clean."

"Damage report, twelve percent starboard. Organic matter lodged—segment 33," the ship voice says, and two more blasts of light precede episodes of violent shaking. Finally, everything is still again.

"Everyone OK?" Dr. Denison's voice comes over the comms.

"We're all right down here. Are they gone?" Tark replies.

"For now, minus a dead tagalong. Let's get everyone aboard."

CHAPTER 13
Landing
Jazz

Research sabbatical? I think but manage to stop the words before they come out of my mouth.

Liam pauses for a second, then begins nodding. "Of course, of course. I was afraid of this. Could you please direct us to your transfer unit? We're already so late."

The man with the water hair raises a dark eyebrow at us, looking from Liam to me, then at Vox. She puckers a kiss at him *like a mollusk,* and now both his eyebrows raise.

"And *you* are?" he asks.

"Consultants on…the project. I'm sorry, but that's all I'm at liberty to discuss with the public. Surely, you understand with the nature of our work." Liam leans on the counter between us and the man with the water hair, who gives us another suspicious look. "Please, we are already risking the contract. It's imperative that you direct us to the transport unit."

"Of course," the man finally says after taking a long, deep breath through his nose. "I assume all your credentials must be in order."

"Naturally…" Liam shrugs. "Would you like to see them?" He feigns looking for something in the chest pocket of his coat.

"Oh," the man says, then smiles at us. "No, no, that won't be necessary. Please give my regards to Mr. Sprague. I, for one, will anxiously be awaiting his new release."

"New release?" Vox asks, and Liam stares knives at her. The man with the water hair shoots her a puzzled look.

"Why, yes. The new virtuo-cine he's researching?"

"Yes, yes. Forgive my assistant, she's new. I'll be sure to put in a good word for you, Mr....?"

"Delaney. Argus Delaney. And thank you so much." The man's lips quiver until he presses the excitement out of them, forcing again a dignified half-smile. Liam nods several times and then straightens.

"Of course, of course. The cines would be nothing without wonderful fans like you. If you would please excuse us, however, I'm afraid we are already quite late." Liam turns abruptly to me. "The survey clearance? You did bring the survey clearance?"

I look at him blankly for a second until his eyes widen just a little and he leans a few inches forward. *Oh, I'm supposed to play along.*

"Yes, of course, what do you think, this is my first day?" I shoot a glance at Vox and give her a thin smile just because I can. She narrows her eyes at me, and the corner of Liam's mouth quirks before he turns back to the man with the water hair.

"Wonderful, then we'll be on our way with your kind help, my friend," he adds, but the water man just stares for a second until Liam clears his throat. "The, uh... direction of your transport?"

The man startles, then blinks several times before he flushes and nods repeatedly. "Yes, just around the corner. Bon voyage!" He waves us down a corridor.

"You just thought of all that off the top of your head?" I ask Liam as we approach a room at the end of the hall. Inside, a steel ring encloses another flat, steel circle with a holographic display rising up from the floor to about shoulder height. Liam punches something into it, and a blue light scans him.

"Didn't have much of a choice. You did pretty well on cue yourself," he says with a quick smile.

"Didn't have much of a choice," I answer, but that's all I can say before Vox sighs loudly.

"So we have to get turned into space dust again? Is that what's happening here with this thing?"

"Good day, Anton Fisk," a young man's voice says from the holographic console. "Please enter your destination coordinates."

"Anton Fisk, Senior Creative Director, Cineworks International?" Liam reads out loud, then sticks out his bottom lip and nods. "Thank you, Dot. All right, let's see where you went, Ludwig Sprague." He pulls a thin, silver rod from his pocket and begins tapping it on the console key panel. After a second, the screen display is replaced with a new block of code.

Liam shakes his head slowly and narrows his eyes.

"What? Don't you see Liddick?" I ask, feeling the blood start to pound in my ears.

"No, he came through this hub...but he came out in the middle of nowhere. It says he hopped to a hub on the Skyboard mountain perimeter. There's nothing out there but..."

"Sand," Vox says under her breath.

"They sent him back to Earth? Topside? What kind of research could he—" I start, but then stop as hope dawns on me. "Do you think maybe he escaped?" I barely say this out loud because I'm afraid I might scare away the possibility.

Liam punches something else into the console with the little rod, and after another second, shakes his head again.

"No, he wasn't the first one to jump to these coordinates. Someone went ahead to receive him on the other side. Three others followed him," he says, reading the console display. "We just missed them by maybe six hours."

"Let's go then. Come on before they get too far," I say, but Liam looks more frustrated than ever.

"We don't know what we're walking into. Give me a second to think," he says after a beat.

"Think about what?" Vox asks almost immediately. "Can we parachute down there?"

"*What?* No," Liam answers.

"So fire up this crate and let's go."

Liam looks at me for a second like I have a rationale comeback for Vox, but actually, I don't. I shrug and nod. He takes a deep breath, then blows it out all at once.

"All right. Follow me in here after it scans you, and hold as still as you can," he says, punching something else into the console. A blue light scans him again, and the young man's voice starts up.

"Welcome, Anton Fisk. Have a good trip. Next

transport, please?" Vox steps into place, and the blue light scans her too. "Welcome, Kitty Spark."

"Ooh, Splice Corps Inc., Cinematics..." she reads. "What does that mean? Am I some bio-grunt?"

Liam rolls his eyes. *"Cinematics...you're a processing editor. Come on."*

"What's a processing editor?"

"In charge of the storyboarders—*come on!"*

"Oh, good. I'm your boyfriend's boss..." Vox says, clicking the side of her mouth at me.

I roll my eyes at her as she finally gets onto the circular platform with Liam, then step in front of the console. The blue light hits me in the eyes, which makes me squint for a second.

Uta Lindall? I read. "TruYou Designs, Glyph Operative Unit," I say out loud, then step onto the platform. "Does that mean I create the characters?"

"No, you program them," Liam answers just before a blinding white light floods everything.

***

Eco or Calyx, or whoever told us port-carnate gets easier with each subsequent transfer, was a liar. When the white light fades and my ears finally stop buzzing, I still feel like I'm frozen in a block of ice...a block of ice that's buried under a building.

As my vision clears, I see a man standing near the far wall of this...little shack? *Where are we?* I think.

"A transfer under the name Ludwig Sprague came through here not too long ago," Liam says to the man. "Where did he go?"

The man taps at his holographic console but can't

seem to get it to do more than flicker at him.

"You scramble my logs? Did you do this?" The man gestures to his console, then widens his eyes at Liam. "Where you coming from? I didn't authorize your hop here."

"This is above your pay grade. Spaulding sent us, and that's all you need to know. *Ludwig Sprague* and his team? Now!" Liam is so adamant, for a second, I almost believe him too.

Feeling starts to come back into my fingertips, and my vision sharpens. The man is much bigger than Liam with greasy, dark hair pulled into a ponytail. With his dingy white shirt and leather vest, he looks like a Badlander. He tries punching something else into his console, but it only glitches at him again.

"I got no authorization for any of you. I only had clearance for the kid and them other sky ferrets."

Oh, I'm stealing that one, Vox thinks, and I bite the inside of my cheek to keep from laughing out loud.

"That's it? What about the rendezvous team?" Liam asks, looking worried.

"The *ronday*-who?" The man scrunches up his face like the word smells bad.

"The others who met them? Are you telling me they didn't show up?" Liam asks, this time more exasperated. He pushes both hands through his sun-streaked hair, then turns to me. "I *told* you we should have gotten here to secure the reception team."

"Uh...I'm...sorry?" I mutter.

He's an even better spinner than I am, Vox thinks, sticking out her bottom lip and nodding just a little to herself. Liam turns back to the Badlander, who has now given up trying to use his console.

"Look, do you have grease in your ears?" Liam asks, taking a step toward him. "I said this comes from the top. From Spaulding. Now if you want to see tomorrow, I suggest you don't make me notify him that not only did you not secure a reception team, but *now* you're delaying the shadow team too!"

I realize my mouth is open and shut it quickly. The man blanches and meets my eyes. I thin my lips and shake my head at him, willing myself with everything I am not to laugh.

"Hey, we *had* a reception team! Grisham sent 'em personally on account it was Liddick! When all his bits was back in place, he and that Admin City handler made for the cannibal tunnels with the three of 'em and the gear they brought. Ain't nobody said to wait for no shadow team. I got no clearance or preloaded entry code on that," the man says, almost pleading.

"Well, at least you didn't bollocks *that* up, then. I guess I won't have to report you to Spaulding after all. Where is Grisham?"

"He was meeting *you all* in Admin City." The man narrows his eyes now at Liam.

"He's *already* meeting with Spaulding? Great," Liam says, pretending to search for something in his coat. He shoots me a worried look. "Do you have the coordinates?"

"Uh...no?" I say, hoping that's the right thing.

"Crite! All right," Liam says, then snaps his finger several times at the man. "You. Which tunnel entry point did they use? We need to catch up to them before they realize nobody is watching their backs out there!"

"You don't know the—?"

"Do you want that on your head? You can kiss this candy job goodbye if something happens to them on your shift!" Liam adds, cutting off the man's protest as he opens the flap of his white coat and pulls out the silver rod he used to hack the port-carnate hub back in Admin City. He holds it to his temple and closes his eyes. "Eight seconds until I connect to Spaulding and let him know how epically you've dropped the net out here!"

"All right! All right!" the man says without even taking a breath. He punches something into his console and starts reading to Liam. "They went to the far east perimeter," he says, then looks up at him. "You ain't gonna be able to catch up to them, though, least of all wearing them daylight suits you got on. You'd be bait out there for them cannibals."

"He doesn't have our *wraps*, either!?" I say, surprising myself as much as Liam. Vox looks at me like a proud parent, and I wrestle with my face to stay indignant. Liam raises his eyebrows at the man and holds out his hands to his sides, waiting for an answer.

"I...uh..." is all the man can manage.

"That's it. I'm calling this in," Liam says, shoving past the man to access his console. He tosses the silver rod to Vox as he passes. "Kitty, pull up a list of doorkeepers who can port down here *right now* and replace this useless one." Vox's lips quirk as she pushes her eyebrows together and raises the long, metal rod to her temple. *"Ensign?"* Liam continues, reading the console. "What kind of name is *Ensign?*"

All the blood drains from the man's face just before he rushes past Vox and me.

"Wait! Wait…uh, *here.* Burlap should do ya. Gonna be awful sweltery with them long coats you already got on, though," he says, pulling the tarps off the counters along the back wall. Dust flies everywhere and stings my eyes. I hold my breath and wave my hands in front of my face to clear it, but it doesn't do much good.

Liam finishes punching something into the console, then takes off his white coat and tosses it on the back counter, making more dust fly in the air. He wraps the tarp around him like a cape and throws one side over his shoulder. Vox and I do the same. A second later, she steps into the doorway looking at Liam and me like we're making her late.

"Are you *coming?*"

CHAPTER 14
The Wraith
Arco

We all move from the airlock to the bridge, which is the same size as the Leviathan's, but with two main center stations sitting on the second tier of the descending floor. I look around for other consoles—the navigation stations that should flank the pilot's station—but there aren't any...just the enormous window that wraps from end to end in front of the long stretch of embedded panels and intermittent controllers.

"Where are the systems consoles?" Avis asks, scanning the bridge.

"They're below," Dr. Denison says, approaching us. He's wearing the same dark red jumpsuit he wore at Gaia.

"What's going on?" I ask. "How are you here?"

"Luck." Denison's white eyebrows jump when he nods, and I forgot how young he looks despite the color of his hair—like he can't be more than ten years older than I am. I shake my head at the absurdity of my whole damn world.

"Luck? What's that supposed to mean?" Jax asks, echoing my irritation.

"Everything is on high alert with you all missing, and now the news about crashing the Grid server flooding the infobits," Denison starts. "We convinced Rheen to pull the regular pilots for these runs and send us in their place."

"And why does she think you'd be fine with shuttling a bunch of Phase Two kids to a lab in the port-cloud for more genetic testing? Your *tenure?*" I ask, narrowing my eyes at him and wondering just how many experiments he's performed on students himself.

"Something like that," is all he says in reply. His face is solemn, and I don't like the way he's looking at me like I'm some kind of pathetic, wounded animal. He looks over my shoulder at Ms. Reynolt, who's climbing the last of the metal stairs that lead below deck. She's wearing the same blue jumpsuit she wore at Gaia. They must have come straight from there.

"We've never been directly involved in the experimentation, Mr. Hart," she says with a weak smile. "We've been working for several years to expose this operation, and now, with your team's help, we can."

"Do you have people below now? People from Phase Two?" Fraya asks.

"They're back at The Seam building already. You made quite a mess of those labs." Denison half-smiles at us, and this time, I smile a little too. "We weren't able to get everyone aboard. Some fled into the biomes. We'll need to run some sweeps before the facility goes back online."

"Phase Two is still *active?*" I ask, incredulous.

"Their systems are badly damaged," Denison says. "The neural freeze Jack launched corrupted much of their programming, but yes, they have basic functions in place...enough to cover their tracks if they have to by reactivating the biomes."

"It wouldn't be the first time," I say, pinning him in place with a cold stare. He meets my eyes and sighs.

"So you learned about the original test subjects then," he states rather than asks. "The Vishan model."

"We learned that the biomes exist so Gaia could get rid of them as evidence? Yes," I answer. "How long have you been part of this?" I ask. "How long have you known and done nothing?"

"Arco, that's not how it is," my sister says.

"Really? Because last I checked, he didn't stop anything while they were making you fireproof. He's part of the problem!"

Arwyn starts to protest, but Denison nods and takes a few steps toward us.

"No, it's all right," he says to her, then looks right at me. "I wasn't there the night they took Lyden and Arwyn, son. Neither was Luz. We were told they'd been transferred to Admin City for *special internships*, and at the time, neither of us had the clearance to investigate." He shakes his head, then turns away and walks to the window that stretches the length of the bridge. "We knew something didn't add up after they had us pursue Jack Ripley, so several of us started listening, then we started asking people the right questions. We made them think we wanted to be involved. It wasn't long before they asked me to supervise Phase One of *The Elements* program—that's what it's called—and I chose my team."

"Unfortunately, this didn't happen in time to keep Liam Wright out of the snare," Ms. Reynolt adds. "But he was the last Gaia Sur cadet to be given a *special internship*. We've run interference ever since using simulated port-call clones, all of them unfortunately passing before they could continue onto Phase Two." She winks, looking from Denison to Tark.

It all seems to make sense, but I still don't fully trust them. I wonder if I just don't fully trust anyone anymore.

"We need to move into position," Lyden says, turning to face us from the main console. "The dock will be waiting for Calyx and us now. I altered the delivery specs for this run, so they won't be expecting a ship of transports anymore."

Denison nods, and Tark gestures to Ellis and Avis.

"Come with me. I'll show you how to run the core. It's similar to the Leviathan, only much smaller. The rest of you should get comfortable below. After we deliver Calyx's group, we'll need to exit the cloud space, then burrow back in."

"Burrow?" Jax asks, confused.

"Mr. Hart and I picked up some piranha wind at our little pit stop in the Sojourner," Tark says over his shoulder, then extends a small box. "A zephyr, as you know it."

Jax's eyes go wide before his expression turns hard.

"You have one of the tornado monsters in there? What are you going to do with *that?*"

"Nothing," Tark answers with a half-smile. "We were hoping you and your father might be able to code it for assassin work." He pauses, nodding to Jack. The blood drains from Jax's face all over again. Tark chuckles. "Can you code it to make a Wraith-sized hole in the port-cloud, then replicate to fill it behind us?"

"You want it to work like an *A-sym* patch?" Jax asks, exchanging glances with his dad.

"We need Rover nanites for that," Jack says, shaking his head.

"I thought you might say that," Denison says. "Skull can get you situated below. The med bay is small, but it's equipped with what you'll need."

Jax looks at his dad again, who nods, but still doesn't look at ease. Jax takes the little box from Denison very carefully and goes below deck with everyone else.

***

Denison slaps me on the shoulder and gestures to the front of the bridge. "Shall we?" he says. I look from him to Ms. Reynolt.

"Uh, I'm flying?"

"You'll need to be acquainted with the system for when the time comes. When we get in range of Phase Three, Luz will move into place, and you'll get out of sight."

"You're a navigator?" I ask her.

"No, a Reader with a Nav latency, but I'm not here to fly this thing."

"Luz will make sure we stay out of trouble," Denison says with a half-smile to her. I look at them both quickly and decide I don't want to know what's going on there. "Have a seat, son." Denison nods to the console next to him, which is smooth with embedded, illuminated buttons and screens. I sit down, and the chair forms to me just like the one on the Leviathan.

"Where's the yoke?" I ask, scanning the controls,

stopping to look at Denison when I can't find it. He exchanges another glance with Ms. Reynolt, then smiles at me.

"You're the yoke, Mr. Hart."

I can only blink at him. "What?" I ask after he doesn't elaborate. He pushes a series of buttons, and it suddenly feels like every system stops spinning. The downshifting hum vibrates in my stomach, and I feel like we're falling.

"What happened? Did we stop?" I ask, trying to turn in my seat. Immediately, the ship jerks and shimmies, and all my blood stops flowing at once. "What the hell...?"

"Just relax, Mr. Hart. Lean slowly forward," Ms. Reynolt says, and a wash of calm comes over me.

"I've transferred control of the ship to you from autopilot," Denison says. "Try to be part of the ship, because it is now part of you."

I look at him quickly, reminding myself not to make any sudden moves.

"It's all right. Just imagine you're flying out here like a bird, Mr. Hart. Feel the direction you want to go, and lean into it in your mind," Reynolt coaches. I try to ignore the criticism I have for this idiotic design and reach for the grips in front of me. I take a deep breath and imagine myself leaning forward a little, like I'm going to dive off the rock ledge back home and drop into the ocean. The ship systems start to hum again, and I feel us pushing forward like we're—*like I'm*—facing down a strong headwind.

"That's it, son. Just keep pushing through..." Denison says from somewhere in the distance, or so it seems. I see him sitting next to me out of the corner of my eye, along with several occasional numbers and symbols, which are always there when I either look directly at them or engage my peripheral vision.

"I'm flying this thing with my *mind?*" I ask, still not quite sure if that's a good question or a stupid one.

"Indeed, and quite well, I might add," Denison says. "Take us to about sixty seconds from the cloud gate— right there on the scope, see it?" he says again, this time gesturing to a holographic green scope just to my left. "Then I'll move her in while Luz readies the airlock to release Calyx and her team."

I nod, noticing in the same second how dry my mouth is. I'm afraid to swallow because what if that causes another staggering jerk-to-halt like turning around a minute ago did? But then I think of Jazz, smiling at me and nodding like that first time on the Leviathan. *You can do it*, she said, and for at least that second, I didn't need to believe it as long as she did. I close my eyes and try to find that person she saw, because she's not here to tell me anything anymore.

CHAPTER 15
The Badlands
Jazz

"This smells like grease and sadness," Vox says, wrinkling her nose away from the burlap wrap near her face. I stifle a laugh and scan the horizon for Seaboard North...for the lights of the Fishers' campfires and the lights from the habitat stacks. I blink, trying to clear my blurry vision, but it doesn't help.

"We're home..." I say under my breath, but Liam hears me anyway.

"Don't get comfortable," he says with an edge in his voice.

"I'm just saying we made it. What's wrong?"

"Why would Spaulding send him into the tunnels?" Liam asks, but after a second I realize he's only talking to himself. "If he wanted to get rid of him, he would have done that in Admin City..."

I jog a few steps to catch up.

"He sent him with handlers, too," I add when Liam doesn't say anything more. "Could it have something to do with Phase Two?"

He just shakes his head. "I don't know. It doesn't make any sense. The transfer logs said there were five in his party, and that walrus back there said there was a reception team with gear. We don't have the equipment to follow them, either. We'll have to find Azeris and regroup."

"Do you know where his hab is?" I ask. "Where are we going?"

"Forward." Liam spits out the word, and I glare at him, which he doesn't see. He picks up his pace specifically, it seems, to get away from me. I'm about to stop in my tracks and tell him we need to figure out what we're doing when Vox's voice sails over my shoulder.

"You know, tunnel sharks aren't the only things under your feet out here!"

Liam stops in his tracks and turns abruptly to her.

"What are you talking about?"

"The *V*," she adds, raising a burgundy eyebrow.

"The people you said *your* people call the Fringe?" I ask, wondering where this is going until she raises her other eyebrow at me and heaves a sigh, blinking obnoxiously.

"What the hell are you two talking about? The cannibals? There aren't any. Tunnel sharks are what pulled people through this sand."

You're talking about the Vishan? I think toward Vox, and she starts slow-clapping. "The supply crews and tunnel shark teams... Liam, they'll help us!"

"Who? The sharks? Uh, afraid not."

"No, Vox's people."

"In the *woods?*"

"No, mollusk. How are you a doctor again?" Vox rolls her eyes at him. "The Vishan in the volcano about six miles that way." she adds, pointing to the ground.

Liam looks at her blankly for a second, then shakes

his head to clear the fog.

"Vishan…? *Allsop* Vishan?" He looks as confused as we are until he jumps like something has bitten him. "Wait, your treatments!"

"What? Who is Allsop Vishan?" Vox asks, ignoring Liam's sudden attack.

"Sorry. He's the original scientist who altered the DNA strand that Jack and I used to code the neural thread—the one we put in the virtuo-cines to warn Liddick…the messages, remember?" He shakes his head, then abandons the question. "Never mind. The DNA was archived. I forgot the original test subjects survived. I forgot there were descendants out there who helped you through the biomes…" he says, all the blood draining from his face. He pushes his hands through his hair again and takes a deep breath.

"OK, how do we contact them?" I ask. "Do we still need to find Azeris?"

"Yes, we need to go there first. Where are we?" Liam asks, but it still seems like he's talking to himself more than he's answering me when he starts looking around. Vox flips the burlap off her shoulder and unzips the front of her white jumpsuit a little, then pulls out her arm. She tilts her head to the side, studying for a second before she points to a spot on her inner arm.

"Here. There's Skyboard Mountain." She points to another spot higher up her shoulder. "Tinkerers are on the other side of the forest there." Vox nods directly ahead of us. Liam and I both stare at her. "What…he's a Tinkerer, isn't he? I mean, you call him a Badlander, but none of them live in the Badlands. *These* are the

Badlands," she says, shoving her arm back in her sleeve, then holding it out to the spread of sand all around us.

"What just happened?" Liam asks, shooting me a glance. Vox sighs in disgust.

"Follow me. Go exactly where I go, and watch where you step."

***

The sun is setting, and I start to wonder if we'll make it to Azeris's hab before it's completely dark. We need food and supplies if we're going in those tunnels, not to mention...will our nanites even work again? Vox is several yards ahead of us, and even though I can see the little fires along the beach from the Fishers' docks, we are still a world away from home. Cold shoots down my back, and I start to feel sick as a new worry surfaces.

"Are the nanites they gave us at Gaia still working even without our dive suits? Can we actually survive this?" I ask Liam as we follow Vox as closely as we can in the diminishing light. He chuckles at me, then jogs a few steps.

"Probably not," he says. "They need a hub to stay charged. Your suits acted like little battery packs when you were out of range of a facility. Azeris will be able to upgrade them so we can go deep. Just slow down and try to relax for now."

I squint at him. *Relax?* We're about to voluntarily make our way into the one place we've been warned to avoid our whole lives, and now we know why: there really *are* things that will eat you in those tunnels.

"Liam, what if Azeris doesn't know anything else about where Liddick is? What if he doesn't have anything that will help us in the tunnels? Then what are we going to do?" I ask, but Liam just cocks his head sideways as he watches Vox take off her burlap wrap and fold it over one of her arms, then push up her white sleeves. She's going to get us killed.

"Vox! Put that back on! That hub operator said we'd be bait out here in the jumpsuits!"

"It's hot!" is all she says in reply.

"Who put all those map lines on her arms?" Liam asks, still studying her.

"She did. She's a boundary scout for her clan. Are you listening to me? What are we going to do if Azeris can't help us find Liddick?"

"So, they're what, symbolic of her job or something?"

"No, they're *actual* maps of where she's been. Her clan sends kids out to get some kind of flower from the top of Skyboard North when they're thirteen. They can't take anything with them except a little knife," I explain just to get it over with. Liam gawks at me.

"She gave herself those tattoos with a little knife? At thirteen years old?"

"Yeah. I mean, no. I mean, not all the maps when she was thirteen. She added to them on different trips."

Liam nods and sticks out his bottom lip.

"She must be pretty tough. Resourceful..." he adds, nodding at Vox.

"She's insane," I answer without hesitation. I look up at him in the same second he glances at me and gives me a crooked smile like I should have figured all this out by now. "Uh, I'm not her," I answer. "I couldn't do what she did."

"Why not? What makes you any different than she was when she was 13?"

I almost laugh out loud at Liam but manage to swallow half of it.

"Well, for starters, she knew it was coming. She wanted to be a Boundary Scout, and that first, she had to go up the mountain."

"That's it?"

"No, her whole culture expects it. It's just what they do. It was always part of her plan."

"So what do you want, Jazwyn?" Liam asks as the wind blows our burlap wraps into billows behind us.

"*What?*" I squint at him again.

"What are you doing out here? What do you want? What's your plan?" he asks again, and this time he looks at me.

"To find Liddick," I say, shaking my head at him. "Did you miss something back at The Seam building? You know, when we decided all this?"

"So you know where you're going then."

"Liam, no, we *don't* know where we're going. The tunnels are—"

"The tunnels don't matter," he says, stopping in his tracks. "We're going to find Liddick, wherever he is. Sometimes you can only see the next step, though, you know? So for now, we look in the tunnels…"

I stare at him for a second, unsure how to respond because he's right. I can't plan this, but I don't know how to *not* plan it either.

"But what if…?" I start, but then trail off because I realize I'm trying to plan it all again. I really can't, though. Not this. And that's the hardest part. Liam smiles a little at me as we start walking again. He drapes his arm over me like Liddick used to do, and I suddenly see him in a new light. I see the big brother who cut his own eyebrow to calm Liddick down when he fell on the dune. The big brother who told him nobody was going to bleed to death that day because they were just going to hold it together until they got home. One step at a time.

"He doesn't even have our wraps!" Liam laughs and nods. After a few seconds, I start laughing too, and for the first time in what seems like a very long time, I feel like maybe everything is going to be all right. One way or another.

CHAPTER 16
Package 872
Arco

I scan the never-ending screens in front of me, all of them saying different things with different numbers and different symbols that I don't understand, but I know there's enough fuel in the ship. I know the pressurization is sound. I know those things that attacked us outside are long gone, except for the carcass trapped in the fuel sector...but I don't even want to think about that when I don't know how I know any of the rest of the information. I shake my head and blow out the breath in my lungs. How do I know so much and at the same time, absolutely *nothing*? Blood trickles over my upper lip again, and I pinch my nose.

"What the...?" I start, looking around for some kind of cloth.

"There have only been a few others like you in the years I've been at Gaia," Denison says, tossing me one from the little medical kit he fishes out of one of the compartments in his console. I look at him sideways, still a little afraid I will somehow turn the ship upside down if I move the wrong way.

"What do you mean, *like me?*"

"A fast burner—your synced proclivities of Navigator and Coder," Denison replies, raising his chin at the expanse of black before us, at the intermittent stars brighter than the haze that seems to be everywhere underneath us.

"A lot of good it does. I can't explain how any of these screens tell me what I know they're saying. I hate not knowing why."

Denison laughs out loud. "That's a slippery slope," he says without looking at me. "Because the flip side is *why not?* That's the question that started this whole mess. Transcend the environment...why not? Breathe underwater, resist the heat and pressure miles within the earth...withstand cold and oxygen deprivation...hey, why not?" He trails off, shaking his head like it's his fault, though he said he never was part of the experiments.

"And you plan to use my sister to start answering that question?" I ask more loudly than I should because I still don't believe him. The ship suddenly surges, and I don't know why until I realize I'm leaning toward him with my hands gripping the edges of this console seat. I'm anxious all over again at the reminder that I'm actually physiologically linked into this ship.

"It's not my first choice to send her into Phase Three with Calyx, but it's our best option," Denison says, unfazed by the sudden speed of the Wraith. I straighten in my seat, and the ship levels out as he continues. "Rheen and Styx were expecting Lyden and Arwyn several days ago. This will be the only opportunity we have to get through that front door without the rest of our support in place."

"And what would they do if you did have support in

place, storm the facility? Run in there and kill everybody? How does any of this end well?"

Denison looks at me hard, then and takes a breath. "Lyden and your sister will walk out of there. I won't let Gaia keep any of the kids they've taken, and neither will you." He gives me a single nod, like that's supposed to be enough of an answer.

"They're making good progress on the coding," Calyx says, walking up behind us.

"I knew they would. Are you ready to report?" Denison asks, gesturing to one of the screens in front of me. Calyx looks over her shoulder as my sister and Lyden close the distance between us, and the ship starts to shimmy.

"Sit tight, sit tight, Mr. Hart." Denison chuckles, then hits a series of buttons in front of him. I hear a hydraulic shift in the ship under me and the shimmying stops. "Autopilot engaged," he adds, smiling. "You'll hone your focus, don't worry." I sigh as the adrenaline hits my blood and makes it hammer in my ears.

"I don't like this," I say through my teeth as I cut a look at Calyx. "We don't have a backup plan—what if they don't believe you? What if you're caught helping them once you're inside?"

"I won't let that happen," she says, exchanging glances with Denison, and that's all I can take of this *make it up as you go* mentality.

"See, here's the problem with all of you," I say, getting to my feet. "You're so sure you're in control of everything. You remember they blew up our ship after they *watched* us steal it, right? They knew we were

planning to take the Leviathan, and they let us do it just
so they could see what we *could* do. What makes you
think they don't already know you're coming?"

"We don't know that," Denison says before Calyx can
answer. "But the advantage of not knowing is that Rheen
and Styx won't know what we're doing until we're doing
it either. We're going to have to put our faith in that."

"This is insane," is all I can say when everyone just
nods and looks enlightened. "Am I really the only one on
this ship who thinks this is all utterly split? We need a
way out if something goes wrong!"

"We have one," Tark says, clearing the last of the
stairs from below deck. He's holding out the same little
box Fargo gave him.

"It's already done?" Lyden asks, raising both his
eyebrows, which disappear under his dark, messy hair.

"It should make a hole nobody but us will know is
there…straight through the wall of that lab."

"Nobody will be able to see it?" I ask.

"Not with this coding," Tark says. "On the surface we
have the *A-sym* patch that will take on the appearance of
what's around it. The molecules themselves, though, will
move out of our way like displaced water when we walk
through it."

"Great. Once we're in, we'll launch this, and you can
bring Jack and the others through the hole. It will eat
through the wall of the lab, and then you can launch the
wind on the cloud barrier to bring the ship inside. You'll
have a straight shot," Lyden says, nodding to me. I look
at my sister, and find her nodding too.

"And what will Jack and his team do once they're in

there? How do we get them back out?" I ask.

"They will upload the archive into the columns once Lyden and I raise them. Once the archive is loose in the system, we'll all meet you in the labs and board the Wraith," my sister says. "We just need you to get as close as you can without being seen."

As soon as she finishes, I realize I have a huge headache. I close my eyes and rub my temples hard, hoping for something else to come to me. Something I can count on. But nothing does.

"All right," is all I can say after a few minutes. "How far are we from the facility?"

"Nearly there," Denison says, scanning the screens behind us. "Everyone needs to get into position."

"Mr. Hart, stay close because we'll need to move fast after we leave," Tark says, with a nod to Calyx. Lyden and Arwyn hold out their hands, and Calyx levels a flat metal rod against them until it encircles each of their wrists and seals.

"Are those really necessary?" I ask, stopping in my tracks.

"Mr. Hart, if you were a prisoner, would you board that facility if Calyx just asked *pretty please?*" Tark asks with a half-smile. He taps something onto the console before he starts talking into it, still smiling. "Eco, show time."

A few minutes later, Eco walks onto the bridge wearing a red military jumpsuit that looks like he's had it awhile. He drops the duffel bag on the floor at his feet and raises his chin to Calyx.

"Everyone below deck is dressed already. The rest of

these uniforms are yours," he says.

"Where did those come from?" I ask, looking from him to Tark.

"The good doctor made some arrangements for us," Tark says with a nod to Denison, who returns the nod and claps his hands together.

"We should get moving. Get changed and get into position. I have to go get that Organic off the hull before they scan us."

***

Tark punches something into the controls and a few seconds later, a voice floods the cabin.

"Wraith Class 77, state your business," the male voice says.

"This is Skellig Tark delivering package 872, reporting officer Calyx Frome. We have two in custody scheduled for Phase Three trials."

"Stand by..." I glance at Tark, holding my breath. "Says here Briggs Denison was delivering that package. What happened?"

"He was needed at Phase One to deal with a clone malfunction," Tark replies. "It would have been suspicious for him to leave now. He asked me to make the run—authorization seven, seven, alpha BCD."

I push my hands over my face half in disbelief, half in panic. This could be the end of everything. I hold my breath and wait for the voice to come back over the comms.

"All right, it checks out. Prepare for entry. You said just two in custody?"

"That's right. Bringing her down. Wraith Class 77

out." Tark hits another button combination before looking at me. "Just stay calm and quiet for the next little bit, and we'll go to work."

CHAPTER 17
Stranglebush
Jazz

The sand starts to turn into briars and vines like when I was walking with Dell in the Rush—the wet marshland giving way to the gnarled bushes of the next biome. A shiver runs down my back as I shake my head, trying to forget that place.

"You OK?" Liam asks, shooting me a sideways glance.

"This part of the Badlands looks like the Rush…like the—"

"The Tanglebush," he finishes with a nod, narrowing his eyes against the sun in front of us.

"Did you really design the biomes?" I ask after he doesn't say anything else.

"No." This time he answers quickly. "The framework was already there. My brother, Lyden, thought he was working on virtuo-cine templates when he coded some of it. Same with your dad's program—the whispers and everything over the chasm. Neither of them would have ever agreed to make any of that real." He doesn't look at me as he explains, and my chest tightens before he talks again. "Rheen and Styx kept me with the kids that those shark things pulled through the ground," he finally says. And that's all he says. I let my mind wander over the possibility that maybe Dell was in the Phase Two facility when they were making Liam carry out the experiments on people.

I look up at him, and my chest tightens even more. The air seems thicker now, harder to take in.

"Something isn't right here." Vox stops several feet ahead of us, then drives the toe of her black boot into the ground a few times.

"What's wrong?" Liam asks just as the pulse in my throat starts to jump and my heart tries to pound out of my chest. It's the feeling of something coming toward us fast, but there's nothing anywhere. I frantically scan the horizon, seeing only the distant, thick trees and the haze of Seaboard North far in the distance beyond it.

"We should run…" I barely say the words because it feels like something is listening. They don't do any good anyway because my feet are stuck in place like they're rooted to the ground.

"Don't run," Vox adds in an equally quiet voice. She narrows her eyes and scans the scrub at our feet. She takes a step, then swears.

"What's the matt—?" I start, but we're falling straight through the ground before I can finish my sentence. The burlap wrap flies past my face, blocking the light until a second later I stop hard. Dirt falls into my face and down my throat, but I can't get enough of a breath to cough. My lungs start to burn as my throat tightens. I roll to my stomach and try to push to my hands and knees, which helps me get a little air into my lungs. *Shallow breaths, Rip. Shallow breaths…* I hear the echo of Liddick's words back in the Rush, and I try to follow their advice.

Vox is spewing a litany of swear words somewhere in front of me, but I can't see her. When she stops, I hear her in my head.

Are you dead? It doesn't feel like you're dead, so are you? She asks, which steals my newly collected breath and makes it come out in a choked laugh.

I'm not dead. Where's Liam?

He might be dead. I landed on him.

I choke out another laugh and push to my feet.

"Liam, are you OK? Where are you?"

A low groan comes from the same place Vox's swearing was just a minute ago. *Did she really land on him?*

"Hey, are you dead, Liddick's brother?" Vox asks as the dust in the air dissipates, and I see her push her boot tip into his ribs. Liam groans again and rolls away from her prodding. "He's not dead," she answers with a big, stupid smile.

"Liam!" I stumble over to him and roll him onto his back. "Are you OK? Just hold still. Does anything hurt?"

He spits dirt to the side and raises his hand to his face to clear the rest of it, which just pushes it into the dark roots of his blond hair. He blinks several times before opening his eyes, which almost seem to glow blue now against his dirty face. He spits more dirt to the side and tries to push up to his elbows.

"Jazwyn!" Vox shouts from the earthen wall in front of me, which rips my attention away from Liam both because of the urgency in her tone and because she actually used my name instead of *sand dollar*. "Come here! Both of you, come here!" she says, this time through her teeth. Liam and I exchange confused glances until something tightens around my ankle and yanks me away from Liam.

For the second time in a handful of minutes, I land hard and lose my breath, but this time, I'm still vertical. I try to take a step, but my legs are pinned in place to the wall, along with my arms. I lean forward a little, only to feel something smooth and hard slither over my ribs.

"What is it!? A snake!?" I shout, but what I hear myself say just comes out in rasps and gurgles.

"No! Stranglebush! Close your eyes and—" Vox starts, but she's cut off when another vine wraps around her waist and slams her against the wall too. *Relax*, she says in my mind. "Get in the sun," Vox whispers to Liam, who starts to scramble to the patch of light in the center of the pit we've fallen into.

"Crite..." he growls, but finally makes it to the center.

Every breath I take feels like it makes the vines tighter around my ribs, and all I can think about is how it will only be a few more minutes before I can't take in another one at all. I swallow hard, trying to keep my throat from closing up like it's already trying to do with the panic.

I said, relax. They respond to motion like a python, Vox thinks.

These are what caught you before? These are the things you said you convinced to let you go? I answer in my head, but even in my thoughts it sounds spluttered and anything *but* relaxed.

Just stop fast-forwarding to your death, crite. Think about right now. Think about relaxing—about the vines turning dry or something. Vox coaches again, but I can't stop imagining my next several breaths. The vines move a few more inches around my ribs and constrict even more. *Jazz! Stay in right now!* Vox shouts in my mind.

The air fills with dust again as a thudding sound crashes, then another. Liam is on his feet throwing his boots against the ceiling, which makes the opening inches bigger with each impact. The vines recoil to the shadows, and adrenaline fills my chest. *He's trying to flood the pit with sunlight. They'll let us go. They'll let us go!* I think, and the vines loosen enough for me to take a breath.

They clamp down on my ribs again just as fast in response to the motion, but I fight to keep the air in my lungs.

Right now! Stay in right now! Vox shouts in my head. I try to focus on the vines loosening, on the feeling of knowing they're going to loosen like I felt when I saw them recoil in the sunlight. To my amazement, they start to shift in response. I take in another small breath.

It's working...it's working... I think, and the vines loosen even more.

A crash of dirt falls to the ground, blinding me for a minute with the kick-up of debris and sunlight. A high-pitched keening sounds from the vines as they fall away, and I wriggle free. Vox and I both stumble to the center of the pit next to Liam as the vines shrivel and recoil to the walls.

"Are you OK? Anyone hurt?" Liam says, out of breath.

"I'm all right," I say, rubbing my ribs, but I think the pain there is from the original fall through the ground rather than the hold of the strangle bushes.

"I'm good," Vox says, spitting dirt. Her face is pinched as her burgundy eyebrows dart in. I'm surprised by the wave of violence I feel radiating from her.

"Hey…" I say, taking a step toward her until I see her warning look.

"Don't say it, or I'll have to gut you."

"Say what?"

"That I should have seen it coming. I'm a Boundary Scout, aren't I?"

"Vox, nobody could have seen that coming," I say. "We were right on top of it and couldn't tell what was underneath."

"*You're* not Scouts," she says, still looking like she's going to kill me, but I know the anger I'm feeling from her is anger she feels at herself rather than at me.

"You called it out—if you hadn't, we would have been walking when we fell instead of standing still. That probably would have meant a broken leg," Liam offers, and this seems to soften Vox's expression. After a second, the radiating violence subsides from her. She takes a deep breath and sends him a sideways nod.

"It's going to take a while to get out of here," she says, kicking at the wall and sending crumbling earth everywhere.

"Steps?" I ask, remembering the story she told me back at Gaia of how she got out of one of these traps. She nods, but then we both stop all at once and exchange the same bloodless expression.

"What's wrong?" Liam asks, confused. "Are you hurt?"

I scan the wall behind him, visible now with the increased light from the collapsed ceiling. Several slats are carved in varying places, a pair of eyes looking back at us through each one.

CHAPTER 18
The Mouth of the Wolf
Arco

I catch my sister's eyes as she sits with Lyden and Calyx in the corridor behind us. She's afraid but trying not to look afraid. I don't even want to think about the experiments they put her through in order to make her fireproof, but I also won't try to put it out of my head.

"I promise we'll get you out of there," I say.

The corner of her mouth twitches, then turns into a small smile. She wants to believe me, but I'm almost sure she doesn't. She still sees me as that little kid clinging to her waist when she left for Gaia Sur that morning all those years ago. That kid who was crying because she wouldn't come back.

"I know you will," she says, but her conciliatory expression doesn't change.

Eco clangs through the corridor in his dark red uniform, which matches the rest of ours. Lyden and Arwyn almost glow in contrast in the white Seam jumpsuits. I take a closer look at Eco—at the strap across his chest—as Tark starts the descent to Phase Three.

"What is that?" I ask, jerking my chin at Calyx, then nodding at the same strap across her chest.

"Neural ray," she says quietly.

"A what?"

"They stop you...from the inside. Freeze the commands from your brain to your limbs, so you quit moving," Eco explains with the smallest trace of a smirk. I swear, I feel compelled to hit him every time he talks.

"They're armed in there? I thought this was just a medical facility?" I jerk my eyes to Tark, who starts to lean forward as he grips the arm controls of his seat. The Wraith shifts, nose pointed directly at the center of the haze cloud in front of us as the green, holographic display trajectory in front of us tracks the descent. Calyx gets to her feet and reaches over my shoulder, then punches something into the console in front of me. Just as she moves back to her seat along the corridor wall next to Arwyn, a compartment about two feet long and two feet wide opens in the floor next to me. There must be five, ten weapons just like theirs stacked on top of each other in the hole.

"It's a medical facility no one knows about. Even the guards at Phase Two had neural batons," Tark says. "Standard issue for Phase Three—there's a lot more traffic here."

"Wraith Class 77, you are on course for entry," the male voice says over the comms again. I jump in my seat and watch a smile start on Tark's face. "Don't worry, Mr. Hart. If we do our jobs right, we won't need to use them."

"That doesn't make me feel better," I say as I fix my eyes back on the expanse of white haze before me. The trajectory dots disappear one after another on the holographic grid until they're replaced by two parallel bars. All at once, the haze clears and smooth white walls appear in their place. They separate in the middle—dissipating rather than mechanically retracting—giving way to a huge hangar with a series of staircases that run the perimeter on multiple levels. Tark punches another series of buttons, and I hear the ship's hydraulics engage. I watch guards dressed in red uniforms like ours approach the back of the ship through the window in front of us.

"Showtime," Eco says, gripping the strap of his neural ray. He shoves the barrel into Lyden's shoulder, which earns him a glare. He tries to laugh but swallows it after a second. "What? Just getting into character," he says. Lyden shakes his head.

"Do we go with them?" I ask, but Tark doesn't answer me. He brings his finger to his lips and sends me a golden stare in warning. I catch Arwyn's eyes as she looks over her shoulder at me and tries to smile again. I nod to her, a reminder about my promise.

Eco and Calyx walk on either side of Lyden and Arwyn as the other two guards exchange nods, then turn to lead everyone into what looks like a solid wall until they're right in front of it. It dissipates like the hangar wall, then reforms behind them like they were never there at all.

"The package is away," Denison says into the band on his wrist, then punches something into the console above his shoulder. Another holographic screen appears, showing what looks like the path everyone is walking behind Lyden and Arwyn.

"Whose perspective is that? Calyx's?" I ask.

Denison nods. "It's an ocular bug. I installed it while

we were below deck. We'll be able to see everything she sees now. Just a little extra security. I have the feed looped to our contacts back at The Seam building, and to one of our contacts at The State."

"Good. So now what?" I ask. "We launch that wind?"

Tark punches in something else and the ship starts to hum again. "Now, it's our turn. Indeed, Mr. Hart," he adds as the ship begins to pull out of the hangar.

"There's really no way to sneak everyone in *now?* We are *right here?*" I say. "It seems ridiculous to fly around and start trying to penetrate the barrier field, then bust through the wall of the place."

"We've come too far to take the chance of getting caught now," Denison says. "On a normal drop, the ship wouldn't linger on the dock. We have to make this disappear like any normal run."

"Something is wrong," Ms. Reynolt says, making her way through the corridor to us.

Denison darts his attention to the hologram display he pulled up. Calyx and the others are still walking, people passing them left and right wearing red uniforms with white lab coats.

"What is it, Luz?" Denison asks. "Something there, or here?"

"I can't be sure. It started here, and only got worse when Calyx took the others into the facility. The feeling is not subsiding. I'm afraid we've missed something." Reynolt's eyebrows dart together as fear registers in her eyes.

"It's not too late," I say. "We can go in after them. We haven't left this hangar yet." I want to say more, but Tark seems to step on the gas, and we pick up speed. *"Hey!"*

"If something is going down, we need to get clear so we can be in a position to help. We can't get stuck here," Tark explains. Denison nods a few times and then corrals Ms. Reynolt.

"We need to secure the zephyr and get it loaded," he says, walking her back through the corridor to the deck below.

"I still don't feel right about just leaving them here," I say.

Tark exhales. "Listen—let this go. The only thing we'll do by staying now is raise suspicion. If something isn't already going down, you can bet that will tip our hand," he explains. "Take your mark. We have work to do, and I'm going to need your eye."

I pull in a breath and try to think of something to tell myself that will make my guts stop turning. And I can't make sense of any of this make-it-up-as-we-go idiocy. There's no going back, only forward. Always forward. No matter what, no matter if forward is a cliff edge. We just have to figure out how to fly in their minds. I feel like my head is going to split down the middle and fall off either side of my shoulders, so I push my teeth together and lean back in the seat. The Wraith picks up momentum until we're clear of the hangar and back in the middle of the white haze. The screen in front of us shows a clear path as Tark punches something else into the console just before we rocket backward. After a few seconds, the haze is only in front of us with the black eternity of space seeming to push it away as we now slowly ease out of it.

Denison's voice comes over the comms. "The wind is loaded and ready for disbursal."

"Copy that," Tark says. "Another ten minutes and we'll be in position. Running surveillance scans now."

The projection of Eco, Calyx, Lyden, and my sister walking suddenly turns off. I notice it but don't manage to say anything about it before Tark starts barking commands at me.

"Where are you?" he asks, hammering his fingers on the screen in front of me. We're flying level, so I don't know what his problem is until the whole ship suddenly jerks backward, then starts moving forward quickly. "Are you flying this thing, or am I flying this thing, Mr. Hart? We don't have time for daydreams right now."

The accusation hits me like a slap, the heat of it washing over my cheeks a second later.

"Right, sorry. The projection just disappeared and it threw me."

"Probably interference. We're moving fast."

I push forward just a little and feel the ship surge again. Tark nods at me out of the corner of my eye, then detaches from his seat and heads back through the corridor behind me.

A wash of panic hits my chest when I realize I'm flying the ship alone. I scan Tark's side of the controls and see that he has not engaged autopilot. I blow out a breath, then take in one twice as deep. *All right, all right. Just follow the grids. The course is right there. Just get into position,* I think, pushing any thought of the hologram, my sister, of whatever Tark is doing… and Jazz… out of my head. I have work to do.

CHAPTER 19
Into the Tunnels
Jazz

It seems like several hours go by before we finally make a hole big enough for us to fit through. We've rolled up our burlap wraps, and our white jumpsuits are filthy.

"It looks like this tunnel goes both ways," Liam says, peering from left to right, but there's nothing to see in either direction since there's no light. Vox steps over the pile of earth and rubble at our feet and walks through the hole.

"They went this way," she says and starts heading toward the path that leads right.

"How do you know?" I call up to her. "There's no light!"

"Yes, there is!" Vox calls back to me, holding up her palm with a small red flame inside. Liam's jaw drops and I blink my eyes a few times, also surprised.

"She never had a dose of that DNA?" Liam asks, looking at me.

"She never had to. She's Vishan," I answer. Liam darts a glance at Vox before we follow her. I hesitate for a second when something rustles behind me, and I stop in my tracks.

"What is it?" Liam asks, studying my face for an answer that doesn't come. "Jazz, what?"

"I heard something. What are we supposed to do if we run into a tunnel shark down here?" I ask, feeling my heart start to pound in my chest. "We don't have any weapons. Maybe we should go back and find Azeris first after all."

Liam pulls in a breath and exhales through his nose, nodding.

"Why did you stop?" Vox yells back to us, making my blood go cold. "We don't have time to wait. Is somebody bleeding?"

Vox! Stop yelling, I think. *There's something behind us!*

I turn to face the gaping hole in the wall, and the pit beyond it. Shafts of sunlight spill through the opening above, like a sunshine fence keeping the withered, dried strangled bushes at bay against the other side. I try to think of a way we could somehow climb them to get back to the surface, but there's no guarantee we wouldn't waste all the daylight trying.

"We can't cross the Badlands at night," I whisper to Liam. "We would run the risk of getting pulled in by a tunnel shark anyway if we tried, and there would be nobody in the vicinity to help us like there is now. We have to keep going forward. That's the only way we'll find Liddick."

I nod to Vox when she comes into sight as if I'm explaining this to her and Liam instead of to myself, which is what I'm actually doing. They exchange surprised glances.

"All right," Vox says. "Then come on before they're out of range."

***

We stay close together when we walk this time. I remember Cal's warnings about getting too far apart when we crossed the Sand and Tanglebush in the Rush. We can't see far in the light of Vox's little red palm flame, but it's enough, and I feel like we're heading in the right direction.

"How far ahead do you think they are? I ask Vox, just to see if she feels the same way I do about our proximity.

"I don't know. They may have a five or ten-minute head start."

"And you're sure they'll help us?" Liam asks.

"No," Vox answers, which feels like suddenly falling in cold water.

"*No?* What do you mean no?" I ask. "Of course they'll help us. Why wouldn't they help us?"

"They may not be able to do anything without Cal and the NET device. We won't know anything until we catch up with them."

She says this casually, but it still hits me like a boulder in the stomach. She's right, though. Nothing is certain. We can't plan this. I realize that when I close my mouth after noticing it's still hanging open with all the things I'm not saying. Liam sends me a knowing smile.

"We'll figure it out," he says, seemingly just to me. "One way or another, we'll find him."

We walk on in silence for several more minutes in the glow of Vox's little fire. I think we must be descending because the damp smell of cold earth is starting to feel dryer, warmer, thinner. We're getting closer, although I have no idea how far we still have yet to go.

In the distance, a scratching sound pulls my attention

away from my incessant but unproductive obsessing about how we will manage to *not* get ourselves killed down here, from asking all the *what if* questions I can't find answers to, no matter how many times I ask them.

"Did you hear that?" I ask, but Vox and Liam just look at me with confused faces and shake their heads. The scratching sound comes again, this time, louder...closer.

"I heard it that time," Liam says.

"Tunnel sharks also made huge, thudding noises in the Rush," I say. "Nothing sounded only like scratching."

"I don't see how it could be the other Vishan, unless this tunnel loops around. That's the only way they could get behind us," Vox says, pushing to get in front of Liam as she extends her palm full of fire. The scratching sound comes again, this time accompanied by shuffling, like heavy, dragging footsteps. My heart starts pounding in my throat, and my mouth goes dry.

"I don't think that's a tunnel shark," I say, looking around for anything I can use as a weapon. There's nothing but dirt and more dirt. I grab a handful of that so at least I have something to throw in the face of whatever might be planning to attack us.

"It's not a tunnel shark—at least not a healthy one," Vox says. "Whatever that is, it's injured. Nothing healthy moves like that."

The scratching and lumbering sounds give way to low moans, almost words.

"*Wuuuuh...*" a male voice says, and I feel tingles start along the back of my neck and run down my spine.

"That's *human*," Liam says, blowing out a small breath. I feel the tension and fear surrounding us drop a level, but only because at least it's not a tunnel shark.

Liddick? I think, holding my breath and hoping I hear his voice in my head in reply.

"Hey!" Vox shouts, extending her fire and taking a few steps toward the sounds.

"Wuuhhhhhh!" the voice calls again, this time louder and desperate. "WUUHHHHH!"

"Tieg?" I say under my breath. "That sounds like Tieg...he and Dez never arrived at The Seam, Liam. I forgot, with everything that came through about Liddick... What if they never made it out of Phase Two?"

Panic rises in my stomach, offset only by the guilt I feel for not realizing sooner that they were still unaccounted for.

"We all assumed they were on a separate transport—it's not your fault. Everything happened pretty fast up there," Liam says, but I don't feel any better.

"Whhhaaaater..." the voice says again, but this time I push past Liam toward it.

"Jazz! Wait!"

"He said, *'water.'* Tieg! Is that you?"

Vox follows quickly behind me with her palm fire until we both stop cold at a huddled mass against the dirt wall of the tunnel.

"Hey!" Liam shouts as he closes the distance between us, then stumbles to an abrupt stop when he sees what we see. A clicking sound comes from the black mass folded against the wall. We all take a step back. It starts moving, slowly pushing upward until it's clear that *it is* a person.

"Tieg!" I shout, convinced it must be him because he's

much bigger than Liddick. I take a few more steps toward him until Liam grabs my arm and keeps me back. I turn to him and start to pull out of his grip, but he holds up a finger against his lips, then pulls a canteen from his satchel and slides it to the hunched-over person with his back to us. The canteen hits his foot.

"It's water! That's what you said…you wanted water?" Liam calls to the person. He's barely finished the sentence when the crouched mass pounces on the canteen and begins desperately trying to remove the lid. He claws and bites at it until it finally falls to the dirt, and he starts to drink like he's never going to stop.

His face is still in shadows, but his throat is covered in black lines, just like his hands. He starts to cough, but then recovers and tries to take another drink, but the canteen is empty. He growls, desperately shaking it over his mouth until he finally gives up and throws it to the ground.

"Wahhter…no…more water!" he says, shuffling toward us.

"Whoa!" Vox says when he comes into the light of her hand flame.

"Tieg…" I say on the last of a breath. It is Tieg, or at least, it used to be.

CHAPTER 20
Find a Way or Make One
Arco

It seems like the more I try to concentrate on not thinking about her, the harder it gets. I even disabled the tracking windows that appear in my peripheral vision for her group. I couldn't make myself stop checking on her, and it was interfering with my own mission. I have to get it through my head that we *are not* on the same path anymore. She made her choice when she decided to go after Liddick instead of believing the obvious: he betrayed us all.

"The payload is secured," Mr. Denison says over the comms.

"Copy that," Tark says. "What's our ETA, Mr. Hart?" Hearing my name startles me, and the rush of adrenaline once again puts me back to work.

"We're almost in position. About another minute," I answer after a quick look at the holographic displays in front of me. I over-correct our trajectory to make up for the glide time I never should have let happen a minute ago while my mind was wandering. I press my teeth together, aggravated with myself again. I just can't shake the feeling that something is wrong, that she needs help. I shake my head because I'm being stupid. If she needed me, she wouldn't have left. "We're aligned," I say, pushing the words through my teeth as soon as I see the grid sync with our position. "Let her rip."

Nothing happens for a few minutes, but then I hear the sound of water rushing, like it's inside the hull somehow. A few seconds after that, I start to see a hole opening in the white haze in front of us. It's only black for a fraction of a second before it returns to a gray, muddy cloud. Another black patch opens up, only to be filled in again with the same thick fog. A thin, glowing blue circle that's very faint takes shape in the haze, and I wonder if that must be the perimeter of the doorway the zephyr animal just made.

"Now, that's a thing of beauty, don't you think, Mr. Hart?" Tark says, at my shoulder before I realize he's even come aboard the bridge.

"Sure. Except we're going to drive through there and it will probably strip this rig down to its coils, and us right along with it."

Tark chuckles. "Let's hope not."

"Great," I say, leaning forward to control our speed so we don't topple into the perimeter opening. I hold my breath, part of me bracing for a sudden flash of light and deafening crash. This is all too easy.

"Nice and steady," Tark encourages. Why he doesn't just do this himself, I don't know. This infiltration of Phase Three hardly seems like the best time to put a cadet through any training. This is all too important to trust to a student, isn't it?

The nose of the ship penetrates the haze, according to the screens going haywire in front of me, obviously detecting the zephyr wind trying to take a bite out of us.

We are about halfway through the gate before I know it, and I let myself breathe again. *Maybe we really can do this.* Still, there's the small matter of actually getting into the facility. This haze is just the barrier field.

"How are we masked again?" I ask.

"Passing through that opening coated us in the same deflectors the piranha wind uses to mirror the other molecules around it. To anyone staring out their windows in Phase Three, we just look like a black sky dotted with stars."

"So, people will literally not see this ship coming?" I ask, feeling all the muscles in my shoulders finally relax. I realize I'm gripping the arms of this pilot seat when I glance down and see my white knuckles. I force myself to release the chair and take a deep breath. *Slow and even.*

"Exactly," Tark confirms with a decisive nod. He flashes a smile that borders on cocky, and that makes me feel a little more confident too. *We're going to do this. We're going to shut down the whole damn show.* But my confidence doesn't last long.

"We have a small problem," Ms. Reynolt's voice comes over the comms from below deck.

"Go," Tark says.

"I can't reestablish visuals with anyone in Calyx's group. Jack doesn't think the wind is interfering because he wrote code modulations for that."

"Let's get closer to the facility and try again," Tark replies after a long pause. His cocky grin is gone, and lines start to form between his eyebrows. Something isn't right. I thought it was maybe just my reservations about flying this ship, but it's not that. Now Tark must feel it too.

"There's no reason anyone in the Phase Three facility would suspect them, is there?" I ask. "Calyx works there, and we had this drop off scheduled. They were expecting us to deliver Lyden and my sister. Right?"

Tark doesn't answer me at first. He just presses his lips into a line. I get to my feet to get his attention.

"What?" he says. "I mean, right. Don't worry, Mr. Hart. Calyx can handle herself. She isn't alone on the inside."

"Then we just keep going?" I ask.

"That's what I was just saying. Stay on course. One way or another, that place is going to need a back door."

"I assume we're moving forward with the second team?" Denison's voice comes over the comms this time. Tark looks directly at me.

"What? You expect me to make that call?" I ask, incredulous.

"You *are* the golden boy." Tark grins just a little, but his expression returns to neutral just as fast. "The hybridization of your abilities makes you the most qualified to assess the situation."

"Please. Get Ms. Reynolt out here. She's the Empath. She can feel out what's happening in there with her waves or something," I say, nearly choking on the words with the laughter in between each of them. Tark just keeps looking at me in the same, sterile way. Finally, his bottom lip quirks up as he shrugs.

"I'm not making the call, and Denison won't make it without me. Neither will Reynolt. So we either sit here all day, turn around and go back to The Seam building, or we push on." Tark's eyes flash at me. The golden rays almost shoot directly into me like some kind of laser beam straight at my chest. *Why is he putting all this on me? Why* **me?** *Does he need some kind of scapegoat if this all falls through?*

"We don't have all day, Mr. Hart. That hole we just made won't last too much longer in stasis like this. It needs to expand right there on that facility wall." Tark nods out the port window. I follow his trajectory and see the whole Phase Three facility coming into view. It's enormous, wide and stretching into a bowed curve that looks like it goes on for miles. The whole thing is the same height, spreading away from us like an impossibly thick boomerang.

"That's Phase Three?" I ask under my breath, surprised at my own question. I don't know what I was expecting to see, something that looked like Gaia Sur, I guess—tall, cylindrical buildings with attached light extensions—but there's nothing like that there in front of us. "It didn't look like this from the front, where we dropped Calyx off with Lyden and my sister."

"We were level with the structure then. The curve on each end is masked by the port-cloud. We're above the facility now, so we can see the expanse of it against the barrier. Set your grid and follow the scope. We're going to make a little hole in the wall out back." Tark smirks, nodding to my controls. I press the comms to the med bay.

"And they can't see us? We're masked?" I ask again because the feeling that something isn't right is getting stronger the closer we get to the walls of the huge, white boomerang building.

"Roger that, Arco," Jack's voice says over the comms. "I took care of it."

I nod to myself and lean into the control field emanating from the chair. The Wraith pushes forward a little faster, filling the wrapping window with the view of Phase Three.

"All right, if you say so. We should be in position to relaunch the package in about ten seconds," I say. And it's the longest ten seconds of my life.

"The second hole will be much smaller than the one we put in the barrier field," Tark says. "This one will only be big enough for us to connect an airlock."

"So we just sit here in the meantime?"

"We need someone we can trust out there, Mr. Hart. And we're going to need to move once we collect everyone."

"Everything will disintegrate once Jack uploads the DNA into their system—that's still the plan?" I ask, sounding redundant, but I don't care. Something doesn't fit.

"Last I checked, that should tie up everything quite nicely," Tark replies.

We drop into position and I line up the nose of the ship against the projected doorway in the holographic scope. The point of our Wraith touches directly in the middle of a glowing blue X, which I presume marks the heart of the labs on the other side of the facility wall.

"Here goes nothing," I say under my breath, but not quietly enough. Tark chuckles.

"On the contrary, Mr. Hart. Here goes everything."

CHAPTER 21
Tieg
Jazz

I take several steps back, nearly running over Vox. Her hands grip my shoulders, holding me still until I get my bearings again.

"What is that on his hands and neck?" I blurt. "Tieg, what happened to you?"

He doesn't say anything in reply. He just grips the roots and hardened earth of the walls like he's trying to keep from being blown away.

"*Bug...*" he says in a raspy voice. "Tunnel...sand bug."

"Crite," Liam says, covering his mouth with his hand before he pushes it through his streaked blond hair. "It's one of the antlions. It has to be, but they're much farther down than we are here."

Vox exhales hard. "They're in the Rush."

"Those things with the pincers?" I ask, remembering how one of them tried to take Vox's arm off while the rest of us were all in the Vishan tunnels.

"Yep. Looks like he went a few rounds with one," she replies, nodding to Tieg, and now that he's out of the shadows, I can see the wreckage of his torn and frayed dive suit.

"Are you hurt anywhere?" I ask carefully, scanning

him for any obvious signs of injury. He doesn't look like he's bleeding from anywhere, but I can't tell with all the dirt covering him. He stretches out his neck like he's trying to get a deep breath, but then pulls what's left of his dive suit down over his shoulder to reveal two puncture wounds on the outside of his bicep. They're not bleeding, but they're the source of the black lines striating up his neck and *what must be* down his arms to his hands.

"It...bit me," he finally says just before his teeth start chattering uncontrollably. He snarls and lunges at us, but then throws himself into the wall again and grabs a nearby root. He grips it like he will fall through the floor if he lets go, and we all jump back a few steps in shock.

"Tieg!" I shout, holding up both my hands. "The antlion bit you...that's what you're trying to say?"

"Is that your only injury?" Liam adds in a pressed voice.

Tieg struggles to shake his head. He clenches his teeth together as his hands start to shake from the grip he has on the roots.

"He can't talk. What's happening to him? That didn't happen to me when my arm got caught in those pincers," Vox says. Liam shakes his head from side to side, partially in what seems like disbelief, and partially in despair. My stomach drops.

"You have to fix this," I say, not giving him a chance to give up. "There has to be something you can do. You know how all these science project animals work down here."

"That's an actual *bite*, first of all, not a scrape from

pincers. Without equipment, there's not much I can do except maybe slow the progress long enough until we can get back to Azeris." Without looking at anyone for approval, Liam pulls a small knife from his bag and cuts a strip from his burlap wrap. He takes a few steps toward Tieg, holding out one hand. "OK, I need you to be on ice for a minute, all right? I need to tie this on your arm to slow the venom's progression."

Tieg grips the roots in one hand even more tightly as he stretches out his other arm. He finds a new patch of roots to grip with the outstretched arm and turns his face away.

"Do it..." he growls, which sends a chill straight up my spine and into my teeth. Liam moves quickly to tie a tourniquet just above the puncture wounds. Tieg fights his reaction, spitting and cursing with the effort. He finally turns, leaping onto Liam and knocking him to the ground. Tieg's wedge of bioengineered teeth start snapping like they're somehow automated as he lunges again and again for Liam's throat. Liam pushes his forearm against Tieg's throat to keep him at bay, but Tieg is bigger and heavier than Liam.

"Tieg!" I shout, scanning the ground for anything I can use to knock him back, but there's nothing except roots sticking out of the walls in every direction. I glance at Vox, and even though we don't exchange any words, we both know to move to the same side of Tieg. Both of us push his ribs with our boots until he finally falls sideways. It only dislodges him for a second, but it's long enough for Liam to get to his feet as Tieg scratches and pulls at the ground to move toward us again. Vox jumps in front of Liam and me with a huge flame rising from her palm, and all at once Tieg stops scrambling for us. He buries his face under his arm to shade his eyes from the light and howls in pain. Liam and I exchange confused looks.

"The fire is how I finally got away from the antlion in the Rush," Vox says. "It snapped at me just like he did."

"Then we need to get him back to Azeris *now*. There has to be another way out of here," I add, scanning again for something other than these *stupid* roots in every direction. "We'll have to use the vines...we'll have to climb the walls in the hole back there." I shake my head, resigned.

"Come on...*hyah. Hyah!*" Vox says to Tieg, pushing the fire in her hand at him. I narrow my eyes at her.

"He's not a *horse.*"

"Uh, sorry, sand dollar. I don't know the *move-it* sound effect for a bug-man in transit. You got a better idea?"

I glance at Liam, who shrugs. I roll my eyes, then turn hesitantly back to Tieg, who's frozen in place with his eyes still shielded and his bioengineered wedges of teeth bared. They start to chatter again, despite the flexed muscles of his jaw fighting against it.

"Tieg, can you stand up? You have to come with us. We need to get to Azeris. He can help you." I take a few steps toward him alongside Vox. Tieg just snarls at me, which makes him lose control of his chattering teeth again. He jumps straight up, making both Vox and me stumble back. I fall on my elbows, and Vox's flame goes out completely.

"Stay down!" a voice shouts from far behind us. It's a familiar voice, but I can't place it until it shouts again. "Don't move!"

"Cal?" Vox whispers next to me. *"Cal!"*

A deluge of Vishan words pour over us, and then I hear several people running in our direction.

A second later I hear the hiss of fire starting like a struck match, only the match is the size of a shuttle bus.

"What the—?!" Liam starts. I try to push to my feet, only to feel a hand push me right back into place on the ground. I look up and see the long scar on his forehead.

"Keep still, little sister..." he says.

"Dell!"

Another howl rips from Tieg, pulling my eyes back to him. Cal is cinching a knot around Tieg's waist, pinning down his arms at his hips.

"Throw me the leaves!" he shouts to Dell, who chucks a rolled object toward him. He snatches it out of the air and unrolls it, then wraps Tieg's bicep. He pulls out another scrap of rope and ties it in place.

It hits me all at once that neither Cal nor Dell are the source of the bright light...and that all of the footsteps have stopped.

Two other Vishan, both boys, stand about ten feet behind us with each of their hands filled with fire. Vox and I turn to each other at the same time, but before I can ask her if she knows them, she pushes to her feet in one quick bolt and offers me her hand. I take it, and she pulls me up.

"Small subterranean world," Dell says with a snort, breaking the tension.

"What are you *doing* down here?" Vox says, narrowing her yellow eyes, which flash in the firelight. "Did you set that trap back there?"

"No, we came after him when a critter pulled him under," Cal says, snapping his fingers and bringing a tiny flame of light to the tips of them right in front of Tieg's face. "His sister nearly crawled straight out of her skin to chase after him."

"Dezzie!" Tieg whales again, almost incoherently.

"She's all right!" I hold up my hands to get Tieg's attention, but he just looks wildly around the tunnel. "She's with your father..." I add, and Tieg finally stops seething.

"So they made it topside? And Zoe..." Dell asks, but trails off.

"They're all fine," I answer. "They all made it to Admin City with us, except Liddick was rerouted. It's a long story, but he's in these tunnels somewhere...Tieg's father sent him here."

"*How?*" Tieg manages to ask, his chest heaving with what is apparently considerable effort to speak.

"That's what we're trying to find out. But we don't have time to talk about it now. We need to stabilize you," Liam explains, then turns to Dell. "Is there another way to get topside from here besides that trap back there?"

"He's not going topside."

"Why not?" Liam asks, annoyed. "I can help him if we can get to Azeris's hab."

"Too late. That sun will crisp him now," Dell says, looking sideways at the black veins running up Tieg's neck.

"He got this bite days ago. We'll have to take him to Vita," Cal says, looking Tieg up and down.

"Who's *Vita?*" Liam asks.

"Their healer," Vox answers, then cocks an eyebrow and seems to look for something in the air. "And...my aunt or cousin or something?"

"Dezzie..." Tieg mumbles again, using what sounds like the last of his energy.

"Your sister is safe. She's with your father..." Liam says. Tieg all but collapses into Dell at this, and I can't tell if he's relieved or just exhausted.

"We need to move because I'm not tryin' to carry this one down any tunnels," Dell says.

"Wait," I say before I realize it. "What happened to you? And Lidd—" I start to ask about Liddick, but his name lodges in my throat when I remember that it was Tieg's own father who forced Liddick back through these tunnels to *find* him. Cal looks at me blankly, genuinely confused.

"They were all heading topside..." he starts, then looks at Tieg. "His sister was wrecked that maybe he'd get swallowed by something, so we went back to hunt him up."

Popular mollusk, isn't he? Vox thinks, which only makes me clench my teeth against my growing frustration.

"And this venom has been in his system for days?" Liam says with another nod at Tieg's black lines.

"Three by my count," Dell says, catching Tieg when he loses his balance. "We've been tracking him up and down these tunnels from the sands to the edge of the

Vishan cavern."

"We need to get him back to Vita," Cal says, waving the two Vishan boys behind us down the tunnel, the light from their palm fires bouncing red off the dark, root-marred walls.

CHAPTER 22
When One Door Closes…
Arco

The blue, glowing outline starts to take shape in an arc over the white, smooth wall through the window in front of us. I stare at it, still not processing that it's actually consuming the molecules that make up the wall and then replacing them with something that only *looks* the same. I shake my head, marveling.

"We have about three minutes until the wall is passable," Denison's voice says over the comms. "Then we'll connect the airlock."

"Is everyone in position?" I ask. "Ripley…are you, I mean…" I start, but don't have to finish.

"Ready as we'll ever be," Jax answers, then starts to chuckle. "This archive is purple…*purple!*" he adds, which makes everything seem less intense. I glance at Tark, who raises an eyebrow and smiles.

"Forty-five seconds to clearance," Denison says, and Tark nods at me.

"Lock in. We have to be in perfect alignment."

I nod back without looking at him, without even blinking or breathing as we approach the blue arc outline.

PERIMETER SEALED flashes on the holographic screen in front of me, and I finally exhale.

"Aligned," I say with the last of a breath.

"Nice work, Mr. Hart," Tark says. "Aligned, Briggs. Whenever you're ready..."

"Copy that. Airlock deployed. Delivery in three... two...connected. Sweeps are clean. Deploying..."

"They're going in there right now? Jax and his dad with the archive?" I ask, and Tark nods again.

"Calyx is waiting to receive them," he answers. "We'll start unloading the labs while they upload the DNA archive. Then we'll get out of here and watch the fireworks."

"What about the others who work there? They'll... blow up with the facility."

"Calyx alerted The State—there will be security ships en route. They'll have a chance to get aboard and face their crimes, or they'll die as cowards," Tark says without an ounce of hesitation or remorse, and I start to realize just how affected he really is by the genetic testing all these years, and on his watch no less. Jazz is right...being helpless has to be the worst feeling there is.

"We're green—the archives are en route. Are you ready?" Denison says over the comms. Tark gives me a quick glance, then nods once.

"On our way," he answers. "Let's go shut this thing down."

***

The airlock is surreal—perfectly clear like there's nothing between the abrupt maw of the ship and the outside wall of Phase Three. Tark slips a red flack jacket over his jumpsuit and loads two neural batons in the front. He slings a neural ray over his back, and throws me another.

I catch it by the barrel and almost choke on a protest.

"Hey!" I say, despite trying to keep my teeth together.

"Relax, Mr. Hart. You have to enable it before it will neutralize anyone." He smirks.

"I know," I lie, watching as he flicks a small lever near his trigger and locks it into place. An electric hum emanates from the ray until I can feel it in my teeth.

I enable my ray, then sling it over my back. I also grab a neural baton and a small toolset from the weapons hold in the ship.

"Ready?" Tark asks. I look out again at the empty space in front of us, a bottomless pit of space between the edge of the ship and the wall of Phase Three.

"It's just solid all around?" I ask, then feel stupid because of course it is or we'd both be frozen solid right now. Tark just starts walking toward the opening, and I quickly catch up.

"I'll take the right wall and you take the left. There will be a console in your corner of the room," he says as we take our first steps onto the ion field. I stop looking down and pull in a breath. "You need to hack into the enclosure controls and remove the barriers—Calyx has the zone channel pulled up already. You'll just need to override the security clearance. Can you do that?"

"Should be easy enough if I don't have to dig around for the access port."

"Good. Then you're up," he adds as we approach the wall of Phase Three. Everything in me wants to stop because all I can think about is that we're walking directly into a *zephyr wind*. But I press on. If Tark doesn't think this thing is going to shred us straight to the bone, I

just need to put it out of my head too. "Three steps…"
Tark continues. "Two steps…one…"

I force myself to keep my eyes open as we walk
straight through the wall. *Jax and his dad did it,* I think,
letting out all the air in my lungs. When the haze clears,
the interior of Phase Three is nothing like I thought it
would be—it's worse.

Clear cube enclosures line the walls starting about
halfway up the room. Everything is dark except for rings
of lights along the bottoms of each enclosure. Some are
filled with water, and the subjects inside…*crite,* the
people inside. They're all wearing the same silver
jumpsuits, some of them cut into a Y pattern with open
sides. Everyone with this kind of suit has three red lines
running along their ribs. It looks like everyone is asleep. I
stop abruptly when my eyes fall on another enclosure
near the center of the room, along the far wall. It's bigger
than the others, and the clear walls are frosted in places.
Someone inside is pacing until the man inside stops
suddenly and turns to look directly at me. His eyes are
milky and his white hair is cropped short. A pair of blue-
tinged hands slam against the enclosure wall. He pounds
on it again and again, and I start to feel blood pounding
in my ears.

"Now! Go!" Tark shouts through his teeth, then runs
directly toward the enclosure.

"Wait! I can't open it with him like that! He'll kill us!"

"Go *now,* Mr. Hart! I've got it!"

"Crite…" I hiss under my breath and make my way
along the wall toward the columns where Tark said the
console would be. On the other side, I see it. A blue

holographic keypad hovers over the white platform, and the green grid display shows a map of the room. All right, time to work.

I study the layout, then start scrolling through the origin code until I find an automated panel access…if I trip them all at once, this place is going to flood with the water from several of the enclosures. *What do I do…? What if they can't survive outside of that water?"*

There's no other choice—we can't take the entire enclosure. Denison will know what to do when we get them aboard. He'll have to know…

Numbers and symbols start to dance in my peripheral vision again.

97A66H Vertical 975-A-17

The code repeats over and over in scrolling text, each time causing a pinch behind my eyes that gets stronger each time. I punch the code into the console, and everything goes silent. Completely silent—I don't even hear the pounding in my ears anymore.

The man in the larger enclosure pounds on his wall one more time before a hydraulic hum radiates into the air, and all at once, the front panels of the clear enclosures dissipate. I swear, the water seems to hold perfectly still for a fraction of a second before it all spills in a deluge onto the ground, along with the suspended people who were just floating inside. Bodies rush toward me as others step outside of their enclosures, some crying, some shouting. Some still unconscious. Two burst into flame and try to pat each other down.

"Come on! This way!" Denison shouts as he, Avis, Ellis, and Ms. Reynolt start to physically pull people through the opening in the wall and into the emptiness between us and the ship.

"No! No!" one girl starts screaming at the edge of the floor. "I'm on fire! I'm on fire!" she shouts again as flames shoot up her back and down her arms.

"It's all right. There's an ion cloud. We're going to help you!" Denison says in a surprisingly calm voice as he pulls the girl across the threshold, singeing his hands. Ms. Reynolt holds out her arms, and the girl moves toward her.

"Breathe. Just breathe… Concentrate on my voice," she says, and slowly, the girl's flames begin to recede.

"Two here!" Ellis says. "We need more room!"

"This is all we have!" Avis responds from inside the Wraith.

I start to head toward his voice but stop when the whole wall behind the large enclosure, which is completely frosted over now, starts to lift. Tark is nowhere when I scan for him, and the nearly foot of water on the floor immediately flows through the new opening. All I see are several pairs of legs that don't move as the water parts around them, then several more that are stepping wildly. The wall reaches the ceiling to reveal Ms. Rheen and Mr. Styx standing in front of Calyx, Lyden, and my sister, all held in place by metal, faceless riot drones.

"Run!" my sister shouts to me just before one of the drones shoves a neural rod into her ribs. Her shoulders erupt in fire until Mr. Styx grabs her and shoves his thumbs into the inside of her forearm. Her flames instantly disappear, and he pushes her back into the grip of the riot drone.

"There's nowhere to run, Ms. Hart," he says. "I thought you knew that by now."

Tark takes a step toward him. "It's over, Eros. The State knows everything, and they're on their way. We've sent all the evidence they need to convict all of you for crimes against humanity."

"Oh, right, that was *your* job, wasn't it, Ms. Frome?" Rheen sneers. Calyx's eyes go wide in confusion. She looks to Jack, who seems equally lost.

"How—?" she starts, but then Rheen steps out of the way to reveal Eco standing behind her, grinning.

"You always did underestimate me, Cally," he says. Acid fills my veins, and it takes every ounce of my restraint to keep from rushing him and putting out those light-up neural circuits in his cheekbones. "Did you really think I was going to just stand by while these mollusks ruined everything?" he adds, jerking a thumb at Jax, who is held in place by another riot drone. Jax stiffens as his father struggles in place next to him. *I have to do something...*I think, then remember my neural ray. I slide it around to my front and am about to take aim when Fraya comes running through the ion airlock and into the lab.

"Leave him alone!" she shouts, obstructing my shot of Styx.

"Fraya! No!" I yell to her, but it's too late. The frozen man inside the larger container jumps down and rushes her, sloshing in the water at our feet. Fraya tries to scream but can't in the shock of this...*mutation* running straight for her. Jax rips away from the drone holding him and tries to tackle the frozen man, who stops running and faces him. I take aim at the back of the frozen man, but then Tark jumps between him and Jax, and I'm afraid I'll hit him if I shoot. The ice man doesn't fall when Tark makes contact. He just spins around and presses his hands into Tark's temples, making his hair go white and his skin frost over.

"No!" I shout, firing at the ice man. He drops, along with Tark. Denison and I both rush over to him.

"Skull…Skull, can you hear me?" Denison says, checking for a pulse. Tark's eyes are closed, and he's not moving.

"No…no, no…" I hear myself saying over and over again, but the words dry up when I hear Eco's nasally laughter. He meets my eyes.

"Do you know how long I've been waiting for that mountain goat to fall off his cliff already?

Everything goes quiet again, except the blood pounding in my ears. *That* is loud and clear. I don't realize I'm walking toward Eco until I'm already almost in front of him—no conscious plan, just movement. I watch the smug look on his face melt when he registers that I'm not stopping…when it dawns on him that he's going to be hit in the face. I punch him once, then grab his shirt to keep him from falling. I punch him again, and the third time I aim directly for the last of the lights in his cheekbone that are blinking red at me. I hit him, but when I pull back for another punch, arms close around mine and pin them to my ribs, pulling me back. Blood smears Eco's face as the lights flicker, then stop all together. He spits blood and tries to get to his feet. I struggle to break free of the hold on me until I hear Denison's voice loud in my ear.

"Stop—be still, son. Your hand...be still..." he says, walking me back at a fast clip, and I nearly trip when I look down and see the white bones of my center two knuckles sticking out from under a flap of skin. For a second I'm not sure it's even my hand, but everything snaps into focus when I hear Rheen's cackle several yards in front of me. Denison keeps dragging me backward.

"Take him to the oxygen trials," Rheen says, gesturing at Eco. Two squat riot drones roll forward and clamp Eco's arms on each side. Blood runs down his cheek as the wiring unit dangles past his ear, and he's so preoccupied with touching the blood and looking at his hands in disbelief that it takes him a second to process what Rheen has just said.

"What? No...we had a deal! You told me I'd have my own cine studio!" he starts in a normal voice, ramping up to yelling. "You can't do this! People will be looking for me!"

"Don't hold your breath," Rheen says, suddenly exploding in laughter after a beat. She makes eye contact with Styx, who also starts laughing.

"Oh! Oh, that was a good one..." He stumbles through the words as he chokes on more waves of laughter.

"Seal it! Go!" Denison shouts behind us just as I see another few riot drones grab Jack and Fraya. Jax lunges forward, shouting, then stiffens when the drone holding him jabs a neural rod into his ribs.

"No!" I yell, trying to pull out of Denison's grip until

white hot pain shoots up my arm, making me see stars. I blink furiously, then realize I really am seeing stars as we cross backward over the ion field airlock.

"Seal it!" Denison shouts again. Ellis punches something into the wall console, and I hear the sound of air compressing.

"Retracting!" Avis shouts behind us. I finally pull free of Denison, but only because he lets me go in the same second. I stumble forward and fall on my knees but catch myself with my hands. I feel sick for a second, and everything goes black.

CHAPTER 23
...*Another Opens*
Jazz

"There has to be a shorter way to the Vishan cavern than going through the Rush," I protest to Dell and Cal, who seem adamant on going back through these tunnels. "Tieg will never be able to hold out through the biomes like this—especially not through the Sand."

"She's right," Vox says. "We'll be too slow, and I don't exactly want to be watching over my shoulder every eight seconds for him to sprout pincers or something."

"This isn't a joke," Liam snarls. "That venom is *killing* him—do you understand that?"

Vox holds her palms to her sides in surrender and raises her eyebrows. "Zone, Liddick's brother. We want the same thing." She cuts a glance at me.

He's wound because he can't do anything. He just has to watch Tieg get worse, I think. Vox nods and lowers her arms. She crosses back to Cal, and they start talking in Vishan.

"We need to get him to Azeris's hab. It's closer than going six miles into the earth," Liam says, the red light of the Vishan palm fires flickering on the walls.

"We're not going back through the Rush," Cal says. "There's a shorter way through the supply tunnels. They're only about a mile out, and then it's a steady descent."

"And the pressure? The heat? Will our baseline nanites still work without our Gaia jumpsuits?" I ask, holding out my burlap wrap to reveal the now stained white jumpsuit they gave us at The Seam building.

"No. Those will be offline," Liam says, narrowing his eyes, then sighing. "If I had my equipment, I could put together a synthetic...I just—"

Jazz? I hear in my head. It's a warbled voice, but it's... Liddick. My legs nearly give out under me.

"Liddick?" I hear myself say out loud, and Liam stops in the middle of whatever he was saying.

"What did you say?"

"I just heard him...in my head somehow," I answer, but then my vision starts to get hazy, and a buzz starts in my ears.

Cal moves toward me, and the buzzing gets stronger. My vision flickers, and I push the heels of my hands into them, but it doesn't help.

"What's wrong? Can you see?" Liam says, but I almost can't make out his voice anymore with the growing buzz.

Crite...it's you. Rip, where are you? Are you OK? I hear Liddick's voice again, but everything is dark.

Liddick! What's happening? We're in the tunnels coming to find you. Where are you? I think, and then I see him standing against a wall made of the same dirt and roots in our tunnels. It's dark around him with the exception of a glowing light sash across his chest. He's in red military fatigues, and I can't tell if he's really there or if the thinning air is just starting to get to me.

I'm here, he thinks. *You're in my channel or something. Are you with Vox?*

Yes, and Cal and Dell...we're on our way to—

You're with Cal? He has the NET, Rip! It's connecting us, Liddick thinks, then puts one hand on the wall and turns toward me. I feel the cool, hard earth on my fingertips and gasp.

I can feel that...it's just like with Vox when she was hiding at Phase Two. When she touched the cold floor...

Liddick nods, and a smile starts to shake on his lips.

You came after me? Even after... He trails off.

I know you didn't betray us. But I don't know how long this connection will last, so just tell me how to get to you, I think, trying to look around for anything that might give away his location. It's just carved earth as far as I can see.

It's not safe. Dez's father has me in lockstep with these government apes. We've tried to lose them twice already.

We?

Finn...a friend from the Badlands. It's a long story.

What's close? Where are you going?

Spaulding sent me to find Tieg.

Tieg is with us! That's what I started to say. He was bitten by one of the antlions. We're taking him to Vita.

Rip! Liddick nearly shouts, then looks over his shoulder. He's rolling his eyes when he looks back at me. *Sorry...this is all split—anyway. I have an idea. How many are with you?*

Cal, Dell, Tieg—though he's tied up—Liam, and Vox.

*Liam is with you!? All right. Tell Cal we are at...*Liddick thinks, then looks at some kind of panel strapped to his arm. *Crite, I can't see the numbers. Listen, there's a waterfall* *about half a mile back. We dropped about a mile from the hub out there at the base of Skyboard. It's—*

Yes, with Ensign? That's where we came through too.

Yes! We dropped about a mile east of there, heading toward the ocean, and we've been descending for a few hours. I'm going to tell these mollusks I know where Tieg is. Can you get to those falls?

Dell and Cal must know where that is, and if not, with Vox, we should be able to find it.

All right. Tell the others there are four Special Blacks with us, and they're outfitted. Liam will know what that means. They're armed, too, and to them, everyone is expendable except Tieg, OK? We'll need to give him up and move.

Liddick, he's really sick.

The Blacks will take him to his father, and he'll be good as new. Trust me. Spaulding is one of the high rollers for all these genetic mutations, Rip. He's been funding Gaia for years, Liddick explains, then starts walking toward me. I feel the pressure of each step on the bottom of my feet and instinctively look down. They haven't moved, and when I look up again, Liddick is just inches from me. He looks down and takes my hand, but I don't feel it.

You can't feel me because I'm not really holding your hand…just the air in front of me, he thinks, reading my feelings. *But I can hear every echo in your head right now,* he adds, then meets my eyes. He moves his hand to my cheek, but then stops abruptly. His dark eyebrows dart together for a second, and he takes a step back.

What's wrong? I think, confused. He shakes his head.

Nothing. Finn is calling me. It doesn't take this long to take a leak. He smirks, then shrugs one shoulder. *They're coming. Head to the waterfall. Be ready for four outfitted Special Blacks,* he adds with a nod.

"Liddick, wait!" I say out loud this time, but before I can even finish the sentence, he's gone, and my vision is hazy again.

***

When I open my eyes, I'm sitting on the ground leaning against the wall. Liam is crouched in front of me and Vox is at my side.

"You went into his channel?" Vox asks, knocking on something hard in my lap. I look down and see the smooth, metal NET device, the two forks of the Y-shape pointing away from me. I nod.

"It was just like with you, but nothing went abstract. Nothing stretched out like a funhouse."

"You're closer..." Cal says, and I shoot him a look, which makes my head spin for a second.

"What?" I ask, surprised.

"Vox was in Admin City when you tapped into her channel," Liam explains. "Liddick is in these tunnels somewhere."

"That too," Cal says. Vox smirks at me and pulls me to my feet.

"So? What happened?"

"We need to find a waterfall. He's not alone. There are four Outfitted Special Blacks. He said Liam would know what that meant?"

"Crite..." Liam says, then blows out a breath. "We're going to need help then.

"What are they?" I ask.

"Genetically modified soldiers. They're enhanced—

night vision, heat resistant—and they're fast. We don't have anything they can't manage."

"Liddick just told me they're working for Tieg's dad. Their mission is to find Tieg and bring him back," I answer, then look back to find Tieg leaning against the wall with his eyes closed, the black lines seeming to thicken and darken down his throat.

"So...we trade?" Dell asks, holding one of Tieg's arms.

"He's not going to make it to Admin City like this..." Liam says. "Not at this rate."

"Liddick said Tieg's father could help him. He's been funding Gaia's research," I explain, then look at Tieg again to see if he understood me, but he's still nearly unconscious against the wall. "I don't like the idea of just handing him over like this, but it sounds like our only chance to get Liddick away from these people."

"Can't say Vita would be able to reverse the spread of this by the time we could even get him to her, if it's any consolation," Cal says, eyeing Tieg. "Going on day four at least of the infection..."

"Then we need to get to the waterfall Liddick was talking about. He said they'd been descending for a few hours, and they went down about a mile toward the sea from the hub we came through at the base of Skyboard mountain," I add, then glance at Vox. She looks behind us in the direction of the trap we fell into, then anglers her head to Cal.

"Do the tunnels all connect?" she asks.

Cal nods. "And there's a waterfall about halfway to the Vishan cavern," he says, but narrows his eyes. "But you need to be sure those people will take him back to where they came from."

I look up at Liam. "We can't let them know about the Vishan down here."

"We won't. When the time comes, we'll create a diversion. I don't know how yet, but I'll—"

"Hell, if a diversion is all you need," Dell says, then looks past us at the two tall Vishan boys standing several feet in front of us. "Run back and fetch me Calliope's whizzer, and *don't* let her catch you, wise?"

Knowing smiles spread over the boys' faces, and it's all they can do to keep their composure. They nod just before bolting into the depths of the tunnel. Everything dims as they get farther and farther away until Cal pulls up another flame in his hand, restoring the light.

"What's a whizzer?" Vox asks.

"A drill that's also about the worst sound in the history of mankind, next to hearing the sound of your own bones crunching." Dell nods. "Reckon we can label that particular noise any creature we want and make them boys take their prize here and run."

"And they'll think whatever is making that sound will just take care of us...eat us or something, so they won't have to account for us," I say. "That could work."

Liam nods. "Aren't those two going to pass the waterfall? They'll be caught?"

"They'll pass on by, but they won't be caught," Cal says.

"How do you know that?"

"Because they'll be going the same way we will: over it."

CHAPTER 24
Round Two
Arco

It's dark and cold, but there's a red light in the distance. I hear voices going in and out that I recognize but can't place...except one.

"...our only chance...Liddick...away from these people..."

"Jazz?" I hear myself whisper, then see her face in the glow of the red light. I press my teeth together and narrow my eyes, but I can't focus on it long enough to make the image stay.

The words TRACKERS DISABLED suddenly flash in green at the bottom of my vision, which startles me enough that I shake off the rest of the fog clouding my brain. The images from my dream fade into the light of the room around me—metallic and bright.

"No, it's Myra. I had to shut down your tracker system because you kept looking for Jazz. You were calling out for her. It was making your blood pressure spike," Myra says, her eyes red and glassy. She presses her thumbs into my forearm. Ice pushes through my veins a second later, and I jump in surprise.

"What did you do to me? What is that?" I fire at her. She just smiles at me quietly and blinks back tears.

"Morphine and dopamine," she says, nodding to my

hand, which is every shade of red and purple wrapped in a clear pack of gel.

"What—?"

"Dr. Denison patched you up...your new nanites are working on the rest."

I barely process what she's saying in the scramble of everything in my head. I try to sit up on the metal table I'm lying on and nearly hit my head on one of the floating lights a few feet above me.

"Med bay..." I say to myself in confirmation.

"Yes. Because of your hand. You fell on it and passed out when the others..." She trails off, choking on a sob.

"Where—*crite*..." I say, remembering what happened in Phase Three now. "We need to go back for them. Where's Denison?"

"We wouldn't get very far right now," Ms. Reynolt says as she enters the room in a hurry, then starts rifling through the cabinets. The sight of her red uniform and reddish hair cause another surge of adrenaline in me because all I can see is Rheen.

"We need to get back in that building," I insist, trying to get off the table, but stop abruptly when pain shoots through my arm from an IV I've just snagged. "Get this tube out of me. We have to—"

"You need at least ten more minutes right there unless you want those fingers to come off entirely," Denison says, crossing the threshold of the med bay a few minutes after Ms. Reynolt. He pinches a holographic image of what I assume is my hand x-ray floating in front of him, enlarging the center two bones at the knuckle. I lean forward a little to get a better look and see that both bones are detached, bending up and away from the knuckles. I wince, then hesitantly look back at my hand, a little amazed that aside from the discoloration, it looks normal.

"Just don't try to move yet," Myra says, quietly again. "You severed a tendon and broke two bones in your hand, but everything is repairing since Dr. Denison rebooted your baseline nanites. Your body just needs a little help for ten more minutes. That's what this tube is doing."

"All this just from punching that little skod a few times?" I ask, still in disbelief at all the garbage I'm hooked up to and the apparently wrecked state of my hand through the gel packing.

"Eco has a titanium sinus membrane, and those lights you put out were laced on fiber optic neural wire," Denison says, flashing a pen light in my eyes. I squint and turn away. "But falling forward on that hand is what put you out."

"Let me up." I say, but he flattens his hand on my shoulder and puts me right back down.

"Not to mention when you cracked his connection relay, wave fluid contaminated your blood, which is worse than mercury poisoning. We finally got it flushed from your system."

I shake my head. "Eco is an *alpha channel* tester. Why would he be loaded with all that?"

"His physical body isn't in the cines, remember?" Denison says mechanically as he flips through pane after pane on his display. "He would only be exposed to trauma via port-cloud holographic overlay. Getting hit in the face would only *feel* like getting hit in the face while he was nice and comfy in his virtuo-cine station," he adds, ending the last sentence with a renewed bite in his voice. And now I remember why...*Tark.*

Denison clicks his pen light off and shoves it in the chest pocket of his red uniform. I let my head fall back on the now inclined table and just let it all come. *Eco betrayed us. Tark is dead because of him—because of me? I should have shot when I had the chance...when the path was clear. I should have just shot Styx, and maybe Tark never would have jumped in. I should have—*

"This isn't your fault," Ms. Reynolt says from across the room. I'm confused for a second until I realize that she's just doing what Jazz does—*reading* me, or whatever it's called. I press my teeth together like that will somehow keep her out of my head. "We'll find a way to get them all back. We'll find a way to finish this," she adds, reading a bottle and then placing it in the bag slung over her shoulder.

"How? Tark is gone, and they have everyone else. They know about us now, and there's no way we can get back in there. I wasn't fast enough. If I just would have taken the shot—"

A beeping sound cuts me off, and Myra crosses over to me quickly.

"I can take this out now; hold still," she says, disconnecting the tube from my arm. "Just get up slowly, OK?"

I swing my legs over the edge of the table and instantly feel dizzy. My hand starts throbbing in the gel pack, but it doesn't feel like there's ice in my veins anymore.

"Now what?" Avis says, now standing next to Ellis at the threshold of the med bay. Panic hits my blood and I have to take a second to keep from barking at him.

"Is autopilot really the best idea, considering what just happened in that lab? Someone is going to be coming for us, no?" I ask in a level voice.

"We're masked. At least for now" Ms. Reynolt says. "We're waiting to hear back from our State contact to see if any of Calyx's message got through."

"And if it didn't?" I ask. Ms. Reynolt just shakes her head and looks at Denison, who's studying the floor. "Nobody has an answer? There's no other plan?" I press.

"The dust is still settling." Denison's eyes flash to me. He pinches the bridge of his nose and sighs. "All right, we need to regroup. We need to figure out how outnumbered we are."

"What do you mean *how* outnumbered? There are six of us left!" I shout, then try to swallow the violence I feel everywhere in me. I push off the table to my feet, and my head spins. "We can't just leave them there. We have to find a way back in."

"I won't be able to go back to Gaia Sur now, and neither will Luz," Denison adds, nodding at Ms. Reynolt. "We won't be able to use those facilities or the transfer routes—we're on the outside now."

"We need to deliver the test subjects before anything else. We don't have the facilities needed to treat their mutations here," Ms. Reynolt says, all the blood draining from her face. She gathers several thin blanket rolls from a cabinet and a few different small machines that she adds to her bag, which doesn't look like it could hold another thing. "I counted twenty-two, and they're in pain, Briggs."

"How many at the atmospheric stage?"

"Five. Four boys and one girl."

"All right—Reese will have to take them until we hear back from our State contact. If he doesn't have room, the rest can be treated at The Seam."

"Why are you still hiding? Get The State officials involved—you have evidence of Gaia's experimentations now." I interrupt.

"It's not enough. There are too many safeguards in place protecting the people responsible. The test subjects would just...disappear if we exposed them." Denison shakes his head.

"Fine. Then we need to finish this," I say. Ms. Reynolt thins her lips in a weak smile before she leaves the med bay with the bag of materials. Myra follows her, throwing more supplies into a bag of her own on her way out the door.

"We're going to need some help getting back in there," Ellis says. "What are our options?"

"Clones? At least port-call holograms?" Avis's voice pitches with hope. "I mean, we are *inside* the port-cloud."

"Like I said, we don't have access to those resources anymore—not with being locked out of the virtuo-cine network, and not without being able to go back to Gaia Sur," Denison says. I blink, but when I open my eyes I just see the image of that ice man coming for Jax...Tark rushing over, and then...falling.

"What about the Organics—the frozen people out

there?" I grip the med-bay table, immediately seeing the image of those ice-skinned people pounding on the hull of our ship, and have to shake my head to get it to clear. "We'll lure them to the piranha wind door. If there's any humanity left in them, they'll remember those labs."

"No, the piranha wind will have been neutralized by now. That's no longer a viable entrance." Denison shakes his head, and Ellis snorts.

"Too bad. That would have been quite the distraction."

"A distraction...that's it!" I say.

"Hart, Dr. Denison just said the wind is kaput. We can't make another doorway with it."

"We won't have to. They're going to open one for us." The thoughts coming so fast, I can barely put words to them. I turn to Denison. "If there's no port-carnate transfer available in or out of Phase Three—the only way is to go through the front door—we just need to get a few important people pounding on it."

Avis sighs at me. "Who? The State is in their pocket. We just covered this."

"Well, who is *Reese?*" I ask Denison. "A doctor? Biodesigner?"

"Both. He's an ally."

"How many more like him do you know who will help us—how many with a medical practice who know the truth?"

"Two, possibly three, why?" Denison asks.

"Will they make a statement about the Organics? Would they get on the neural feeds and stir the pot if we put one on a burner?"

"It would depend—what would…" Denison trails off as realization dawns on him. "We would cause a panic." He nods, meeting my eyes again.

"We can't just lead these ice people to Admin City," Ellis protests. "They are *clearly* dangerous."

"We don't have to do that," I say. "Look, we believed everything was fine when we were escaping Gaia because Rheen and Styx knew exactly what we were going to do. They counted on it, and we played right into their hands. Right now, they know we have the test subjects, so they'll be preparing for some kind of backlash…but only from the people who know what they're doing. The public doesn't know about Phase Three. Hell, I'm sure once the public *finds out*, the buffers at The State won't risk being affiliated."

"We force them out into the open…" Avis says.

"Exactly. We cause public panic with medical statements about the genetic anomalies that seem to have drifted from the port-cloud. How often does the cargo scan clear on this ship?" I ask. "Do we have a recording of the Organics attacking the Sojourner?"

"We won't need those. We have one of the bodies," Denison explains.

"What?"

"The one we dislodged from the hull after we launched the neural pulse… The lights, remember?" Denison answers. "We can place the body at the perimeter of Admin City and go from there."

"Good, then people's imaginations will do the rest. Someone behind the scenes will be on the next private shuttle to Phase Three demanding to see for themselves what's going on there."

"That still doesn't help us get in," Avis says.

"Of course it does," I say. "We go in masked in the wake of that shuttle, then make our way back through the facility. We get our people and get out."

"And the DNA archive? What about disintegrating the facility and the port-cloud?" Ellis asks.

"We have another sample of the archive at The Seam building," Denison adds. "When we drop off the test subjects for treatment, we'll take it with us."

"All right then... Round two." A grin peels across Avis's face. I nod, feeling optimistic for the first time since we got on this stupid ship.

"Round two. For Tark..."

CHAPTER 25
Liddick
Jazz

I can hear the falls in the distance and know that we must be getting close. The air is getting thicker, warmer, and it's harder to breathe.

"You said we'd be going above the falls somehow?" Liam asks over his shoulder.

"We're already above them," Cal explains. "There's a fissure up ahead—we can get a scope out everything before making any acquaintances."

"How did we get above the falls?" I ask. "We've just been walking straight all this time?"

"If Liddick went down a chute way off toward the ocean like he was saying, those tunnels go nearly straight down to shark holding coves—the daylight landings—then it's a straight shot to the mountain. 'Bout the quickest way to get there from the surface," Cal says. "The tunnel we're in now was made by the hunting parties over time."

The Vishan stories of being tested, of being *chosen* by the tunnel sharks to prove themselves to their *Bestower* come rushing back. If Liddick were here now, he'd be hard-pressed to keep his sarcasm about it to himself.

"There," Vox says, then darts toward a horizontal crack of blue light in the earthen wall ahead of us. We move quickly and quietly to peer through it.

The pouring water of the falls obscures almost everyone below, but I see two of the guards Liddick mentioned. They're dressed in black clothes that look like our dive suits from Gaia, except these are layered with strapped-on gear over dark vests. Both guards have neural batons attached to their legs and some kind of gun slung over their backs. I scan for Liddick and finally see him as he walks into view from the path apparently on the other side of the water. It must be a corner or something. My stomach jumps and my heart pounds in my chest. Liddick slows and looks up from the ground, but not all the way.

Rip, I hear him in my head.

We're here...above you.

He doesn't look up, but crosses to another person who looks about his age. This must be the friend he mentioned from the Badlands. All of them are dressed in the same black gear, only Liddick is in red, and he doesn't have weapons like the others.

He's not armed, do you see that? He's telling the truth about being forced to do this, I think toward Vox. She doesn't reply.

"I count five with him," Dell says.

"The smaller one with the long hair is his friend— he'll help us," I whisper.

"But the others are armed," Cal adds, peering through the fissure. "They don't know about us, so you go down with Tieg. We'll make a racket with that after you pass him over." He gestures to the drill the other Vishan boys brought back with them.

"That thing better make one hell of a grind," Vox says, narrowing her eyes at the small drill that looks like it's held together with putty and joint tape.

"Trust me," Dell answers.

Liddick, we're coming down with Tieg. After we release him, Cal and Dell are going to cause a distraction. You can run with us then, I think.

All right. Be careful.

"Let's go," I say to the others. "Tieg, can you hear me? We're going to get you help, all right? Your dad is going to treat whatever is happening to you, OK? There will be three men who will take you to your dad. We're going to them now."

Tieg doesn't answer me. From the look on his face and the rigid way he's standing, I wonder if he even can anymore. His bar wedges of teeth are locked together, and his engineered, nearly-glowing blue eyes widen at me. He presses against the restraints, trying to move his arms, but he quickly gives up, exhausted. The sight of the black, vein-like lines that started on his neck have moved over his jawline now, and I shudder at the sight of them.

"He's getting worse," Liam says. "Come on, come on…"

Cal points us in the direction that leads down to the level below, and we follow the tunnel around a short spiral. After several yards, I start to feel the spray from the falls against my face. And then we're in front of them.

"Don't move!" one of the guards yells, pointing his neural ray directly at me. The other two follow, aiming next to me at Liam, but then I see the tips of their guns lift to aim at Tieg, behind us. "What the…?"

"It's Tieg Spaulding. He's sick. You have to help him!" I say as calmly as possible. "He was bitten by a tunnel shark and the venom is doing something to him. Can you help him?"

None of them talk. They just stare for a second until one of them takes a few steps forward.

"Scan..." he says into the long, metallic device strapped to his forearm. A blue light passes over Tieg, and the man's face wrinkles. "Davis, send a feed; extraction at zero bravo. Package acquired," he adds, snapping the blue light scanner closed. "Why is he tied down?" the man barks at me as one of the others comes forward, presumably to cut Tieg loose.

"I wouldn't do that," Liam says, holding up a hand. "He's a danger to himself and everyone around him—he doesn't know what he's doing anymore."

"I think we can handle him," the man says with a pinched smile. Tieg starts to rock from side to side as one of the guards cuts the restraints loose, and I suddenly have a very bad feeling.

Get away from him, Rip, Liddick thinks, evidently feeling the same thing I am. I take a few big steps toward the waterfall as Tieg starts to growl low in his throat. A few seconds later, the drill sounds. The deep reverberation bounces all around us and actually does sound like something guttural.

"Analyze!" one of the guards shouts into his arm unit, but before he can get a readout, Tieg lunges at him, gripping his shoulders and trying to bite the man's neck.

Come on! Come on! I think at Liddick, and we all run behind the falls.

***

We wait a few seconds, peering through the fissure to see if the guards manage to contain Tieg. They use a neural baton on him, then secure his arms around his waist with something. They look around for another few seconds before finally turning around, presumably to go back the way they came with Tieg in tow.

I stand with my palms against the wall, frozen in place. I'm afraid to take a breath in case they might hear it, though I know that's completely irrational. We're too close. We've come too far to risk anything else now.

Hey... Liddick says, brushing my hair away from my face. I turn to him slowly. His fingers fold behind my ear, and I can't look away from him. His eyes are intense again, looking straight into me the way he does. I always look away. It's always too much, but not this time. He moves his other hand to my cheek and presses his lips against mine. I don't know why I let him. Maybe to know that he's really there. That we came all this way and really found him because it seemed too easy just now. The adrenaline of coming to this point...from leaving Admin City, from running in disguise, from jumping into actions without knowing if we would ever land safely. It all hits my blood in this second and makes me lightheaded. I wrap my arms around Liddick and feel myself fall into him. He's warm and strong and here, and I've never been so exhausted in my life.

I let my head rest on his shoulder as he pulls me against him. He holds me so tightly I can feel his arms around my ribs starting to tremble.

Are you all right? he thinks. I nod into his shoulder

and feel the hot tears start to stream down my cheeks like the vise in my chest that has been clamping them down has finally been released. They come, and I let them, and he starts to *laugh*.

I pull back from him, stunned, and wipe my face with the palms of my hands.

"What's so funny?"

He studies my face for a second before he answers. "I knew you'd come, but I can't believe you're here."

A laugh bubbles in my stomach at this, but it turns to a sob by the time it gets to my chest, and I'm crying all over again. He kisses me one more time, but now I pull back. Back from escape and into reality. *This isn't what I want. Liddick isn't...* I abandon the thought when I hear my name like a far away whisper.

When I look out toward the direction of the sound, *Arco* is standing there—right there in the tunnel!

"Arco!" I shout and run to him. He just looks at me, surprised.

"You can see me?" he asks, but I don't understand.

"It must be the channel! You must be in mine because I can only see you. What do you see?" I ramble.

"Liddick. You and Liddick," he answers after several long seconds. His face hardens, which makes me feel like I've been hit in the chest. *How long has he been in my channel?* I wonder just as he starts to disappear.

"Arco! Wait!" I call to him, blathering about finding Tieg, about how it was his father who took Liddick, as if any of that would make him seeing me kiss Liddick any better.

"We have to get to Admin City. I have to explain..." I

stumble, turning to face everyone.

"Explain what? Are you all right?" Liam says, helping me up. It's only then that I realize I'm sitting on the ground.

"What?" I ask, looking around, then nearly jump to my feet. "I saw Arco. He was in my channel just now, like when I saw Vox in the Sand biome and again when she got to Admin City with Azeris."

Everyone looks at me blankly except Vox.

He saw you... she thinks, giving me a sympathetic look. I feel my composure crack and tears start to stream down my face again. I turn to Vox and blow out a breath. She nods at me, letting the corner of her mouth tack up just a little. *We're not done yet,* she thinks after a long beat. *It's not over.*

CHAPTER 26
Drop Point
Arco

It's hard to breathe, and the walls are hard-packed earth. People are laughing in the distance, so I start walking toward them, and then I hear her... I hear her laughing. "Jazz?" A second later, she comes into view, folded into Liddick, who's *kissing* her. I stop in my tracks and let her name fall off my lips one more time. "Jazz..." *This has to be a dream. Just wake up...* I tell myself. *Wake up and stop this.* But to my surprise, she looks around like she can hear me this time. I take a step toward her.

She smiles at him, and a wave of violence runs through me. I don't move. I can't move.

"Why?" is what I think, but I hear myself say the word, despite myself.

"Arco!" she says, then rushes from Liddick's side straight to me.

"You can you see me?" I ask, feeling like I'm free-falling. I can't get a deep enough breath before she throws her arms around my waist and presses her cheek hard into my chest. I can't feel her, so I wonder if she's really there. I move my hand to the back of her head and can't feel her thick hair between my fingers. I hold it out in front of me and watch it slip through, but still, there's just *nothing*. She pulls back from me and looks up, her face streaming with tears.

"It's the channel. You must be in mine because I can't see anything but you. What do you see?" she blurts all at once, and I'm answering before I even know what I'm saying.

"Liddick...you and *Liddick...*"

Her face falls immediately, and I can't find any more words, though I know there's plenty more to say. And then she's gone. The dark tunnel, Liddick, everything is gone except a dull, hazy light that's getting brighter, along with a low, slow-motion voice that I can't make out. After a few more seconds, both the pitch and the decibel of the voice change, and I hear my name loud and clear.

"Mr. Hart! Wheels down, son," Denison says, the intense brightness in the room making it a fight to open my eyes.

I'm on a cot that I don't remember getting onto...until I do. *Crite.* **Was** *that a dream?*

"Right. Coming," I say, pushing my hands over my face. "How long have I been asleep?"

"Maybe four hours," Denison answers.

We land the Wraith at Reese's private dock back in Admin City. The small hangar is state-of-the-art with the entire roof opening to accommodate our landing, then closing once we're clear. Before I can even get out of the pilot's seat, the scans show me that people are already outside the ship helping the testing victims off the platform.

I run down the ramp and survey the perimeter, just waiting for riot drones to surround us, but it looks like we're the only ones even remotely nearby. The cylindrical buildings we saw when we first arrived in Admin City are far off in the distance, and from the look of the rectangular glass building in the distance, this place seems like some kind of Skyboard North resort. I gawk at it for a second more until I notice the commotion Denison and Ms. Reynolt are making to help some of the test subjects into the arms of people dressed in differently-colored jumpsuits... *Are they his staff?* There must be twenty of them coming and going.

A tall man with thick, white hair like Denison's runs from the building in the distance to us. He's in a long, white tunic and pants with a slim, silver control panel strapped to his forearm.

"Let me scan her," he says to Denison, punching buttons on the arm control. Data starts populating a series of blue hologram grids that appear over the girl under Denison's arm. "I knew it..." the man says to himself, then looks up at Denison. "They used tardigrades."

Denison nods. "The other four are male—their mutations are more advanced than hers. Reese, they've progressed even since we pulled them from the labs," he adds.

"We can stabilize them once we stop the catalyst," the man Denison called *Reese* says as he grabs two of the staff wheeling a gurney by. "Take her and the other four like her first—look for the blue-tinged lips and throat." The men nod, taking the girl with them toward the building.

"Prometheus therapy?" Denison asks. Reese nods, then steps to the other testing victim being escorted out and pulls up a new set of holograms that populate with data. He sighs, then motions for more staff to take the girl he just scanned to the building behind him.

"Briggs, some of these mutations—"

"I know. We just have to do the best we can. When can you get the word out on the neural feeds?"

"Tomorrow morning at the earliest. I'll have the body moved tonight. You have the body?" Reese asks. Denison steps back, then leads Reese up the ramp of the ship. He darts a glance at me. "Who is he?"

"Arco Hart—one of the Gaia cadets I told you about. Arwyn is his sister," Denison answers.

Reese's hard expression changes to one of compassion, almost apology. He smiles a little at me.

"Thank you," he says in a careful voice as he offers me his hand. "Reese Halliday. Your sister was slotted to be one of my interns before…this. You and your friends were very brave to come for her. For all the testing victims."

"It's the only choice we had," I explain, shaking his hand. "What Gaia is doing is wrong."

"That, it is. And now, we can stop them," he adds with another nod. "Fuel up. I'll have some provisions loaded when your dock is clear. Do you need room for the Phase Two group?" he asks Denison.

"No, they're stabilized at The Seam—we transferred them first. You'll have your hands full here."

"All right. Watch the feeds—I'll send word." Reese claps Denison on the shoulder just before turning to me again. "Arco, was it?" he asks. I nod. "You get your sister to me. We'll reverse what they did to her. I promise."

I clear my throat so I don't choke when I answer him. "I will. Thank you."

He turns then, running up the dimly-lit path after the last of his staff in the distance.

***

Denison makes his way back to the dock of the Wraith as I'm loading the last of the boxes that Reese sent down.

"Reese just issued a statement about the body of the Organic his crew deposited on the edge of the district. We need to get into position before it goes to the feeds, and someone decides to pay Rheen and Styx a visit to find out what's happening in Phase Three."

He gives me a decisive nod before he leaves. I start to follow him, but sit on one of the boxes and push the heels of my hands into my eyes, like that will dislodge the sick feeling in my head after that dream. I can still see the smug look on his face... his hands on her. Anger shoots through me again, just like then, and I want to throw something through a wall. I push to my feet and make my way to the bridge.

Denison has already managed to get into the co-pilot seat by the time I get there. I slip into the seat next to him, feeling like this whole arrangement is wrong.

"Why aren't you flying this thing? You were the one teaching me back at Gaia," I ask.

"You're already a better pilot than I am, son. You just don't know it yet."

"What is that supposed to mean?" I answer with too much of an edge.

"My specialty is in systems integration...neural connections and synapses. What I was showing you during the *around the block* we took on the Leviathan back at Gaia Sur was how to mentally engage with the ship."

"Uh, you were definitely showing me how to navigate up and down, and generally, how not to kill everyone."

"Well, yes." Denison chuckles. "Those were the tools we used for integration. What I *taught* you was how to keep your panic and fear in check. Remember your hesitation to pull forward, even though the gate hadn't opened yet?"

I nod. "You just kept telling me it would."

"Right. You had to learn to trust the ship. The system log reported that you were the one who found the hole in the termite code Rheen planted, even when the others thought you were delusional. How do you think you knew it was trying to compromise the ship before anyone else saw it?"

"It was just…a feeling, I guess. I knew it was there."

"Exactly. Because you were neurally linked to the ship. That's your proclivity, son: Navigation integration, particularly now that your hemispheres are also merging."

I can't help but laugh out loud at this, and finally, I start to feel a little less like putting my fist through the front window of this ship. "So, Avis wasn't too far off when he said I was psychic?"

"Not too far off at all." Denison laughs now too. "So, get us into a nice dark corner on the northwest bank of that Phase Three doorway. You won't be able to find it on the scanners through the barrier field now that the hole we made is likely repaired. But you'll know it when you feel it." He nods to me, then grins after a second. "Take us in."

Denison looks back through the window at the port-cloud in the distance, and I scan the controls jutting from the console. The grids are all clear, the ship mask is holding... Apparently, I can pilot anything if I just let myself, but I still feel tense...like there's something out there waiting to swallow us or blow us into oblivion. Then I remember the smile on her face after he kissed her, and I know the only crosshairs I won't be able to outmaneuver are the ones I keep walking right back into. *Let her go, man. Just let her go.*

CHAPTER 27
Going Deeper
Jazz

I brush the dirt from my pants and scan the ground for my burlap wrap. Liam hands it to me and studies my face.

"What was that? You were talking to Arco... Did you see him?"

"Yes. He was in my channel like Vox was before. He was standing right there." I nod a few feet in front of us where the two tall Vishan boys are now standing.

"What did he say? What's happening up there?"

"He was gone before I could ask him. I don't know how it happened—he looked just as surprised as I did when I saw him, so I don't think he initiated the connection," I add, still feeling hollow.

"They must be somewhere close to Phase Three," Liam says, looking around the tunnel like there could possibly be an answer in the walls. "Whoa!" he suddenly shouts before quickly rushing past me. It's then that I see *Liddick* on the ground, leaning against the earthen wall.

"What happened to him?" I almost shout, moving to kneel next to him, but no one seems to have an answer. A man in the same dark military fatigues as the Special Blacks kneels down next to him too, already shaking his head at me like I'm about to accuse him of something.

"He was standing right there when you went down, and then he just dropped," he says, confused. "This happened once before, but he popped right back up."

"Well, let's pop him up again," Dell adds, crossing to poke Liddick in the ribs with his boot. "Yo...wakey time, princess."

"That's not helping." I glare at him, and the other man in dark fatigues starts to flick water from a canteen in Liddick's face.

"Dell?" Liddick whispers, startling all of us. Dell raises his eyebrows at me and smirks.

"What happened? Are you sick?" I ask, returning my attention to Liddick as a panic rises in my chest.

"No...Azeris...found us." He stands, then immediately wobbles and finds the wall to steady himself. "Whoa. Apparently, channel hops never get easier."

"You saw Azeris? In your channel like before?" the man with him asks.

"Who's he?" Liam asks.

"This is Finn. He's an old friend from the Badlands. He'll help us." Liddick scrubs his hands over his face like he's trying to wake up, then turns to Finn. "It was all of a sudden. No buzz like before... This time the connection came out of nowhere."

"That's how it was for me too just now with Arco," I say, and Liddick's attention darts back to me.

"You saw *Hart* in your channel?"

"He saw...us. It was only for a minute, and then he was gone again."

Liddick raises his eyebrows and blows out a breath.

"All right…where was he?"

"I couldn't tell. The last we saw them they were going to take down the port-cloud manually."

"Take down the port-cloud now? That will cause global chaos. That's if they can even get near it," Finn says, his dark eyes widening so much he almost looks like he's going to lunge at me.

"No, it's the only way to stop the genetic testing," Liddick says. "Azeris has been trying to make contact with The Seam, but they're offline."

"You unplugged them when you reset the server to the Grid. Oh! Did you see my dragon!?" Vox asks, popping to attention, which causes dirt to crumble from the ceiling and hit her cheeks. She brushes it away, and Liddick rolls his eyes.

"I didn't mean for any of this to happen. I *thought* it was all Gaia's propaganda that I was shutting down," he adds, turning to me. "It wasn't until I saw you really there in front of me in the cine that I… Anyway, but even then, I wasn't sure."

"It's all right. I know. And we'll make sure everyone else knows. We just need to find out how to get reconnected. How did Arco access my channel? He's not a Reader."

"Neither is Azeris," Liam says. "It doesn't depend on that, I don't think. I mean, it helps, but it's about finding the right frequency. Arco must be close to Phase Three— to the transmission equipment housed there."

"But how would that reach us? We're standing at least a half-mile underground." Finn pulls the dark hair off his neck and ties it into a ponytail.

"It's the NET," Vox adds, raising her chin to Cal. "Proximity to that thing... Didn't somebody say it enhances the channel signal or whatever?"

"Like an antenna—that has to be it," I say.

"Can I see that?" Liam turns to Cal and extends a hand. Cal pulls the slim, silver, Y-shaped device from the leather bag slung over his shoulder and hands it to him. "Where did you get this?"

"Like I told Jack, our people have always had it—it's from the ancestors."

Liam starts nodding slowly, then switches to shaking his head. "You called it the *NET*? Well, that makes sense, a *Neural Enhancement Tuner*. But this one must be a few hundred years old."

"That's about the age of the Origin Wall, according to the Vishan records," Cal adds. "The NET is one of the artifacts left to us by the original families."

"The ones who escaped... I know this story." Liam closes his eyes in a long blink, and Cal's face tightens. He does *not* want to revisit the subject.

"Didn't you say that unit had been modified?" Liddick asks Cal, evidently feeling the same tension from him that I do. Cal darts a glance at him, then nods after a second of consideration.

"Don't ask me how. I just know if you have this with you, anyone on the Lookout Pier will be able to find you."

"What is the Lookout Pier?" Liam asks.

"It'll be easier to show you. We need to get back to the Vishan right now." Liddick rubs the back of his head.

"We aren't even equipped to go that deep." Liam

almost laughs at the ridiculous suggestion, and I completely agree with him.

"We need to get back to Admin City with the others. Isn't that what Azeris contacted you about?" I ask. Liddick shakes his head.

"Just the opposite. Not only did that thing help bolster our signal so he could find us, it also must have amplified the signal for Spaulding's men. When he broke into my channel, he overheard them reporting that they had Tieg now, but not Finn and me anymore." He nods toward the man who had been kneeling next to him. "Spaulding is sending a team to sweep Tinkerer Square in the Badlands because he thinks we'll go straight to Azeris—he and Zoe need to get out of there now before they find them. Spaulding is also sending teams to sweep Phase Two *and* the Vishan tunnels. But if we can get there before them, we can save them."

"Those skods are coming through the tunnels? *Now?*" Cal nearly yells. "We need to get everyone out."

"How? We can't take anyone up through the shark routes…they'll be trapped at the surface. No way we can hide them in the Rush either," Dell adds, his eyes darting to everyone in search of an answer no one has.

"No, listen! Azeris found a tunnel. It's underneath the Lookout Pier," Liddick explains.

"That pier is solid *rock*," Cal protests.

"Wait…" I think, turning to Liddick. "The first time we were all up there, we felt a vibration and heard a loud hum, do you remember? I thought for sure I saw something in the wall move. Maybe it was a door, or a hatch of some kind. Something hidden?" I look to Cal.

"Has Jove or anyone in the Council ever mentioned anything about a secret door up there?"

Cal shakes his head. "There's no door or secret anything up there, as far as I know. Just the platform where you're supposed to stand with the NET if you're tryin' to scout after somebody in the Rush."

"Well, there must be an access point if Azeris saw the tunnel in his scans," Finn says.

"It runs under the Rush and connects to Phase Two. The connection point is right below a port-carnate hub there. We could transport everyone to the Admin City bridge...if it's still there," Liddick says, then turns to Liam. "Could you reverse their DNA encryptions?"

"Theoretically, yes, but that would depend on if we could access the databases. Jack froze everything with a chaser code when we escaped."

"All right. We'll just have to figure it out when we get there. Cal, can you use the NET to warn Jove that Spaulding's men are coming?"

"No...it doesn't work like that. It just tells them where we are."

"It *has* to work like that," Vox says. "How else did I connect with Jazz when I was out there in that rainforest, or on the dune?"

Cal stares at her for a long second before shaking his head. "I don't know. The Council was still trying to sort that when we all lit out after you."

"Well, let me see it. Maybe you just shake it or something?" Vox reaches for the NET, but Cal grabs it from Liam before she can take it. He shoves it back into his satchel, muttering something in Vishan. Vox snorts, but Cal just rolls his eyes at her.

"If those toadies are coming to Vishan, we need to get there before they do," he adds, motioning for everyone to follow him deeper into the tunnel. "You all coming, or are we waiting for one of the antlions to circle back?"

CHAPTER 28
The Between
Arco

We sit masked and on standby for several more hours before the feeds finally start reporting the body of the dead Organic found drifting just off the perimeter of Admin City. I close my eyes to pull the feed images out of my peripheral vision and enable the sound. A reporter with pink, jagged layered hair is standing on the edge of the glowing light field. She gestures to the hazy port-cloud in the distance. Denison's friend Reese is standing with her in the same white tunic he wore to help us unload the testing subjects we pulled from Phase Three. I still can't hear the reporter talking, even though I've closed my eyes, so I blink a few times to refresh the queue. Finally, it kicks in.

"—ectra Brown reporting from the Orion Deck, where the body of what appears to be a frozen *man* was found adrift just beyond the ion perimeter field. Dr. Halliday, could you please give us your professional medical opinion about...well, what happened to this man since it's impossible for anyone to just *fall* through the ion field?"

"Like you, Electra, I can't imagine how this man could have accidentally found his way off the platform to tumble through space, but what is more concerning to me are the physical...well, *alterations* he seems to exhibit," Reese says, raising his white eyebrows.

"I'm sorry, did you say *alterations?*"

"Yes, I'm afraid he has mutations that appear specifically designed to help him withstand the freezing temperatures of space. To cope with the lack of oxygen, for example, the liquid in his body is not, in fact, liquid, but a complex gelatinous material."

The reporter's face blanches. "Could this be an effect of the port-cloud, Dr. Halliday? Radiation perhaps?"

"It's hard to say, Electra, but from what I have been able to see, I can't imagine how this could be natural. It seems the result of outside intervention."

"Do you mean...aliens?"

"I can only report *what* I've seen, Electra. It will be up to you and your fine team to find out *who* did this."

"Thank you, Dr. Halliday. Devereux, back to you with in-house guests, Doctors Cora Fields and Aldos Landers, whom I understand have also examined the body."

The feed scatters and regroups, this time in a white studio with the guests, but the whole thing wipes when I nearly fall out of my chair at the sound of a high-pitched alarm.

"PERIMETER ALERT," the ship's calm, casual voice says after the loud bell.

"Show time, Mr. Hart!" Denison runs up the stairs at the back of the bridge like something is chasing him.

"How? The feed is still playing!" I stumble, scrambling to boot the Wraith's systems and make sure we are aligned with the Phase Three docking bay doors.

"Headline teaser feeds started streaming an hour ago.

Are we in position?"

"Uh...yeah. Yeah, now we are," I say, adjusting the last of my scopes. "Spider waiting for the fly and all that."

"Good. When that fly comes along, we'll have about five seconds to get into its wake before Phase Three's perimeter scan does all the math, understand? We need to be in that shadow before it figures out just how big the other ship is."

"I'll line us up—don't worry."

"PROXIMITY ALERT," the woman's ship voice says again, but my heart is still trying to hammer through my ribs.

"I don't see anything—what's coming?" I say, scanning the scopes for a ship.

"Wait for it..." Denison says. "It's coming."

A full minute passes, but it feels like twenty before a ship finally appears on our center scope.

"There!"

"TARGET IN RANGE," the ship's voice says.

"Yeah, yeah..." I lean forward a little in my seat and feel the engines fire underneath us.

"Easy, easy," Denison says. "Feel it. You'll have to feel this one through... Get into the wake as soon as the ship passes into the Between—don't rely on the Wraith to tell you where that ship is. Run the numbers, son; we only have five seconds to play with."

"Got it," I answer. But crite, why did he have to say *that?* The blood pounding in my ears gets louder as numbers and geometrical symbols start flooding my peripheral vision. They appear this time like those invisible, floating specs that you can never really look directly at, so I don't even try. I lean forward, and we pick up a little speed. Too much speed.

"Hot... We're coming in too hot!" Denison says in the distance along with a dull, echoing bell alarm. His voice sounds muffled, and the pounding in my ears starts slowing down. Everything slows down as pieces of the geometrical symbols break apart, then fall into a kind of landing strip in my head. I look directly at the scopes, but what I see isn't there...I'm generating it. "Mr. Hart! Pull back!"

The last of the peripheral graphics align, and finally, I lean back. The bell sound gets louder, but then eventually stops.

"ALIGNMENT LOCKED," the calm ship's voice says, and I blow out the breath that has been burning my lungs.

"Crite..." Denison exhales and leans forward into his hands.

"Sorry," I say, a little curious how close we actually came to the back end of the other ship if Denison is all but in the fetal position over there. "It took a while to line up."

He nods into his hands, then finally sits back in his co-pilot seat and shoots me a glance.

"Evidently, it did," he finally says, then blows out a big breath on the edge of a few bubbles of laughter.

"What the actual hell up there!?" Avis shouts over the comms. Denison and I both almost choke on laughter this time. I hit the relay button to reply but don't get a chance before he hears me. "Oh, it's funny? You think it's funny to break the damn sound barrier with no warning at *all?* I smashed my face with my own hand, Hart!" Avis shouts again, and my eyes start to burn from laughter. Denison's face is bright red when I look over at him, which makes him start laughing all over again. "Yeah! It's funny! Really funny, Hart! Mollusk!" he fires again all in the same breath, then starts all over in Chinese, and any shot I had at regaining my composure is utterly, irrevocably lost.

***

We pass through the docking gate undetected and settle behind the small personal carrier vessel that doesn't look much bigger than a Sojourner. The mask on the ship seems to be working, because I don't see an army of riot drones storming our perimeter.

"What kind of mask is this?" I ask marveling at how such a huge ship can be invisible in plain sight.

"Government grade," is all Denison says before a set of guards in red jumpsuits comes through a door in the hangar about two flights up. They skitter over to the little craft in front of us just in time for the side panel door to open. Four men in long white tunics and pants walk out with purpose toward the stairs along the hangar wall. The guards turn on their heels and move quickly after them.

"Is that Cole Daniels?" I ask, noticing my mouth starting to dry out because it's hanging open. I snap it shut.

"The Weasel of State himself," Denison says. "Looks like we cut ourselves a big, juicy fly, Mr. Hart."

I shake off my astonishment and get to my feet. "OK,

we need to move. We need to find my sister and the others. Where's the archive DNA?"

"Luz has it below. We can grab it on the way out. Are you ready for this?" Denison asks with a decisive nod.

"Ready as I'm going to get for infiltrating an illegal lab full of people who want to kill me."

"Excellent. Let's go."

Denison and I make our way to the airlock of the Wraith and stop when we hear Ellis come over the comms. "Their security feed will loop out in about ten seconds. You will have sixty more to get from here to that door up there. On my mark..." he says, and after a few beats more, "Three...two...go!"

The airlock opens in a *whoosh,* and Denison and I both sprint toward the stairs. We take them three at a time, but the door is locked once we reach it.

Denison swears and hits the comm system on his arm. "We need access—can you locate the panel?"

"Not from here. Wait. I'll try to pull up the source code," Avis says.

"We don't have time for that," I say, scanning the open hangar below us. "You're going to have to hit that puddle jumper with some juice and then get the hell out of here before they close the outer door."

"That will bust the ion seal—you'll suffocate!" Ellis says over the comms.

I grit my teeth. "Not if you move fast. It'll seal behind you. Go!"

"But we won't be able to get back in!"

"Damn it! Figure that out later! Hit that ship now and run!"

A few seconds later, a small pulse of light seems to come out of nowhere, then explodes the entire back end of the little jet-like ship just below us. Ripples of electricity run over the Wraith like lightning, and I start to see its outline.

"Get out of here!" Denison says into the comm system on his forearm. The popping sound of the Wraith pushing back through the ion field is almost deafening, but everything drops to the background with the sudden blast of freezing air, which feels like a cold hand reaching straight down my throat to crush my lungs. Denison grabs a fistful of my jumpsuit collar and pulls me against the wall just before the door flies open and several more guards in red uniforms pour down the stairs behind us.

As quickly as it came, the burning cold is gone, and I can breathe again as I watch the last of the rippling lightning disappear into the haze beyond the hangar opening. Before the door closes, Denison and I rush through...straight into another group of guards in red uniforms.

CHAPTER 29
Outfitting
Jazz

We get about another fifty feet before I remember we can't go any deeper than we are without being in range of a hub like Gaia Sur, or at least a remote hub like the dive suits we had. The baseline nanites they gave us at Gaia Sur won't work without it.

"Wait. How are we going to go any deeper without a hub?" I ask, turning to Liam. "Our nanites are offline?"

"How deep are these Vishan tunnels?" he asks.

"Five or six miles," Cal answers. "If we go by way of the supply tunnels, it's almost a straight shot—that's the trajectory we're on now."

Liam shakes his head. "Yeah, we can't make that depth. Not without a suit of some kind."

"I don't have the equipment for a treatment, either," Cal adds, and to everyone's surprise, one of Vishan boys suddenly elbows the other in the arm. They both start yelling back and forth in their language.

"Criminy, stop! You sound like chickens scalding on a tin roof!" Dell interrupts after a few more seconds of this.

"You knew we'd need *what?*" Cal presses them when they finally stop talking, and they both start to answer at the same time. "Dev! You speak…"

The Vishan boy who started the fight reaches into his

satchel and pulls out Vita's treatment kit...the reeds, the stones, even the special pain root and the little bowl. Everyone's eyes go wide. "When the Seaboarders came to us the first time, Veece flared five kinds of red about them getting treatments, but you did it anyway," he says to Cal. "They made it through the Rush because of you. Vita even sat Veece down about it sayin' how sometimes you just have to make the call like that. So, when we grabbed the whizzer, we figured she wouldn't mind us borrowing this in case things didn't mix out right, and we had to bring those new Seaboarders back to the cavern." He nods first to Finn, then to Liam.

Dell's mouth hangs open until he tucks his top lip into the bottom one and nods like a proud father at the boy, who must be just barely thirteen judging from the fairly fresh, pink arrow scarring on his face and throat.

"Is *that* what you thought?" Cal answers, tight lipped. The boys both take a step back from him as he holds his hand out for the satchel. The boy hesitantly takes it off his shoulder and extends it. Cal snatches the bag and takes another look inside, then looks up at the boys, whose normally-tanned faces, like all the Vishan, are white with fear. After another second, Cal laughs and shoves the bigger boy's shoulder. Blood rushes back into both of their faces as they let out a breath.

"Uh, I hate to break it to everyone," I say. "But didn't you say Spaulding's men are making their way south anytime now? We don't have twenty-four hours to wait for these treatments to kick in again."

"They won't take that long," Liddick says almost immediately. "At least...not for you. Cal retreated us when we went back into the Rush to make our way up through the tunnels… The fire didn't work right away, but it didn't take all night the second time, and I didn't feel like I fell off a cliff afterward."

"Jack told me about these treatments," Liam says. "You heat blood over some hematite and boron, then inject it? Somehow it's supposed to bond? That's ridiculous."

"Who cares how it works as long as it does? But even still, we don't have the time for it to kick in for us," I press, and Finn startles with an idea.

"Wait! These suits are outfitted for going deep." He points at the chest of the black fatigues he's wearing.

"*Those?*" Vox narrows her eyes. "It's just a coverall."

"No…these." Finn pulls down the collar of the heavier top shirt to reveal a slim red base layer that looks a lot like the blue ones we had at Gaia Sur. He nods to Liam. "Take this suit. It should fit you. Spaulding's men will report back that they saw you. You'll just endanger everyone topside if you turn back, so I'll go. I'll say you knocked me out, and when I woke up you were gone. They don't know I helped you," Finn says to Liddick, taking off the top layer of his fatigues. "I'll get Azeris into Grisham's hab and we'll find you again," he adds, unfastening his belt.

I hold up a hand. "Whoa, wait. Maybe you can—"

"Perfect. Strip!" Vox declares, cutting me off. She turns to Cal and rolls up her white sleeve. "I'll do the honors this time."

Cal gives her a curt head shake. "No, we don't know if it will work since your line has evolved topside. I'll do it."

Vox rolls her eyes. "If I can survive in your caverns, not to mention in the Rush without a treatment, my blood has *obviously* evolved to be just as unsquishable as yours," she protests. Cal closes his eyes in a long blink and mutters something in Vishan. She shrugs at him and puffs air in his general direction. "*Pffft.* Fine, if you want to put unnecessary holes in yourself," she says, rolling up her sleeve as if she's now racing Cal, who has also started rolling his.

"What's happening?" I ask, looking from one of them to the other.

"I'm topping it off just in case." He narrows his eyes at Vox, though I see him forcing back a smile once she looks away.

"Ha! I'm first," she says, offering her map-tattooed arm to Cal. He sighs and stops rolling his sleeve as she gives him a pressed smile, then glances at me. "Hurry up, sand dollar. We have to move."

***

When I open my eyes, I can't see anything except for fire crawling about three feet over my face until it dissipates and new flames replace it. I gasp, inhaling a mouth full of dust that makes me choke, and when I try to reach for something solid, I only grasp scratchy fabric on either side of me. It's then that I realize I'm in some kind of hammock...and I'm moving.

"What—?"

"Stop, stop!" Liddick says, then drops to one knee to take off a backpack, but my legs drop as I realize the backpack is connected to the hammock. The heels of my boots hit the ground, and I leap off the fabric to whirl around in front of Liam, who was apparently supporting my other end. He pulls his arms through the makeshift straps of the burlap wrap and chucks it to the ground.

"You're a lot heavier than you look." He chuckles.

"How do you feel?" Liddick asks. "Stiff? Sore?"

"Not really...not like the first time by the stream," I answer, the memory of him helping me that night flooding back. I shake my head and refocus on the burlap knotted together on the ground. "What did you do?" I ask. "And how long were you carrying me in that thing?"

"You were only out a few hours after the treatment— we tied your wrap together with Liam's and Vox's to make the sling," Liddick explains, beads of sweat collecting, then streaming down his temples. I immediately feel guilty.

"Oh...sorry. I didn't want you to have to carry me."

"Stop. It was the only way. We're about a mile out yet. Can you walk?"

"Yeah, of course," I answer, though I'm still a little dizzy. There's no way I'm getting back in that sling for them to carry me again, though. I hold out my palm and try to concentrate on making my palm itch to bring back the Vishan fire, but nothing happens.

"That will take a while..."

"Took an antlion to light it for him this last time." Dell chuckles as we all start walking again.

"What?!" I gasp at Liddick.

"Uh, yeah we had a run-in... Everything was fine."

"After he yelled at it," Dell adds, laughing openly now. "Just went all Tarzan!"

I stare at Liddick, whose lips quirk. "It wasn't a Tarzan yell, thank you very much."

"Right, right. More like the ape's." Dell laughs so hard this time, he makes himself cough, and Cal narrows his eyes in a glare at them both.

"What's a Tarzan?" Cal asks. Everyone except he and the two Vishan boys laugh now. "What? Why is that funny?"

"Nothing, nothing," Liddick says, slapping Cal on the back and swallowing the rest of his laughter. "I'll explain it later."

Cal gives him a side eye and scans everyone still choking on bubbles of laughter, but his expression changes when he abruptly stops.

"Vox—hey…" he crosses quickly to her. Her face is paler than normal, and she's swaying with each step.

"I'm good!" she slurs.

"What's wrong with her?" I cross to her on the other side of Cal, who moves under her arm.

"You started to wake up a few minutes after we treated you, so we had to supplement with some of Vox's blood," he says. "It takes a toll."

"You took out maybe two ounces," Liam balks.

"It takes time to replace. Two ounces of our blood is like several pints of yours."

"Well, *that* explains a lot!" Vox slurs again, then starts laughing. Cal talks quietly to her in Vishan, saying something that just makes her laugh-snort. He rolls his eyes.

"My sister will give her Avo juice and she'll be fine—we're almost there."

"Is that the stuff that smells like dead fish?" Vox snorts again. "Because, thanks, no."

I feel more guilt well up in my chest seeing her like this, and between that and being closed up again in these narrow tunnels, everything starts to feel claustrophobic.

Take a breath, Rip, Liddick thinks, reading me. *She's fine. You heard Cal. There's nothing to feel guilty about.*

His confirmation should make me feel better, but it doesn't, and as soon as I realize this, Vox has already read me too and is slurring again.

"Just call him back, sand dollar."

I turn to her, and she widens her yellow cat eyes at me like I've missed something obvious. "What?"

"Tell him you were just happy to be right when he kissed you. Easy!"

I'm frozen, unsure of what to say to her after that, mainly because I don't know how to tell her she's wrong. I don't know if she *is* wrong, and with every second of trying to think of something, I realize more and more that she's exactly *right*. Kissing Liddick wasn't about him. It was about me. About knowing I was right that he didn't betray us like everyone thought he did. *It was...victory?*

"Victory!!" Vox says *much* too loudly.

"Stow it!" I hiss at her, feeling my face flush as Dell and Liddick catch up to us.

"Right about what?" Liddick asks.

"Nothing—how close are we to the cavern now?"

Liam looks at me and sighs. "Not close enough."

CHAPTER 30
Trackers
Arco

I count four guards who rush us as we come through the door. For a second I struggle with them, but then realize they're not trying to drag us off—they're just trying to push us out of the way. Denison and I look at each other, astonished—*they must think we're guards*. We quickly start walking away from the door panel after it closes behind them.

"It's the red uniforms," Denison says.

"I forgot we were dressed like them." I say, looking down at my clothes. I take a deep breath and let it out slowly, trying to keep my pace steady. "Where are we going? We need to get everyone out before we plant that archive."

"The first thing we need to do is get out of sight." Denison steers us around a series of corners until we come upon a small hallway. He scans the ceiling and then nods at me. I shake my head at him, confused.

"What are you looking for?"

"Surveillance. I don't see any here, but we still shouldn't stay long. We have to keep moving so they don't discover we got off that ship."

Denison opens his hand and pushes the thin line of a faded incision in the base of his palm. A second later, a conical blue field appears with a grid inside. After another second, several blinking red dots appear, then take on the shape of everyone's faces: my sister's, Jax's, Jack's, Lyden's.

"When did you get our tracker uplink? You weren't in The Seam building when we had those put in."

"I've had this awhile. Calyx just uploaded your locator code to my feed. Look!" He watches the final dot take on the shape of a face in the base of the cone. *"Eco..."*

"Why isn't he with everyone else? Where is that?"

"He's in the oxygen trials wing. That's the first stage of treatments for the Organics we saw," Denison says, and I can't understand how he has managed to be affiliated with a place like this all these years, just biding his time. I press my teeth together to keep my questions to myself. We don't have time for an ethics discussion right now.

"So then where are the others? What is this part?" I ask, pointing to the center of the cone where everyone's avatars are.

"Recovery rooms..." Denison meets my eyes in the same second the dread of what this means hits us.

"No way. There hasn't been enough time to put them through any procedures. It hasn't even been twenty-four hours," I say as soon as the idea registers. Denison thins his lips and nods in agreement, but that doesn't make me feel any better. I push down the nerves because we don't have time for *them* either. "We need more weapons. The guards who rushed through the door back there had neural rays."

The console on Denison's arm blinks. "The Wraith is

clear—they're going back to The Seam to regroup."

"Then we won't have a ride back anytime soon. We need to find a backup in case they can't get through the barrier again," I say. "Are there ships here?" I ask, my mind going a mile a minute and in three different directions.

"Without port-carnate tech on site, there would have to be," Denison answers. "Calyx would know. We need to move."

Denison slips around the corner first, waving at me to follow him. We walk casually through the corridor without making eye contact with anyone else in red until a few balding men in long, white lab coats approach. It's harder not to focus on them, considering they're no doubt the ones actually executing the genetic experiments up here. I catch the eyes of one of the doctors and look away immediately, but it's too late. His face contorts in confusion at first, but then his eyes widen.

"That's two of them—" he starts to say to the other doctor next to him. Before they can call attention to us, Denison and I pull them back around the corner. It doesn't take much to subdue them since they're both thin and, well, not young. To my surprise, Denison grabs the throat of the doctor closest to him and *squeezes* until the man gasps for air.

"Briggs," the doctor wheezes. "You…traitor."

"*I'm* the traitor? You swore an oath to protect these kids, not exploit them, you selfish parasite!" Denison snarls, reaching into the man's coat and yanking off some kind of badge with a little black stick attached to it. He jabs the stick under the man's chin while the smaller doctor in front of me tries to make a run for it. I grab his lapel and slam him against the wall, pushing my fist into his throat.

"You stay right there!" I say through my teeth, then rifle through his coat for the lanyard he must be wearing too. I jerk it from his neck and find the little black stick attached, which seems to be a miniature neural baton. I shove it into his neck.

"Take off the coats. Slowly," Denison says to the men. They carefully slide their arms out of the white lab jackets and hold them out to us.

"What's that door?" I ask, angling my head down the corridor to our left.

"Storage," the doctor in front of me croaks.

Denison takes a look, then shoves the doctor with him toward it while sticking the miniature neural baton into his ribs.

"Let's go," I add to the one with me, catching up to Denison just as he opens the door with the doctor's badge.

Inside are several console stations covered in plastic dust covers. Far in the corner is a clear cube like the one my sister and Lyden were in back at Phase Two.

"Open that up," Denison says, jabbing the miniature neural baton into the doctor's ribs. "If you don't mind, that is, *Dr.* Howard."

"You're going to pay for this, Briggs," the man says. Denison just jabs him in the ribs again, and the man finally punches a code into a holographic keypad that appears when he covers his hand over the door. Denison jerks his chin toward the cube.

"Both of you get in."

Once the doctors are inside, the door seals, and Denison turns to one of the consoles behind us. He pulls the clear, plastic dust cover off and presses the badge he took from the doctor flat against the desk, then begins typing something on another holographic keypad that appears.

"What are you do—?" I start to ask but am cut off by a loud, pulsing alarm. The doctors start laughing in the cube, but Denison just keeps typing.

"We got it, we got it," he shouts, now punching something into the miniature console unit on his arm. "All right, this whole place is going on lock down, so we need to move."

"What? What did we get?" I ask, looking toward the door and wondering why we're not bolting toward it.

"The arrow map for this place. We need to get the archive to the core room—flatten your palm here," Denison says, pressing his hand against the console's floating screen display. I do the same when he moves his hand and feel a stream of cold shoot up my arm until it stops with a tickle in my ear.

"*Ugh*, what the hell?"

"Relax. It's just a navigation app. The same thing was embedded in your nanite package at Gaia Sur. You heard the arrow voices there, right?"

"Yeah, but it didn't feel like *this*."

"This schematic has Howard's security clearances— bigger file. Let's get to the core room."

"Wait, no," I protest. "We need to get to the recovery

room first to get everyone out, then we need to find a ship. Calyx should know about the ships, right? Once the archive hits the core, this place is going to fry."

Denison presses his lips into a flat line and shakes his head at me. "There's no time now—we'll have to split up. Keep your head down and get to the recovery room. I can give you thirty minutes. Go!"

"You're not *coming!?*"

"Listen to me." Denison grips my shoulder and gives me a steely look. His forehead wrinkles as he pushes the badge around my neck into my chest. "Get everyone out of here—get clear."

"We're not leaving you here!"

"I'll find the hangar when the archive is uploaded. If you're not there, I'll find another ship. Now go!" he says, shoving me. "Go, before those clone guards figure out you're coming!"

I stumble back a few steps, then rush to the door. Red lights are flashing everywhere, and there are three times as many guards running around in the same red uniform as mine. I'm not going to get very far with this stupid miniature shock stick, though, so I scan for the closest clone guard carrying a neural ray. I walk toward him facing the ground, then call to him.

"They're in here!" I shout, waving him to me. As soon as he's within reach, I grab his arm and press the miniature black baton behind his ear. He drops, jerking a few more times until he stops moving. *Did I just kill him? Is it even killing if it's a clone?* I wonder for a second, then watch his face and neck start to cave in before it actually begins disappearing in bigger and bigger patches. A chill runs straight up my back and into my teeth.

I grab the neural ray from him and sling it over my shoulder, snag the gear belt from around his waist, and take off into the mix of red uniforms running everywhere.

CHAPTER 31
You Can Never Go Back
Jazz

We walk in silence for the next several minutes, but it feels like hours before Liddick startles me with a chuckle.

"What?" I ask, but then immediately regret it because my stomach starts to twist. Whatever he's laughing at isn't funny.

"You finally did it," he says without looking at me.

"Did what?"

"Figured out how to block your thoughts from me. I've been trying to read you since we left, but all I get is this general...anxiety. Well, and violence toward Vox." He chuckles again. "But I couldn't hear your words."

"I don't know how I did it, if that makes you feel any better," I say, and this time he looks at me from under a dark eyebrow.

I don't know what to say to him. I don't know how I've blocked my thoughts, unless it was just the desperate feeling for him not to know anything about my little epiphany back there. About my personal confession. But it would hurt him to know that kiss didn't mean what I know he thought—what I let him think—and that's all my fault.

"What's going on with you, Rip?" he asks, slowing his pace.

"Nothing. I mean, I just...I don't want to hurt you." The twisting in my stomach gets worse, but I'm not sure if these are his feelings or mine. Or both of ours.

"Looks like maybe I didn't completely misread you after all," he says after a long pause. "I understood what Vox meant...the part about victory. That was easy to feel in you."

"Don't oversimplify this," I say before he can get another breath. "Of course I was happy we found you. How could I not be?"

"No, I get it. But there was more. And that's what I can't find in you now. That's what you're closing off from me."

"This is stupid," I fire back. "Why does it even matter what else I felt? You're with us now. We can catch up with the others, and you can explain everything."

Liddick all but stops walking now and stares straight through me in that way that is too intense. I want to keep walking, but I can't.

"They don't agree with you, do they?" he asks. "They think I sabotaged them," he says.

"It doesn't matter."

"Spaulding said they would. And when I saw you here...I knew you had to make a choice, Rip. I thought you chose me."

Liddick searches my face for the answer he wants, but I can't give it to him.

"We can't do this here, Liddick. It's too complicated."

"Why? What's complicated about you choosing to come after me, even when the rest of them wrote me off? I can just hear Hart now." He chuffs another short laugh, and something about the whole way he's pushing me makes my palms start to itch. I ball my hands into fists before the fire comes, like I know it will, if I don't calm down. Liddick darts a glance up and down my arms, then raises his dark eyebrows at me. "Your fire is back already?" He nods to himself and lets the corner of his mouth tack to the side. "I must have really clipped you off."

The itch subsides slowly as I feel a lightness start in my chest. I take a deep breath to reset myself.

"Tell me what happened exactly in that last cine, Liddick. Why did you throw the server reset switch? And before that, why did you rewrite the narrative to support Gaia and incriminate Arco and me?"

He sighs and starts to pick up his pace again. "That's not what I meant to do," he says in a low, tight voice. "I was helping someone who was supposed to find Dez after she ran away from us. A quid-pro-quo kind of thing. But once I got in there, it seemed like the cine was *already* propaganda. I thought they made the characters who were like you and Hart from my head somehow," he says, then turns to me. "Rip, I had no idea you were already in the Grid."

My stomach starts to twist again, but this time with the weight of his guilt. He's telling the truth, and I don't know why that's even something I needed to confirm.

"The Seam had been working on this subliminal messaging system to organically get the public to start questioning Gaia and their affiliates," I explain, not sure if he even understood why we were in the Grid in the first place. "We accidentally tripped it before they were ready, and only part of the message was getting out. A *pro-Gaia* message. We were going in to patch the glyphs with the rest of the message when everything got shut down."

He shakes his head and blows out a breath. "I'm so sorry, Rip. I never meant to—"

"It's OK," I interrupt him this time because the twist in my stomach starts to reach into my chest. "Once we get back to Admin City, you can explain to everyone that you were forced into the virtuo-cines, and things can go back to the way they were."

"Rip…" He starts to laugh tentatively. "If there's anything we've learned since we left the dock at Seaboard North, it's that we can never go back to the way things were."

The red firelight ahead of us weakens to a dim glow, and I realize how slowly we've been walking.

"We need to catch up to them," I say.

"Something is catching up to us…" Liddick adds when a red glow spills over the walls in front of us. We both turn around and see…*Veece?*

He's wearing the same style woven shirt and tactical pants as the hunting parties the Vishan send out. Kesh and Jesse round the corner just behind him, and now I know he's not just out for a stroll.

"Are you both all right? Where are Cal and Dell?" Veece asks. His eyebrows push together, wrinkling the diamond and chevron tribal scars on his forehead.

"We're fine—they're just ahead. How did you find us?" Liddick asks.

"Took about three minutes for a rabble to start about

who made Calliope's drill go missing. Someone heard the scouts talking about your situation on their way back to you with the drill and told the Council. They sent me after you. We have two more teams behind us."

"No, no, no...they need to go back to the Vishan tunnels to protect everyone. Those men are coming *there*," I say. "We're on our way back to you right now!"

"Evacuate? Who's coming?"

"The same men who took me after we made our way out of Phase Two—er, your Motherland."

"Their Motherland? You were *there*? Dell said that place doesn't exist." Jesse scowls.

Liddick and I exchange glances and he blows out a breath.

"OK, this is a really long story, but in short, Dell was right. About everything." Veece's nearly translucent blue eyes widen. "I know, I know," Liddick continues. "But right now your people are in a lot of danger. We know a way to get them out before the topsiders find them, and we have to hurry."

Veece takes another second, then turns to Kesh.

"Circle back to the other parties and take them to the cavern. Tell my father I said the prophecy is coming true. He'll understand what that means. We'll follow you."

Kesh pushes the bandana around her neck onto her forehead and tucks the tail into a band, then nods to Veece.

Jesse cracks his neck. "Does the prophecy involve scrappin' with folks? Been a while since I landed a good punch."

"Not if we can help it," Veece answers seriously.

"Please, hurry."

Kesh and Jesse start back the way they came as the rest of us jog to catch up to our group.

Cal and Veece greet each other first with a few shoulder grips, then Veece quickly looks around, confused.

"Where's Zoe?"

Cal and Dell exchange glances, then both look to me.

"She's topside...with her father," I say.

Veece narrows his eyes. *"Topside!?"*

"It's all right," Liddick says. "My brother found a way to reverse her treatment. She can go into the sun now."

All the blood drains from Veece's face. The muscles in his sharp jaw flex, and his chest rises with a single deep breath.

"That is for the best. That is her place." He shifts his eyes to the ground after an awkwardly long pause, and my chest feel like the air is thinning more with each breath. He nods once to us, then ushers Cal a few yards ahead of the group as we follow.

CHAPTER 32
Recovery Rooms
Arco

The door to the recovery rooms opens with the badge I took from the doctor, but inside, all I see are empty clear holding cubes along the far wall. There must be at least five lined up in a row, but something is off. It's too still... too quiet in here.

I move a few steps along the wall, gripping the neural ray until I hear whimpering. I stop in place and listen, just to make sure I actually heard it. It comes again, and I pick up my pace.

Around the corner are two more holding tanks, bigger than the ones near the entrance to the room. They're partitioned off from the entryway, and I imagine there must be even more on the other side of them.

Another doctor in a long, white lab coat is typing at a console station behind the partition, and four clone guards in red uniforms stand ready outside both of the enclosures. All of them are brandishing neural rays like mine. Inside, Calyx stands with Lyden and my sister against the clear wall of the first cube, while Jax, his father, and Fraya stand close to each other in the other cube. I blow out a silent breath and try to decide how to get the guards out of the way but still keep the doctor in place so he can open the enclosures.

Calyx pounds on her enclosure, causing one of the clone guards to step toward her.

"Stand down, specimen 8796," it says, the voice monotone and deep. All five of the other guards train their neural rays on her, but Calyx just pounds her fists on the clear wall of her enclosure again.

"Don't bother," the doctor says with a chuckle. "Let her knock herself silly. It won't affect the cellular mutations."

After another second, a blue light starts to glow at the base of her platform. A holographic grid display appears in front of the doctor's console and starts populating with images I can't make out this far away.

I have a clean shot at the first two guards, and I take it. They drop quickly as the other four shoot their neural rays in my direction, and things get more complicated. I dart back behind the corner and watch the blasts dissipate into the wall in front of me. When I hear their footsteps speed up, I get low and spray a continuous blast along the ground. It hits three of the guards across the shins, and they drop too. They try to stand but can't, and though they can still shoot, their mobility is impaired. *I don't have a lot of time,* I think, but that's all I can think before I feel something hit me in the shoulder, then a heat rush down my arm and across my chest. I look down and notice a smoldering circle growing in circumference. *I just got shot?*

I bite the inside of my cheek to keep from yelling out, then taste blood in my mouth. My fingers start to tingle, so I instinctively close my hand into a fist. The streams of heat feel like a current pulsing up my arm, and I start to panic that they won't stop. Without thinking, I grab the barrel of my neural ray and balance it on my hip, aiming it in the general direction of the guards in front of me, then press the trigger. It's all I can think to do, even though I know it's probably the last thing I'll ever do.

It's a strange feeling to know you're going to die. You would think there would be screaming or begging, at the very least fighting, but I can't find any of that in me. Everything just seems to slow down. I look up at the guard running toward me and wait for another blast to hit me in the chest or the stomach. I wait for everything to go numb and dark, but the guard suddenly drops right in front of me.

I nearly choke on my tongue, not sure what just happened. *Did he trip?* I wonder until the hollows of his cheeks start to cave in just like the other clone, and I choke again in complete astonishment. *I hit him? I must have hit him?* I think.

The heat in my arm starts to shoot down my leg, and my chest tightens. Blood pounds in my ears as I try to push myself forward, the neural ray still balanced on my hip and my fingers wrapped around the trigger guard.

"Open the doors!" I shout, surprised at the sound of my own voice, which is ragged and a lot lower than normal. I sound like one of the clones. "Now!"

The doctor throws his hands in the air, then abruptly turns back to the console. I move as quickly as I can to his side and push the barrel of the neural ray between his shoulder blades.

"You won't be able to leave this facility. They have alerts on every level." The doctor almost whimpers, holding his hands at his sides. Over his shoulder, I'm drawn to the code he just entered onto the console, and before I know *how* I know what he typed, I know it needs to be stopped.

"Why couldn't you just open the doors?" I say too loudly next to his ear, then shoot him in the ribs with the neural ray. He drops to the ground in a convulsive fit, and then totally passes out. The code keeps scrolling.

Jax rushes the wall of the enclosure next to Calyx and pounds against the glass, exploding in cheers when he sees me. I scan for my sister and feel sick when I don't see her, until she and Lyden come out from behind the others. Lyden tries to mouth something to me, but I can't make it out.

The console starts beeping and blinking as the columns of code scroll quickly upward. Something is wrong. *This is a countdown.*

I sling the neural ray to my back and try to clear my head...to see something in the chaos of symbols and numbers, but the harder I push, the more chaotic it all becomes.

"Damn it!" I shout, then hear more pounding on the glass. I turn to see Lyden looking at me hard. He points his first two fingers at me, then redirects them to his eyes. *Watch him? Why?*

I shake my head, confused until I start to feel like everything is slowing down again. My breathing, the pounding in my ears. I take a deep breath just as he points me back to the console. Even the code has slowed down, and I start to see a pattern in the symbols. *Crite, did he just push me?* I think, but I let it go because numbers start to glow, and I know what to enter to kill whatever this is counting down to.

I hammer the glowing number sequence into the keyboard, and the code stops scrolling all together. I scan for the root menu tags and delete the remaining code, which takes me to the main system command portal. I enter a kill command, and the power in the room goes out. The thrum of the hydraulics slows to a whine, then completely stops. When the emergency lights turn on, I rush to the enclosures and push the doors ajar.

"Let's go! Let's go!" Jax shouts, reaching for Fraya. He almost tackles me when his feet hit the floor. He thumbs the strap of my neural ray, then slaps my chest in approval. "Look at you, cinestar! Dice McClain *who?*"

I laugh and roll my eyes at him as my sister throws her arms around my neck, but looks at me like I'm a ghost when she pulls back.

"What?" I ask. "Did they hurt you?"

"Your nose," she says. I bring my hand to my face, confused again until I see the blood. My vision starts to blur the second I do, and a wave of nausea hits me hard. I squeeze my eyes closed to get some clarity.

"It's the fuse," Jack says. "The Coder and Navigator proclivities are trying to use the same part of his brain. He can't engage one without the other now," he adds. "Get him on the table."

"No, I'm fine," I say, forcing my eyes open. "They're coming. We need to find a ship. Where's Calyx?"

"He's right. They may have already sent a signal out. We should move. There's a small med bay aboard their ships," Calyx says, jumping out of the enclosure and pushing her streaked, white-blonde hair out of her eyes when she lands. "Where's Briggs?"

"He went to upload the archive," I say, wiping the last of the blood from my nose as we make our way out of the lab.

"The *archive?* How? Rheen purged it."

"Denison got more of the sample. He's going to meet us at the hangar," I say, surprised to feel winded when we've only run about fifty feet. "But that's probably still flooded with guards from when we fired on Cole Daniels's glider."

Calyx smirks and gives me a sideways look. "Then we're just going to have to get creative."

***

Guards are still swarming around the entrance to the hangar when we peer around the corner.

"We won't be able to take them all down," I say to Calyx.

"No, and Briggs won't be able to get through there either. We need a distraction."

"Do you still have the clearance badge?" Jack asks me. I nod, pulling the lanyard from under my shirt. "If we can get to a console, I can help with that distraction."

We're not far from the room Denison and I pushed the doctors into, but we would have to walk right in front of the swarm of guards around the hangar entrance to get there. We'd never make it.

"I know another place. This way," Calyx says, doubling back until we turn down an offshoot corridor. "Is the badge you have a researcher credential?" she asks, grabbing the lanyard at my chest. She nods a few times, then moves to the door just up the hall. "Open this one. Hurry!"

I jog to her side and press the badge against the reader, which lights up green before the hydraulics engage the door and open it. Inside, amphitheater style seating surrounds the sunken floor just like the Phase Two port-carnate room...just like Tark's classroom back at Gaia. At the bottom are two more clear holding cubes on a center platform with several consoles wrapping the length of each bench that encircles them.

"Is this some kind of teaching lab? It looks like a stage here," Jax asks, scanning the room as we rush to the closest console.

"For all intents and purposes, yes," Calyx answers, waving her hand frantically over the console screen, which does not turn on. She swears, then jerks around to me. "Toss me the lanyard. I've already been wiped from the system."

"I'm amazed you're not setting off alarms everywhere since Rheen knows you turned on them," I say.

"Oh, I'm sure she's convinced they've already turned me into a popsicle. But everybody we knocked out will wake up eventually, and then you'll hear some alarms." She finishes off typing whatever she's entering into the broad console keypad. "Jack, can you make a clone without a full DNA workup?"

"On a hybrid console?" Jack asks, looking around the room and up at the ceiling. "I can make it work. I don't see a dedicated cloning system in here. Everyone give me a hair."

"You're going to clone *us*?" I ask, confused.

"Yes, but the clones won't have time to map us before Denison will be heading for the hangar," Calyx says, pulling up a tracking display in the palm of her hand. "We'll have to send them into the fray empty."

Lyden must register my confusion, because he starts explaining. "They won't be able to talk or reflect our personalities, gauge our probable responses or emotions in a situation," he says. "They'll just be blank cartridges dressed up like us."

"That's all we need—draw the attention away from the hangar door so we can get in, then get out," Calyx adds.

"Do we at least have time to program them to fight?" I ask.

"The standard program has self-defense built into the baseline code. If someone tries to attack them, they'll fight back," Jack says. "Replicating the clothing will be a bit more of a challenge without a dedicated device, though. I'll have to print them...without any."

"Wait, what? Naked?" Arwyn asks.

Jack chuckles. "I'm afraid so."

I glance at my sister, who is beet red standing next to Lyden. He meets my eyes and holds up a hand.

"Don't worry. I'm a gentleman." He nods, then winks at Arwyn. She and Fraya start laughing, and Jax snorts from somewhere behind me.

CHAPTER 33
Returning
Jazz

We pass the waterfall my brother fell down the first time we made our way through these tunnels—when we escaped from the Leviathan wreckage.

It's surreal to see it now, the pool writhing and splashing against the stone perimeter, pushing foam to the edges. I look at the wall where Liddick covered my mouth to keep me from talking and outing us to the Vishan waiting in the wings.

We move quickly and silently to the cave opening behind the falls, and I wonder if the story of the water worm that hunts by sound really was just something they told us to keep us in line. In any case, I'm not willing to find out, so I follow Cal and Veece through the fissure with the others. A chill runs down my back as we make our way down the corridor where Dell and Cal dragged Liddick and me all those months ago. I glance at him, but he just scans the walls. I can't read him now either, and I know he's probably blocking me on purpose.

Jove meets us at the opening to the Vishan caverns, pushing aside the tapestry covering the threshold as we approach.

How did he know we were coming right now? I think at random.

Vox hears me and answers. *It must be the NET device. Cal said it acts like a beacon—they've probably been tracking him.*

"You have returned," Jove says, narrowing his electric blue eyes at us as his deep voice reverberates off the walls. He wears the same beige tunic as I remember, but his tanned, tribal scarred face is terse instead of welcoming. He glances at Liam, who looks like he's seen a ghost. "And you have brought another."

"This is my brother," Liddick speaks up, nodding to Liam. "He was trapped in the mountain—in your Motherland," he adds, but he doesn't explain anything else. Jove gives him a hard, unblinking look but doesn't say anything else. The air turns thick with tension, which Veece tries to cut.

"Did the hunting parties return? Is the platform ready?" he asks, almost out of breath with anticipation.

"Yes, we are making preparations in light of their reports," Jove answers. "We will need the artifact to activate the platform."

Cal takes a few steps forward and pulls the slim, Y-shaped NET device from his satchel and hands it to Jove.

"Who are you trying to call with that thing? We're all out of the Rush now," Vox asks, too abruptly. Jove nods in her direction, then turns to Veece.

"We are creating a place for your group on the edge of the Council circle. Secure your hunting parties and then join us. We have much to do."

Jove turns toward the small corridor that I remember leads up to Circle Hall, the enormous cavern where everyone sleeps.

"Who *else* is out there?" Vox asks again after Jove leaves. She nudges Cal in the ribs.

He shakes his head and shoots a sudden glance at Veece. "They think there's still a Motherland out there, and it doesn't matter what I tell them. It doesn't matter how many times I come back from that mountain to tell them there are *no* ancestors waiting. They'll never believe it's just a story."

"*Everything* is a story until it happens," Veece growls. "Then, it is the truth."

"You know as well as I do there is nothing up on that Lookout Pier except *rock*," Cal says.

"Then how do you explain *her?*" Veece fires, gesturing to Vox. "She was the beginning of the prophecy, and others are coming now. We have to trust the Origin Wall." Veece takes a few steps to follow his father up the small corridor into Circle Hall, then turns back to us. "Stay close. We don't have long to prepare the platform… or our people."

Cal pushes his hands through his white-blond hair and blows out a breath. Liddick looks at me from under a raised, dark eyebrow.

The Lookout Pier is about thirty feet up another narrow corridor, if I remember the schematics. There's no way a few hundred Vishan will all fit up there at the same time, he thinks.

And what are they planning to do once they do get up there? Toss them off the pier and into the Rush below? All at once, terror washes over me.

"Are they going to move everyone to the Lookout Pier?" Liddick asks out loud, putting words to my fears.

Cal turns and gives him a grave look. "Like I said, all I know is there's a platform up there for scouting somebody with the NET. Ain't a thing else except what's wild beyond the Bale field threshold."

"But Vox just told him there's no one *in* the Rush anymore," I say. "Why is Jove getting the platform up there ready to look for people?"

"It's the prophecy," Cal explains with an exhausted sigh. "We get into our positions, and it will connect the Motherland with our lands here. The prophecy says this will open the tunnel to the stars."

Dell shakes his head, his expression crumpled like he's bracing against a loud noise. "How is everyone standing up there all particular and such supposed to attach that mountain with this one?" He throws a hand out toward the Lookout Pier corridor.

Liddick shakes his head too and exchanges glances with Liam. "There has to be something we don't know. Azeris showed me the tunnel under these lands that runs the length of the Rush. Something *is* down there."

"Not like we can just start digging," Cal replies soberly. "It's rock all around, save the ash field under the Bale crops. There's nothing about fighting off zephyrs to connect the two mountains in the prophecy, I'll tell you that right now."

"Well, while you all are debating the details," Dell says, "we have firsthand account that some undesirables are making their way here now or soon thereabouts. I'm going to help Veece with the hunting parties." He looks over his shoulder. "I'll meet you up there. If folks are coming to do no good, we best get fortified."

The rest of us make our way back to Center Hall, which is scrambling with Vishan gathering up their belongings. Kesh and her crew are ushering people to line up at the threshold of the Lookout Pier corridor, but it's still mainly chaos. Cal starts shouting something in Vishan as he, Liddick, and Liam cross to aid the organization efforts.

"Come on," Vox says, darting for the far corner of the area. I follow her trajectory and see Vita helping the others load their belongings into woven baskets. She sees us approaching, and the tan color of her face blanches.

"You're alive..." she says quietly, then drops the basket in her hands and rushes us, throwing her arms around Vox. "The Council did not think you would survive the Rush..." She exhales.

"The Council can kiss my—"

"Vita!" I say, cutting Vox off. "We need to ask you something."

Vita holds Vox at arm's length and looks her up and down.

"Is this suit from the Motherland?"

"Not exactly," Vox says, glancing down at her white jumpsuit from The Seam, which is marred in dirt from the tunnels. "Vita, Dell was right. There are scientists in the volcano. Bad ones. They've been hurting people there for a long time."

Vita's face blanches, but I can tell it's not out of surprise. She nods a few times and lets go of Vox's shoulders.

"People are coming—people like the bad scientists," I say. "Veece said this was a prophecy? But where's everyone going? Is there a way to escape on the Lookout Pier?"

She looks at me for several seconds before she nods one more time. "Come with me," she says, leading us to the Swim, the opening in the rock floor on the other side of Circle Hall, which slides to the lower level of the Vishan cavern.

She and Vox step off the edge like it's the first step in a staircase, then quickly vanish into the black hole. I never did get used to this. I sit on the edge, then slowly push off it with my hands. Immediately, everything gives way, and I'm flying through the darkness.

A few seconds later, I slow to a stop at the bottom of the slide and inch my way to the edge. Vita and Vox offer a hand to help me out, and we all move through the corridor that leads past the natural spring pool where Zoe tossed me in the water. A chill runs through me at the memory of having to get the microscopic *bugs* from that water so the Bale stalks outside, just at the perimeter of the Rush, wouldn't attack us when we went to collect the harvest.

"Where are we going?" I ask, but we're at the Origin Wall room before Vita can answer.

"This is the prophecy," she says, pulling up a small fire in the palm of her hand. She moves it close to the etchings under the wall, which dance in the shadows. "It says that people from the topside world will come, following the one who is like us, but different," she says, glancing at Vox. "When this happens, it will no longer be safe for us here."

"We already know this. But how are you supposed to

get to the stars? Veece is taking everyone to the Lookout Pier," I ask. "Where does it say how everyone gets out?"

"Here," Vita says, pointing to the diamond scar in the middle of her forehead and holding the little flame in her hand under the same diamond etching in the wall. It sits between two sets of arrows—the arrows above pointing up, and the arrows below pointing down, just like the scar design, and just like Vox's tattoos.

"So what does that mean?" Vox presses. "The diamond is the topside world, right? How is that supposed to get us out of here?"

Vita points to the top two inverted arrows carved into the Origin Wall. "These are the first and the second skies," she says, then points to the inverted arrows under the diamond. "This is the first barrier and the second barrier…"

"Vita," Vox says impatiently. "We don't have time for a cartography lesson. Those skods are *coming.*"

"*This* is all we know," Vita says firmly, darting her eyes to Vox and pressing her palm flat against the Origin Wall. "The answer must be in our maps…our paths."

"But they're just—" Vox starts, then quickly looks at me. "Wait, there are two ways to the stars. The first barrier from the topside world…" She lifts her hand to trace the diamond tattoo on her forehead, then closes her eyes. Almost immediately, I can feel her flood with emotion—fear, pride…

"What? What is it?" I ask.

"My grandmother told me the first barrier to the stars is the *water*. The second is the earth…" she says without opening her eyes. Her fingers trace the inverted arrows just under the diamond tattoo on her forehead. "We came through the water, and down here under the seafloor— we must already be through the second barrier. Something *is* here." She opens her eyes to look at Vita, who nods.

"Azeris said as much, but that doesn't help us. We don't know how to get to it," I say. "Is there something else on the wall about how we do *that?*"

Vita shakes her head. "The one who is like us, but different, holds the key. This is the one who must open the door to the stars. That's all that is written."

"Vox, that's you. Maybe something up on the Lookout Pier activates for you? A secret door or something?"

"It never did anything when I was up there before," she says, her yellow-green eyes narrowing. "I don't know any secrets," she says.

"Maybe you don't have to. Maybe *you* are the secret," I say. "Come on. We need to get up to the Lookout Pier."

CHAPTER 34
Distractions
Arco

"OK, so you're going to print *naked* clones of us, and then what? Slap everyone on the butt and send them streaking past the clone guards?" I ask, shaking my head in disbelief at this plan.

"Basically." Jack nods, pushing out his bottom lip like he's been mulling this over awhile. I'm speechless at the stupidity of this idea, but I don't have a better plan.

"Crite...how long will this take?"

"Two, maybe three hours."

I shake my head. "We don't have that kind of time. Do we even need all of us cloned?"

"The smallest of us will take the least amount of time to print, and even less time if I only program a basic framework for the tissue overlay—no organs," Jack says.

"OK, but how long?"

"Twenty minutes, if I interface both of these printing mechanisms," Jack answers, gesturing to the clear enclosures down on the center platform of the room.

"That will have to work..." I say, glancing at Fraya, who's the smallest here. Jax raises an eyebrow at me and wraps a big gorilla arm around her.

"Uh, no," he says. "Print me."

Calyx chuckles, looking him up and down. "Kid,

we'll be here for days. I'll do it," she says. Fraya blows out a breath watching her pull out one of her white-blonde hairs and hand it to Jack. "I'm not that much bigger than she is, and I know the layout of this place. Maybe there will be some baseline synapses that carryover into the clone."

Jack nods. "I need those enclosures unlocked. There are cellulose pads in the platforms that will work well enough," he says to Calyx. She crosses to me and takes the lanyard from around my neck, then tosses it to Jack.

"We have to hurry," she says, turning back to me. "Keep an eye out for Briggs. We should have felt at least one small tremor by now if he was able to upload the archive."

"I have a bad feeling about this," I say, shaking my head. "He was never programmed into my tracker system. Do you see him?"

Calyx opens her palm and presses into her wrist to activate her locators. Several blue dots appear on the miniature, green grid display, then start to flesh out with our faces. I brace myself to see Jazz, but her face never appears. Calyx points to a dot far at the bottom, well below her hand.

"He's still in the core room," she says. "You're right—something is wrong. He's been in there way too long."

"Do you know how to fly the ships in the hangar?" I ask.

Calyx nods. "Not like you, but I can put them in the air."

"Can you get a ship back to The Seam? Or back to the Skyboard North doctor where we left the testing patients?"

"Why?" she asks, her black eyebrows darting together. "What are you planning?"

"I don't know," I say, trying to settle the churn in my stomach. I pull Calyx several steps away from the others and whisper to her. "I'm going to go find Denison. Can you get everyone on board and get them out or not?"

"You need a brain scan, literally," she adds after a beat. "That proclivity merge in your head is happening too fast. It's not a good idea to be alone. I'll go. You fly them out of here."

"I'm fine. It's helping get things done, and if something does melt down, I don't want to be the only one keeping a ship in the air. Autopilot won't engage in the ion field here."

"Then I'll go with you."

"No, are you listening to me?" I ask. "*You* need to fly. Everyone with us is either an Omnicoder or a Biodesigner—nobody else can *pilot* a ship. I'll find Denison and we'll get back to the hangar somehow. He'll be able to fly if I check out."

She gives me a narrowed look, but before she can protest again, Jack starts laughing out loud. "It's working!" he almost shouts as he points to the cube enclosure on the right. Feet and ankles have already begun to form in the center, and with each laser line coming from the top of the clear cube, more of the legs start to take shape in seconds. After only a few more minutes, both knees are in place.

"OK..." I shake my head at everyone to pull out of the surreal fog that seeing an *actual body* being printed just put me in. "I'm going to find Denison. He's still in the core room, so something must have gone wrong—he should have been in the hangar by now."

"I'll go with you," Jax says.

"No, get everyone out. It might not be a clean shot even with a distraction, and they'll need all the muscle they can get," I say. He starts to protest, so I cross to him. "Please, man. Get everyone back. Get your dad back home."

"And what if you have some kind of brain thing happen again?"

"How much longer?" I ignore his question and call to Jack, who's still typing away at the console. I glance at the Calyx clone before I realize it and look away even faster.

"Five minutes, all that is left is her head," Jack answers.

I blow out a breath, then see my sister approaching over Jax's shoulder.

"Take this. It's all I have ready right now, but give me a few more minutes," she says, handing me a small, white disc.

"What is it?"

"A neural blocker. It's like a pain-killer, but I altered it with some of their equipment over there." She pushes her chin to the bay of consoles where Jack is still typing. "I don't have a way to keep it charged, but it will buffer your hemisphere merge until it dies. If you don't surge, it could last seven or eight hours."

"And if I do surge?"

"Maybe a half-life after each episode. Four hours after

the first time, and two after another."

"So, third strike, and I'm out?" I smile at her, and tears fill her eyes.

"Stow it. Hurry up and swallow it, will you?" she says, giving me a trembling smile.

It tastes like something dead and rotting, and I cough to the point that I gag. Jax laughs and slaps me on the back. "You OK?"

The first thing I see when I recover is Calyx's clone, now complete with a head, but still no clothes, and I cough again on the shocked breath I suck in.

"Yeah, here," I say, taking off the lab coat I took from the doctor. "Put this on her."

"You'll need that to get past the guards," Jack answers.

"The guards are going to be chasing her. Can she—er, *it* talk?"

"No," Jack says, catching the coat I toss to him. "But I programmed a trajectory into its base code. Basically, it can run, and it can fight."

"Great," I manage, around the last of my coughing. "Can any of you pull up Jazz, Vox, and Liam on your tracking?"

"I've been trying. They're all out of range," he answers.

"How can they be out of range? The whole point of getting these trackers put in was to—" I start, but my sister cuts me off.

"Arco," she says just as I feel blood run over my lip. I wipe it on my sleeve. "Crite, this is asinine."

"Sometimes pain can trigger a surge," she says,

crossing to me with something small in her hands. "Here, this is done loading now. Hold still."

Arwyn shoves the little tube into my nose without a warning, and a second later, it feels like the whole inside of my head is flushed with ice.

"*Wha—!?*" I start, but the cold pushes into my throat and cuts off my words.

"Your rebooted nanites aren't keeping up," Arwyn says, taking a few steps toward me. "There's no time to splice any either, so take this," she adds, handing me the little cylinder. "There's enough for two more shots. It won't stop the damage from the surge, but it will stop the bleeding. Between that and the neural blocker, you should be OK for now."

"What is it?" I choke.

"Oxygen, mainly. It's a primitive composition, but that's the best we could do with what's here—or at least, what we could find," she says, looking around at the stark walls. "They must have a way to print what they need on demand."

"Are we ready?" Lyden says, peering through the cracked door at the top of the stairs.

"Almost," Jack says, hammering something into the console. The clone of Calyx opens its eyes, then starts marching toward Lyden at the top of the stairs.

"What's it doing?" he asks, registering a little panic.

"It's all right. She's going to start by walking, and when she registers that she's been noticed, she'll start running to draw the guards away. Don't engage her," Jack says. Lyden takes several steps back from the door, letting the Calyx clone have plenty of room.

The real Calyx stands up behind a console near Jack and stares at the clone in awe. "I'll be damned, Jack. No wonder they pinched you for Gaia even after you told them to go to hell."

"It's just a few neural connections and the right organic tech," he says with a shrug.

The breeze from the corridor blows the clone's lab coat open just as it passes me. I reach to button it, but my sister grips my wrist.

"No, don't engage or it will start running, remember?" she says. I nod, feeling stupid.

"Right, right. OK, come on. We need to get in the wake of that thing," I say, waving everyone toward the lab door. Jax moves to my side, opening the door the rest of the way for the clone.

It walks over the threshold, keeping a normal pace for about twenty-five yards until several guards start to take notice.

"You remember the last play against Seaboard East last year?" I say to Jax. "All right. Let's go."

He grins. "Set 'em up, knock 'em down."

"You there! Stop!" one of the guards shouts to the Calyx clone, but instead of stopping, it starts running, taking most of the guards with it.

"Now! Come on! We still have a few at the door!" I call back to everyone. Jax runs next to me until I go wide, hoping one of the guards will try to shoot at me. "Hey, test tube!" I shout. The clone guard jerks his ray toward me just as Jax bulldozes him. He falls, skidding across the slick floor. Jax flies past him, grabbing up his neural ray. "Go! Go!"

"You too! Hurry up!" he calls back, taking out the other three clone guards alongside Lyden and Jack. I watch them make their way through the hangar door before I turn down a corridor and realize I have no idea where I am.

"Crite..." I breathe, then remember the arrow uplink we took from the doctors. "Core Room," I say out loud.

"This way to the Core Room, Dr. Beckett," the arrow voice in my head says as a blue arrow materializes in the corner of my vision, and again, I'm running.

The Core Room is down multiple flights of steps, and I manage to stay ahead of any clone guards. I use the credential I took back from Calyx to open the Core Room door and duck to the side just in case there's someone on the other side who isn't Denison. The room is full of consoles and one giant, white, churning cylinder in the middle of the room, which reminds me of the virtuo-cine platform back in Admin City. It's surrounded by controls that Denison is hammering over and over again.

"Come on!" he shouts. I take another quick look around the area but only see a few unconscious clone guards on the ground. Denison has a neural ray slung over his back.

I pick up the other one next to one of the downed guards and rush over to him. "What's wrong?"

"The sample is corrupt—shriveled."

"How? We took it directly from The Seam's containment room!"

"I know. I was there," he barks, then swears. "It had to be Eco. He exposed the other sample to ultraviolet light. He must have done the whole thing at once."

"Useless skod!" I grip the back of my neck, which helps me think when I don't have a two-inch tracker incision healing exactly there. A shot of adrenaline pushes pounding blood to my ears with the initial jolt of pain. "All right, well, we need to abort then. There's no recovering the sample, right? No restoring it?"

"No, I've been trying since I got here," Denison answers, stopping for a second to push his hands through his cropped, white hair. He pulls them down over his face and blows out a breath.

"Then let's go. Calyx is securing a ship in the hangar right n—" I'm cut off by another blinding light that feels like an ice pick through the center of my head. It drills through my skull to the base of my neck, then freezes my spine for a second until more numbers appear in my peripheral vision. A wave, an arrow cap, three curved lines, and a flame? The first three are the key signatures for seaboard communities, mountain communities, and underwater homesteads... *What's the flame? What's the flame!?*

"What's happening? Are you all right?" Denison asks. I push the heels of my hands into my eyes to clear my vision, then move behind the console. My hands are moving over the screen before I know what I'm doing, pressing numbers, entering equations, hitting button after button and swiping screen after screen until another database system appears.

SECURITY BYPASS...ALPHA TWELVE...EXODUS PROJECT...UPLINK CONNECTION...PROXY SCRIPT...LOCATING HOST...CONNECTED... ACTIVATE ARC SEQUENCE?

I pull back when the last button appears with the flame symbol embedded in the center. *Activate Arc Sequence? What does that mean?* I think, as the rest of the numbers and symbols on the console screen stop scrolling. Whenever I try to swipe the screen away or look for anything else on it—an exit symbol, something—the piercing ice headache returns. It only stops when I look directly at the blinking button. It's the only way…so I push it.

ARC SEQUENCE ACTIVATED. PREPARE FOR LAUNCH IN T-MINUS THIRTY MINUTES.

"Wait, what? *What?*" I say out loud, then turn to Denison. "What's the Arc? Is it another ship?"

He looks at me blankly and shakes his head.

"I have no idea. What happened?" He moves in front of the console and sees the same message.

"I just activated some kind of countdown sequence."

"What is this? How did you get to this screen? It's not even in the Phase Three database."

"I don't know. The numbers were just in my head, *under* the screen somehow. Lots of layers under. That doesn't make sense…" I trip over my words. "I don't know. I just saw them," I try again, only vaguely registering the sudden reverberation of the yell I let out and the pain in my knees when they hit the ground. The ice headache comes again, washing out everything.

CHAPTER 35
The Platform
Jazz

"What is that?" I ask Vox as a small tremor rattles the rock under our feet.

"I don't know. Do you hear the buzzing?"

I nod, feeling the thrum again just behind my eyes. I press my palm to the black, smooth wall and feel the vibration run up my arm.

"Something is happening," I say, turning back to Vita.

"Has anything like this ever happened before? Is it an earthquake?"

"No, not in my lifetime," she says. "But the prophecy says these lands will be destroyed when we rejoin the ancestors."

Vox and I exchange glances.

"Destroyed how?"

"First, the earth will break away…"

"Break away?" I ask. "The tremors…" I add, looking again at Vox.

"And then, a great flood."

"Vita!" Vox almost shouts.

"Don't you think that was maybe critical information back at the Origin Wall?"

"I tried to tell you. You didn't want a cart—a cargotro…"

"Ugh…a *cartography* lesson," Vox answers, rolling her eyes. "We have to get out of here. We have to get everyone out."

We make our way up the long corridor that circles back to Center Hall where everyone is being lined up with their belongings at the foot of the Lookout Pier.

"Where are they going?" I ask Vita. She opens her mouth to answer, but Vox cuts her off.

"And don't say to the stars."

Vita closes her mouth.

"Crite," I say, blowing out a breath.

"Vox!" Cal shouts, making us all jump as he appears from around the corner of the Lookout Pier staircase, which is buried in the black slab of the rock wall. We follow him while all the Vishan lined up against it stare silently at us as we pass, some of them looking hopeful, and others looking at us like we're on our way to be executed.

This isn't right, I think. *The younger Vishan look happy. The older ones…don't.*

They know something, Vox answers in my mind. I feel a wash of panic from her before it's buried under a cold, muted weight in my stomach.

There's nothing up there. If they're sending everyone up there, it can only be to push them off or something. Like a ritual suicide? I think in a panic.

I don't think they would do that, Vox answers.

These people brand their faces and throats, Vox! I don't think they'd think twice about taking a swan dive off that pier! Especially if the whole damn ocean is going to bust through here.

"Finally. Come up here!" Cal clears the top of the stairs and disappears around the corner just as the sound of fighting breaks out in the distance. I jerk around but can't see Center Hall anymore.

"They're almost here. Spaulding's men..." I say to Vox. We sprint up the next several steps of the stairwell with Vita just a few feet behind us. I press my hands against the smooth, black obsidian to keep from falling, and feel the electric current vibrating against my palm again. The sharp edges of the glass-like stone glint in the light of the Lookout Pier, but then fall into shadows when Liddick comes bolting halfway down the stairwell to us.

"Crite, Rip...where did you go?" he asks, gripping my shoulders.

"We went to the Origin Wall to find out more about this prophecy. It has something to do with Vox—somehow, she's supposed to go to the stars."

"I know, they're looking for her," he says, darting a glance over his shoulder. "There's a storm gathering too, just like the one when we went into the Rush. You can feel the electricity in your teeth up there."

"What's happening? What do they want?" Vox asks Vita.

"It's the prophecy...they're preparing for you to open the door."

"*How!?*" Vox asks, throwing up her hands. Vita shakes her head. I touch the wall of the corridor and feel the electric current again just like before. The hum is getting even louder now in my ears.

"Do you feel that? It's happening again. The hum—

can you hear the hum?"

Liddick nods and glances over his shoulder again. "OK, we need to make a decision here. That way is Spaulding's goons," he says, jerking his chin behind us, then tossing a glance over his shoulder at the rest of the stairwell leading to the Lookout Pier. "That way is maybe some kind of magic carpet ride out of here."

"Or some kind of human sacrifice!" I almost yell. "Their prophecy said these lands are going to break away, and then there's going to be some kind of flood. Something *is not right* here, Liddick!"

"*Everything* is not right here, Rip," he says, gesturing again to the stairwell and Center Hall behind us. "Spaulding's men are *coming right now*, and they'll kill everyone. We can't go back…" He moves his hand over my face. "There's just forward, Rip."

Vox makes a roarfing noise and shoves past Liddick.

"Crite, I'd rather be human-sacrificed. Just come on."

We cross the threshold at the top of the stone stairwell. Off the edge, the ribboned, dark gray clouds are bunched like several rolled blankets pushed together. They crackle with lightning flickers, which are followed by more low rumbles I can feel reverberating off the rock.

"Are those zephyrs?" I ask, turning back to Vita.

Her clear blue eyes widen as she shakes her head in disbelief. "No. This is a storm, but I have never seen one so dense."

A huge whip of lightning spiderwebs through the dark, rolled clouds, and I feel the crackles over my lips and in my ears. It sounds like fifty cannons going off one after the other just a second afterward.

"Take your positions on the platform," Jove says, holding his arms out to his sides with his palms facing the mass of gathering cloud ribbons over our heads. The electricity in the air feels like small prickles in my skin, and in seconds, the low rumble all around turns into violent shaking.

"Spaulding's men are here!" Liddick calls to Liam, who's against the smooth, black rock next to the threshold.

Liam looks around for a second, then shakes his head. "There's nowhere to go!" he shouts over the rumbling sky. In the center of the Lookout Pier, a square stone column comes up from the ground like a peg being pushed from its hole. It's about three feet across in any direction, glinting in the gathering storm clouds that spark again with the same kind of lightning that we hoped would hide us from the zephyrs in the Rush.

"What is this!?" I shout to Liddick, but I can't hear his answer until he says it in my mind.

I don't know! Hang on! He pulls me against him as everything rattles, and the electric buzz behind my eyes just gets stronger.

Four more black, stone columns erupt from the ground, smaller than the larger one in the center that has only risen about two feet into the air. Each of the pillars is marked with a symbol—one that looks like a wave, one that looks like the top of an arrow, three wavy lines, and something that looks like a flame. *I've seen these before...*

"Child of Vishan! Take your position on the platform!" Jove shouts to Vox over the howling wind. He moves behind one of the smaller columns as Veece and

Vita move into place behind two more. Veece points to the other one for Cal, who reluctantly crosses into position.

"What are they doing?" Liam shouts to us.

"Some kind of ritual for their prophecy!" I answer, trying to remember what Vita told us in front of the Origin Wall.

Veece leaves his column and walks directly toward us against the wall. He takes Vox's hand and starts walking with her toward the platform in the center of the pier. She starts to pull away from him but can't break free.

"Something is wrong!" I yell to Liddick and Liam, feeling her fear knotting at the same time it starts spinning in my stomach.

"What happens on that platform!?" Vox shouts to Veece, but he doesn't answer. As strong and able to fight as she is, she can't escape Veece's hold. We all start to move toward them, but Liam is already there in just a few long strides. He pushes Veece a few steps back, which breaks his hold on Vox, but Veece seizes her wrist again and throws Liam to the ground like he's made of cloth.

"Let her go!" Cal protests, then starts looking at his legs as his expression changes from anger to shock.

What's wrong with him? I think, and Liddick answers almost immediately.

He's stuck in place. His feet are stuck in place!

I pull away from Liddick to run to Vox, but the ground starts to crack in places between the short columns where she's standing with Veece.

"Watch out!" I yell to her.

I take a step away from Liddick, just to make sure I can. The ground holds, but I can feel the tremor in the rockface running through my feet straight to my teeth.

"Get back!" Vox yells. "It's crumbling!"

Veece pulls Vox onto the platform, and before I know it, I'm running toward him as fast as I can. I ram my shoulder into his back, making him stumble, then trip and fall to the ground. I land on my hands and knees as the hum in my ears turns into a deafening, incapacitating buzz.

"Jazz!" I hear, and force myself to look up.

"Arco?"

CHAPTER 36
The Channel
Arco

"Whoa! Lie back—lie back!" Denison shouts, but it's a faraway sound, like it's coming through a few closed doors. I hear the echo of it one more time, but then it's gone, replaced by *Jazz screaming*. I blink to clear my blurred vision and see her running straight toward the cliff edge of the *Lookout Pier*...toward the open air of the Rush. *This is why she's out of range? What the hell is she doing back there?*

"*Jazz!*" I shout her name after she falls forward onto her hands. I scramble toward her as she looks around frantically, like she can hear me but can't see me. I call to her again, and this time, she looks right at me. "What are you doing!?" I yell to her again.

"Arco?" she calls back to me, then jerks her eyes away. I follow them to find Vox stumbling back from some kind of raised stone box in the center of the Lookout Pier. "This is the channel again...you have to be in my channel because I can't see anything where you are. Can you see anything here? *What can you see*, Arco?" she insists without so much as taking a breath.

"I can see you, Vox, and the *Lookout Pier*—why are you trying to run off the edge? Are you split? Do you see the storm!? What are you doing here?" I fire at her.

"That's not what I was doing. Veece is trying to pull Vox into the center...to that box platform, can you see it? Can you see the columns? The big one in the middle and the four smaller ones surrounding it?" she asks, but I don't see anything until she turns around and looks at it again herself.

"It's there! I see it all now... *What the...?"* I add under my breath, amazed to see Jove, Vita, and Cal already standing behind the little pillars, while the short, wide square one in the center stands empty. "Where did all that come from? What's *happening* up here?"

"They have a prophecy," she says turning back to me. "It started coming true when Vox arrived—now, Spaulding's men are coming here too."

"Spaulding? As in Tieg and Dez Spaulding?"

"*Yes,* I was trying to tell you the last time in my channel. Their father is the one who hijacked Liddick's port-carnate transfer to Admin City. He's the one who forced him to shut down the Grid server."

"Jazz—"

"Arco, *listen* to me. Azeris intercepted their feed— they were on their way to the Badlands, and some are coming here. They'll be coming for you too," she says, finally taking a breath. "Where are you? What's happening with the port-cloud?"

I try to think of somewhere to begin, but any variation of the story is too long. "We're in Phase Three, but we need more Vishan DNA to take it down. Eco ruined the archive we had," I manage, then see numbers and symbols starting to flicker in my peripheral vision. Pressure builds behind my eyes almost immediately. *No, not yet…not yet*, I think, afraid that this will be the end of our channel connection.

More numbers start compiling, separated by periods…by…*coordinates?*

In that second Veece yells something in Vishan. Red flames jump from Jazz's shoulders, which somehow makes the numbers in the corners of my eyes turn over faster.

"Fire? *How?*" I ask, squinting against the pressure in my head. "Your treatment was reversed like the rest of ours." I stumble over the words, trying to pat out her flames until I realize, like an idiot, that I'm really only in her head.

"Vox and Cal had to treat me again in the tunnels on the way down. She's immune to the pressure, and Liam put on a suit that Liddick and his friend got from Spaulding's men."

"Liddick's fr—?" I start, confused, but then decide I don't care. I don't have time to care right now. "Jazz, if they're coming, you need to get out of there. You should all be moving—Cal and Veece should be leading Spaulding's men back to the falls where that worm thing is. What the *hell* are you all doing up here?"

"I told you, it's their prophecy! They said they're trying to send Vox to the stars or something, and then everyone else will follow her."

I feel my whole face pinch with the effort to understand what she's just said. These people don't even have electricity, let alone a port-carnate hub, and they want to send someone into *space?*

"How? With that NET thing? Jazz, you all need to

leave! Now!" I say. She turns around, abruptly this time. The blackness behind her immediately gives way to the circle of little columns again, but this time, Veece is wiping blood from his head and moving toward us. I try to move into his path, but he walks right *through* me.

"Hey!" I shout, then remember he can't hear me because I'm only in *Jazz's* channel.

"What's happening to the ground?" Vox yells as small fissures spring from the connection points all along the rest of the wall face and in the ground below. The splits in the smooth, black rock run like rivers all the way into the Bale field.

"Jazz! We need to get everyone off this pier!" I shout, but she doesn't even seem to hear me now.

"Leave her alone!" she shouts, and the whole scene shifts to Veece pulling Vox by the wrist and hoisting her behind his shoulders, clamping her arms and legs down like she's hogtied. She knees him in the face, and he drops her onto the square platform in the middle of the Lookout Pier. She sweeps his legs, and he falls beside her.

"You have to fulfill the prophecy or we will all die!" he shouts.

"We're going to die if we don't get off this pier, you mollusk! Look!"

Vox points to the growing fissures all around the platform. She scrambles to her feet seconds before Veece and kicks him in the face. He stands up anyway, blood pouring over his lips.

"You are the only one who can save us!"

A flash of lightning blinds me for a second, and the rattle that follows just makes the cracks in the ground widen.

"Take your position!" Jove yells to Veece. He moves behind the last little pillar, and Jazz rushes to her.

"No! It's cracking more—stay back!" Vox yells.

"Wait!" Liddick and I both shout to her, but it's too late. She jumps over two widening cracks, losing her footing on the second one. She slips into it, and everything in me stops hard. *No...no...* I think, racing toward her. I reach for her, but my hands pass through hers. "No! Jazz!"

"Rip!" Liddick shouts, jumping over the fissures.

"Hurry!" I call to him, but he doesn't hear me. He stands where I'm standing. I watch his arms reach for hers...reach through mine, his hands through mine... except his take hold where mine don't.

"Hang on, Rip!" he says as another fissure opens under his feet. He catches himself with his knee but loses one of Jazz's arms.

"No!"

"Arco!" she shouts.

Wake up...wake up... I think, but it doesn't end. She's still falling, just like in my interview scenario. For a second I wonder if it's a flashback, if it's not real, and my stomach jumps with the hope, only to fall when she screams my name again.

"Wright! Pull her up!" I yell, reaching for her, but my hands go through hers. Finally, he connects, gripping both her wrists and pulling her up from the fissure.

"Hold on!" someone yells from behind us. I turn to see his brother, Liam, throwing out a length of rope. He pushes the satchel over his shoulder around to his back and calls to them. "Liddick! Get the rope!"

He catches it, wrapping an arm around Jazz's waist, and tries to pull her away.

"Let's go! Let's go!"

"We can't leave her!" Jazz yells. "Just go! Go back and then throw us the rope again!"

"Rip, no! I'll get her. Take this!"

More coordinates flash in front of my eyes, and then geometry formulas spread over the ground along the fissures. White veins appear in the black stone ground under our feet, branching off again into the Bale field, and I know those are where the next cracks will appear. The whole thing is going to give way except for the little columns and the center platform.

"Jazz! Go with him! Get out of the middle—it's going to collapse!" I shout to her. She looks at me and nods, but then pulls out of Liddick's arm and lunges back toward Vox on the center platform. "No! Jazz! *Jazz!*"

She leaps away from him and is suspended for a minute that seems to last an eternity in the air, but I don't see her land. The clouds roll down, engulfing everything in a haze, and for a few more seconds I can hear the rumbling all around until the pressure behind my eyes swallows everything in another blinding white light.

CHAPTER 37
The Core Room
Jazz

The last thing I hear is Arco calling my name as I jump toward the platform where Vox is standing. I turn to tell him I'm all right, but he's gone as fast as he appeared.

He's gone… He was just there! I think.

Arco? But you're awake? Vox says in my mind.

I don't understand it either…

It has to be something with the NET out here on this platform, she thinks, helping me to my feet. The platform shakes beneath us again, and we drop to our hands and knees.

We need to get off of here.

"There!" Liam shouts from across the pier. I look up to find him pointing at the rock slab between the platform Vox and I are standing on and the other four pillars encircling us.

"Rip! Don't move!" Liddick calls to me.

"What's happening!?"

"It's the opening to the tunnel Azeris found!"

Jove brings something to his mouth and blows, making a loud horn sound that reverberates off the black rock walls. Seconds later, the rest of the Vishan come pouring through the opening to the Lookout Pier and stand with Liam and Liddick against the wall.

The ground separates even more, falling away between the center platform and all four pillars. When the dust clears, I see a set of stairs leading down from the outside perimeter of Jove, Veece, Vita, and Cal, leaving Vox and I standing on top of a *now* very tall square pillar.

"Liddick!"

"Hold on!" he shouts to us.

"Sit down! It's better if we get low!" Vox says, slowly moving her legs under her.

I drop down and grip the edge of the platform when everything shakes around us again.

"They're here! The others are here!" Rav, Vita's son, says as he runs toward the stairs with another Vishan woman. Jove's family follows just behind them.

"The hunting parties have blocked the entrance to Center Hall. But the others have weapons," Flora says, directing the children to go with Liv, Rav, and some of the other Council members down the stairs that surround the pillar Vox and I are on.

"Then we must hurry," Jove says, striking the Net device hard on the stone column in front of him. The vibration starts in the pillar Vox and I are on and moves through my knees and up my arms, then rattles my skull. Vox growls through her teeth.

What are they doing!? I shout to Liddick in my head because I can't seem to use my voice.

Spaulding's men are here, Rip. Dell and the others just made it back and are down the stairs, he answers. I force my eyes open against the crippling buzz to look for them, but everyone is blurry. *We don't have a lot of time before they break down the barrier the hunting party made. Liam and I are going to go down the stairs, and I need you two to jump to us, OK?*

I can't see that far—it's all blurry, I answer. Liddick swears.

All right. We'll move right under you then. You'll just drop straight down. On my count, get ready...

I turn to Vox, whose eyes are also narrowed against the buzz she must be hearing too.

Liam and Liddick are going to catch us, I think toward her. *We're going to jump straight down.*

"Rip! We're here! On three! One!" Liddick shouts, but I can barely hear him over the crushing buzz in my head. "Two...three!"

Vox shifts away from me, then jumps. I try to do the same, but Jove must strike the NET device again because another deafening buzz hits me, freezing me in place and blurring my vision even more. Everything is heavy, cold...and the blur of everything around me fades to white.

***

"I've got you. It's all right," Arco says, but it can't be Arco. I try to talk, though nothing comes out. My head feels heavy, like it's filled with sand—like it felt after the port-carnate transfer to Admin City after we made it through the Rush.

I open my eyes and see Arco's face, his mossy hazel eyes starting to glass over.

"Arco?" I whisper, my voice feeling like gravel in my throat. "Is this your channel?" I ask, noticing the white walls and technical equipment behind him.

"Don't try to talk yet," another man's voice says. I

look over to the source and see Dr. Denison, then feel panic swell in my chest.

"It's OK; he's with us," Arco adds before I can say anything. "He's with The Seam. Crite, I can't believe it worked…"

"What? Where is this place? Am I in your channel?" I ask, feeling the weight in the back of my head and limbs finally start to lift.

"No, this is the Phase Three facility, Ms. Ripley. And I'm afraid we don't have much time," Dr. Denison says, moving toward me. "Can you bring her here?" he asks Arco, who nods.

"Wait, what? Arco?" I say, turning to him.

"It's all right—I was trying to bring Vox and Veece, too, but you said you had the Vishan treatment, right?"

"Yes. *What* are you talking about?"

"Your coordinates loaded into my head somehow when I was in your channel. When I woke up here, I just knew what to do at the console…the Vishan DNA is as close to the archive as we're going to get. Can you stand?" Arco asks, helping me to my feet.

We're standing inside a cube enclosure just like the ones from the Phase Two facility on the other side of the Rush. I pull in a quick, sharp breath and nearly start coughing.

"I transferred? *Port-carnate* transferred? Wait, but the treatment!"

"It's all right, Ms. Ripley. That baseline is already aligned with the system here. The transfer recognized without issue," Dr. Denison says. "Now please, we need a physical sample."

He moves toward me with a syringe, and I flinch.

"A sample of what? What's in that needle?" I ask, backing away from him. This is all happening too fast.

"You have incoming!" Calyx's voice comes from somewhere. I look around but don't see her. Denison swears and punches something into the flat, silver panel unit strapped to his forearm.

"You have comms? When did comms connect?" Arco asks abruptly.

"Right now, apparently," Denison answers, taking another step toward me with the syringe. I pull back again.

"What's in that? Tell me what's going on!" I shout. Arco steps in between us and rubs my arms, lowering his chin to meet my eyes.

"Listen, it's all right, OK? I rigged a port-carnate bridge to bring you here. After I woke up from being in your channel, that NET device was sending a buoy signal, so I anchored the system to it and plugged in the coordinates that kept flashing in my head," he says, nearly out of breath. "They were *your* coordinates, Jazz."

"Ow!" I jolt, feeling the needle plunge into the back of my shoulder. "Arco?" I search his face for an answer, not sure if the rock that settles into my stomach is my feeling of betrayal or his guilt. He shakes his head.

"It's not what you think, OK? Denison needs a syringe of your blood because it's been spliced with the Vishan DNA—the treatment, Jazz—that DNA needs to be routed into the core of this place."

"Loading!" Denison says, injecting the syringe of my blood into a cylindrical container, which he then races across the room to insert into some kind of column receptacle. It vanishes in a vacuuming *whoosh*, and Denison runs directly at us. "Time to go!"

"Can you walk?" Arco asks, slipping his arm around my ribs and taking a few steps forward. I put one foot in front of the other, but my legs feel like they're made of rubber.

"Whoa..."

"OK, I've got you. Come on. We need to move."

After a few more steps, I feel a little steadier, but everything is still happening too fast. Dr. Denison waves something over the wall in front of us, and a door panel appears, then slides open. Beyond the door is a long, white corridor that reminds me of the dorm wing of Gaia Sur, but beyond it I hear yelling.

"We can't go this way. There are too many clones now," Dr. Denison says, then swears again as he looks back at us.

"Crite," Arco says, wiping blood from his nose.

"Arco!" I gasp, moving to face him.

"It's all right. It's just the surge," he says, bringing a small, metal cylinder to his nose and inhaling. He grits his teeth, but the blood stops.

"What was that?"

"Oxygen or something, I don't know. My sister gave it to me. Come on. I know another way," he says. Dr. Denison's face is suddenly both hopeful and worried, but there's no time to find out why when a guard in a red jumpsuit rushes around the corner and aims at us with the biggest gun I've ever seen.

Dr. Denison tackles him around the waist, then sits

across his chest and drives the base of his hand into the guard's nose.

"Crite!" I shout. Dr. Denison takes the gun and gets to his feet.

"They're clones. He didn't feel a thing," he adds, catching up to us. "Lead on while that surge lasts."

"What is a *surge*?" I ask. "Arco, what is going on?"

"I'll explain when we're not about to be vaporized," he says. "Can you run?"

I nod back at him as we all take off down the corridor. We make our way through several winding hallways and finally, down a flight of metal stairs.

"This came to you in the surge?" Dr. Denison asks Arco when we stop at a wall. Arco waves a badge from around his neck over a panel, which then opens.

"Yeah—I can't explain how else I knew where to go. It was just there. Come on. We need to get on that ship."

Arco gestures to a large, teardrop-shaped craft that looks a lot like the big brother to the Stingrays from Gaia Sur. I only hope it doesn't have the same toy operating system inside.

"This one is closer," I say, pointing to another ship that's right in front of us.

"I know, but Calyx and the others are on the one over there. Trust me."

CHAPTER 38
The Space Between: Part One
Arco

The door closes behind us as we rush to the small barrier wall, which is about chest-high. It surrounds the hangar in sections, and with any luck, we'll be able to align with an opening that leads to the ship in the middle of the docked vessels. Calyx and the others have to be aboard that one—it's the only one with a clear path to the launching dock.

We move to the closest break in the wall, which doesn't line us up perfectly, but it's as close as we're going to get. Clone guards are everywhere in the hangar, boarding and searching the ships.

"We're at the dock, and you're about to have some company," Denison says into his wrist comms.

"Copy that. We already have you mapped," Calyx replies. "You cover incoming and we'll get your back."

"Copy." Denison turns to me. "You take the right. I'll take the left." He nods to to the neural ray slung over my shoulder. I bring it forward and make sure it's charged.

"Jazz, you stay in the middle of us, OK?" I say, handing her the neural baton from the side of my gear pack. "I hope you won't need this." She cracks it against her leg, and it buzzes to life.

"He goes left, you go right, I'll get the middle," she

says with a flat smile.

I grin at her. "Let's get out of here."

She smiles, and before I can think, I'm sliding my hand behind her ear and kissing her just like by the moon pool at Gaia Sur.

She's here. I don't know if she wanted to be here, but right now I don't care. Right now, in this minute, I don't care about Liddick Wright or anything that has led up to this point. If we make it on board that ship in one piece, we can figure it all out later.

"Hey!" Denison shoves my shoulder with the butt of his neural ray. "Our window is closing, Romeo. Time to go."

Jazz smiles up at me again and tries not to laugh. Her face flushes, and it's all I can do to keep myself from kissing her again. She turns to face the scatter of clone guards beyond our barrier wall and blows out a breath.

"It's not even their fault," she says, gesturing to the neural baton. "They were engineered too." Denison jerks his head back and gives her a side eye, but then just sighs.

"These are military grade clones. Like I said, they won't feel a thing, Ms. Ripley—pain receptors would be a handicap," he says with obvious restraint. "All right, let's move."

We rush into the fray of guards mobilizing toward us, and seconds later, the air ignites with a beam of light from the ship in front of us. It's far over our heads, but I can still feel the heat from it singeing my forehead, chest, and stomach. I take out a line of clone guards who rush us from behind the landing gear. In the span of a few seconds, we clear the boarding platform, only to have more clone guards take their place.

"Jazz, go!" I shout, gesturing to the stairs, but she won't take them. "What are you doing? Come on!"

"We have to help him!" she says, making me see that Denison's ray isn't firing. He doesn't realize it either until a few clones rush straight for him even though he's firing directly at them.

Jazz starts running toward Denison, jabbing and waving her neural baton in every direction.

"Jazz!" I shout up to her, but she can't hear me. She downs a few guards with the baton, making her way to Denison just in time to keep one of them from picking him off from behind. She takes out the clone's legs, but it doesn't stop him trying to take aim with his ray. "Jazz, look out!"

I fire on the clone, and he drops. Jazz whips around, surprised for a second until she's suddenly running toward me.

"It's OK...it's OK..." she says, but I don't know what she's talking about.

"Are you all right?" I ask, and she looks at me blankly.

Denison runs up behind her and seizes her wrist.

"Crite... All right, keep pressure right there," he says, pressing her hand high on my chest.

"What?" I say, but then touch the wet fabric of my jumpsuit. I pull my hand away and see...*blood?* The fabric of this guard uniform is red too, so I have to squint to see any contrast. "What happened?" I ask out loud. At least, I think it's out loud. Everything starts slowing down, like

I'm either waking up or falling asleep.

Denison is pulling me along with him. My legs are turning over. I'm taking steps. Jazz's mouth is moving when I look over at her, but all I can hear is a muffled alarm in the back of my head. Another bright beam of light shoots from the ship and my forehead, chest, and stomach are on fire again.

"Just a few more steps, son...Calyx! Send Arwyn to the med bay and have Jax Ripley and Lyden meet us on the landing platform now!" Denison's voice is loud next to my ear. The shock of it all of a sudden is like a slap in the face. I push up the stairs and nearly fall forward on the platform, but Denison catches me. "I got it," he adds, pressing into my chest. The burning feeling shifts to a sharp pain, and all my fog clears for a second. The clarity is gone as fast as it comes, and my legs feel like they're filled with water. Everything starts spinning, and I can't seem to get a grip on anything.

"Arco! *Arco,* hold on!" Jazz says, sliding her arm around my back. I try to put my arm around her, but Denison has it pinned to my ribs. She presses her hand over my chest again, and I hear her crying. "It's OK. You're going to be OK."

I turn toward her voice and find her face—her dark brown eyes, narrowed and spilling tears. "What happened?" I ask, but she just shakes her head at me as tears run down her cheeks.

"I don't know...I don't know. Something hit you, but you're going to be OK."

I look down again but don't see anything other than blood moving between her fingers and pushing out from under her palm. *Why is there so much blood?* I think.

"Be careful—the projectile shifted, but it's still embedded," Denison says to Jax and Lyden.

"Crite, what happened?" Jax asks, taking Denison's place.

"How is he hit? I thought they only had neural weapons?" Lyden follows, but then everyone's voices just start running together until I can't make out any words.

"Arco...*Arco!*" Jazz says, loud and clear, and it's the last thing I hear before everything gets dark and quiet.

***

I push the heels of my palms into my eyes and press to clear my vision. It's not as dark as it was, but it's not exactly bright in here either.

The room is small with one row of steel cabinets on the wall and another set of what look like refrigeration units below.

"What is this?" I hear myself say, and a second later pieces start coming back to me. My hand moves to my chest to see if there's still blood, but I only feel my skin and some kind of cloth...tape? I try to sit up but stop when I see her there curled in a chair next to me. "Jazz?"

She opens her eyes, then bolts up out of the chair. "You're OK. You're OK..."

"What happened? What is all this?"

"We're in the med bay on the Phoenix ship we took from Phase Three."

"But what *happened*? The last thing I saw was one of those clones trying to fire on you, and then everyone was dragging me into the ship. And the blood..." I look down at my chest again just to make sure I didn't miss it last time.

She wipes more tears from her face with the back of her hand and puts the other one on my chest.

"That was from when Calyx fired on the clone guards. Part of one of their neural rays broke off and hit you here. It wasn't a big piece, but it punctured your artery. Your body rejected the blood from the synth unit."

"The synth *what*?"

"Dr. Denison called it the blood cloner machine," Jazz answers, this time letting the corner of her mouth drift to an almost-smile.

I follow the tube in my arm and see an IV bag of what looks like blood. "Then what's that?"

She just looks at me now, finally letting the smile take hold. She shrugs. "I guess we're the same," she says. "Blood type, you know?"

I can only stare at her for a few seconds when she looks up at me again. The corner of her mouth quirks, and she bites her bottom lip nervously, like she's trying to think of something else to say...or maybe she's just waiting for me to reply. I brush the dark strands of hair from her cheek and stroke her bottom lip with my thumb.

She's so damn beautiful. Her long, dark hair falls over her shoulder onto my chest. I thread pieces of it through my fingers, watching it weave around my knuckles until a tear falls on the back of my hand.

"What's all this?" I ask, wiping one of them from her cheek. She leans into my hand and lowers her chin, then just lets the rest of it come. "Hey...hey...come here."

She buries her face under my jaw, and her hair falls across my throat. I comb down her back with my hand and pull her closer to me.

"If I lost you…" she whispers. "Arco…I'm sorry…I'm so sorry…" she says through heaving sobs.

My chest hurts again, but not because of the shrapnel or fused artery, or whatever else was wrecked in there. I take as deep of a breath as I can without coughing and press my lips to her forehead. "It would take more than this to keep me from you, OK? A hell of a lot more than this."

She crawls onto the gurney and curls into me, still crying so hard, she hitches for breath. I close my eyes when I feel them start to burn and blur, too, then pull her closer, stroking her hair until she falls asleep in my arms.

CHAPTER 39
The Space Between: Part Two
Jazz

I forget where I am when I open my eyes and see the metal cabinets and long, metal counter space along the wall. *Arco...* I think, but he's not lying on the gurney with me anymore. I jump down and rush into the corridor, scrambling to remember where I am and how I got down here. *We came up from the landing platform and they took him... Where did we go? Where did we turn?* I think, feeling the blood pounding in my ears.

I turn down another metallic corridor, this one with ducting and some kind of storage bins built into the walls. Just as I turn the corner, I run straight into Jax.

"Whoa!"

"Where is he?" I ask. "Where's Arco?"

"I was just coming to get you..."

"Jax!"

"OK, OK, zone. He's fine. He's in the galley." I run a few steps past him, then realize I don't know where the galley is either. I stop and look at Jax over my shoulder. He shrugs and starts talking again like this is all a big joke. "I mean, I *told* them to wake you up, but he insisted that they let you sleep. I'm only your twin brother, though, so what do I know about what you might want...and—"

"*Jax!*" I grind his name between my teeth, and he laughs.

"Oh! Would you like me to show you where the galley is?" he asks with mock surprise. "Sure. Follow me."

I punch him in the arm when he gets close enough, and he laughs again, throwing his arm around me and nearly crushing me in a half-bear hug.

We wind down a few more corridors until one corner opens into a large room with more metal fixtures. A metal countertop sits in front of a deep sink, and there are tall metal cabinets overhead. Everyone except Calyx and Lyden are sitting with Arco, who's wrapped in a blanket with a bowl of something steaming in front of him.

"Arco..." I say on the last of a breath.

He stands up, wincing a little, but then he throws off the blanket and walks toward me.

"Careful. The fuses are still bonding," Dr. Denison says sternly, but then a smile starts to move across his angular face.

"Hey..." Arco says in a quiet voice just a few inches from me.

"Hey..."

My heart pounds against my ribs being with him again. It feels like it's been years, but at the same time, like we've never been apart at all. I don't know what to do with myself standing here, somehow in between it all. I glance through the set of windows on the far end of the galley, but see only the expanse of black space.

"Where are we?"

"Somewhere they can't find us," he answers, bringing

one hand to my face and brushing my bottom lip with his thumb again. "You saved my life."

I look up at him, into his hazel eyes that are warm and kind, but now also a little sad.

"What's wrong?" I whisper. He shakes his head just a little.

"Nothing. Not one thing," he adds, then leans close and kisses me. His arm moves around my waist and pulls me close, so close and tight, I'm afraid I'll aggravate his injuries. His other hand is light over my face, his fingers combing over my jaw and down my throat, through my hair. I feel like my chest will explode until a huge clamor of applause and cheers startles us both. We laugh for a second, and he clears his throat. Mine feels like it's starting to close as tears burn my eyes *again*.

"I love you," I whisper before my throat constricts the rest of the way. "I love you, Arco."

His smile starts slowly, then lights his whole face like a sunrise. He winces through a deep breath and swallows, then pulls me into a hug.

"I tried so hard to let you go," he says quietly into my hair. "But I couldn't. I can't..." he adds, tightening his arms around me. "I won't."

The rest of the world falls away until it's just us. He still smells like the sea, and I don't think I'll ever understand how that's possible. I grip the fabric of his open shirt and pull myself as closely to him as I can as tears run down my cheeks. I feel like I might never stop crying, but I blink until I can make out what the sudden flash through the far windows could be. Arco feels me startle and lets me go.

"What is it?"

"Look..."

He turns toward the galley windows, and another flash lights up the hazy white port-cloud.

"I guess those are the fireworks," he says, taking my hand with a small chuckle.

"Fireworks?"

"The Vishan DNA we put into the Phase Three core. Yours was grafted to it when we uploaded it into the four column channels, so it will be a slower burn until it hits the port-cloud and gets direct sun," he says, smiling proudly at the imploding bursts of light. "We were just talking about how we wouldn't have made it out of there alive if we'd used the original Ignis Archive."

This makes me remember what Arco said in my channel about how Eco exposed the original DNA and ruined it.

"What happened to Eco?" I ask hesitantly. Arco doesn't answer for a long time.

"Rheen sent him to the oxygen trials—they were modifying people to withstand the cold and the lack of air in space. We didn't see him again after he sided with her."

Now it's my turn to wince. "And the doctors?"

"Our contacts at The State intercepted another Phoenix class ship that was evacuating. Rheen, Styx, and all the medical officers on staff were aboard," Calyx says, smiling at Dr. Denison. "Thanks to Briggs..."

Everyone turns to look at Dr. Denison, who just shakes his head and holds up his hands.

"All I did was upload the neural thread Jack's team

coded with the lab files and authorizations."

"Neural thread? Like the one that was originally made for Liddick?" I ask.

"Not quite..." my dad says. "This one functions more like an advertisement rather than a subliminal message. We programmed it so the download codes for the files could be consciously recognized," he adds, putting an arm around my brother, who's sitting next to him. "The State will be cleaning house once they view everything, and Reese Halliday says Admin City is being evacuated as we speak."

"So Phase Three is really gone? And the port-cloud?" I ask, looking again through the staggered explosions through the windows on the far side of the galley.

"It's a chain reaction of small disintegrations, so I imagine Phase Three itself will be completely gone in a matter of hours," my dad says. "Once the reaction hits the port-cloud—well, if you think *these* are fireworks..."

My chest swells to the point that it almost aches with happiness, but at the bottom is still a hollow feeling that I don't even have a chance to address before Arco takes my hand and faces the rest of the group.

"This part may be over," he says. "But we still have people in those tunnels on Earth. Things were critical down there—did Azeris say anything else?"

"Just that the tremors aren't sporadic, at last report," Dr. Denison answers, then taps the silver panel on his forearm. "Cally, Lyden...any report updates from Azeris? Did Liam's group and the indigenous make the rally point at Phase Two?"

"We're actually getting something right now, but it's

coming in scrambled," Lyden answers. "Here's what we have so far..."

A few seconds later, a hologram appears over the metal galley table. A beach...a mountain in the distance...

"That's Seaboard North," I say, then swallow my next question when a reporter with pink hair walks in front of the scene.

"We're here bringing you live feed from Seaboard North," she says, "where State officials are en route to assess the pulsing mini-quakes, which are occurring every hour on the hour with increasing severity. Gaia Sur and The State campus are undergoing evacuation procedures until more information is available. Monty?"

The live feed cuts out, and Lyden's voice comes over the comms again.

"We just got more. Azeris reached Liddick. The Vishan tunnels are...*flooded*. Liddick said everyone made it into the tunnel. But it's not what they thought..."

"*What?*" I ask, feeling my stomach twisting. "Where are they?"

"Azeris said Liddick's channel showed an airlock sealing behind them once they entered. They walked about a mile to another airlock, and on the other side of that was...a *ship*."

"That's impossible," I say. "That far out from the Lookout Pier is just the Rush. The *biomes*..."

"I know. But they're safe. There's life support," he says, then exhales hard. "It's a beast according to Azeris's pings. Four miles long with a mile of what looks like support infrastructure at each end—there are apparently two tunnels. The other comes out under the Phase Two facility. The ship has also started emitting some kind of pulse that's displacing the rock above the cavern. They're *moving.*"

"The Vishan prophecy…it connects their caverns with their Motherland," I say under my breath. "Wait, did you say they're *moving?* Through the cavern ceiling?"

"Yes, and no. Azeris said the cavern ceiling just… opened. But, there's an electromagnetic pulse emitting from the ship that seems to be trying to work on the seafloor."

"It's synced now…" Arco says as a drop of blood runs over his lip.

"Arco—" I turn to him and gasp, but he just keeps talking.

"That's why there had to be four columns. That's why they had to be aligned in that sequence," he adds, looking straight ahead.

Arwyn moves quickly in front of him and sprays a small, metallic cylinder into his nostrils. He waves her hand away, and the drop of blood turns into a stream.

"Crite. Arco, look at me," she asks, but he ignores her.

"There were four columns on the Lookout Pier. The coordinates were for those columns…" he rambles.

"Arco! *Look at me!*"

"It was a program…a launch system…"

"Help me with him," Dr. Denison says to Jax. They both rush to his side and start walking back toward the med bay.

"Arco, what's happening? What program?" I almost shout as blood starts streaming onto the floor. "Arco!"

He meets my eyes for a fraction of a second until his head falls forward.

Dr. Denison swears. "I should have taken the damn thing out with that shrapnel!"

"What's happening to him!?" I ask again, and this time, I'm shouting.

"It's the surge—his brain hemispheres…" Arwyn finally explains, catching up to me.

"What does that *mean!?*"

She speeds up until she falls into line with Dr. Denison and Jax. I start to speed up too until my dad catches my arm and pulls me against him.

"Stop, stop…" he says. "Listen, it's a fast burn. His mind, Jazwyn. It's evolving faster than his body can keep handle. It's a natural process for Gaia cadets under normal circumstances, but not this fast. It happens over a lifetime…not days."

"Why? Why is that happening to him?"

"He's a hybrid—a Navigator/Coder. With the Empath Latency, it's just the right cocktail. These traits are naturally occurring, but the nanites you all received were designed to produce growth with organic situational stimuli—even though his were wiped, the neural pathways have already been created. "

"*Dad!* Just tell me!"

"Calm down. Calm down. You've all been through so much that the situations have triggered an advanced survival system in his brain. He can sense direction and location at what seems like a psychic level now. He can read code like a story. It's all just survival mechanisms—"

"Then *why* is he *bleeding* like that!?" I scream. My dad

pulls me into a tight hug. I push against him until I can't anymore. It's all too close to the surface, and I just let the tears come. Again. I let the weight crush my chest until I collapse against him. We've come this far. We've destroyed the Phase Three labs. The port-cloud is disintegrating. We've won. *We're supposed to have won.*

"Listen to me, Jazwyn. He'll be fine. This is what Briggs does, OK? Everything will be all right. He'll be all right..."

CHAPTER 40
The Surge
Arco

Blood is in my teeth. I can taste the tinge of metal, but more compelling is the string of molecular symbols and numbers that scroll over my vision whenever I think about there being blood in my teeth.

OXYGEN.
IRON.
WATER < 1 HYDROGEN, 2 OXYGEN.
SODIUM.
NITROGEN.

The list goes on, factoring into just numbers and random letters that I know is the chemical makeup of my *own* blood down to the molecule—the *weight* of each molecule.

I stop thinking about the blood, and the scrolling list disappears. The image of the four pillars rising out of the Vishan Lookout Pier washes back into my line of sight. Coordinates scroll in the lower third of the image, and though I don't read them, I know they are location points for each individual column and the platform rising up in the center.

If I look at any one person running down the steps that have opened from the center platform, the scrolling at the bottom of my vision turns into another chemical analysis of their bone and muscle weight...their water volume...their brain chemistry... My head starts to hurt. *Too much at once. Too many equations.* I focus on the platform again...on the numbers and colors between it and each column. Magnetic waves. *I'm looking at magnetic waves?*

The tunnel is a ship, not a tunnel. The columns are receivers. They were programmed. I did this. I launched that ship, I think, feeling like my head is flooding with water. *I have to tell someone. They're going to crack the ocean floor. They're going to kill everyone.*

"He's seizing!" My sister's voice is loud and sharp. It makes the scrolling and the colors wipe away like a page turn, along with the image of the columns and the ship just below.

My chest is tight. My fists are clenched. *Am I being electrocuted?*

"Right here, son. Look right here." Denison's voice is quieter than my sister's. "Look right here," he says again just before a purple light floods my vision. My chest loosens, and my hands relax.

"Ship..." I hear myself say.

"What ship? What ship, Arco?" my sister asks, bringing something silver to my face. Before I can answer, a cold blast shoots up my nose and cools the heat in the back of my head. It's the best feeling in the world.

"The tunnel he found. It's a ship. I launched it."

I can't blink. I can't blink my eyes.

"Who, Azeris? The tunnel Azeris found?"

"Yes. I launched it. The Phase Three columns...I

aligned them with…the platform pillars. An old… permission relay," I mumble, and finally, I can close my eyes.

"A *what?*" my sister asks.

"He's talking about a clearance code," Denison says. "Tell Lyden to run a trace for code acknowledgements coming into Phase Three before the explosions. All right. He's stabilizing," he says again. My eyes are closed, but I can still see the opaque purple light—no codes, no images, no more symbols or numbers. And I'm dead tired.

***

The purple light is gone when I open my eyes, and my head is pounding. The first thing I see are more tubes running up my arm, but everything hurts so much, I don't even care. Even blinking is painful. My throat feels like I've been chugging sand, and I try to clear it.

"You're awake…" Jazz says. I turn to her too fast. "Try not to move, you have a lot of…attachments."

"Why?" is all I can manage to say.

"They said you *surged*. Denison took your tracker out while you were asleep, so it shouldn't happen again."

"No!" I say as loudly as I can, which makes me cough. Pain shoots through my neck and into my chest like a spear through the back of my head.

"It's OK…*it's OK*. You won't lose your Nav or Coder abilities," she says, gripping my hand. "You just won't be able to use them at the same time anymore. At least not for a while."

"I need to be able to do that! We're not finished!"

"Arco…it's done. The port-cloud is going to come

down. Do you remember the DNA? The columns?"

"*That's* what I'm talking about—the columns I saw in your channel, Jazz. The platform. That wasn't a tunnel underneath the Lookout Pier. It was a *ship*. That was the Arc Sequence…crite, I launched it when I brought you here."

"Arco, we know…you have to relax," she says, shaking her head at me like I'm delusional.

"*Damn it,* no! Where's my sister? I need all this unhooked. I need to talk to Denison."

A blue hologram grid on the wall turns red and starts beeping.

"Stop—Arco, *stop!*" Jazz says, gripping my wrists so I can't pull out the stupid IV and taped-on monitor pads.

"We need to warn people. The ship is unfathomably big, do you understand? It will—"

She moves in fast and kisses me hard.

I stop searching for tubes to pull. I stop everything. Her fingers brush my face and I find her waist, pulling her down over me. Pain shoots through my chest again and wraps around the back of my head, but I don't care. I don't even remember why it hurts.

"Hey, you're going to rip open your sutures," my sister says, half-laughing. Crite, if one more person interrupts us, I'm going to kill them.

Jazz pulls back abruptly and stands up next to me. Arwyn taps a bunch of things onto the holographic grid display, and it goes back to normal just as Denison walks in.

"You have a penchant for self-destruction," he says through a grin. "Too bad the nanites will take care of any battle scars you could tell your kids about someday after all this," he adds. "Pretty nasty laser burn on your shoulder, we removed a shard of a neural ray that was lodged in your chest, and for at least a little while longer, you'll have a two-inch incision at the base of your skull."

I look up at my sister in surprise. She raises her eyebrows and nods at me.

"From the tracker?" is all I can say. My sister and Jazz nod while Denison turns to the holographic display on the wall and taps until a scrolling block of text appears.

"Looks like you've leveled out—how do you feel?" he asks.

"Fine," I answer. He cocks a white eyebrow at me. I roll my eyes. "OK, sore, I guess, but not enough to stay in this bed anymore. We need to warn people on the surface. That ship is going to launch."

"It already has," Denison says without hesitation. "You don't remember Azeris's report?"

"*What?*" I press. Denison exchanges glances with my sister. "I can handle it. Just tell me."

"His pings are showing that the electromagnetic pulse from the ship is displacing a meter of ocean floor every twelve hours."

"Vox and everyone made it into the ship," Jazz says. "They're all safe."

"What are we still doing up here? We need to warn everyone on the coast. That pulse is going to cause a tsunami that will level *everything*. We only have so much time!"

I try to do the math, to pull up the equations in my peripheral vision like I could before, but I just get an ice pick between my eyes. I suck in a sharp breath through my teeth and press my hands to my forehead.

"Don't do that," Denison says. "That connection isn't there anymore. The nerves are going to take at least another day to rebuild even with the new nanites."

"Did you hear what I said!? People are going to die!"

"No, they're not. The displacement rate isn't fast enough; we ran the numbers."

"Your numbers are *wrong!*"

"Arco, listen," Jazz says, taking my hand again. "We're going right now to rendezvous with Ms. Reynolt, Myra, Avis, and Ellis. You can talk with Avis about it, OK?"

"I'm not talking to anyone until they get people out of Seaboard North, "I insist." Do they at least know what's coming? Do people know about that ship?"

Denison crosses to tap something into the holographic grid on the wall. The charts and monitors disappear, giving way to a reporter in the middle of a sentence.

"—scene has been tense with what seismic experts are calling *tectonic tremors,* causing the rising tide to lash the shoreline. Concentrated efforts to secure the local fisher community as well as the Seaboard North residents are in effect with the Skyboard Council setting up shelters and donating food, water, clothing, and personal items to aid the effort during this very strange event, Monty."

"Thank you, Electra," another reporter says as the screen flashes back to a studio with the Seaboard North coastline in the backdrop. "We have Spokesperson Cole Daniels with us in the studio now to help shed some light on what might be causing the tremors. Spokesperson, what could it be?"

"*Daniels* was in the hangar! Why isn't he locked up?" I look over at Denison, who just shakes his head.

"We've been assured by several sources that it's just a little tectonic friction," Daniels says, "likely to subside in a few days or so, Monty. We're evacuating the shoreland communities, as well as Gaia Sur and The State complex strictly as a precaution."

The reporter raises an eyebrow. "Spokesperson, we've received intel from our own sources that *sinkholes* have appeared in the ocean floor that span several miles. Can you confirm?"

"Yes, Monty, these are occurring approximately twenty miles from The State and Gaia Sur campus. We do not expect damage to these areas, but again, we have evacuated just as a precaution. Everything is contained. No cause for worry." Daniels smiles directly into the feed, and I suddenly feel violently ill.

Something beeps, so Denison kills the feed and brings back the holographic charts.

I point to the now blank feed screen. "I told you. Sinkholes that go miles deep. The water is already breaking high on the beach, you *heard* her..."

"*Miles deep* is impossible at that rate of the displacement. I only turned the feed on so you could see the evacuation loop report," Denison says, tapping onto the charts. "Your levels are rising again."

"OK...one thing at a time. How much longer until we connect with the Wraith?" I ask.

Denison checks his arm panel and sighs. "Looks like they heard about the ship too. They're going topside."

CHAPTER 41
Debriefing
Jazz

"That's the Wraith," Arco says, pointing to the huge, almost metallic ship that's already docked at a private hangar in Skyboard North. Dr. Denison lands our Phoenix next to it, and a tall man with thick, white hair is waiting for us when we come down the ramp.

"Well, you're a bit worse for wear," the man says, seeing the bandages through Arco's open shirt. He offers his hand.

"Good to see you again, Dr. Halliday," Arco says, taking it.

"And who might this be?"

"This is Jazwyn Ripley. Jazz, this is Dr. Halliday. He helped us with the testing victims from Phase Three. This is his facility." Arco turns back to Dr. Halliday. "How are the test subjects doing?"

"Several of them are stable," he answers, then sighs. "And...some of them are not. We're doing the best we can." Arco nods, and for several seconds it feels like someone has sucked out all the air around us. *"Ripley..."* Dr. Halliday says, raising an eyebrow at me. "Any relation to Jack Ripley?" he asks just as my dad and Jax make their way toward us down the ship's ramp. "I'll be damned...it's true."

"Good to see you, Reese," my dad says, walking into Dr. Halliday's huge hug.

"Jazz!" Myra's voice comes from nowhere, and I spin around in the direction of it to find her running toward me from the Wraith. She barely stops before throwing her arms around me so suddenly that I stumble backward. *"Jazz!"* she shouts my name again too close to my ear and immediately starts sobbing. "Did you see the explosions? Did you see them start?"

"I did..." I answer, feeling my throat start to constrict again.

"And they're safe. They're safe, Jazz. They found a ship down there! A ship..." She trails off in a mixture of laughing and crying.

"I know, I know..." I keep saying, hugging her as tightly as I can. Avis and Ellis poke Myra on either side of her ribs until she laughs and lets me go.

"There is a *line* forming here, Myra," Ellis says, wrapping one long arm around me as Avis does the same on my other side.

"Did you shrink? I think you shrunk. Space stunts your growth, you know," Avis says, flipping his blue-edged wing of black hair out of his eyes to compare our heights.

"Mollusk, we were not at zero gravity," Ellis says, and Avis rolls his eyes.

"It was a *joke*, crite. Can you program some nanites with a sense of humor please?" he says, glancing again at me and whispering, "You know I know about gravity. It was a joke."

We all laugh at this. Even Ellis cracks a smile and

shoves Avis's shoulder. They lead on ahead of me, taking turns pushing each other off balance.

Jazwyn... I hear in my head, and I don't even need to look to know it's Ms. Reynolt. I turn around and see her open her arms, and I rush into them.

I can't breathe, not even a little. The air just hits a wall when it reaches my chest. I start the breath over and over again, but it just results in a convulsive cycle of sobbing that flushes out everything that has happened since we sat for our interviews. How many decades have gone by since that day? How many millennia? Everything from that life seems so small and so far away now.

She grips my shoulders and smiles just before touching her forehead to mine. She cups my chin like my mother used to do when I was small and smiles at me in the same proud way. She doesn't think or say another word, and she doesn't have to for me to understand that there just aren't any that could contain how this feels right now.

"This way," Dr. Halliday says. I've made arrangements for you to stay at...a *former colleague's* hab. The heliocar is already loaded with the destination." He says, offering his arm to Ms. Reynolt. She takes it, and Arco wraps his arm around my shoulder again. I lean my head against his chest as we walk past a huge angular house, which is hidden behind several palm trees.

I keep looking up from there, scanning the sky for the pending port-cloud explosions, but there's only the perma-haze that blankets everything.

"Shouldn't the port-cloud be coming down by now?" I ask.

Arco scans the sky too. "Not yet. Phase Three isn't even finished disintegrating. Once it starts going down, there will be chaos. The Grid is up there."

Dr. Halliday opens the door to a dark, pear-shaped heliocar with a wave of his hand, then nods to Ms. Reynolt. "After you."

Dr. Denison, Calyx, my dad, Jax, and Fraya also load into the heliocar, which fills it to capacity.

"Guess that means you're with us," Azeris says, hovering to a stop next to us in another heliocar, only this one is red.

"*Azeris!*" I say, "Is Zoe…?" I trail off, suddenly afraid to ask.

"Riding shotgun, uh, yes," she says, vaulting to the front. "One of you all can babysit that gear," she says with a quick chin jerk over her shoulder. She taps the side of the red heliocar once, and the door slides up and away. In the center of the seat circle is a box of blinking panels and metal pieces with wires everywhere.

"Excuse the mess," Azeris says. "We were in a bit of a hurry on account of fleeing for our lives and whatnot. You coming or…?"

"Excellent!" Avis says, heading straight for the box. "This is a Class Seven Seismograph! Only The State has these!"

"Is that a Neural Wave Calibrator?" Ellis asks, following Avis into the heliocar. Lyden and Arwyn exchange knowing smiles and get in on the other side of them. This leaves only one seat left, and Arco raises an eyebrow at me.

"Looks like I'll have to sit on your lap." He smiles. I

can't hold back the laugh, and especially not when he pokes me in the ribs and takes the last seat. He extends a hand to me. "Come on…"

Once we're inside, the door slides closed, and Azeris taps the long, wraparound dashboard.

"All in?" he asks. "All right. Brenda, let's go."

"Of course, Dr. Wright," the heliocar says in almost the same arrow voice from Gaia. "Beginning course for home."

***

We're in the air before I can sort out the details of what just happened…that this is Liam's *clone's* car, which means we're going to Liam's clone's *hab* too? *He's* the former colleague Dr. Halliday was talking about? The stacked rectangular building comes into view as we come through a grove of palm trees, the front of it almost entirely made of glass.

"So…I'm going to go ahead and ask," Arco says. "What happened to the clone?"

"That doctor called it over for some emergency construction—"

"*Consultation*…" Azeris corrects.

"Right, consultation," Zoe continues, "and stuck a needle full of carbon something-something in its eyeball."

"Carbon *disulfide?*" Ellis asks in disbelief.

"Yeah, that. Right in its *eyeball!* Killed it dead to ash right there in the hangar."

"Crite…" Myra whispers, bringing her hands to her mouth. "Then that means this is…his hab?" she adds as we clear the palm trees and start lowering to the ground.

"Arrived, Dr. Wright. Enjoy your evening," the heliocar says.

"So how are we supposed to get in there?" Arco asks.

"Bioprint!" Azeris pulls out a surgical glove and slides it on, flashing a wide smile. "We had a little time before his hand disintegrated." He shrugs.

Arco opens his mouth to say something but just closes it and blinks a few times. He presses his lips into a flat smile and nods. "All right then."

"Careful with the gear, campers," Azeris says to Avis and Ellis. They scoff at him like they've never been more insulted. Myra meets my eyes with amazement, and we both stifle a laugh at this whole situation.

"Well, come on 'fore the Bale bites ya," Zoe says, already out of the heliocar and several steps toward the hab. She doesn't get another step before the ground seems to open up and swallow everything. Her smiling face withers when she realizes what she's said about the predatory grain crop from the Vishan cavern. I feel the ache start in her like needing to breathe, but not being able to. Before I can say anything to offset it for her, she's clearing her throat and waving us on again. "Well, come on."

We make our way up the lamp-lit walk, which brightens as we approach and dims as we pass. Azeris presses his gloved hand to the door panel, making it slide open.

"Good evening, Dr. Wright," a woman's voice says. I startle and immediately feel my heart start pounding in my chest.

Arco grips my hand and gives me a sideways smile as

we walk into the front room of the hab, which opens to a sitting area with four long, white couches and a coffee table in the center.

"Why does a clone need this much space?" Avis asks, coming up behind us with the others.

"Appearances, probably," Arco answers.

"Does that mean it eats for appearances too?" Jax asks. "That looks like a matter board to me, kids. Get set up and I'll program some sandwiches."

He walks toward the kitchen counter area with Fraya and Myra not far behind while the rest of us move into the sitting area. Avis, Ellis, and Azeris begin assembling whatever seismic neural thing is in the box they've set down, and Arco searches for a neural feed panel in the wall. He waves his hand over it, which turns on a report that's already happening.

"Thank you, Monty. Breaking news tonight: Highland shelter evacuation efforts for all Seaboard North and inland communities have now been expedited to priority one, despite assurances from Spokesperson Daniels's office that these are only precautionary in nature. Spokesperson Daniels *himself* could not be reached for further comment. The Maritime Council tells us the source of the tremors seems to be originating from beneath the ocean floor roughly 1,500 miles offshore, though specifics regarding that source are still being investigated. The waves here continue to grow in strength each hour, and as you can see, Monty," she says, gesturing behind her, "these breakers are now nearly six feet high from just two-foot whitecaps earlier today. Stay tuned to Network Eight for—"

Dr. Denison waves a hand over the feed, making it vanish when Jax, Fraya, and Myra return passing out plates of sandwiches and drinks.

Arco shakes his head, still looking in the direction of where the feed was playing.

"They're too close. Skyboard is too close. Six-foot waves are nothing. It's going to be a *tsunami*," he says, pushing his hands over his face. "Ling, tell them," he says after another second, looking up at Avis.

"Tell them what?"

"The tremors are getting stronger, you heard that? And a few hours ago the waves were less than half the size. Do the math, man."

Avis looks over his shoulder from the feed assembly he's working on and shrugs. "Can't *assume* the waves will just keep compounding, but if they do, yeah, that's going to get hostile."

"There, she's ready," Azeris says, connecting a final cord and then flipping several switches on the side of the assembly, which looks like a small satellite dish on top of two rows of thick, coiled spring. A screen display panel sits over the front of the coils and is attached in the back with metal S-clips.

I know it doesn't look very sophisticated, Lyden thinks, *but it's powerful.* I glance up at him and half-smile, forgetting completely that he can read me just like Liddick can.

"What does it do?" Fraya asks.

"Measures and tracks the electromagnetic pulse coming through the water, mainly. I'm still working on it, but sometimes we're also able to capture that ship's feed," he adds, and after another few seconds, some grid lines waver in and out.

"On the Phoenix I was trying to trace the developer of the permission relay Arco discovered, but the code is at least a hundred years old," Lyden adds.

"Well, looks like she's in a good mood tonight." Azeris nods, then laughs to himself while tapping something else into the side of the assembly. "See what you can make of this."

CHAPTER 42
The Hole in the Sky
Arco

The display screen fills with columns of code and what look like blueprint images...*layouts?*

"What are those?" Jazz asks.

"Plans," I answer, moving closer. "And trajectory maps for the pilots."

The lines in the code fold and bend into boxes, triangles, ovals, and rectangles until they all zoom out and take the shape of a...*city?*

"Maps to where?" Calyx asks, making the image warble with her voice.

"Somewhere that doesn't exist...but will. Phase Three was only the beginning," I say as quietly as I can so I don't affect the graphics.

"How can he be reading that fast?" Jazz asks. I narrow my eyes to push her voice out too.

"Shut it off," my sister says, nearly wiping the entire display I'm seeing, but not before I understand what they were building and why.

"They were going to colonize it..."

"Colonize the *port-cloud?*" Avis asks.

"He's bleeding!" Fraya says.

"Shut it off!" Denison says this time. The images of the small city rattle and blur until they completely wash

away and the display screen, which is frozen now, comes back into focus.

"Here..." Fraya says, handing me a tissue. Arwyn crosses to me with another blast of oxygen or whatever is in that little metal cylinder. It stops the bleeding, but I feel like I've just fallen out of a window and landed on my head.

"I thought you said that would stop happening when you took the tracker out," Jazz says, her voice restrained and tight. Denison looks at me, baffled.

"It...It should have," he says, exchanging glances with Arwyn. "Unless..."

"His neurons remembered the pathways and...*remade* them," Arwyn says quietly.

"Arco, look at me," Jazz says, and a second later she's straddling my legs to sit directly in front of me. *"Arco..."*

I pull in a deep breath and close my eyes to clear my head, then finally look at her.

"There were blueprints...coordinates. They even uploaded docking instructions," I say.

"Wait, he's right," Azeris says, reading the frozen assembly screen and comparing it with a newly projected holographic display of...*Admin City?* "The embedded coordinates align with an area about half a click from there..." He pauses. "But there's nothing out there, according to these scans. "

"There's a trading post..." I say, studying the display above our heads and remembering when Tark and I picked up the zephyr from Fargo there.

Calyx sucks in a quick breath. "That post is almost right on top of the port-cloud."

"Oh, no," Jazz says, all the blood draining from her face. "How long before the DNA reaches it?"

"Hard to say since we can't see the destruction progress on Phase Three anymore," Lyden says.

"Wait, are you saying that ship is heading into an explosion?" Zoe asks, holding out both hands, as if that will keep the answer from jumping at her.

"This can't be happening," Ms. Reynolt says, then covers her mouth.

"Turn the feed back on," I say. "Maybe I can find a way to follow the trajectory path and—"

"No," my sister cuts me off. "Your hemispheres are syncing again *without* the tracker interface. You might not come out of it this time."

"Then at least turn on the audio," I insist, but she just stares at me. "*Arwyn*, we need to know when that cloud is going to explode. They're going to head right into it!" After another second, she reluctantly agrees, nodding to Azeris.

The audio warbles at first, and then I actually hear another frequency fall into sync. "Standby...we got 'em. We got 'em!" Azeris almost sings.

"Wait, what? Then turn on visuals too," I say, getting to my feet. My sister opens her mouth, no doubt to protest, but I stop her before she can start. "We fired it up for trajectory feedback, but he just *linked with the ship itself*. Azeris, turn it back on!"

"No!" Arwyn shouts me down. "I'm not risking your life after we've come this far!" Her voice catches on a sob.

"—faster than—the threshold speed is holding, but not sure how—can last..."

"That's Liddick's voice!" Jazz says.

"*Riptide!* How—there? I thought—off the—Pier!"

"Long story we ain't got time to explain right now," Azeris says. "We got a job here for you."

"Is he *piloting*?" Lyden asks.

"No," Azeris answers. "The feedback says it's on autopilot until the crew signatures are entered...but even with those, they don't know how to pilot that thing."

"Vox is with them," Jazz says. "She's a Navigator."

"As a secondary proclivity," Ms. Reynolt says. "Her primary is Reader Empath."

"Azeris—still hear me? We're showing trajectories through—undertows. Seeing effects—chop—happening topside?"

"We've got six-foot breakers and climbing, along with tremors from that electromagnetic pulse your heap is emitting."

"—can't stop—ic pulses—"

"Listen," Azeris starts, then exchanges glances with Denison and Jack.

"Tell him," Denison says. "Vox's Nav class may be secondary, but Liam's primary class is Coder. Between the two of them, maybe they can work on the trajectory."

"All right, listen, there ain't an easy way to say this... you have to try to reprogram the trajectory, wise? That ship is trying to take you to ground zero of the port-cloud explosion."

No one else talks for a few seconds, and it's just long enough for me to listen to the frequency again, as broken as it is. *How fast are they going? Where are they?* I think.

Equations start to populate in the dark—the dark

water leaking through the rock fissures all around them and boring them up toward the seafloor. I hear the electromagnetic pulse of the ship under their voices, under the frequency warble. I hear the rock cracking and crumbling above them, which makes more equations fly into focus. I don't do the calculations. I just watch them solve themselves and come to life like the most jacked virtuo-cine ever made.

"Arco!" Jazz gasps, the shock of it sending a spike of adrenaline through me. All the equations collapse back into symbols and numbers...into the totals of a scrolling report.

"I lost the audio—" Azeris starts, but I push the rest of whatever he says away so I can focus on the totals coming into view.

"They're going to break through six miles of seafloor in seven hours, at an impact of eighty-seven knots. The debris field is getting softer, less compacted. The electromagnetic pulse is going farther. They're picking up speed," I hear myself say, but I'm watching the impact of that ship take shape behind my eyelids, the symbols and speed formulas breaking apart and forming the images just like before.

"Arco, *stop*. You're bleeding again!" Jazz says, but I push her voice away because it makes the images blur and fade.

"The impact will hit all points along the six-mile stretch at the same time with equalized displacement value..." I laugh in disbelief. "The ship accounted for variances in the rock thickness...incredible."

"What's happening? The visuals are off! How is he

getting *any* of that?" my sister says.

"I think he's...*hearing* it," Ms. Reynolt says.

"We need to stop that bleeding. Help me with him," Denison says. People grip my arms from both sides. I struggle until the effort distorts and fades the images too, and I try to refocus on the sound of the feed. *It's working...it's working.*

"Wait—a six-mile breach in seven hours at eighty-seven knots...they're about 7,000 meters down..." Avis says. "Figure gravity at 9.81 meters per second...they're 1,500 miles out. No...crite...it's too fast. The wave from that impact would wipe out everything like, almost a mile up the Skyboard mountain."

"2,087 feet..." I say, watching the square root symbol in the corner of my vision stretch and bow upward, blocking out the setting sun against the water in the image. "It's coming."

"Turn it off!" Jazz's scream wipes the images out of my head for good this time. I open my eyes and Denison has a small, purple penlight in my face, and the room is spinning.

"Hey, *whoa...*" Jax says, gripping my arm.

"Let...me up..." I say.

"Arco...be still. Can you hear me?" Jazz asks, pushing something *else* into my face.

"*Stop...* Everybody, stop. It's OK."

"No, it's *not* OK," she says, pulling back a cloth full of blood. I take it from her and force myself to sit up.

"I'm OK, listen to me... *Damn it*, where's that oxygen thing?" I find it on the coffee table and shoot a blast of it to stop the nosebleed that has already half-soaked the little towel I took from Jazz. "The wave that's coming... that will be the biggest wave in history. A train of them has already started. The swells are growing. They will *keep* growing as long as that pulse keeps coming. The culminating tsunami will level everything for several miles inland *and* nearly a mile up the Skyboard mountain."

Everyone just stares at me until Ellis breaks the silence.

"If he's right," he says, "then the people being evacuated are not at high enough ground. The shelters are only just within the Skyboard Mountain limits. We have to inform the Maritime Council."

"And tell them what?" Avis asks. "We know it's true because our friend with the psychic nosebleed powers told us?" He shakes his head.

"Aren't there people whose *whole job* is predicting this stuff? They'll have to realize the evacuations aren't going high enough, right?" Jax asks, obviously trying to keep his voice level.

"They don't even know what's causing the tremors," I say. "And they won't be able to see the trajectory until it's too late."

"All right. Everyone, stop talking for a minute," Denison says, then scrubs his hands over his face. "The first problem is this hemorrhaging. Those oxygen freezes are a bandage, and I don't have much more than some basic diagnostic tools and bandages in my gear. We need to get back to Reese's clinic."

"Is anyone listening to what I'm saying?" I press.

"Son, do you understand you may not be around to

say much more if we don't get that brain bleed under control?" Denison snaps, then takes a controlled breath. "You want to help people, then let us help you first, all right? I need equipment." He turns his attention to Ms. Reynolt. "Luz, have you had any contact with Sandra?"

"She's not answering her cues."

"Is this another teacher?" I ask.

"No, she's one of our insiders with The State. She can get help rerouting the evacuees," Ms. Reynolt answers. "In the meantime, I have contacts at Skyboard Secondary Prep who can help us relocate people there. It's three miles above sea level."

Denison nods to her. "Good. I'll cue Reese and let him know we're coming back."

CHAPTER 43
Three Places at Once
Jazz

Arco paces back and forth from the door to the far end of the sitting room while we wait for Dr. Denison to return from cueing Dr. Halliday.

"How did that ship even get down there?" he asks, shaking his head.

"What we know is that it's at least a hundred years old, if we're going by the age of its navigation code," Lyden says.

"But people have been in the tunnels down there for *two hundred* years…" I add. "Doesn't that mean the Phase Two facility and whatever that dome thing is had to be there *at least* that long for *a ship* to be buried in the rock?"

Lyden shakes his head at the ground. *"Two* hundred years ago…they would have had to lower rigs down through that volcano to print the facility and the dome. The biomes and the ship *could* have come later, but…"

"Either way, they were going to leave Earth at some point—maybe it was an emergency escape plan in case they were caught?" Fraya says.

Ellis raises his eyebrows. "A ship that big? It's more likely they were using passage as a bribe for partnership. As in, when everything goes to hell here, you and yours can come with us…to our paradise rock landing in space.

"Right." Arco nods. "We triggered their launch too early, and look how long it's taking to get airborne. That ship was meant to leave for good, regardless of the fallout, and without anything in pursuit."

"We have another problem," Dr. Denison says, gripping the frame of the doorway to the sitting room. "Reese picked up the cue and then disconnected it, but it was long enough for him to tell me there were a few State Patrols there looking around. They must have traced the Phoenix and the Wraith somehow."

"What does that mean?" Myra asks.

"It means we're not safe here. Where those ships came from is not common knowledge—either someone went looking for them and is not going to stop until they find who brought them here, or Van Spaulding saw the newsfeed with Reese and didn't like his speculations about that Organic we left on the perimeter."

"Those Patrols *will kill* them, Briggs," Ms. Reynolt says.

"I know…I know…I'm thinking."

The floor starts to vibrate, just a little at first to where I'm not even sure it's really happening, but after a few seconds, the feeling shoots through my knees and makes me grip the edge of the couch.

"What's happening?" Myra asks in a pinched voice.

Glass breaks somewhere in the room, and the neural feed on the wall turns on again by itself.

"—I repeat, *not* naturally occurring tremors, Monty, but updated reports from The Maritime Council have determined that the source of the disturbances is originating about 1,500 miles offshore. The swells continue to grow and are expected to culminate in an estimated tsunami scale wave that is predicted to hit landfall in approximately two and a half hours. As investigations continue, Shoreland Council personnel have mandated evacuation for Seaboard North and all inland communities. Shuttles are running on a loop to the Southern Skyboard North evacuation centers. Please only bring critical items with you so shuttles may accommodate as many people—"

The feed turns off again with a sudden, stronger rumble, which then fades completely away. Everything is still again as we all get to our feet slowly, just to be sure.

"Did you hear that? She said that wave is going to hit in *two and a half* hours!" Ellis says.

"If we're lucky," Avis says, shaking his head. "If that tremor was the pulse effect all the way up here, it has to be battle ramming the ocean floor."

"We have to leave now," Arco says, commanding everyone's attention. "Azeris, if Spaulding's men are already watching your hab, is there somewhere else we can go with tech capabilities to stop that ship?"

"There's one place, but it's inland. We won't have much time."

"Thank you, thank you, Sandra. We'll be ready," Ms. Reynolt says, coming back into the room. She lowers her hand from her temple and turns to us. "Sandra got my cues. They've just realized the destruction will be more than anticipated and have already opened the school. They're rerouting people, but it's not going to be a small job."

Denison blows out a surprised, relieved breath.

"Finally, some good news."

"There's more," she says, furrowing her brow. "There's been an accident near the Seaboard school just off the coast—a shuttle collision on the tracks. There's a massive fire they're trying to put out, but with so much smoke, they can't get back to the shore for a final sweep like they've been doing in the outlying areas."

"But that's exactly where our families live," I say, feeling the blood suddenly pounding in my ears.

"I asked about their estimates of how many people are still there. They've already done a few sweeps, and air support doesn't see anyone on the ground."

"But how will we know for sure?" Myra asks. "Can we find out if they're already at the evacuation sites?"

"We'll have to figure out what to do on the way—she sent a transport that will be here any minute for us."

"One transport? What if we need to carry more people? Even just our families alone wouldn't fit," I say, shaking my head at Ms. Reynolt. She can only draw her brows together in reply.

"We'll figure it out," Jax says.

"We'll find them." My father presses his lips into a determined line.

"This is the only way to be in three places at once." Arco nods. "Who's going to Reese's clinic?"

Before I can even process what he's just said, Calyx is already volunteering.

"I'll go. We have a few from The Seam in the area. They'll help," she says, tapping her temple to access her cue line.

"Arwyn, you need to make sure Mom and Dad get to

the school, all right? You have to make sure they get out," Arco says.

"Your surges…" she starts to reply, but trails off when her voice breaks. My stomach sinks and twists… Helplessness *again.*

"I'll go with him," Denison says, gripping her shoulder. "Don't worry. I'll keep him on a short leash." The corner of his mouth twitches as he gives Arco a sideways smile.

My head is spinning with the reality of this whole discussion setting in. There's no question I have to go with my father and brother to make sure the rest of our family gets to higher ground…to make sure everyone in our stacks gets to higher ground. *But that means I have to leave Arco. Again.*

"And you'll meet us there," Lyden says to Arco, briefly meeting my eyes. His lips quirk in an almost smile as I take a deep breath and feel the tightness in my chest start to dissipate. The reassuring feeling has to be from him, and I don't care if it's not real… I don't care if he's pushing it on me. It's the only thought keeping me from drowning in the alternative.

"In two hours," I say abruptly, interrupting the dismissive agreement Arco has already started to give Lyden with his nodding. My throat starts to tighten again, and my words crack. "No more than two hours, Arco."

He sighs, all dismissiveness aside now. He crosses to me and pulls me into his arms. "It's OK," he says, brushing his thumbs over my cheeks, and it's only then that I realize there are tears running down my face. "I'll be there," he whispers into my hair. "You think a stupid 2,000-foot tsunami can keep me away from you?" He laughs, and for some reason, the sound of it makes my chest seize with tears that can't seem to find their way out. I grip the back of his shirt and pull closer to him.

"Promise me."

"I promise. *I promise…*"

"Uh, we interrupt this beautiful moment to inform you that we only have one heliocar," Avis says, opening the front door and extending his hand like the vehicle is going to fly right in at any second, then quickly shuts the door. "Crite, they're here! They found us!"

Calyx rushes to the window. "Settle down, killjoy— that's my ride." She blows out a breath and winks.

Avis blanches. "*How* are they here already?"

"I said they were in the area," she shrugs. "Everyone, meet at the school in two hours, no matter what. All our destinations right now are going to be wiped out when that wave hits, all right?"

"And our trackers are still connected, correct?" Ellis asks. She nods to him, and a second later is out the door.

Avis and Ellis stand next to me with Arco, along with Zoe, Azeris, and Dr. Denison. My chest feels hollow again as we watch her go, like I'm falling, and everything inside me has been left somewhere above.

***

A large, black shuttle bus glides to a stop at the end of the walkway several minutes later. I've never seen a heliocar this big before, and I panic for a second that it won't stay in the air. In the same moment I remember the Phoenix ship we landed in and push the fear away.

"Jazz, hurry," my brother says, waving me toward the door. I start to jog and catch up with him after a handful of strides. He gets in after me and shuts the door.

"This is Jazz and her brother, Jax Ripley," Ms. Reynolt says to the driver. He seems familiar with his ponytailed hair sticking out from the back of his hat. It's dark like my father's, but that's not why he's familiar.

"Fancy meeting you here, ain't it?" he says, and then I remember.

"You're Liddick's friend from the tunnels."

"In the flesh."

"He's one of your contacts?" I ask Ms. Reynolt. She shakes her head at me as we start to move.

"No, he's one of Sandra's. He's with The Seam."

"But how—?" I start, then realize I have no idea how to say anything about this economically.

"Liddick didn't know I'm with The Seam," he says. "I got involved because of him, though. When he went looking for Liam those years back. The Seam would have recruited him too if he hadn't been tapped for Gaia Sur. He asked the right questions," Finn adds, looking over his shoulder again at me with a small, remorseful smile.

"He was in the *Vishan* tunnels with you and Liddick?" my father asks. "How?"

"He helped us get away from Spaulding's men," I say. Finn clears his throat.

"*And* served as double agent extraordinaire when our golden boy came off of the Grid freshly minted as a new Biotech subliminal storyboarder. I never want to see *that* look on his face again, crite."

"You were there! Then you know..." I say, turning to

Jax and the others. "See, I told you. I told you Liddick didn't betray us. Spaulding tricked him."

"That's the truth," Finn says. "Whoa..." he adds when we fly over an endless line of vehicles trying to get through the Skyboard North checkpoint.

"They'll never make it in..." I say, glancing at the waves pummeling the shore. "Crite, do you see that?"

"Your brother was right," Lyden says, taking Arwyn's hand. "This is going to be more than anyone is prepared for."

"Where are you going?" I ask Finn, making myself look away from the water and the line of gridlocked vehicles.

"Skyboard South shelter. That was the plan, I thought? Load 'em up, move 'em out?"

"No. I mean, yes, but we need to make sure people got out of the area near the shuttle crash," I insist. "Our families live there."

"Sandra said that air support was blind in there. They've been working on controlling the fire," Ms. Reynolt elaborates.

Finn blows out a big breath, then sucks in another just as big. "All righty... Hang on to something," he says, veering toward the roaring waves and the haze that's starting to thicken in the night sky.

CHAPTER 44
Another Hole in the Sky
Arco

Azeris punches what I assume is an address into the wrap-around console of the heliocar, making it flash in my eyes.

"Sorry, security override," he says with a shrug.

"Where are we going?" I glare at him.

"Somewhere that doesn't exist."

"We don't have time for riddles, man," I say, already losing patience, so I take a deep breath. *Get it together, Hart...focus.*

"There's another hole in the sky not far from here," Azeris explains, raising an eyebrow. "A Seam operative who was running between Van Spaulding and an old associate of mine set it up. Tell you what, the more power people get, the stupider they get."

"It's arrogance. They think they're gods who can do anything—that's when they get sloppy," Denison says.

We approach the ion gate leading into and out of Skyboard North. Shuttles and heliocars are backed up as far as I can see.

"Why don't they just widen the dome clearance?" I say, feeling an ache start in the back of my head as I try to process the *champion* level idiocy of the people in charge of this place. "Why are they even bothering with the damn gate *now?"*

"Look at the breakers!" Avis says, pushing over Ellis to get a better look out the wrapping window. I turn to look out the window on my side of the heliocar and stop breathing for a second.

"Crite…those have to be fifteen feet high."

"Can you see the trough? Look at the bottom of the breakers…" Avis says.

"It's too dark," I answer.

"Then open the sky port." Avis runs his hands back and forth over the roof. "Isn't there a skyport in this thing?"

"Doesn't look like it," Azeris says, scanning the dashboard console.

"Then can you hear the water? Can you hear, like, a growl?"

"I just hear the sirens," Zoe says, narrowing her eyes against the vacillating, pitching wail that has just started.

"How far out are we?" I ask as we move easily through the abandoned gate. I try to scan the shuttles coming in for anyone from Seaboard North, but we pass too quickly. "They need to raise this dome clearance or those people will never get through in time."

I see the probability equations taking shape in my peripheral vision, but I shut my eyes hard to push them aside. I don't want to know the estimates.

Denison blows out a breath. "They'll figure that out as soon as Sandra gets a visual of this. Luz will make that happen, don't worry."

"All right, five minutes should get us there," I say.

The streets below are deserted, and I only hope the

rooftops are too. Only we're not heading for the rooftop.

We come to a stop in front of two buildings with stone pillars at the base of each. A second later, both doors of the heliocar wing upward to let us out.

"Which one is it?" I say, staring at two more rundown buildings.

"Neither," Azeris answers. I sigh audibly without even trying to hide my impatience. I'm getting tired of his stupid riddles. "It's in the middle of them, stretch."

"Wh—?"

"Come on."

Azeris walks toward the two buildings like he's going to walk between them, but there's only sand and sky between them.

"There's nothing there," I say a little louder than I should. He doesn't stop. When we get a little closer, I see that there actually is a structure between the two buildings. Dark, concrete blocks edge either side of a glass tower that goes about halfway up, then turns into more dark blocks on the second floor. From the street, it looks like that half of the building isn't even there. *The hole in the sky...*

"Keep moving," Azeris says to everyone, then walks directly *into* the concrete blocks in front of us.

"Uh, what just happened?" Avis asks, trading shocked expressions with me. Ellis laughs.

"Heh, it's a hologram," he says, putting his hand through the stone. We follow him through to see, on the other side, a set of stairs that just leads to another wall. I watch Azeris and the others walk right through *that*, too. A feeling of total body exhaustion hits me. *When will things be what they seem to be again? Or...were they ever what they seem?*

Through the wall at the top of the stairs is a small room loaded with equipment: different pieces of consoles, discs, piping, button panels, and more wiring bundles than I can count. There's a chiller in the far corner that sits at the end of a sink, counter, and a makeshift table. The main space has two chairs and a couch surrounding a beat-up wooden coffee table that looks about as old as this decrepit building. Avis crosses directly to the tech equipment, nearly squealing.

"So the gear you brought in the box was your *scrap?*" he says, wide-eyed. "This is military grade field equipment—an oxygen scale...a *nanite encryptor?* Are you serious?"

"That's nothing. Here," Azeris says, crossing to the far side of the room to retrieve a cart. He wheels it over, then removes the tarp over it.

Avis swoops in. "This is not here. No way is this in front of me."

I study the mass of twisting coils and slim, metal lines emerging from the cart for a second, and I understand why Avis is about to wet himself.

"Where the hell did you get a *sonic arc relay?*" I ask, moving in to take a closer look.

"I built it," Azeris says, waving Avis away so he can get the machine powered up. "How do you think I found your crew when they synced with the NET device?"

"Is this what you used to find the ship then?"

"Initially, but it only worked because it synced to the NET—somebody on board must have it. I used that baseline to capture the ship's feed with the mobile unit back in the box. Should be able to reconnect with this now," Azeris explains, pushing a final series of buttons and clamping a wire. The front panel of buttons starts to glow, and a blue, 3D hologram bubble appears over the device.

"Don't get any ideas—and I mean that literally," Denison says. I turn to him, confused. "We need a filter if you're going to do anything with that machine, and I don't have the equipment here to put one in your head."

"What if we can put something on the machine?" Ellis says, looking around the junkyard that is this room. "If you have a nanite encryptor here, there must be something we can use to block his neural connection to the code."

"It might work," Denison says, joining Ellis in picking through the heaps of tech equipment littering every surface. I shake my head and return to the hologram, which isn't reporting much more than the ship's coordinates.

"They moved twelve feet with that last quake," I say, reading the time-lapse of the last tremor and the distance traveled.

"The oceanic crust is getting thinner closer to the top..." Avis adds. "Look at the number of pore pockets compared to here." He traces a grid line from the earth above the ship to that below it.

"Can you access the controls?" I ask. "There has to be an engineer database in there somewhere."

Azeris nods and starts tapping away at the detached key panel lying flat on the cart in front of the machine.

The monitor screen floods with code a few seconds later, which translates to a blueprint layout with key boxes and diagrams in the hologram field above it.

"Ha!" Azeris says. "Thatta girl…"

I skim the diagrams and the data entry field for trajectory input and see the coordinates for that slab of rock near Phase Three.

"OK, enter an all-stop command. It should work like a remote control, right?

"Already ahead of you, stretch," Azeris says, typing into the keypad.

The controls don't move, even though the data entry field populates with the command.

"The ship isn't reading that. Are you sure you're connected to the control schematic?" I ask.

Azeris looks at me like I just asked him to dance. "Wouldn't you move your britches before watering the weeds?"

I close my eyes in a long blink and let out the breath in my lungs. "If it's connected, the *controls* should have moved. Can you get them online? We can talk them through how to stop manually."

"That *is* the itch I've been workin' to scratch," he says like I'm pestering him. I press my teeth together.

A frequency wave flares, and the high-pitched squeal makes me cover my ears. It levels out into the crackle of static and a lower frequency wave. Azeris looks at me, surprised.

"I think that means it worked," he says, then nods in confirmation. "All right…Liddick? You picking this up?"

There's no answer at first, but the frequency wave

starts to send images into the lower half of my peripheral vision—a metal floor with rectangular skid-rugs just in front of a row of seats behind a wrapping console. And then, endless black.

"Azeris!?" Liddick says, and the sound of his voice makes the images in my vision blur and fade out. "This ship is coming through the ocean floor. *Fast.*"

"We know. I found the control schematic, but we're locked out of remote access."

"Do you see the all-stop command in the input field?" I ask.

"Hart?"

"Listen to me. You just plowed through twelve feet of oceanic crust since the last pulse that ship emitted, and the breakers here are up to fifteen feet. You need to stop that ship."

"I don't know what to tell you, Hart. We're running blind down—wait, we got it! We got the relay! Liam is entering it now."

I close my eyes and listen to the frequency mixing again with the static. Liam is a blur at the console as something heavy settles in my chest.

"What's wrong?" I say without opening my eyes.

"It's not working. He entered it twice and is try—"

The feed visuals warp and bend like a funhouse mirror in my head.

"Now what's happening?" I ask, looking over at Azeris.

"Incoming," Avis answers, studying a device he's arranged on the coffee table. He barely finishes the sentence before I feel the vibration start in the floor, traveling up my legs all the way to my teeth.

"It hasn't even been an hour since the last one!" I shout over the growing rumble, which is already stronger than the peak of the one that hit back on Skyboard Mountain.

"We're at sea level! It hits here first!"

"Steady the machine!" Ellis says, pushing toward it with Denison. I lean against the wall, gripping the arm of the couch and the side of the cart to stabilize it.

Denison turns to Azeris. "Where's the output hub? Hurry!" he shouts.

Azeris crosses to the cart slowly, stumbling as the room shakes. He holds out his hand for the sheet of steel mesh in Denison's hands and attaches it.

"We can't stay here!" Zoe shouts over the rumbling, which finally starts to subside. "We gotta get back to higher ground."

Azeris makes his way to the other side of the room and opens a panel in the wall next to the chiller. Several screens appear, along with a control console below each. The far screen shows the view from the abandoned street, and the center screen shows a blue grid field with several moving dots. The far-right screen shows nothing until Azeris taps something into the console below it. When he finishes, a series of lights grow in unison.

"What is that?" Ellis shouts to him. I move closer to the screen and feel my stomach sink.

"That's the Maritime Council's surface scanner," I say, then watch the lights continue to grow: *37...42...59...* "That wave is going to be seventy feet high when it breaks. *Jazz...*"

CHAPTER 45
Seaboard
Jazz

Finn lands behind the strip of Seaboard North habitat
stacks, which are lit up by search lights from airbuses
running paths back and forth to the Skyboard mountain.
I look for the relay dome light in the water, which should
be glowing red or blue, but it's nowhere to be found.
Even the rock pier has been swallowed by the surf.

"The swells are building," Lyden says, studying the
water against the dark sky and the various search lights.

"Then we need to hurry," my father says as the doors
of the shuttle slide open. We jump out and head for the
doors of our hab just as a spotlight from one of the
aircrafts hits us.

"Return to your hovercraft and evacuate this area
immediately!" a booming voice says.

"Hurry!" Lyden shouts, motioning to Arwyn to
follow us. "I'm going to check my parents' house!" he
says.

"You can't go alone!"

"I'll go with him—hurry!" Ms. Reynolt says as she
and Lyden begin running up the beach to the detached
housing strip, reserved for Council members.

"Return to your hovercraft immediately or you will
be forcibly removed!" the aircraft voice calls again.

We push through the corridor leading to our hab. Fraya and Arwyn race up the stairs. I get to the retina scanner first, barely able to stand still long enough for it to scan me. The door slides open after what seems like an eternity.

"Mom! Nann!" I shout, tearing through the rooms, which are dark and empty.

"Nann!" Jax shouts, moving into the back hall toward the bedrooms. He returns almost immediately. "They're not here. I'm going to check the other habs," he adds, going to pound on the neighbors' doors.

"Then they have to be in transit," my dad says. "Come on."

Fraya, Myra, and Arwyn meet us in the corridor without their parents.

"They're all already gone..." Fraya says. "Avis's and Ellis's family are out too. There's no one on the whole top two floors."

The open doorway to the hab complex is flooded in light from the aircraft above, and in the light, I can see the black water in the distance moving in.

"Crite, come on! Come on!" my father shouts. "Jaxon!"

Jax rushes back down the corridor, shaking his head. "They're all gone!"

"Good, good, come on," my dad says, motioning everyone back into the shuttle.

"Wait! We have to get Lyden and Reynolt!" Arwyn shouts as we close the doors.

"Hang on!" Finn turns the shuttle and flies up the beach where Lyden and Ms. Reynolt are trying to carry a large man down the stairs of one of the houses.

"That's not his father," I say, trying to figure out who they're carrying.

"That's Paxton!" Jax says. "How was he not the first one out of here?

"Ed Paxton is still the Council leader?" my dad asks, but abandons the question when the doors to the shuttle fly open again and Jax jumps out. He takes the arm Ms. Reynolt was trying to brace over her shoulder and moves Mr. Paxton, who seems unconscious, onto the shuttle with us.

"Go! Go!" Lyden says as the surf crashes behind him in a wall of white. The water splashes into the heliocar with him and gets into my mouth. I start coughing in shock because the shoreline is normally *at least* three hundred feet from our habitat stacks.

"The waves!" I choke. "Hurry!"

Lyden closes the door as the aircraft spotlights shine blindingly through the windows of the heliocar, then move over the houses and stacks we've just left. The beams climb higher into the sky, then over the buildings toward the forest at the edge of Seaboard North.

"Where is it going!?" Lyden shouts. "There could still be people in the other buildings!"

"There are people in that forest, too. Vox's people." I cough again, watching the aircraft's searchlight stop.

"Hold on! We're blind!" Finn says, flying into thick, black smoke as we try to make our way from the beach. He makes a hard turn, and we all push into each other before we level out again.

"*What...?*" Mr. Paxton rouses, his round face shiny

with sweat. His meaty hands push over his forehead and through his thinning hair as he looks at us in amazement.

"Jack Ripley..." he says with the ghost of a breath. "I...*I'm dead?*"

"Not yet!" Finn yells as we pull out of the smoke long enough to see the aircraft searchlights illuminating a wall of black, roaring water. "Crite! Hold on!"

I look at Jax at the same time he looks at me, and we both know we won't be able to escape the wave.

The movements of his face slows so that I notice every wrinkle between his eyes as it forms. Every beat of his heart in the pulse at his neck, and the stretch it causes in the tip of the Vishan's *S*-shaped treatment scar just over his collarbone. I hear the roar of the water fall to the background of my own, quick breaths that are getting ahead of me—that are competing with the swell in my chest for space in my lungs.

Breathe...I mouth to him as the window behind him turns from the wall of dark green to white. *Breathe...*

***

Arco grips the edges of a tall metal machine on a standing table. His eyes are closed and his head is bent in front of it. Something tells me not to talk, not to get his attention, but I don't know why. The feeling in the air is tight, constricting, like he's holding a bomb. I take a step because I have to go to him, but then stop myself when he warps and bends like Vox did when she was in my channel at Admin City. I take another step and the machine blurs out entirely until it takes the shape of something else...of a console? I walk toward it, even though everything in me says to stop, but I have to see.

The blur spreads, and there are people—*Liam*—typing. Liddick shakes his head, both of them moving in slow motion. They're talking, but I can't understand the muffled, distorted words.

The window in front of them is black, and it's not until then that I realize they're on the ship that was under the Lookout Pier.

Are you dying, sand dollar? Vox says in my thoughts. I look for her but don't see her anywhere.

I don't know, I answer.

"Jazz?" Arco says from behind me, and I turn over my shoulder just as he's raising his chin from his chest. He looks directly at me, then reaches for me from the room *I* was just in with him. I try to walk toward him, but he warps and blurs again.

"What's happening?" I ask, but my voice sounds so far away. He takes several steps toward me, and when he's finally close enough, he moves his fingers over my cheek. His thumb brushes my bottom lip and the corners of his mouth almost tack into a small smile. But then he moves past me and starts typing into the console. His hands move normally at first, but then so fast, I don't understand how he could possibly know what he's entering.

"It's cracking!" Liam yells, but again it's muffled and in slow motion. Everything is in slow motion except for Arco's hands over the console.

A loud roaring crashes against the dark window, filling the room with the reverberation. Liddick and Liam stumble and reach for two of the seats that line the console station to steady themselves.

It's all right, I think toward Liddick. He looks up and around, but he can't seem to see me. *Here!* I say again. *I'm here.*

I know you are, Rip, he answers. *You're always with me.*

I turn to see Arco again in the bright distance several feet away. He's still gripping the side of the standing table. I turn around to see that he's also still typing feverishly at the console.

"Arco?" I say, turning back to find him standing in the bright room.

"I'm here," he says as blood starts streaming down his nose and over his lips. "I'm always here with you."

"Arco!" I try to go to him, but I can't get through the space. It's like we're separated by a window now. "No...*no!*" I pound on the glass with my fists as the ship rumbles again. I stumble backward, falling on my elbows. I scramble to my feet and see the other Arco finish typing. He just stands there and watches the window, which is still black, but is now streaming with periodic white bubbles.

"We're in the water..." Liam says, standing not ten feet from me, but sounding so much farther away.

"Arco," I say, but he doesn't move. "*Arco!*" I move between him and the console, and over his shoulder, see the other version of him with blood completely covering his mouth and chin and soaking the front of his shirt.

"He won't let go!" Avis says in the distance.

"He pulled off the filter!" Dr. Denison shouts from even farther away.

"Arco..." I turn to the version of him standing in front of me. "You have to go. Arco, you have to go now!"

He doesn't move, so I start pushing his chest until he takes a step backward.

"Turn it off! Azeris, now!" Dr. Denison yells in the background.

"Arco, please!" I shout, and when he still doesn't move, I kiss him, gripping his shirt between my fingers and holding on like if I didn't, he would fall down a hole and be gone forever. I feel his hands close over my shoulders—actually feel them, which doesn't make any sense. I pull back and look at him, into his eyes that are the same mossy color they've always been, but different...*distant*. He moves with me until we get to the opening with the other version of him still gripping the table and bleeding everywhere. "You have to go," I whisper. "You have to go back."

"Not without you," he says.

"I'll be there."

"Promise me..."

"I promise. *I promise...*" I say, feeling the tears choking off my words. I push him as hard as I can back through the opening to the room. It seals the second after he falls through—after he falls and disappears into the bleeding version of himself, who finally lets go of the table and falls into blackness, washed away in white.

CHAPTER 46
Somewhere Between Us
Arco

"Keep his head steady!" Denison says against the backdrop of roaring wind. We're moving, swaying... I hear the ocean surf and feel the spray on my face.

"Pull him up!" someone far in the distance says. Bright light comes out of nowhere, and even with my eyes closed, I have to turn away.

"What...?" I say, but there's no one to hear me. I turn my head the other way and feel stabbing pain behind my eyes. Black closes in from the edges, but not before I see Denison clipped to a platform that's directly below me and the heliocar following us.

"Easy...easy..." a woman's voice says. "All right, we're unlocked. Slide it on three, one...two...three..."

"Where is she?" I ask, trying to open my eyes, but the throbbing in my head spikes every time I try. "The wave is...coming. She's on the beach..."

"Don't talk, son," Denison says. "Breathe..."

Something cold presses over my face—my nose and mouth—and the air is thinner, cooler. The pain in my head lessens enough that I can open my eyes, but what I see isn't what I expect.

"What is this?" I say, but I can't hear myself through whatever is on my face. I reach up to pull it off, but my arms are strapped down. I try to lift my head to get a better look, and the icepick between my eyes returns, bringing the tunnel vision back. Someone in red moves over me.

"Let's not do that," she says, but I can't make out her face. She moves something cold to either side of my head and runs another strap between them over my forehead. I can't look to the side anymore and I can't sit up.

"*Where is she!?*" I shout this time, pushing against the straps holding me down. Everything flashes white, and a searing pain shoots between my eyes.

"Stop! Stop, son!" It's Denison. The cover over my mouth moves away, and the air is thick and heavy again. The first breath I take feels like it's pouring in and pooling at the back of my head.

"Jazz..." I say while I can, while I can still keep the words out of the deepening water. *The water...*

I see her again, pressing her hands against the glass. Her head is bleeding, but her eyes are open, searching. Debris washes past in the lights of the shuttle, in the muted light from the surface. *Where are you...? Where are you...?* I watch the streams of white bubbles pushing through the green and black water. They crash and dissipate against a dark shuttle. *Where are you...?*

The bubbles move into symbols, numbers...into coordinates.

"What is this? Look at the screen. Where is it coming from?" the woman's voice says, making the image of Jazz in the shuttle warp and ripple in the rushing water.

"I'll find you..." I say, pushing out her voice and focusing again on the shuttle—on the speed of the racing water and the turn of the current.

"It's what he's seeing," Denison says, warping the images and the numbers again. This time I almost lose the image of her completely.

No! Stay there… I'll find you… I think, holding out my hands to meet hers on the other side of the glass.

"That's the Seaboard coast—ground zero, Briggs," the woman's voice says.

They can see this? I think, which costs me a little clarity in the image, but this time the numbers don't freeze. I stop resisting their voices.

"He's…stabilizing? I don't understand it," the woman's voice says.

I concentrate on the coordinates. *Can you see them?* I think. *Go there. Go there!*

A wash of white bubbles floods the image of the shuttle. The water currents scatter the numbers in a hundred directions. Another wave. It wasn't the tsunami yet, then… It's still coming.

"Arco?" I hear her call my name, but the image is still lost in the white wash of the wave that has just crashed.

"I'm here. We're coming… Hold on. We're coming."

"Are we moving?" she says in a tight voice.

"Another wave crashed over you."

"Then we're moving… Arco, you have to get out of the water," she says, her voice getting thin.

"I'll find you no matter where you go, do you hear me? *Hold on!*"

"You're so cold… Why are you so cold?" she asks. "You have to get out of the water, Arco…"

"Jazz…I'm not in the water. Listen to me. I'm—I don't

know where I am. Somewhere between...*us.* Your head is bleeding. You have to stay awake, all right? You have to hold on," I say, moving in closer and pressing my hands again to the glass. Her hands drop and splash the water rising around her waist. "No, no, no...Jazz—Jazz, stay awake! Damn it, we didn't come from six miles under the ocean for you to drown here! Jazz! *Denison! Where are you!?*" I shout into the water and pound on the window with my fists. With the last crash, all the water disappears. All of it, just...gone.

"There! There in the trough! Send them! Send them!" the woman's voice says again. "Watch that swell! We only have about five minutes!"

"We found them, son. Hold on—all of you, hold on!"

Beams of light spill over the shuttle, which is wedged in the sand. Four men in red flight suits drop down in a raft-sized basket, which lands near the roof of the shuttle. They break the windows and send two of the men into the shuttle while the other two wait outside just as a bone-shattering roar floods everything and wipes away the image.

"No!" I say, but I barely hear my voice, only the continued roar all around. I blink a few times to make sure that the wall of water moving toward us on the horizon is actually what I'm seeing—the arcing dark mass rising in slow motion.

"He's awake! Briggs! He's fighting!" a woman says, but again, I can barely hear it over the noise flooding the air-transport we're on.

"Let me up!" I shout, realizing the straps on my wrists are cutting into me as I struggle against them.

"Are you trying to get yourself killed?" Denison shouts as he appears at my side.

"Let me up! I'm all right! Do you see any blood? Damn it, let me up before that tsunami gets here! You need this bed!"

Denison's eyes flash to the screen next to me, and his face blanches. He shakes his head, pulling his hand down over his mouth and off his chin. He starts unstrapping my arms.

"OK, slow! Slow!" He holds up his hands as I push up. He shakes his head at me again and grabs an earpiece from the wall. He hooks it over my ear and taps the side. "You listen to me," he says in a clear, booming voice. "I don't know what kind of scrambled eggs you've made of your brain, or how you've managed to unscramble them —if you've even managed to unscramble them. The *only* reason you're out of that flatbed is because the probabilities read you wouldn't relapse, but if you stayed in it, you would. I don't understand that, so you sit there and don't do *anything* until I can figure it out, all right?"

Before I can answer, the long basket platform is back at the threshold. The two men standing on the perimeter are holding on to the ropes. They jump down into the transport and turn back to the basket platform.

Two more from inside it help lift Jax to the men who are waiting in the transport. They strap him onto one of the flatbeds, repeating the process for his dad, then Ms. Reynolt, Myra, and Fraya. Lyden and my sister are conscious, so they climb onto the platform quickly with the help of the men, who return their efforts to lift out someone I don't know, and...*Mr. Paxton?* Jazz is the last one out of the basket. I move to the flatbed before they put her in it and shut the door. Denison crosses to us carefully between the flatbeds, where the men who have just closed the door begin attaching oxygen masks for everyone.

"Secure! Go! Go!" a woman says over the earpiece. Denison passes ear pieces to Lyden and Arwyn, who lean against the wall. Lyden clutches his chest and gasps.

"Breathe through your nose...in and out. Watch me," Arwyn says. He complies and slowly starts breathing normally.

"Jazz..." I hold her face in my hands, feeling for her pulse. It's strong, crite. "Hey, come on...come on," I say, but then realize she probably can't hear me. I grab another ear piece off the wall and slide it into place. Denison moves to her side and punches something into the small panel on the side of the flatbed. A hologram grid appears behind her head, populating with images.

"Category two concussion, and something strange here between her hemispheres...but that's not related to the injury. She'll feel that bump in the morning, though," Denison says. "Put this on her," he adds, handing me an oxygen mask.

"Jax? My dad?" she asks before I can secure it.

"A little waterlogged, but otherwise, they're clean," Denison says, blowing out a breath.

"You're all right," I say, looking back at Jazz. Her eyes are still closed, and I brush the dark hair away from her face to position the mask over her nose and mouth. It secures itself around the back of her head."Everyone is all right. We did it... We did it."

"Arco, look," my sister says, but the only thing I can look at is Jazz as she opens her eyes slowly.

I watch the smile start in them before it spreads to corners of her mouth, covered by the mask. My chest constricts, pushing up a laugh, then another. I swallow hard to keep my throat from following suit and shutting off my words. But I only get one out before I lose that battle altogether. "Hey..."

CHAPTER 47
Transport
Jazz

I don't know if he's really there, looking down and smiling at me with bloodshot, glassy eyes. Maybe this is all happening in the space between us again. Wherever it is, as long as he's with me, I'll stay as long as it lasts.

"Hey…" he says. I smile, feeling something covering my face. I try to raise my hand to it but can't move my arms. "Oxygen. And it's *free.*" He chuckles.

I laugh, but it makes my head hurt. He takes off the body straps holding me in place, then the mask, and it's immediately harder to breathe. But I don't care.

"Jax…and my dad?" I say, trying to look for them.

"They're OK. Denison is checking on them now. Everyone is OK."

I take a deep breath because it finally feels like I can. His fingers brush the hair from my forehead and move over my cheek. He's *really* here.

"I saw you there…" I say. "Under the water."

"I saw you in the ship," he replies, cocking an eyebrow for a second as he looks to the side in contemplation. "I guess that's still technically under the water."

"Arco—you need to *look,*" Arwyn says, then angles her head toward the cockpit window. I push to my elbows, which makes everything spin.

"Here, wait." Arco moves his arm behind me, but then he suddenly stops and holds me against him. "Crite...there it is."

I don't see anything at first, but just as I'm about to ask what we're supposed to be looking at, a burst of light erupts in the sky, sending out whips of lightning in several directions. Against the illuminated sky, the horizon is warping upward in an arc.

"Rally, Unit 792," a woman's voice says over the comms system in my ear. "Please be on the lookout for abnormal electrical activity surrounding you. We have tsunami confirmation with trough exposure. Estimated culmination within ten minutes. You should have visuals westbound. What's your SA?"

"What's she saying? That it will hit in 10 minutes?" I ask.

Arco nods. "It's coming..."

"Copy, Control," the pilot says. "In that case, we *will not be* out of range yet without a lift for the hitchhiker we picked up. Medical is stable and we have two Capables aboard. Please prioritize."

"Copy that, 792. Phoenix Seven, confirm coordinates received and begin route to intercept 792's drag. 792, you are cleared for landing on the roof of Skyboard Prep. Triage units are in place and they could use the Capables."

"Phoenix Seven responding. Copy that, Control," another ship says over the comms.

"Unit 792 responding, what he said, Control. Thank you."

Arco blows out a breath, relieved just before another flash of light streaks across the dark sky and lights up the enormous bowing horizon.

"What hitchhiker? What does that mean?" I ask, pushing with my hands to sit up more.

"The heliocar we took. Azeris is still in it with Avis and Ellis. They brought me up on a platform like you. Denison came up with me."

"You were in that room. I don't know how—our channels, or whatever—you were just bleeding so much..."

"I didn't have a choice...and then I didn't want one," Arco says, looking away.

Another flash streaks across the sky, lighting up everything like the middle of the day for several seconds. The wave on the horizon bends more steeply, moving like it's floating in slow motion toward the shore.

"Arco..."

"It's like I was inside that ship, Jazz. Like it was inside me. I wouldn't have let go." He chuffs a laugh and shakes his head. "I know that doesn't make sense, but when you kissed me, it just—you cut me loose. You brought me back."

Another crash of light blows up the sky, spider-webbing innumerable lightning streams.

"Crite, it's the cloud..." Dr. Denison says, then moves quickly to the cockpit. "Listen, that's not an electrical storm up there. How soon until we can get on solid ground?"

"Running at least ten minutes in the headwinds," the pilot answers.

The glowing outline of the explosion and lightning hangs in the air until another bright explosion obliterates them. In the light, the wave on the horizon stretches and sharpens to a peak.

"Where's the ship?" I ask, feeling my chest start to hollow. "It was set to launch right into the explosions. Where's the ship, Arco?"

"I killed the launch—the engines are offline."

"But where *is it?*" I press.

"It's...under the water somewhere. It has to be."

"Phoenix Seven to 792, be advised we are relieving you of your hitchhiker—locking on. Stand by," the comms chatter again.

"Copy that, Phoenix Seven. Standing by. Try not to get cooked in your flying oven."

"Copy that, 792, we will take that into consideration."

The comms go quiet again for several seconds as the transport jerks and rattles. Several smaller pops of light stretch across the sky, but they don't produce lightning flashes.

"What happens if we're still in the air when the cloud comes down?" I ask.

Arco turns to me. "If the Grid goes down, so do their Nav controls. They'll have to land blind."

A flood of light fills another part of the sky, this one lingering longer than all the others. Lightning races from all sides, shooting into the horizon and straight overhead. No matter where I look, breaking diving and rolling waves streak the ocean surface, seemingly just to gather all the water ahead to feed it to the growing wall in their wake.

"Phoenix Seven to 792, be advised your hitchhiker has moved into our basement," the comms start again. "Give us a three-second head start, then buster like your ass is on fire."

"Copy that, Phoenix Seven. Much obliged. Meet you at the bird's nest. 792 out."

The transport hovers for another few seconds before turning sharply and picking up speed. The lights from the other transport are almost gone.

I turn around and get to my knees to see through the back window. The sky is now as bright as daylight with the periodic explosions of lightning.

"It's happening... It's all happening," I say under my breath, watching the wave moving upward like it will never stop. We keep climbing higher and higher until I can see the entire stretch of ocean pulled in like a vacuum in front of the building-sized wave. It finally bends, rolling into itself and pushing forward, engulfing all the habitat stacks and separate houses. It pushes through them, swallowing the tall building ruins like they're sand castles.

"Crite..." Arco breathes, moving next to me.

"What is that?" Arwyn asks. "Do you see that? That's not water. There! It's going to hit us!"

The black water diverges from the rushing water swallowing the shore. But it arcs up instead of forward, widening as it comes out of the water, then tapering.

"It's the ship," Lyden says in disbelief.

"No! It can't launch!" Arco says. "It *can't* launch!"

Prickles run under my skin, hot and cold at the same time. Liddick, Vox, Liam...Dell and Cal, Vita and Rav...

all the Vishan are inside that ship.

"Where's the airlock tunnel?" Arco asks, looking at the ship. "It's gone. There was a mile of it on each side."

"It must have separated—or broke off," Denison says, marveling.

Fire erupts through the center of the ship in a half-circle from side to side.

"Crite, it's breaking!" I gasp, fear stabbing through my chest. *Vox!* I shout in my mind. *Liddick!*

"No! I killed that launch! *I killed that launch!*" Arco's hands ball into fists.

"Unit 792 to Control, we have a bogey in our wake," the pilot says over the comms.

"Unit 792, did you say a *bogey?*"

"Copy that, Control. It is incendiary."

The line of fire stretching across the center of the ship brightens like it's spreading, but then I realize the line is actually *rockets.*

"It's separating!" I shout, which makes my head pound and my vision blur.

The other half of the ship is still attached, tapering to what looks like a section of the airlock that must have broken off too.

"What did you tell it?" Denison says, gripping Arco's shoulder. "Did you program a separation?"

"I—I don't know. I killed the trajectory. I'm telling you, I *killed* that launch."

"Did you program the *separation?*"

"Your connection..." I say. "Arco, you said you wouldn't have let go...that you felt like I cut you loose in your channel—in that space between us. You said it's why you came back. That must have worked its way into your program."

"That's impossible because I had already entered the codes!"

"Unit 792, be advised aerial teams confirm the bogey appears to be domestic and the incendiaries are propulsion. We are scanning for a comms port. Do not engage. I repeat, do not engage and hold your trajectory."

"Copy that, Control," the pilot says. "But we just lost our trajectory map. Please advise."

"Crite, the Grid is gone," Arco says, pushing his hands through his hair."

"Confirm, Unit 792, we just lost you and the bogey. Say your state."

"Control, we have…one point three seven to splash. Skyboard Mountain is in the goo, and it appears this bogey is…*following* us."

Denison shakes his head and turns to Arco. "It's following *you.*"

CHAPTER 48
The Connection
Arco

The water pours over the seaboard, swallowing everything in its path—it's too surreal, like paint spilling over a board game from high in the air.

About a quarter mile offshore, the remaining half of the ship juts out of the ocean like a tree limb in a stream, causing white impact water to rush at each side.

Periodic explosions send more fractals of light leaping across the sky for as far as I can see in any direction. It's hard to believe that we're here now, on the edge of everything.

"Arco," Jazz says, snapping me out of the hypnotic light show. "Did you hear what he said? Dr. Denison thinks the ship is following you?"

The face I make must be compelling because both my sister and Denison jump to counter whatever they think I might be about to say.

"You're neurally linked to that ship—that's the only explanation," Denison says. "You shifted its trajectory, so the autopilot is now—well...*you.*"

"Well, how do I steer it because that ship isn't going to fit on that roof with us," I say, watching Skyboard Prep come into view.

"Confirm, Unit 792," the comms start again. "At last

check, the bogey was following your stream. We are speculating that it must have locked on to *your* trajectory since the Grid is offline. Prepare backup systems to come in without guides."

"Copy, Control, but that's going to be a problem. Smoke is obstructing the target and pings are ricocheting right back at us. Are we getting music from that ship?"

"Unknown, 792. Can you tail Phoenix Seven?"

"No joy, Control. Phoenix Seven has left our line of sight."

"Standby, 792..."

Denison exchanges glances with my sister, then lowers his hand from his earpiece. "Did you say you can *see* the school roof from here?"

"This doesn't make sense," I say, looking out the window again. "There's a thick blanket of smoke rolling between Seaboard North and the base of Skyboard Mountain. It stops about halfway up," I add, but something isn't right with that. *Smoke doesn't just stop.*

"Come with me." Denison pushes to his feet and makes his way to the cockpit. "Let him fly—he's a Gaia-trained Navigator, and he can see that rooftop," he says to the pilots. They both look at him blankly for a second until he slaps the side of the co-pilot's chair. "Do you want to play Ring-Around-the-Mountain with that rig in tow if another wave decides to chase us? Let's go! Let's go!"

The co-pilot unclips from her seat and moves past Denison.

I shake my head. "Wait, I—?"

"If you can see that roof, Mr. Hart, you can land this

ship. And that one," he says, raising his chin to the back window.

"I look quickly over my shoulder at the enormous crescent-shaped ship in our wake with what could be over two hundred people aboard. My heart hammers in my chest. I glance toward my peripheral vision hoping for more equations to take shape—to solve themselves like they did before, but Azeris's machine isn't here anymore, and they don't appear. There's no overlay whatsoever.

I look away and find Jazz's eyes.

"It's gone," I say shaking, my head. "I can't see the numbers without Azeris's machine. I don't have the connection anymore."

"Yes, you *do*," she says without even a second passing. "You don't need the machine. You see the roof because the smoke just stops—none of us can see that. *You* are the connection, Arco."

The comms crackle again. "Unit 792, we cannot get you on the scopes and cannot coach you in. What is your fuel situation now?"

"Control, fuel is at twenty-five percent, but we have a bigger problem right now: an incoming echo wave at 2:00," the pilot says. I look out the window to our right and see another breaker picking up speed on the surface.

"Confirm, 792...stand by."

"Are you kidding me?" the pilot says, her voice clipped. "OK, pick a seat, Navigator."

"All right, all right." I climb into the co-pilot's seat. The controls are simpler than any of the other ships I've piloted: just the Y-shaped yoke, fuel gauges, and a few landing gear controls since everything else is offline. I pull up on the yoke to catch the air current, and the ship soars upward, fast.

"Throttle back, Nav. That mountain could be right on top of us!"

"It's not...not yet," I say, checking the back window to make sure the other ship is still in our wake. It is, but the school roof is almost out of range for us to make the turn without the other ship clipping the side of the mountain. It's going to have to fly on its side...and if it's following me, I have to do that too. *Crite.* "Denison! Secure everybody—we need to get creative!"

"Uh, we're in the soup here, tiger. What's your plan?" the pilot asks.

"Bank left sixty degrees on my count, or that ship is going to clip the mountain."

"Bank *what?*"

"Just do it!" I say. "Three...two...now!" I hold my breath as the pilot dips the left wing at the same time I pull up on the yoke. We turn hard on our side until I can see the ship behind us angling too. "Level out," I add, blowing out the breath I've been holding. "Bring her down on the north end of the roof so that ship lands on the gravity ball field to the south."

"Copy that..." the pilot says, then angles her head at me. "What's your name, Nav?"

"Arco Hart."

"Hart, huh?" She nods at me. "I'm Major Reynolt. Sandra Reynolt."

"*Reynolt?*"

"Luz is my sister-in-law," she says with a wink, then

turns her attention back to the comms system. "Control, this is Unit 792. The soup is clearing and we have visuals on the school. We are setting up for VTOL on the north side to accommodate our bogey on the game field."

"Copy that, 792. Security is en route. Impressive, ladies."

"We would love to take credit, Control, but that belongs to a Gaia Nav-cone we were fortunate enough to pick up. Arco Hart. Say hello to the fans at home, Mr. Hart," Major Reynolt says. I try not to laugh.

"A *student* brought you in? Well...attaboy, Mr. Hart. I'd say this was a hell of a test, wouldn't you?"

"Uh, yes, ma'am," I say, but I don't try to hold back the laugh this time.

"Unit 792, visuals report that you are coming in clean, and so is the very big dog that followed you home."

"Copy that, Control," Major Reynolt says. "Three locked and down. Unit 792 out."

***

Medical volunteers are already unloading everyone from the ship when Jazz, Denison, and I come down the ramp.

"Where are they gong?" Jazz asks, grabbing the sleeve of the closest volunteer.

"Evaluation," he says. "Straight ahead."

"Listen, I'm all right—" Jack argues with one of the volunteers. "Let me up. I can *help* here." I shake my head and stifle a laugh because it's too familiar.

"Is everyone OK?" Avis shouts, rushing over to us with Ellis, Azeris, and Zoe not far behind.

"Where is everyone?" Ellis asks.

"Jack's Omniclass nanites are already working on his

concussion over there," Denison answers, angling his head. "Same for Luz. Everyone else is stable but will need a reboot."

"And Seaboard North?" Avis asks. "Did everyone get out?"

"Our stacks were empty when we checked," Jazz answers. "Everyone was out."

Ellis and Avis both visibly relax.

We make our way over to Jack and the others, who are all waking up now.

"Ugh... How many shuttle busses hit me?" Jax mumbles, holding a hand to his head.

"*Pshhh.* It was just a seventy-foot wave." I shrug. "I've hit you harder on the field."

He laughs, then groans and brings the other hand to his head.

"Speaking of that—have you seen the size of that thing?" Avis asks, throwing a hand in the direction of the field and the enormous ship that covers it.

"I've never seen a ship that—" I start, but he jumps right back in.

"Their *gravity ball field!* How is it even regulation and our field is half that size?" he gapes. "How does that even fit on the side of a mountain anyway? They terraformed it. I'm telling you. That's gospel."

"*Guhhh,* stop making me laugh," Jax groans, which only makes me laugh more. Denison is talking with Ms. Reynolt when we cross to them. A medical assistant is using some kind of little white wand to close the cuts on Myra's head, and Fraya looks like she has a pretty good bruise starting under her eye.

"I'm pretty sure you both won the round," I say to them. They smile and wince almost at the same time.

"Where is Finn?" Jazz asks, looking around. "And Mr. Paxton?"

"Good question… Where are Lyden and my sister?" I add, scanning the rooftop tents, but I don't see them either. Just then, the transport we landed in takes off, and I panic for a second that the enormous ship on the field will follow it.

"They're all in good hands," Ms. Reynolt says, winking at Jazz and me.

"Damn it, I'm going to say it one more time, and then I'm going to tip this gurney over and show you just how fast these nanites work…" Jack says, still arguing with the same medical assistant.

"Excuse me," Denison says, making his way over to him and unfastening the cinches still holding Jack's arms and legs down. "You know he left you in this for fear of his life and not your concussion, right?" They both laugh.

I walk up behind Jazz and wrap my arm around the front of her shoulders, pulling her into me. I kiss the top of her head, and she folds her fingers over my forearm.

"What happens now?" she asks, turning her head to watch our transport join several other vehicles that are surrounding the ship in the distance, which is even more massive in context on the gravity ball field.

"I don't know," I answer. "I imagine those people are going to want to get in there, and the people in there will want to get out."

"I imagine they're all going to need your help with that?"

"Let's see, who's aboard that beast… Liam took you to the Slide, which was basically the most dangerous place in the entire world," I answer, kissing her temple. "Vox hijacked my face with her mind control just so you could walk in on it…and then there's Liddick Wright," I add, kissing down her cheek and neck, "whose rap sheet is far, far too long to list."

She laughs, leaning into me. "And Cal, and Dell, and Vita are on that ship…all the Vishan." She laughs again, but then it all catches up with me and a shot of adrenaline hits my blood.

"Jazz…your treatment. You can't be in the sun when it comes up," I say, looking at the glow starting on the horizon. "Denison!"

CHAPTER 49
Aftermath
Jazz

"Electra Brown coming to you again from high above Seaboard North, where as you can see below, Monty, the devastation is astounding in the aftermath of what seismologists are calling *the largest tsunami in history*. Coastal quadrants, and even the original evacuation sites located in the Skyboard lowlands were swallowed by the still-receding water. Were it not for the quick thinking of State search and rescue crews rerouting to Skyboard Secondary Prep and nearby primary schools, truly, all would have been lost."

"Come in. It's all over the feeds," I say as Arco pokes his head through the curtain, then moves to sit on the edge of my bed. He puts his arm around me, and I lean into him.

"How's your head?" he asks.

"*Shhh,*" I say, putting a finger over his mouth. He laughs, wrapping his hand around mine and kissing it, then bringing it to his chest. The feed switches to footage of a dark-haired man in a suit being led away in handcuffs from a boardroom, and then to an aerial shot of Liddick, Vox, and Liam coming out of the ship on the field and being wrapped in blankets by two people.

"That's the pilot from our ship! The woman next to

Liam!" Arco says abruptly.

"Is that Dr. Halliday with her?" I ask, watching Liam adamantly say something to both of them. The pilot nods, and Dr. Halliday waves several people into the ship with wheeled carts and medical machinery.

"As if the largest tsunami in history isn't enough to dominate the newsfeeds, Biotech CEO Van Spaulding has been taken into custody for his connection to what experts now believe may have been the *cause* of the tsunami, and ultimately, the destruction of the port-cloud. Crews of medical personnel have ventured into the craft that surfaced, and we have received word from ground crews that Skyboard North's rising biodesigner, Liam Wright, as well as two Gaia Sur cadets—Liddick Wright and Vox Dyer—were somehow aboard the ship *as it* launched. Decrypted data from the ship's schematics shows they were able to break into the ship's trajectory code and alter its original path, which was directed at the port-cloud. Details on just how these young people found themselves on the ship are forthcoming. Faris Temple is on the scene at Seaboard North with more."

The feed switches to a split screen with visuals of a slim man with cropped black hair standing against the backdrop of the coast, which is still flooded past the habitat stacks. The other half of the ship arcs out of the now calm water behind him with boats and hovercraft everywhere. "Thanks, Monty. Sources are telling us the ship that was able to land on the Skyboard Prep gravity ball field was in fact only *part* of the massive ship that came through the ocean floor. Believe it or not, even though the ship on the field measures more than a hundred yards long and seventy yards wide, an even *more* massive component is still lodged in the Atlantic coast just behind me. Officials believe the ship now on the Skyboard field is actually an *emergency escape* pod. The question on everyone's mind, however, is how it got underneath the ocean floor. State investigators are decrypting the ship's records, which so far reveal the ship was built as a cooperative effort by Biotech Global founder Franz Spaulding and former CEO of the Carboderm Corporation, Rex LeMar. It was intended for use within the next hundred and fifty years when the planet's environmental stability was, *then*, expected to collapse. Spaulding and LeMar appear to have written legacy plans guaranteeing a place aboard the craft for their descendants. These plans were extended over the years by these descendants to include several individuals who supported the evolution of an illegal genetic experimentation program known as *The Elements Project*, namely, renowned geneticist Allsop Vishan, one of the founding members Gaia Sur. The State has received a data package also implicating several of Gaia Sur's past and current administration, as well as Spokesperson *Cole Daniels* in *The Elements Project*. We've also been advised that new Biotech leadership, Zeb and Bev Spaulding, claim to be completely unaware of this The Elements Project and will be releasing a statement on behalf of the corporation this afternoon after a closed-door meeting with the *president*. Monty?"

The feed switches back to the studio setting with Monty, the dark-haired reporter.

"Thank you, Faris. In related news today, the neural

network is still down as crews report *continued* combustion in the port-cloud after nearly forty-eight hours of chain-reaction catalysts. These appear to be linked to the launch of the embedded sea-to-space vessel unearthed about 1,500 miles off the Atlantic Coast two days ago. Reconstructed data thumbprints implicate known hacker, Howard Grisham, who was working to directly implement subliminal Biotech Global propaganda messages into popular virtuo-cines."

I look quickly at Arco, who's already smiling. "You erased *Ludwig Sprague*? Did you erase all that when you were typing on the ship console?" Arco shrugs and lets his smile spread. *"Tell* me!" I laugh, elbowing him in the ribs.

"I mean, the uplink connection to Phase Three was right there, already in the coordinates bridge. And Phase Three was already connected to the port-cloud, so...I just cleaned up the breadcrumbs a little."

"But you didn't believe Liddick's story," I say, looking up at him. He turns to me and smiles.

"No. But you did..."

"Knock knock? Are you decent?" Jax asks, actually knocking on the curtain.

"No," Arco says. I smack his arm and laugh.

"Uh, *yes,* come in," I answer, muting the feed.

Jax and Fraya push aside the curtain and stand at the end of my bed.

"It's going to take a while to get used to flatfeeds without the 3D neural connection," he says, glancing at the screen on the wall. "So, feel all brand new with your freshly scrubbed DNA?"

I smile at him. "I mean, I'll probably miss not being able to throw a fireball at you, but…"

"Oh, good, bad jokes! Guess that means you'll make a full recovery."

"If I have anything to say about it," my dad says, coming into the room with Dr. Denison, both of them in white lab coats. I flinch a little until I realize it's them, and so does Arco. "Omniclass nanites should have you out of here within the hour."

"*Omniclass?*" I ask.

"Well, we had to mix up an extra strength batch for an exceptionally stubborn pilot I know," Dr. Denison says, smirking at Arco. "And I'm afraid it's all we had on hand. Hopefully, they'll do."

"You still can't make fireballs, though—just saying…" Jax raises his eyebrows and shakes his head at me.

"Is everyone else OK? Mom and Nann? Myra, Vox?" I ask.

"Major Reynolt arranged for a team to bring our families here," Arco says. "It should be any time now… I don't even know how to begin telling them about everything," he adds with a sigh.

"The only thing I'm sure they'll be interested in today is that you're all safe…and home, son," Dr. Denison says.

Fraya wipes a tear and curls into Jax, who pulls her close. "And Myra was discharged with Jax and me a little while ago," she says. "Zoe, Avis, and Ellis are with her while Azeris is getting the heliocar. It's really over, Jazz… It's really over."

Tears start to burn my eyes too, but I push them back. I'm afraid to ask about the ship and everyone aboard since no one has mentioned it yet. Were there windows in the ship? Did they survive the sunlight? Why did all those medical officials rush in there? I realize now that I let the whole thing slip away after the initial newsfeed report because if I'm honest, I'm terrified to know the answers.

Everything that has gotten me to this point, though, has involved asking the questions that I've been afraid to answer, and I know it's the only way to go forward now.

"And Liddick? Vox, and Dell, and Liam…" I barely say their names because it feels like their fates are tied to disrupting as little of the air as possible. It's only seconds before my father takes a deep breath and responds, but it feels like it lasts forever.

"They're all still at the ship site with the other Vishan and Badlanders," he *finally* says. "Reese's team is giving those who need them the same treatments they gave you and Zoe in order to reverse the volatility in their DNA."

I exhale the breath I've been holding throughout his response. "So…they'll be able to go in the sun?"

"Not as quickly as you will with the Omniclass nanites, but yes…soon. We'll be able to see them tonight at the integration dinner the new Skyboard Council leader and the leaders from Vox's clan are arranging."

"The new Council leader?" Fraya asks. My dad presses his lips together into a quick smile and nods.

"Their previous one *and* Ed Paxton have a lot of explaining to do at The State tribunal alongside Cole Daniels, Van Spaulding, Giselle Rheen, and Eros Styx."

"I can't believe this…" I say, still unsure if this is really happening or if I'm really just dreaming, or in a virtuo-cine, or in someone's channel. "This is real? It's real, isn't it?"

Arco interlaces his fingers with mine and brushes his thumb under my bottom lip. "This is real," he says. "I promise. It's real."

Heat fills my chest and races up my throat, threatening to close off anything else I want to say. I ask about his sister and Ms. Reynolt as fast as I can before that happens.

"Luz's nanites fixed her concussion before we even got to the hospital last night," Dr. Denison says. "She's at Reese's clinic with Lyden and Arwyn," he adds, then stiffly nods. "It's going to take awhile to undo what they did to them. But if anyone can reverse it, it's Reese and his team. Liam will also be on staff to help oversee things."

"And Calyx?" Arco asks. "Plus the test subjects from Phase Three and The Seam building?"

"The patients housed at The Seam are mostly discharged and currently at The State's remote office here at Skyboard giving statements about their experiences," Dr. Denison says. "As for the ones with Reese?" He chuckles. "Calyx messaged that an *Alpha Class* security detail has been in place around the clinic since early this morning after The State decrypted the backup files of evidence from Phase Three that we sent."

"But what happened with the patrols who were there?" I ask.

"Bound in IV tubing and left on the doorstep to wait for the security detail," he says, letting his chuckles roll into a laugh, which infects us all.

"The best biodesigners from around the world are transporting in, too, at the request of The State," my dad adds. "Turns out they're very grateful for the feeds we sent of Cole Daniels at the Phase Three facility."

"Is that Eco?" Fraya asks, turning to the flatfeed. I turn the volume back on and blink to make sure what I'm seeing is actually what I'm seeing.

"—barely escaped with my *life*. Honestly, and I've seen a lot considering my years as a top alpha channel tester for the virtuo-cines, this was by far one of the most corrupt and revolting operations I've ever experienced," Eco says.

"Is he *actually* trying to *cry?*" Arco gapes.

"Giselle Rheen and Eros Styx are the epitome of what's wrong with this world," Eco continues. "Morally bankrupt people who were only ever interested in personally profiting from others' misery."

"That pathetic little skod!" Arco says, shaking his head in astonishment as I mute the feed. "I should have hit him harder."

"So he just gets away with everything?" Jax asks.

"He doesn't need the bars at Lima. His life is his prison," I say, noticing the ache at the bottom of my chest as I watch him...a desperate, never-filling hole where Eco's sense of self—a real acceptance, a real understanding of himself instead of just free-falling through the worlds of others—would be. I watch the muted feed of him wiping non-existent tears from his face for a few more seconds before turning it off. I try to imagine what it must be like to be so completely disconnected from anything real. To live explicitly in a world where you're only ever a player in someone else's game. "That has to be the loneliest thing in the world..." I whisper. "It has to be the worst punishment of all."

"Jazwyn?" a woman wearing long, dark braids with blue beads intertwined knocks at the door, and I feel the breath catch in my chest.

"Ms. *Wren...?* How—"

"I was volunteering at the evacuation center. There are a few people out here who are very interested in seeing you all."

CHAPTER 50
The Leader
Arco

Fraya stays behind to help Jazz get dressed. I wait for them outside her room with Jax while Denison and Jack go with Ms. Wren, our Communications teacher from Seaboard North. On the other side of those doors, Jazz's mom and little sister are waiting with Fraya's parents and Myra's. Ellis's and Avis's will be coming up with Azeris and Zoe, no doubt, and mine should be there too.

I don't think I'm the same person who left on that shuttle sub all those months ago. I don't know if they'll know me anymore…if I'll know how to tell them who I am now, what I've seen, or what I've done that has made me so different than the person they hugged goodbye that morning on the shore.

We've spent our whole lives pushing forward to get to a place that never existed, and now all I can seem to do is stand right here while what *is* real waits for me on the other side of the door.

I blow out a breath and try to think of what to say, but no words come to me. When the girls come out of the room, Jazz takes my hand and smiles up at me. In that second, I start to understand why I can't think of anything. Sometimes there aren't any words. Sometimes, there's only taking one step after another…forward.

"Are you ready?" she asks. I nod. Jax throws an arm around my shoulder as Fraya takes his hand, and we make our way to the door.

"Arwyn?" I say to myself when I see her locked in a hug with my mom and dad. She hears me and turns around.

"I have to go back for follow-up treatments to remove all the DNA integrations—they're not as cleanly fused as the Vishan treatments, but they were able to remove the volatility strand so far." She wipes her tear-streaked face and tries to restore her composure.

"They keep saying that Dr. Halliday is the best," I say, swallowing hard to dislodge the knot forming in my chest. I clear my throat.

"He wants you to come in with Dr. Denison and me later in the week for a scan, just to make sure everything is healed up there." She cocks an eyebrow and messes up my hair. Not even a second passes before tears start streaming down her face again. "It's so weird to reach up to do that..."

I press my teeth together like a dam against the tears closing off my throat, but it doesn't work. I squeeze my eyes shut for a second as a last-ditch effort and pull her to me in a tight hug. Over her shoulder, my mom is covering her mouth with tears streaming down her face. My dad's arm is around her with Denison on his other side gripping his shoulder.

"Your son is a hero, Mr. and Mrs. Hart. They are all heroes," Denison says.

I don't know what to do with that. I laugh, but not because it's funny, and the dam just breaks.

My parents come over and wrap their arms around Arwyn and me as I watch Jack walk slowly toward Nann, Jazz's little sister, and kneel in front of her. He takes her small hand and kisses it, nodding and smiling at her. She throws her arms around him. He lifts her up in a hug as her mom moves to his side, and Jax pulls Jazz in under his arm.

***

Ms. Wren and Denison lead us to the lobby of the hospital, where Major Reynolt is waiting in uniform with several State Patrol officers. Everyone slows to a stop, and I exchange a wary glance with Jax.

"No cause for alarm, gentlemen," Major Reynolt says. "They're not here to arrest any of you. They're here to escort you to see the president."

"The *what?*" Avis asks.

"If now is a good time, of course?" Major Reynolt smiles.

"Uh, *yes!*" he answers. Ellis elbows him and gives him a narrowed glare. "*What?* Sorry, you have a date so we should reschedule?"

Ellis rolls his eyes, and his mom and dad laugh.

"Please follow the Sergeant at Arms, in that case," Major Reynolt says as one of the Patrols turns on point and heads for the door. The others move in lockstep on either side of our group as we all follow him.

The black heliocar waiting outside is even sleeker than Liam's clone's car. It's flatter, wider, almost like an airship. The doors glide upward, and there's enough room inside for all of us to slide in around a center console with oxygen mask portables, *chocolates*—with one

Zero Gravity caramel bar peeking out among them—and beverages. I don't even have to look up at Jax before I start noticing the geometry of his hand in proximity to the Zero G bar...the length of his arm, the probability of his reach velocity. The numbers and symbols work themselves into an equation, and I look up, grinning. He's wide-eyed when he glances from the chocolate to me, possibly more amazed than he's been since we left Seaboard North in the first place.

"That's a Zero G bar, man..." he says conspiratorially to me. I nod at him and cock an eyebrow. He nods back at me, and I reach for the bar a fraction of a second before he does, snatching it right out of his closing hand.

"Ha!"

"No way!" he protests, falling against the back of the seat in disbelief while throwing his arms in the air. "You did some Nav-jitsu math right there! Everybody see that?" He chuckles.

"All right, all right." I laugh, breaking the bar and tossing half of it to him.

A few minutes later we're at the temporary State facility several miles up the Skyboard mountain. The Sergeant at Arms and the rest of the Patrol escort us into the white building, the back half of which is still being printed by three land rigs in the distance.

The Patrols march on either side of us, corralling us through the winding white hallways, which haven't been decorated yet. They head toward a doorway and flank each side as a receptionist with a bun as tight as Sarin Nu's presses a button on her desk panel.

"Mr. President, the Gaia cadets are here," she says.

"Brilliant. Send them in, Grace."

The Sergeant at Arms nods to the receptionist and opens the door for us.

Inside the office, President DeAngelis gets to his feet and crosses to us, shaking each of our hands.

"Have a seat, have a seat," he says, waving us to the high-back white couches. Calyx is sitting on one of them with Finn, Ms. Reynolt, a Cloudy woman with long, black hair and radioactive green eyes like Pitt had, plus another Cloudy man with blond hair and a tanned complexion, but with ice blue eyes like...*Dez?*

She stands up on the other side of the Cloudy man with her glowing blue eyes filled with tears.

"Dez!" Myra says, running to her with open arms.

"I'm so sorry," Dez sobs. "I didn't know...we didn't know..."

Jazz looks up at me just as shocked as I am.

"Thank you all for meeting with me today," President DeAngelis says. He takes off his suit coat and hangs it on the back of his desk chair, then passes a hand over his salt-and-pepper hair. "Please, sit."

We all take a seat as Dez wipes her face with a tissue she snags from behind the table.

"This is my oldest brother and sister, Zed and Bev Spaulding," she says, her voice crumbling into erratic chuckles. "They're twins, believe it or not."

Jazz laughs and starts wiping tears away with the back of her hand as Dez blows out a breath and tries to reset her composure.

"Tieg was bitten by an antlion," she says tentatively, nodding to the president. "One of the creatures from the biomes I mentioned. He's OK. Our brother Lief is treating him at his clinic. But he wanted me to thank you all for helping him...even after what our father did," she adds to us, lowering her eyes.

"It won't make up for what you've all been through, but as acting CEOs of Biotech Global," Zed says, taking Dez's pale hand in his tanned one. "Bev and I have authorized BTG's board of directors to make rebuilding Seaboard North our company's top priority...for as long as it takes."

"In cooperation with The State," Bev says, pushing a lock of straight, black hair behind her shoulder when she nods to President DeAngelis, "and the new acting CEO of the Carboderm Corporation—"

"New acting CEO?" I interrupt before I can stop myself.

"Yes," President DeAngelis says. "Their former CEO is currently...indisposed as we work through the rest of the files our crews are decrypting," he says delicately and nods to the group.

Bev Spaulding tries to smile as she continues. "Well, in cooperation with The State and the new Carboderm leadership, we're already working to rebuild The State campus, and we'll be starting on the new Gaia campus soon...*topside*. We're breaking ground as soon as we can get it to dry out." She smiles.

"But...the air?" Jazz asks.

"That's one of the reasons we asked you here today, Ms. Ripley," President DeAngelis says. Major Reynolt here has advised me that your group has developed keen abilities during your tenure, albeit brief, at Gaia Sur, and throughout your subsequent ordeal. I would like to invite you to finish your schooling at the new *Skellig Tark Institute* once it's complete, under the leadership of its directors, Briggs Denison and Luz Reynolt. That is, if they would do us the honor?" He lowers his chin in a question to them.

Denison and Reynolt both startle, obviously not knowing about this ahead of time.

"Sir, the honor would be ours, I'm sure," Denison says. "Though I don't want to speak for Luz—" he starts, but she takes his arm and tries to contain the huge smile threatening to take over her face.

She clears her throat. "It would be the greatest of honors, sir."

"I'm so happy to hear that. Well, then…about the air. As I mentioned, our teams have been toiling over the endless records that were housed in the ship's databases. They go back over a hundred years. While the port-cloud brought civilization into the future, it also shortened it considerably for most of its inhabitants. In light of the technology Arco Hart and Azeris Frank have been able to unearth, it would simply be going backward to even attempt reconstruction of the port-cloud."

"That's incredible!" Jax says.

"Well, that's not all. As you can see by looking out any window, we have a lot of rebuilding to do. Our neural telecommunications system depended on the Grid, which has been damaged beyond salvage. Sometimes, that's what it takes to move forward, however, and that's what we plan to do with your help, Mr. Ripley. Would you consider working with my office to redesign and implement our new neural network?"

"I...I don't know what to say." Jack almost laughs.

"Well, I hope you'll say yes." President DeAngelis grins.

"Ah, yes...yes, of course. Thank you, sir."

"Excellent. Now that just leaves a few more things in order to put this community back together. Mr. Frank, I understand you have a strong relationship with the Tinkerer community as well as with some of our leading, shall we say...*technical professionals* here on the Skyboard Hill." President DeAngelis offers a raised eyebrow and a knowing smile.

"Ah...that I do, sir."

"Good. Would you do us the great service of choosing a team and coordinating efforts with my office to standardize a port-carnate technology system for global distribution?"

"Wait, what?" Azeris flinches.

"Dad!" Zoe squeezes the words through her teeth as she elbows Azeris in the chest. He clears his throat.

"I mean, yes. Absolutely can do, sir," he finally says, still in disbelief.

"Wonderful." President DeAngelis laughs. "Finally, we'll need expert agricultural and botanical experience after this water recedes. Mrs. Ripley, I understand you ran the very successful greenbeds for the community before this tragedy struck?"

"Yes, sir," my mother says. "But of course, they wouldn't have been possible without our hard-working interns."

"I was hoping you would say that. I would like to

send a few representatives from our Department of Natural Resources to coordinate the immediate materials and labor needed to move forward. They could use a project advisor, and we would greatly appreciate your help in overseeing these endeavors, plus land quality inspections as we move forward with reconstruction. What do you say?"

Jazz's mom beams, which, aside from the last few days, I haven't seen happen in five years. "It would be my pleasure, sir," she says, clasping Jack's hand.

"Excellent...then this is the beginning! I'll have all the contracts drawn up for dispersal. Today, we will roll up our sleeves and start leading the world to a bright tomorrow," he says with a wide smile to us all. "Your nation thanks you, and we are in your debt."

Everyone stands shaking their heads in disbelief as he nods and turns to leave.

"Thank you, Mr. President," I say abruptly before he makes his way out the door.

"Thank *you*, for your leadership, Mr. Hart."

CHAPTER 51
The Beginning
Jazz

I sit next to Arco with my head on his shoulder watching Vox's clan get acquainted with the Vishan, all of them either laughing or crying, or just marveling at each other. I haven't seen Vox or Liam or Liddick yet, and I can't seem to make contact with Vox or Liddick telepathically either.

He knows you're here, Lyden thinks, approaching us with Arwyn supporting his arm and his parents on his other side. Mine are just a few steps behind.

"Lyden!" I say out loud, startling Arco. We get up and cross to them.

"You're discharged already?" Arco says, noticing the way Lyden is holding his torso with his other arm.

"Not permanently, but I wasn't about to miss tonight. It's not every day my little brothers get to introduce an entire lost society to the whole watching world." He laughs as my parents approach and stand with us.

"Jazwyn, Arco..." Lyden's mother says, glancing at my mom and dad. She's tall and thin with swept-up dark hair and clear blue eyes just like Liddick's. "I can't begin to—" she starts, but then is overcome with emotion. "I'm sorry... I'm sorry," she says, trying to regain her composure.

Lyden's dad wraps his arm around his wife and puts a hand on my shoulder. He's also tall with dark hair that's gray at the tips and temples, his long, blue tunic setting off the blue of his eyes under thick, dark brows.

"We can't begin to thank you for everything you did to get our boys back," he says, gripping my shoulder, and then offering a hand to Arco.

He takes it and nods respectfully. "We all helped each other out there."

Lyden's mom abandons her struggle with her composure and hugs Arco, kissing his cheek, and then doing the same to me.

"We owe you everything...*everything*," she says, dabbing at her tears as her husband nods his agreement, then signals to Lyden where they're going to be seated.

Liddick will be here soon, Lyden thinks. *He's been asking about you in my head since they surfaced.*

I can't find him...or he's just not answering me? I think.

Lyden just smiles quietly at me as he and Arwyn go to sit with their parents, and I understand without him having to answer my question. Liddick hasn't figured out what to say to me any more than I've figured out what to say to him...now that it's all really done. We're home, and we can start over.

We all watch the Wrights take their seats, their absence leaving a kind of ravine between my parents and me...empty with all the years we've been apart in one way or another. There are so many things to say that it's hard to know where to begin, so I'm surprised when my mother moves toward me and puts her hands on my face. She looks into my eyes and takes a long, slow breath as a smile moves quietly over her face.

"You changed my world when you were born, Jazwyn," she says, her eyes filling with tears. All the breath is pushed out of my lungs as a sea of my own tears rise up in my chest. "And now, you've changed everyone's."

I swallow hard to prevent the deluge threatening tears, but it's useless as I feel them run down my face. She folds her arms around me and pulls me close, which fills the distance between us. All five years.

She smiles brightly at me when she lowers her arms to look at me again, and I can't help but smile too. Arco puts a hand on my back, and I'm finally able to take a deep breath.

"I'm so proud of you two," my dad says, beaming at us.

"Dad, you're going to make me cry again." I try to laugh. "Apparently, I have an inexhaustible supply of tears, so..."

"As any good Empath would," my mom says with a wink and a glancing smile that lasts a second too long. Wait a minute...

Mom, can you hear me? I think. Her smile just widens as she grips Arco's other hand for a second, then turns toward the seating area. I laugh under my breath and shake my head, watching them sit with Fraya and her parents. Jax is with them holding Nann on his lap. Since we left the hospital, she's been draped all over him listening to stories about life-sized mosquitoes and giant, mutant manta rays who roam the ocean helping people, and he wouldn't have it any other way. I scan the crowd for Avis and Ellis and find them sitting with their parents, not far from mine, but Quinn and Sarin are not with their parents.

"Do you know where they are?" I ask Arco, raising my chin. Arco follows my eyes.

"Quinn and Sarin? Major Reynolt said they were on the ship with Rheen and Styx when it was seized, but they sent them to psych evals instead of criminal holding," he answers, trying not to look at their parents for too long. "They won't be released until they're cleared, though, and only then after the trials since they're testifying."

"Psych evals?" I ask. "The State really thinks it was brainwashing? Because I bet Sarin wouldn't have thought twice about getting on that ship under the Rush and leaving everyone here behind to deal with the end of the world."

"I'd bet the same thing, but I guess that's why they were so easy to manipulate." He laughs.

"What's so funny?"

"I just remembered your go-around with her in class at Gaia Sur," he says, touching four fingers to his thumb to make a hole. *"Crawl in a hole and die?"* He cracks up all over again. I roll my eyes and nudge him.

"Hey, she started it."

His laughter trails off as he looks at me seriously again, the hard lines of his face even sharper now, making him look older.

"That seems like a lifetime ago," he says, shaking his head as he chuffs a laugh. "I guess it was."

"I've thought that so many times over the last few

months."

We stand there without talking for another several seconds before he leans down.

"And now?" he asks through my hair. "What do you think happens now?"

I lean my head back on his chest to think about it. I've been trying to answer that question since we found out Gaia wasn't what it appeared to be. That the life we planned was never there waiting for us.

"I don't know..." I finally answer, and am a little surprised that not knowing actually feels OK now.

"Jazwyn Ripley *doesn't know* her next step?" he asks, poking me in the side. I squirm and nudge him again.

"I really don't...aside from I don't see how we can pass up the opportunity to finish school at the new topside Gaia. I just want to learn how to use what we can do to help people. And there are plenty of people who need help now."

"We?" he asks in the quiet voice again, this time so closely that I can feel his warm breath next to my ear. I settle back against him, and he wraps his arms around me.

"I mean, unless you *wanted* to figure out how to brain-fly all the ships you see from now through trial and nosebleed?"

"Definitely not." He laughs, combing my hair back with his fingers and leaning close to my ear again.

"What do you want?" I ask, turning my head a little toward him.

"You know what's funny?" he asks after a long pause. "Even though everything is gone—I mean *everything* we knew—I still want the same thing."

"A base career where you can come home at night?" I ask, remembering what he told me that night after he first kissed me by the moon pool at Gaia Sur. He chuckles.

"Exactly," he says, kissing my temple. He's quiet for a few more seconds before he takes in deep breath and starts again. "And I think I want to see what I could really do out there, you know? I guess I've never really pushed too many limits before now. Tark made me see that."

"He'd be proud of you."

Arco doesn't say anything else in response to this. I feel a hollow start in my chest, but it's quickly filled with a spreading warmth when he pulls me closer to him. Grief...and love.

"You two just going to sit back here and pet each other all night then?" Vox says from nowhere.

I whip around and see her standing right next to us. "Vox!" I almost scream. "How do you even *do* that?"

"Do what? Do you think I have the time to plan out a special, silent route whenever I approach you *just* so you never see me coming?"

"*Yes!*" Arco and I both say at the same time, which makes her genuinely smile instead of giving her trademark smirk. She cocks an eyebrow and shrugs one shoulder.

"I mean...it's not *every* time." She hooks my arm in hers. "Come on."

I narrow my eyes at her. "*Why?*"

"Because I'm actually going to roarf in a hard, straight

line if I have to watch you two breathing all over each other anymore. Crite, go find sunken treasure or something," she adds, cocking another eyebrow at Arco and trying not to smile.

"Copy that, Vox," he says, giving her a two-finger salute like the Badlanders. He gets about five steps from us when she calls out to him.

"Hey," she says, and he turns back to us. "Thank you...for bringing us home."

He takes a long, deep breath at that and nods, pressing his lips into a hard-lined smile before he turns and walks over to his family.

Vox blows out a breath and marshals me in the opposite direction.

"Where are we going?" I ask.

"Somewhere you need to go."

"That doesn't answer my question, though."

"There's something you need to see."

"What?"

"Sand dollar, can you just stow it for, like, twenty seconds until we get there? Because you're taking up all my poignant time."

I actually almost choke on the laugh that lodges in my throat and raise my hand in surrender.

"OK, OK..." I finish choking.

She rolls her yellow-green eyes at me. "First of all, I'm glad you didn't die," she says, giving me a quick glance as we walk out the auditorium door toward the guard rail at the edge of Skyboard Mountain. I try to keep my expression neutral, but when the corner of her mouth tacks in a restrained smile, I know she feels the same closeness I do. "Second, I'm not going to the new Gaia."

"Vox... *Why?*"

"Because you were right. I never wanted to go in the first place. And now that the Vishan are here... I just..."

"You have to help them find their way," I say. "That's what a boundary scout does."

She slows her pace and watches our footsteps. Her lips quirk and her forehead wrinkles, but only for a second before she sniffs and wipes her nose with the back of her hand. *Ewww,* I think.

She laughs out loud and lets go of my arm, shoving me a few steps to the side. "Cal's never had to escape a stranglebush," she says, cocking a knowing eyebrow at me. I laugh, and so does she. We walk a few more yards before we both trail off, and she takes in a big breath. "Here you go," she says as we round the corner.

The sun is no more than thirty minutes from disappearing under the horizon, which makes the sky a wash of orange, pink, and purple. I gasp and stop cold where I stand.

"I never thought I'd see another one of these," I say to Vox, but when I turn around, she's gone.

"I know," Liddick says from just a few steps more around the bend.

"Liddick..." I say his name with the rest of the breath in my lungs. The way he looks at me is almost unreadable—it's everything all at once. But that's how it always is with him. He sighs, slipping one hand in his pocket as he leans back against the railing, which he grips with the other hand.

"I've been in more virtue-cines than I can count, Rip,"

he says with a smile and eyes that seem to flash just for a second. "But this…" He shakes his head and almost laughs "All this with you has been the best adventure of my life." He holds out a hand to me, and I try as hard as I can not to breathe because I know that any space I make in my chest will just constrict and suffocate me right here on the cliff edge. "Come over and watch this with me."

I move to his side, and we both lean forward on our forearms.

"I was so afraid I'd never see you again," I say, threatening the control I have over my composure. I take a deep breath to try to stabilize, but it doesn't really help.

"For a while there, I was too. But I felt you there. In the ship just before the trajectory reprogrammed itself, or, I guess I should say before Hart reprogrammed it." His dark eyebrows dart together as he shakes his head, confused. "That's when it all kind of hit me, I think…that you really do love him."

"Liddick…"

"No, it's OK," he says, covering one of my hands with his as we watch the sunset. "I just mean I can accept it now after seeing him through your lens…literally."

"You could see me in his channel?"

Liddick nods. "In a way. I think the NET, or the ship relay, or something made it so you were connected to both of us at the same time, and because of that, I could see him, but only through you. You were like, a conduit. I could feel that he's not as black and white as I thought he was," he says, gripping my hand. "And…that you really do love him just as much as I love you."

Tears burn my eyes despite my best efforts. They

stream down my cheeks and instantly cool in the breeze. How can this be so painful but also so hopeful at the same time?

Because endings and beginnings are things that happen at the same time, Riptide, he thinks, eavesdropping on my thoughts. Or maybe this is one that I let him find in me.

"What will you do now?" I ask, almost afraid that no matter what he says, I won't know how to feel about it.

"Well, there's the Presidential Gaia 2.0 scholarship slot if I want it. And Dez's family felt so bad about what her father did that they offered Lyden and me positions in the new cinematics industry they're building in Admin City. Next generation virtuo-cines." A flash of panic hits me at this, but I catch myself before I ask him the question he already knows I'm going to ask. He looks at me sideways and smiles. "Don't worry, Rip. I'm never going back there again. I found what I went looking for in the cines."

"So you'll come to the new Gaia with us?"

"I don't know. I think it'll depend on the schedule."

"What?" I ask, trying to keep the laugh out of my voice. Liddick shrugs, stifling his own laughter.

"Thanks to Hart, Ludwig Sprague is an unmarred man with wicked security clearances," he says, nodding to the water. "Grisham and Tarriff are never getting out of Lima after this all goes to tribunal. Someone needs to watch your back out there."

"Watch my back?"

"And everybody's in the Badlands. Finn and I had plans to clean it up and make sure people got a fair shot. Grisham used to be on board with that until he got selfish."

"So, you'd become the new Grisham?"

Liddick turns to me with a wide, Liddick-caliber smile.

"Riptide, are you afraid of what I might add to the subliminal feeds once the Grid is back up and running?" He raises both dark eyebrows at me.

"No." I roll my eyes and laugh.

"Well, you should be," he says, knocking into me, but then he sobers. "But I mean that about always having your back."

"I know," I say, leaning into him. "And I've always got yours."

He wraps his arm around me against the breeze coming off the endless water, which is dancing with sparkles and the riot of color reflected from the sky. The sun starts to dip below the water, and there's no more haze to conceal the first star appearing just above the horizon.

"It's funny, you know…that the first star we see out here isn't even a star," I say, leaning my cheek on his shoulder just like I did that night on the dune before we left for Gaia Sur. "It's a planet."

"Venus."

"There are so many things that aren't what they appear to be in this world…" I think out loud.

He nods slowly, resting the side of his head against mine as the rest of the sun slips away. "Yeah, but sometimes, they're better."

Be sure to sign up for Tracy Korn's Newsletter for exclusive bonuses, plus the latest on new releases!

http://bit.ly/TracyKornNews

Visit The Elements Series on social media!

http://www.facebook.com/TheElementsBookSeries
http://twitter.com/ElementsSeries
http://elementsseries.tumblr.com
http://instagram.com/elementsseries

Books in this series:

- ◆ AQUA: Book 1
- ◆ TERRA: Book 2
- ◆ AER: Book 3
- ◆ IGNIS: Book 4

If you liked The Elements series, you may also like the following books by Snowy Wings Publishing authors:

- ◆ Fourth World by Lyssa Chiavari
- ◆ Phoenix Descending by Dorothy Dreyer
- ◆ Starswept by Mary Fan
- ◆ Fangs & Fins by Amy McNulty

Acknowledgments

Thank you so much to my awesome beta readers: Ron and Deb Commons, Emily Gangloff, Alicia Hooley, Manie Kilian, Margarita McClain, Tracy Siri, Jon Skelly, Anna Swenson, Cassidy White, Christian Yoder, and Christine Yoder. I so appreciate your time, keen eyes, honesty, and support! Also, many thanks to the indie community for being such a big family, especially the AAYAA group, 20Books group, and the Dystopian Bookworms group, authors Dr. Dennis Chamberland, Dave Chesson, Ira Heinichen, Alison Ingleby, Michael W. Huard, Logan Keys, Alex Lidell, Craig Martelle, Brian Meeks, Derek Murphy, Sarah Schmitt, Tawny Stokes, Jesikah Sundin, and so many others I'm sure I'm missing who have been generous with their time, insight, advice, and support. My amazing audiobook narrator and long lost little sister, Dana Dae, I just love you! To infinity and beyond with all we do. To my publishing pals in the Snowy Wings group, especially Amy McNulty, editor extraordinaire, and my INFJ sister friend, Lyssa Chiavari. I'm holding you to the drinks and the sure-to-ensue dago laugh riot (no, the world is *not* ready). As always, my undying gratitude to my former students involved with this project, especially Arianna, Derek, Devlin, Josh, Katie, Kayla, Liam, Olivia, Timmy, Will, and Zoe. Every time I wrote a line for these characters, you were there; none of them would have existed without you. To my long-time writing partner, the irreplaceable Ryan Bachtel, the value of your insight to me is second only to your friendship. I'm going to move to that mountain view one of these days, and we can swap manuscripts on our front porches with the pups. Of course, thanks does not begin to express my appreciation for my family: Mom and Dad, for always having my back. James, Laura, and Michael, thank you for your encouragement, support, and daily inspiration (and for putting up with my erratic sleeping habits). Love you guys.

Wow. It's so hard to believe this is really the end of the series...I guess it's time to start a new one!

Thanks for hanging out with me in this world for the past four years.

About the Author

Tracy Korn is a veteran English teacher, robotics coach, novice cinematographer, and all around science geek. Her high action/adventure YA fiction (beginning with AQUA, book one of The Elements series) was inspired by her students' everyday superpowers of empathy and problem solving. When she's not spending time with family, writing, reading, teaching, or coaching, she can be found playing with her family's two big puppies.

Tracy holds Master's degrees from Indiana University in Secondary Education, in Language, Culture, and Literacy Education, and in English. She lives in Indiana with her husband and their two very own superheroes. Stay in touch at **www.TracyKorn.com.**

Facebook: **http://www.facebook.com/AuthorTracyKorn**
Twitter: **http://twitter.com/Tracybonics**
Instagram: **http://instagram.com/tracy_korn**
Goodreads: **http://bit.ly/TracyKornGoodreads**
BookBub: **http://bit.ly/TracyKornBookBub**
Amazon: **amazon.com/author/tracykorn**